WET BLADES GLISTENING, ARTHUR AND THE DARK ELF FOUGHT ON. . . .

As Diana stepped forward, Arthur danced sideways to avoid a lunge and tripped over a discarded tote bag.

He began to fall. His sword rose to block a descending blow, but the angle was wrong and everyone could see it.

The Immortal King was about to die.

A simple "no" could prevent disaster.

Diana could feel the word rising.

But that "no" could provide the enemy with power enought to complete the segue.

She had nothing in her pouch, nothing that might . . .

The wand. The wand belonged to the Otherside.

Yanking it from her pocket, Diana pointed the pink star at the dark elf, tried very had not to think how stupid this had to look, and opened herself to extreme possibilities. . . .

TANYA HUFF

Long Hot Summoning

The Keeper's Chronicles #3

DAW BOOKS, INC.

DONALD A. WOLLHEIM, FOUNDER

375 Hudson Street, New York, NY 10014

ELIZABETH R. WOLLHEIM
SHEILA E. GILBERT
PUBLISHERS

http://www.dawbooks.com

First Printing, May 2003
1 2 3 4 5 6 7 8 9

Back in the summer of 2001, I attended a convention in Toronto called TT15. Or possibly TT2001 . . . it used to be called Toronto Trek and that's how I remember it. Anyway, after my reading, during the question and answer session, I talked about this book which I'd just started writing. I gave a brief synopsis of what it was about and mentioned that it didn't, as yet, have a title. A woman in the back of the room called out, "What about LONG HOT SUMMONING?"

The perfect title.

I don't know who you are, but if you're reading this, this one's for you!

ONE

Throwing her backpack over one shoulder, Diana raced out the front door and rocked to a halt at the sight of the orange tabby crossing the front lawn. Or more specifically, at the sight of what dangled from the cat's mouth. With one of its disproportionately long arms barely attached and dragging on the grass, and something that looked like intestine wrapped around one bare ankle, the bogey was unquestionably dead. An eyeball bounced gently against its bloody forehead with every step. "Nice catch," she noted, half her attention on the approaching bus. "Where did you find it?"

"Ood 'ile," Sam told her proudly, his voice distorted by the body.

"You know you can't eat it, right?"

Amber eyes narrowed, he let the bogey drop and fixed Diana with an incredulous glare. "Do I look like an idiot?"

"No, but you haven't been a cat for very long . . ." Six months ago, he'd been an angel. Angels didn't concern themselves with the small things that slipped through the possibilities. ". . . and you know how my mother feels about that whole puking on the white wool rug thing."

"Once! I did it once!"

"Yeah, so did I, and she's never let me forget it either." With a scream of abused brake linings, the bus stopped more or less at the end of the driveway. "I don't have time to bury it now, so try to leave it where Mom's not going to trip over it." Turning, she took two steps and turned again, pulled around by the weight of Sam's regard. "Oh, right. Sorry. You are a mighty hunter. Your skill with tooth and claw is amazing. Fast. Deadly. I stand in awe."

"Hey! Sarcasm."

"Not sarcasm," Diana protested hurriedly. There were any number of imaginative places the dead bogey could be left. "But I've got to go. Mr. Watson won't wait forever."

"I'm amazed Mr. Watson stops at all."

"Yeah, well, need provides and all that. Remember, I'll be home early," she added, trotting backward up the path, "just in case there's anything you don't want me to catch you doing."

A presented cat butt made his opinion of that fairly plain.

Mr. Watson looked more nervous than impatient. He nodded a silent reply to Diana's cheerful good morning, closed the door practically on her heels, and jerked the bus into gear. Had Diana not already been reaching into the possibilities, she'd have landed on her ass as he burned rubber trying to outrun half-buried memories. Fully burying them would have messed with his ability to drive, so only the less likely edges had been fuzzed out, leaving him in a perpetual state of nearly remembering things he'd rather not. Which was actually a state fairly common among school bus drivers.

Diana tried not to resent his attitude, but it wasn't easy. This semester alone she'd stopped a black pudding from devouring an eighth grader, saved Chrissy Selwick from a three-headed dog attracted to the aconite in the herbal body mist she'd been given for Christmas—might as well have had "eat me" tattooed on her forehead—and prevented a Gameboy™ from taking over the world. Handheld computer games were more competitive than most people thought.

She'd also stopped Nick Packwood from hanging a second grader out the window by his heels, but since she still wasn't entirely certain the kid hadn't deserved it, she usually left that particular incident off her "reasons Mr. Watson should thank his gods I'm on the bus" list.

Making her way back through the rugrats, Diana noticed without surprise that the last six rows—the rows reserved for the high school students on the route—were nearly empty. On this, the last day of the high school year, only two freshmen had been unable to find alternative transportation.

"My brother was going to give me a ride," said the first as she passed. "But he had to go to work really early."

"Yeah. I was going to ride my bike, but I had, like, an asthma attack," the other explained, holding up his inhaler for corroboration.

Diana ignored them both. First, because a senior acknowledging freshmen would open up all sorts of possibilities she had no desire to deal with. Second, as the youngest, and therefore most powerful Keeper, as one of the Lineage who maintained the mystical balance of the world, as someone who had helped close a hole to Hell and faced down demons, she didn't need to justify her reasons for taking the bus.

Settling into her regular seat, she thanked any gods who might be listening that this would be the last day she'd ever be at the mercy of public education.

Frowning, Diana crossed the main hall toward the stairs, trying to get a fix on the faint wrongness she could feel. It wasn't a full-out accident site; no holes had been opened into the lower ends of the possibilities allowing evil to lap up against closed doors leading to empty classrooms, but something was out of place and, as long as she was in the building, finding it and fixing it was in the job description. Actually, it pretty much was the job description.

As far as Diana was concerned, all high schools needed Keepers. Nothing poked holes in the fabric of reality faster than a few thousand hormonally challenged teenagers all crammed into one ugly cinder-block building. Unattended, that was exactly the sort of situation likely to create the kind of person who developed an operating system that crashed every time someone attempted to download an Amanda Tapping screen saver.

The sudden appearance of a guidance counselor actually emerging from his office and heading straight for her nearly sent Diana running toward the nearest washroom. She didn't want her last day ruined by yet another pointless confrontation. Fortunately, she realized he felt the same way before her feet started moving. *Fuck it. What's the point?* flashed into the thought balloon over his head and he slid past without meeting her gaze.

The thought balloons had appeared back in grade nine when, after half an hour of platitudes, she'd wondered just what exactly he was thinking. An unexpected puberty-propelled power surge had anchored the balloons so firmly she'd never been able to get rid of them and she'd spent the last four years finding out rather more than she wanted to about the fantasy lives of middle-aged men.

Pamela Anderson.

And hockey.

Occasionally, Pamela Anderson playing hockey.

Some of the visuals were admittedly interesting.

The wrongness led her up the stairs, through the first cafeteria and into the second—weirdly, the hangout of both the jocks and the music geeks—

empty now except for a group of girls who'd laid claim to the far corner by the northwest windows. A flash of aubergine light pulled her toward them. The senior girls' basketball team, Diana realized as she drew closer. Probably hanging around in order to *remain* the senior girls' basketball team. Over two thirds of them were graduating, so once they stepped out the door, they'd be a team no longer.

". . . so I said to him, I'm not putting *that* in my mouth." Tall, blonde, ponytail—Diana didn't know her name. "First of all, I don't know where it's been and secondly, this lipstick cost twenty-one dollars."

"And what did he say?" asked one of her listeners.

"Oh, you know guys. He took it so personally. All like, 'you would if you loved me.' "

"So what did you say?"

"That I loved my lipstick more."

In the midst of the laughter and catcalls that followed her matter-of-fact pronouncement, Blonde Ponytail looked up and spotted Diana.

"Did you want something?" she asked icily.

"Uh, yeah." Diana leaned a little closer; trying to get a better look at the heavy bangle Blonde Ponytail wore around her left wrist. "*Please* tell me where you got your bracelet."

"This? At Erlking's Emporium in the Gardener's Village Mall. I got it last weekend when I was visiting my father in Kingston."

Great.

Kingston.

Where there used to be a hole to Hell.

Oh, sure. It *could* be coincidence.

"It's silver, you know."

Well, it was silver colored; the broad band embossed with large flowers each centered with a demon's eye topaz. It was quite possibly the ugliest piece of jewelry Diana had ever seen. "No, it isn't. It only looks like silver."

"What? You mean that troll lied to me?"

Troll.

With any luck, that was a colorful exaggeration rather than the mystical version of a Freudian slip.

Diana didn't feel particularly lucky. Stretching out a finger, she lightly touched the edge of one metallic petal.

A much larger flash of aubergine light.

A moment later, Diana found herself pressed face first into one of the cafeteria's orange plastic chairs discovering far more than she wanted to about the olfactory signature of the last person sitting in it. Then she realized she was actually under the chair and heaved it to one side.

"Are you okay?"

"Fine. Just a little bruised." Accepting the offered hand, she pulled herself to her feet. "Static electricity," she explained, trailing power through the basketball team. "I must have completed some kind of circuit."

Several heads, probably the ones who hadn't passed physics, nodded sagely.

The insistent trill of a cell phone broke the tableau.

"Mine," Diana admitted, digging her backpack out from under the table. Eyes widened as she unzipped an outside pocket. After the unfortunate 1-800-TEACHME incident back in the spring of 2001, students were not permitted to use their cell phones while on school property. *Oh, yeah, I'm a rebel,* she thought flipping it open, then added aloud, "It's my mother."

When the team seemed inclined to linger, she threw a little power into, "Everything's cool. You can go now."

"Diana? What just happened?"

"You felt that at home?" She headed back toward the other cafeteria as the girls reclaimed their table, Blonde Ponytail muttering, "What a piece of cheap junk; I'm going to wring that troll's neck."

"Felt it? Yes, I'd say we felt it. Sam's hanging from the top of the living-room curtains and the coffeepot's bringing in radio broadcasts from 1520—apparently Martin Luther was just excommunicated. I missed part of Suleiman the Magnificent's birth announcement as your father called to say he'd felt it in the next county. Are you all right?"

"I'm fine. I touched a piece of jewelry from the Otherside and there was a bit of a reaction. Don't worry, I covered everything up, and the jewelry's been totally nullified."

"Where . . . ?"

"Was the jewelry?" Diana interrupted. "Around the wrist of a fellow student. How did she lay her hands on a bracelet—and an incredibly ugly bracelet, I might add—that came from the Otherside? She bought it in a store called Erlking's Emporium. Just where exactly is Erlking's Emporium? Kingston."

"*Oh, Hell.*"

"Probably." Leaving the cafeteria, she headed for the main stairs and the front doors. "I figure I just blew a crack through their shielding and that Claire ought to be getting the Summons any minute."

"*Claire's not in Kingston right now; she's answering a Summons in Marmora.*"

"Well, if it's important, I'm sure the id . . . powers-that-be will give it to someone else."

"*You're not getting anything?*"

"Nope, nothing." There was no one in the main hall. Another fifteen meters and she'd be out the doors and home free.

"*Good. And while I have you, I thought we'd agreed you weren't going to wear that T-shirt to school?*"

"Sorry, Mom; the school has a 'no cell phone' rule. Gotta go." Flipping the phone closed, Diana paused in front of her reflection in the glass of the trophy case. The writing across her chest—red on black—said, *My sister's boy toy went to Hell and all I got was a lousy T-shirt.* She seemed to be the only one in the family who found it funny.

"Ms. Hansen."

Phone still in her hand, Diana spun around and smiled up at the vice-principal. "It was my mother, Ms. Neal. I had to take the call."

"Yes, I'm sure. But that's not what I wanted to speak with you about. You're an intelligent young woman, Diana, and while your years here have not been without . . . incident . . ."

The pause nearly collapsed under the memory of the whole football team thing. Some changes lingered, even in the minds of the most prosaic Bystander.

"Yes, well, your marks are good," the vice-principal continued after a long moment, "in spite of your frequent absences, and I can't help but feel it's a real shame that you've decided not to go on to college or university."

Diana shuddered. More time spent under academic authority? So not going to happen. "I'm afraid I'm just not the higher education type, Ms. Neal." Sliding sideways, she moved a little closer to the door.

"Job prospects . . ."

"I have a job. Family business. Pays well, chance to travel, making the world a better place and all that." Also demons, dangers, and the possibility of dying young but it still beat pretty much any other profession as far as Diana was concerned. Well, maybe not sitcom star or Hollywood script doctor but everything else. "You might say it's the kind of job I was born to do," she added reassuringly.

From the sudden contentment on Ms. Neal's face, a little too reassuringly.

"It's nice to know that at least one of my students will be leaving the school for a bright and beautiful future," she sighed. "I'll never forget you, Diana."

Diana smiled. "Actually, you'll forget me the moment I step out the door."

"I don't think . . ."

And then the threshold was between them.

Ms. Neal's brow furrowed. She stared at Diana for a long moment, shook her head, and walked away.

Although not by nature a bouncy person, Diana almost skipped down the steps of the school. It was two thirty on Thursday, June the twenty-third, and she was finally free to be what she'd been intended to be from birth. Crossing the threshold for that last time had moved her from reserve to active Keeper status.

At two thirty-one, the Summons hit.

Both hands clamped to her temples, she tried to uncross her eyes. "Okay. I probably should have expected that."

"Mom? You home?"

"She's at the Pough house," Sam told her, coming out of the living room. "There was some kind of emergency involving ravens and bad poetry. She said . . ." He paused, stared at Diana for a moment, then rubbed up against her shins. "We've got a Summons!"

"We do." She told him about the bracelet as they pounded upstairs.

"Kingston?" Sam jumped up on the end of the bed. "Shouldn't it be Claire's Summons, then?"

"No. It's mine."

"Yeah, but . . . you know . . . it's just . . ."

"Austin." Diana dumped assorted end-of-year crap out of her backpack and shoved in her laptop, a pair of clean jeans, socks, underwear, and her hiking boots. There were places Otherside where even heavy rubber sandals wouldn't be enough. Actually, there were places where hazmat suits wouldn't be enough, but she planned on staying away from the Girl Guide camp. "You're afraid to go onto his territory."

"I am *not* afraid. But he doesn't like me."

Zippered sweatshirt. Pajama bottoms. Tank tops. "He's old. He doesn't like anyone except Claire."

"He likes you," Sam protested following her into the bathroom.

"He tolerates me because I can operate a can opener." Shampoo. Toothbrush. Toothpaste. Soap. Towel. "Don't worry. We'll be in and out before Claire and Austin even know we're there."

Eyeing the toilet suspiciously—who knew porcelain could be so slippery—Sam jumped up onto the edge of the sink. "You know, a hole big enough to pass physical objects through might be harder to close than you think."

Diana snorted, threw in a couple of rolls of toilet paper just in case, and headed for the kitchen where she packed a box of crackers, a jar of peanut butter, a nearly full bag of chocolate chip cookies, and six tins of cat food.

"Less chicken, more fish," Sam told her.

"Fish gives you cat food breath."

He looked up from licking his butt. "And that's a problem because . . . ?"

"Good point." She made the change, pulled the small litter box and a bag of litter out of the broom closet and packed them as well. "I think that's everything. Now I just need to leave a note for the 'rents."

"Make sure they can see it." A few moments later, his pupils closed down to vertical slits, Sam stared up at the brilliant letters chasing themselves around the refrigerator door. "That seems a little much."

"Well, they'll be able to see it."

"Yeah; from orbit."

"Some cats are never happy." About to pick up the pack, she paused. "You want to get in now? Our first ride'll meet us at the end of the driveway."

"Might as well." He flowed in through the open zipper, and the green nylon sides bulged as he made himself comfortable. "Hey . . ." Folded space distorted his voice. "What's with the rubber tree and the hat stand?"

"They're holding open the possibilities." Zipping up all but the top six inches, Diana swung the pack over her shoulders and headed for the road.

Their first ride took them into Lucan.

Their second, to London.

In London, they got a lift from a trucker carrying steel pipe to Montreal. Diana spent the trip strengthening the cables that held the pipes to the flatbed—a little accident prevention—and Sam horked up a hairball on the artificial lamb's wool seat cover. Which was how they found themselves standing by the side of the road in Napanee, a small town forty minutes east of Kingston.

At Sam's insistence, they stopped for supper at Mom's Restaurant . . .

"No, that's not a cat in my backpack. It's an orange sweater that just happens to enjoy tuna."

. . . where they met someone willing to take them the rest of the way.

Her back to the West Gardener's Mall parking lot, Diana waved as the metallic green Honda merged into Highway Two traffic. "That was fun. I don't think I've ever heard 'It's Raining Men' sung with so much enthusiasm."

"My ears hurt," Sam muttered, jumping out onto the grass.

"I suppose you'd rather have angelic choirs?"

"Are you nuts? All those trumpets—it's like John Philip Sousa does choral music." Carefully aligning his back end, he sprayed the base of a streetlight. "It's all praise God and pass the oom pah pah."

"I'm not even sure I know what that means, but just on principle, please tell me you're kidding."

"Okay, I'm kidding."

She turned to face the mall. "Now say it like you mea . . ." And froze. "Oy, mama. That's not good."

The circles of light that overlapped throughout the parking lot had all been touched with red, creating a sinister—although faintly clichéd—effect. At just past nine, with the mall officially closed, the acres of crimson-tinted asphalt were empty of everything but half a dozen . . .

"Minivans. It's worse than I thought."

*   *   *

He had stood at this door, at this time, every Friday night for the last twenty-one years. There had been other doors in the long years before, but there would be no other doors after. He would make his last stand here. The door was open only to allow late shoppers to exit; he, a human lock, protected the mall from those who would enter after hours.

He watched the girl stride toward him. His lips curled at the sight of bare legs between sandals and shorts. His eyes narrowed in disgust at the way her breasts moved under her T-shirt. He snorted at her backpack and her youth.

Were it up to him, he'd never let her kind into the mall. He knew what they got up to. Talking. Laughing. Standing in groups. Standing in pairs. Pairs tucked away in Bozo's School Bus using lips and hands.

He stiffened as she stopped barely an arm's length away.

"The mall is closed. It will reopen tomorrow at nine a.m."

Pink lips parted. "*Please* move out of my way."

Twenty-one years at this door. "The mall is closed. It will reopen tomorrow at nine a.m."

Dark brows rose and dark eyes tried to meet his, but he stared at the drop of sweat running down her throat to pool against her collarbone and refused to be drawn in.

"Okay, fine. We'll just have to do this the hard way."

"The mall is closed. It will reopen tomorrow at nine a.m."

"Yeah, gramps, I got it the first time."

His eyes burned and he blinked, only a single blink, but when his vision cleared, the girl was gone.

Good. It was good that she was gone. Gone with her shorts and her breasts and all her infinite possibilities.

Diana stopped just the other side of Bozo's School Bus, set her backpack down on the yellow plastic kiddie ride, and waited while Sam climbed out.

"That was creepy," he muttered, licking at a bit of ruffled fur.

"Very. And aren't people that old supposed to be retired or something?"

"Or something," the cat agreed. "Hey." Front paws on the Plexiglas window, Sam peered into the bus. "This thing has seat belts. They don't take it out of the building, do they?"

"Uh, no."

"Then why seat belts?"

"I have no idea. But you know what's really whacked? My bus—the one I rode down potholed dirt roads at a hundred and twenty klicks every morning and afternoon with a whole lot of very small bouncy children—no belts." Swinging her pack back onto her shoulders, she headed for the main concourse. "Stay close and no one will see you."

Sam fell into step by her right ankle. "Considering

what that thing smelled like, I can think of one reason for seat belts. This place is huge. How are we
going to find the Erlking Emporium?"

"Easy. We find the you-are-here sign. It's probably
at the end of this side hall."

It wasn't.

Although the side hall and one of the huge anchor
stores spilled out into the main concourse at the same
place, there was nothing to help mall patrons find their
way through the two-story maze of stores they now
faced.

"Maybe someone from the Otherside took it," Sam
offered when it became clear they were directionally
on their own.

"It's possible." Motioning for Sam to be quiet,
Diana froze as a final shopper slipped through the
partially barricaded Kitchen Shop storefront, clutching a cheap manual can opener and trailing the ill
wishes of the teenage clerk like black smoke behind
her as she hurried down the side hall. "She feels like
the last one in here. We'd better get moving before
that creepy old security guard heads this way."

Sam butted his head reassuringly against her leg.
"You can take him."

"Well, yeah. But I'd rather not. Come on. Blonde
Ponytail said . . ."

"Who?"

"The jock with the bracelet. I never got her name.
She said the store was on the lower level, so let's
find some stairs."

Behind reinforced glass or steel bars, the stores themselves were places of shadow.

Unless the bracelet was the only piece of the Otherside they were selling, Diana should have been able to sense the Emporium, her Summons directing her like a child's game of Warm and Cool where the parts of "Warm" and "Cool" were played by "I Can Live With the Headache if I Have to" and "Shoot Me Now." Unfortunately, the Summons was unable to poke through the interference from the back rooms where a hundred part-time teenagers counted up a hundred cash drawers and ninety-seven of them came up short. By the time the cash had to be counted for the third time, the emanation of frustrated pissiness was so strong Diana couldn't have sensed a trio of bears if they were sneaking up beside her.

"Hey, Rodney River has orange polyester bell-bottoms on sale for $29.99."

"Is that good?" Sam wondered.

Diana shuddered. "I can't see how." Pleased to see that the escalators had already been turned off—cat on escalator equaled accident waiting to happen—she led the way to the stairs.

Only the emergency lights were lit on the lower level, and the footprint of the mall seemed to have subtly changed.

"There's too many corners down here. And if I can smell the food court, why can't we find it?"

"I don't . . . Someone's coming." Scooping up the

cat, Diana backed into a triangular shadow and wrapped the possibilities around them both half a heartbeat before a flashlight beam swept by.

"I know you're here." One shoe dragging *shunk kree* against the fake slate tiles, the elderly security guard emerged from a side hall. Massive black flashlight held out in front of him, he walked bent forward, his head moving constantly from side to side on a neck accordion-pleated with wrinkles.

Diana would have said the motion looked snake-like except that she rather liked snakes.

Shunk kree. Shunk kree. "I will find you; never doubt it. I know you've hidden your lithe bodies away in the shadows."

Sam twisted in Diana's arms until he could stare up at her. His expression saying as clearly as if he'd spoken, "Lithe?" She shrugged.

"Long, loose limbs stacked unseen against the wall." *Shunk kree.*

Who was he looking for? It couldn't be her and Sam—he thought *they* were gone.

The flashlight beam flicked up, caught the pale face of a store mannequin, and stopped moving.

"Can't run now, can you?" He shuffled past so close to her hiding place that Diana could almost count the dark gray hairs growing from his ear. "Can't run with your muscles moving inside the soft skin."

Diana gave him a count of twenty, then prepared to slip out and away. She had a foot actually in the air when cool fingers wrapped around her upper arm and held her in place.

Shunk. The security guard pivoted on one heel, turning suddenly to face back the way he'd come, flashlight beam exposing circles of the lower concourse. "Not too smart for me with your young brains," he muttered, turning again and *shunk kreeing* his way toward the mannequin.

The cool fingers were gone as though they'd never existed. Since Diana was certain she and Sam had been alone in their sanctuary, the logical response seemed to be that they never had. That they'd been a construct of self-preservation. Her own highly developed subconscious holding her back from discovery. On the other hand, logic had very little to do with possibility, so Diana murmured a quiet thanks to the fingers as she left the shadow.

Cat in her arms, staying close to the storefronts, she raced down the concourse toward a side hall they hadn't tried, at least half her attention listening for the *shunk kree* following behind her. After weaving through a locked-down display of hot tubs, she sagged against a pillar, adding its bulk to the space she'd already put between them and the old man.

"Okay," she whispered into the top of Sam's head. "I am officially squicked out. Where did they find that guy? He's like every creepy, clichéd old man rolled into one wrinkly package and wrapped in a security guard's uniform. I mean, I know he's just a Bystander and I handled him at the door, but still . . ."

"Still what?"

"You know, *still*."

"If I knew, I wouldn't have asked," Sam pointed out, squirming to be let down. "And by the way, we've found the food court."

Only six of the seven food kiosks were currently occupied. Directly across from them, a poster on plywood announced the future site of a Darby's Deli. At some point, a local artist had used a black marker to make a few additions to the poster's picture of Darby Dill, creating a remarkably well hung condiment. Tearing her gaze away from the anatomically correct pickle, Diana spotted yet another hall on the far side of the food court, the rectangular opening tucked into the corner between Consumer's Drug Mart and a sporting goods store.

"It's got to be down there."

"Why?"

"Because it isn't anywhere . . . What are you eating?"

Sam swallowed. "Nothing."

As they entered the hall, the tile turned to a rough concrete floor. The bench and its flanking planters of plastic trees, although outwardly no different from other benches and other trees, had a temporary look. Only three stores long, the hall ended in a gray plywood wall stenciled with a large sign that read, "Construction Site: No Entry." The last store before the wall was the Emporium.

Tucked into another convenient shadow, Diana studied the storefront through narrowed eyes. "I can't sense a power signature, so I'm guessing the power surge only went one way."

"If they'd known you were coming, they'd have baked a cake?"

She stared down at the cat. "Something like that, yeah. Who . . . ?"

"Your father."

"Well, do me a favor and don't pick up any more of his speech patterns because that would be too weird."

"Why?"

"Sam, you sleep on my bed. Just don't, okay?"

He shrugged, clearly humoring her. "Okay."

Diana turned her attention back to the store. "They're not being very subtle, are they? If any of the Lineage had ever window-shopped their way down here, the name alone would have given the whole thing away."

"The Lineage is big into window shopping?"

"Not my point."

"Okay. But I think Erlking Emporium has a marketable ring to it."

"Marketable? First of all, you're a cat; marketable for you involves a higher percentage of beef byproducts. Second; do you even know what an Erlking is?"

Sam shot her an insulted amber glare, the tip of his tail flicking back and forth in short, choppy arcs. "According to German legend, it's a malevolent goblin who lures people, especially children, to their destruction."

Which it was. "Sorry. I keep forgetting about that whole used-to-be-an-angel had-higher-knowledge thing."

"Yeah, you do. But I learned that off a PBS special on mythology."

"While I was where?"

"Cleaning the splattered remains of a history essay off your bedroom walls."

"Right." A lapse in concentration and the Riel Rebellion had spilled out of her closet. It had taken her the entire weekend to clean up the mess, and most of it had turned out to be nonrecyclable. "I think I've seen enough. Let's go."

The purely physical lock on the door took only a trickle of power to open.

Sam radiated disapproval as he slipped through into the store. "Breaking and entering."

"Technically, only entering." Locking the door behind them, Diana tried not to sneeze at the overpowering odor of gardenia coming off the display of candles immediately to her left. A quick glance showed that the gardenia had easily overpowered vanilla, cinnamon, bayberry, lilac, belladonna, monkshood, pholiotina, and yohimbe. Unless the Colonial Candle Company was branching out into herbal hallucinogens, at least half the display had clearly been brought over from the Otherside.

Not just the bracelet, then.

Rubbing her nose, she moved cautiously into the store, skirting a locked glass cabinet filled with crystal balls, and ending up nearly treading on Sam's tail as, hissing, he backed away from . . . Diana bent over to take a closer look and had no better idea what animal the pile of stuffed creatures was supposed to represent. In spite of neon fur, they looked remarkably lifelike—given a loose enough definition of both life and like.

"I was just startled," Sam muttered, vigorously washing a front paw.

"If I was closer to the ground, they'd have startled me, too."

"I wasn't afraid."

"I know." She stroked down the raised hair along his back as she straightened. "I think we can safely say the hole's not out here. Let's check out the storeroom."

"It's not back there either."

Not Sam. Not unless Sam's voice had deepened, aged, and moved up near the ceiling.

Diana dropped down behind a rack of resin frogs dressed in historical military uniforms and began to gather power.

"Think about it for a minute, Keeper; if I wasn't on your side, I'd have already sounded the alarm. Why don't you drop the fireworks and come over here so we can talk."

He—whoever he was—had a point. Diana stood, slowly, and looked around. The shadows made it difficult to tell for certain, but she'd have been willing to bet actual cash money that she and Sam were alone in the store. "Where are you?"

"Up in the corner."

The only thing she could see in the corner was the convex circle of a security mirror. Just as she was realizing the reflection seemed a little off, a familiar pair of blue-on-blue eyes appeared. "You've got to be kidding me. They're using a magic mirror for security?"

"Ain't life a bitch," the mirror agreed. "Got pulled out of a well-deserved retirement—quiet hall, nice view out an oriel window—and got stuffed up here by Gaston the Wondertroll."

"So there's a real troll?"

"Large as life, and twice as ugly. Actually, larger than life if we're reflecting accurately."

"Great."

"I wouldn't worry about him, kid; he's just the front man." Faint blue frown lines. "Front troll. Those actually running this segue are keeping their heads tucked well down until it's too late for your lot to stop it."

Good thing she'd touched that bracelet, then. The energy discharged had been enough to crack the shielding and send the Summons. No touching, no Summons, no chance to stop the . . . "Wait a minute. Did you say, *segue*?"

"I did."

"Okay. This is one of those times when I really wish I could swear." She took three quick steps away from the mirror. Three quick steps back. "I should have known there was more to this than a cheesy gift shop selling . . ." A glance down. ". . . fake fairies on sticks."

"Look again."

Under the lacquer and the glitter . . .

"Eww."

"Duck!"

"Where?" Diana didn't even want to think about what these guys could do to a duck. A sudden circle of light hit the back wall of the store and she dropped to the ground. Oh. *Duck.*

The emporium's door rattled as someone shook it, testing the lock.

Now who could that be? Two guesses and the first one doesn't count. Flat against the carpet to keep the curve of her backpack behind cover, she tried not to think about the dark stain just off the end of her nose.

"Think you can get away with anything. Young bodies, supple, lissome."

Adding that to lithe and limber, there seemed to be a thesaurus specifically for dirty old men.

"You can't hide forever." The circle of light swept across the store and disappeared. Through the glass came a muffled *shunk kree, shunk kree* as the security guard moved away.

Remembering the warning delivered by imaginary fingers, Diana hissed, "Sam, stay down," a heartbeat before the light flashed back through the window. She counted a slow ten after *that* light disappeared before she stood. "Sam?"

He crawled out from behind a box of glow-in-the-dark Silly Putty and shook his fur back into place. "Don't worry about me. I'm way faster than a geriatric rent-a-cop."

"Good. So." Arms folded, she stared up at the mirror. "Let's cut to the chase before we're interrupted again."

"Fine with me, Keeper. Here's the deal: I give you what help I can; in return, you get me out of here when you shut this place down."

"Agreed."

"And you recognize that when the shit hits the fan, I'm breakable and more than just a little exposed."

She nodded. "We'll be careful."

"We? That would be you and the cat?"

"Us, too." Diana took one last look around the store and decided she really didn't need to know just what exactly the weights on the wind chimes were made of. "I think we're going to need a little help."

TWO

Dropping his spray bottle of window cleaner onto the old-fashioned wooden counter, Dean Mc-Issac crossed the small office and caught the phone on the second ring. "Elysian Fields Guest House." A small frown of concentration appeared as he flipped open the reservation book, a leather-bound tome with the phases of the moon prominently displayed by each date. "Yes, sir, we still have rooms available for next Wednesday. We can certainly accommodate you and your mother. Sorry? Oh. Your mummy. No, that's fine; many of our guests arrive after dark. We'll hold the rooms until midnight. A dehumidifier? That can be arranged, I understand how mold and mildew could be a problem. No, unfortunately, I can't guarantee the Keeper will be here, but I'm sure you'll find our . . ." His cheeks flushed. "Thank you, sir. I'll see you Wednesday."

"Flushed is a good look on you."

"Claire!" The receiver fell the last six inches into the cradle as Dean flag-jumped the counter and gathered the smiling Keeper into his arms.

"You made good time," he murmured when they finally came up for air.

"I had a good reason."

"One that I should know about?"

Dark brown eyes gleamed suggestively up at him. "Definitely."

His fingers tightened on her shoulders and he began to pull her close again.

"Hel-lo! Crushing the cat here!"

Dean released his hold like he had springs in his fingers, and Claire leaped back, exposing the indignant, black-and-white cat cradled between them. "I'm sorry, Austin. I just got excited about being home."

"Oh, yeah," he muttered as she set him carefully on the counter. "It's home that gets you excited. Tell us another one. No, wait . . ." He turned and glared at her from a single emerald eye. ". . . don't."

"Okay." Her hands free, she slid them up the sculpted muscle of Dean's torso and around the back of his neck, fingers entwined in thick hair. "I can't resist a man in a pink T-shirt."

He shifted his grip to her waist, thumbs working against the damp line of flesh between cropped tank and skirt. "Someone buried a red catnip square in the laundry basket."

"That's right. Blame the cat. The starving cat!" Austin snapped after a moment when it became quite clear he'd been forgotten again. "The old starving cat who just spent three hours in a car listening to sappy tales of dear, departed Muffy—who probably threw herself in front of that truck in an effort to escape the schmaltz with what was left of her dignity. The old starving cat who's going to give you a count of three before he starts making pointed comments about your technique!"

"Austin, there's a package of calf liver in the fridge." Dean slid his hands down to the backs of Claire's thighs and lifted her up onto the counter, hiking her skirt up over her knees. "It's after being yours if you'll disappear for ten minutes."

"Fifteen," Claire growled, licking at the sweat beading Dean's throat. She kicked off her sandals, crossed her ankles behind him, and dragged him closer.

"You guys do know this is a hotel, right? Like, get a room!"

Forehead to forehead, Dean stared deep into Claire's eyes. "You didn't lock the door?"

"Apparently not."

Lip curled in disgust, Diana closed the front door, pointedly locked it, and strode across the lobby toward the long hall that led to the back of the guesthouse. "We've got a bit of shopping-mall-takes-over-the-world situation here, but you guys go right ahead and continue with that whole blatant heterosexuality thing; there's probably time. I'll just make myself a sandwich and feed the cats. Coming, Austin?"

"Finally," he snorted, jumping carefully down off the counter, "someone who has their priorities straight!"

"Are they always like that?" Sam wondered as the older cat fell into step beside him.

"Are you kidding? They've only been apart for three days—you should see them after a week. Spontaneous combustion."

Sam frowned. "Wouldn't that kill them?"

"You'd think."

As the footsteps of the two cats and her sister faded toward the kitchen, Claire sighed. "Well, I'm no longer in the mood. You?"

"Not so much. That was after ending things for me." He lifted her down off the counter and steadied her while she slipped her sandals back on. "Just so I'm clear on this; strangling your sister is not an option, then?"

"If you want to strangle my sister," Claire told him as they left the lobby, "you'll have to wait in line."

"I hope you guys postponed instead of finishing," Diana snorted as they entered the kitchen, "because if that was it, Claire should file a complaint. I mean it's not like I'm an expert on these things," she continued, assaulting a leftover roast with the carving knife, "but someone's getting left a little short. No offense." She grinned up at Dean.

"And yet, I'm offended anyway." Grasping her wrist with one hand, he confiscated the knife with the other and jerked his head toward the dining room table. "You sit. I'll do this."

"I don't know, Dean. I like my sandwiches made slowly and with care."

"And you might want to reconsider further commentary," Claire interjected from the dining room, "since he's eight inches taller than you and holding a knife."

"Please," Diana scoffed, grabbing a bottle of juice from the fridge and coming around the counter that separated the two rooms, "Dean's a pussycat."

"Now, *I'm* offended," Austin muttered.

Sam looked up from his cat food and frowned. "I thought you liked him."

"Yeah. So?"

"I don't understand."

"You're not supposed to," Claire told the younger cat comfortingly. "Let it go and move on." Pulling out one of the antique table's dozen chairs, she folded a leg up onto the red velvet seat and sat, indicating that Diana should do the same.

Diana didn't so much sit as gang up with gravity to assault the furniture.

Claire winced as the chair protested, but hundred-year-old joints and wood glue held. "You said something about a shopping mall taking over the world?"

"I'm amazed you heard me."

"You have a talent for attracting attention. I assume this concerns your first Summons as an active Keeper?"

"Got it in one." Smiling her thanks at Dean for the sandwich, she waited until he sat down and pulled his seat up close behind Claire's before she continued. "It all started this afternoon on what was, thank God, my very last day of school . . ."

When the story arrived at the mall, Claire interrupted.

"You should have called me."

"Chill, uberKeeper. You weren't in Kingston, and until I actually got to the Emporium, all I had was a piece of ugly jewelry. I'd have been further ahead closing down the Home Shopping Network. Unfortunately, once at the Emporium, I discovered we're talking about a little more than a mere accident site—according to the magic mirror they're using for security . . ."

"Magic mirror?" Dean leaned forward, one hand on Claire's shoulder. "Like in the fairy tales?"

"Just like. Well, not exactly like," Diana amended after chewing and swallowing the last mouthful of sandwich. "He's a little pissed about being yanked out of retirement by Gaston the Wondertroll and is willing to do what he can to close the whole thing down."

"Troll?"

She nodded. "They're not just under bridges anymore."

"According to the magic mirror," Claire prompted, poking her sister with a Tahiti Sands-tipped finger.

"Ow."

"Diana . . ."

"Okay, fine. According the mirror, whose name is Jack, it's a segue."

"A segue?" When Diana nodded, her expression making it clear she wasn't kidding around, the older Keeper ran a hand up through her hair. "I have a sudden need for profanity."

"Yeah. That was my reaction. That mall's got to cover at least four acres. Maybe as much as six."

"Segue?" Dean asked, dragging his chair around far enough to see Claire's face.

"A metaphysical overlap intended to displace reality."

He switched his attention to Diana.

She scratched thoughtfully at her left elbow and tried to come up with an explanation he could understand. "You know how the Otherside is neither here nor there? That everyone—good guys, bad guys, the Swiss—can all get in but can only get back out into their own reality, the one they left from? Well, in a segue, someone, or something, matches up a piece of the Otherside to this reality and blends them together until enough of the copy occupies the space of the original whereupon the copy takes over. That puts a piece of the Otherside inside this reality so that anyone can enter it from their reality and exit here. The Erlking Emporium is anchoring the biggest segue I've ever heard of."

"The biggest?"

"Well, you can't count Las Vegas, that's a metaphysical heritage site. All that bad taste in one place put a real strain on reality."

It took Dean about half a heartbeat to decide that was one of those comments he didn't need to understand. "But how did the segue in the mall get so big without you guys noticing?"

"Hell," Austin answered before either Keeper could.

He put his front paws up on Claire's knee and she lifted him onto her lap. "They hid a smaller bad inside the noise of the biggest bad. They probably set the anchor last fall while we were closing the hole and after that, it was just a matter of keeping things moving ahead, slow and steady."

"And they are?"

"Your guess is as good as mine. Oh, wait. No it isn't." He paused and licked at the quarter-sized bit of black fur on his front leg. "For simplicity's sake, let's just call them the bad guys."

"But the Otherside isn't necessarily bad."

"Doesn't matter; with a segue *anything* can cross over. Bad, good . . ."

"Hey!" Sam protested, coming out of the kitchen. "This world could use a little more good in it. I ought to know."

Austin sighed. "Yeah, yeah. Light. Angel. Cat. Yadda. We all know the story and you're missing the point. A little good is fine. A lot of good isn't."

"Keepers maintain the balance, Sam. A functional segue could tip it in either direction, and if they're using trolls, well, I'm guessing we're not heading for hugs and cheesecake." Claire rubbed her thumb gently over the velvet fur between Austin's ears. "Shutting them down is a tricky business," she added thoughtfully. "It can't be done from this side; I'll have to cross over and go to the source."

Diana rolled her eyes. "*You'll* have to? Try *we'll* have to. If I can't close something this big on my own, you certainly can't—Basic Folklore 101, the younger sibling is always more powerful. I have the power, you have the experience. United we stand, divided we fall, yadda yadda. So I suggest you get over yourself, drop the whole I'm-the-only-one-who-can-save-the-world crap, and recognize that *we've* got trouble."

"Right here in River City," Sam added.

"Show tunes?" Austin glared down at the orange cat. "You have got to be kidding."

"I have three words for you, Austin." Diana leaned a little closer to Claire's lap and flicked up a finger for each word. "Andrew Lloyd Webber. But that's so not what we're talking about. We need to get back into that mall and close that segue. It's going to take some time, so I suggest we start tonight."

"Ignoring your less than flattering opinion of my character," Claire muttered darkly, "I agree."

"I don't."

"Listen much, Dean? Segue bad. Keepers good. And I don't know where I was going with that, but the sooner we get the sucker closed down the better."

"Not arguing," Dean told the young Keeper calmly. "You said it's going to take some time—that means you'll be there for a while?"

Diana shrugged. "Yeah, but . . ."

"So you can't just rush in all unprepared."

"I guess not."

"You'll have to pack."

Claire twisted around until she could see his face. "We have everything here . . ."

"It'll still take time." He glanced over at the old school clock hanging on the wall in the kitchen. "It's past eleven now. It'll be close to midnight when you're ready to leave. By the time you get to the mall, you've both already been up for what—sixteen, seventeen hours? You'll be facing whoever created this thing when you're tired. You won't be thinking as quickly or as clearly. The bad guys could win before you even get started and then where's the world? Up sh . . . the creek without a paddle." Taking a deep breath, he let it out slowly, holding Claire's gaze with his, lacing the fingers of his right hand through the fingers of her left. "You've got to weigh the delay against going in tired and unprepared. You should sleep tonight and go in tomorrow morning."

Diana opened her mouth to deliver a blistering reply, and snapped it shut again as Austin said, "He's right."

"He's a Bystander!"

"And I'm a cat, so listen up." He climbed from Claire's lap up onto the table, leaving sweaty paw prints on the polished wood. "Going in tired and unprepared is a good way to get our collective butts kicked but, more importantly, going in tonight gives the advantage to the other side."

"You mean the Otherside?" Diana sniped.

"Don't interrupt. Two Keepers and two cats head into an empty mall in the middle of the night and we might as well call first to tell them we're coming. There's no way even the most idiotic, written for television, evil overlord isn't going to notice something like that. The moment we cross over, BAM! And that's if we're lucky. We all know there's a whole lot worse than BAM waiting out there."

"No, we don't." Ears saddled, Sam sat down on Diana's foot. "What's worse than BAM?"

"Splat. Crunch. Grind. Chew." When no one seemed inclined to argue, Austin continued. "We get a good night's sleep and go in tomorrow morning with all the other shoppers, hiding in plain sight. We slip across with no one the wiser, you two close down the segue, and we're home by lunch."

"Lunch?"

Austin snorted. "Okay, it's a metaphorical lunch some days in the future."

"Look, it's my Summons," Diana protested, tumbling Sam off her foot and jerking her chair away from the table. She had a strong suspicion that had come out sounding whinier than she'd intended.

"You came here for help," Claire reminded her. "You were there, in the mall; is there a chance the copy will be matched up before morning?"

"No. But . . ."

"Then I vote we wait. But you're right." She raised the hand not holding Dean's in surrender. "It's your Summons. Only you can make the final decision."

"Don't patronize me."

"Then stop acting so childish. When you got here, you were willing to stop for a sandwich, and now you're set on charging in where angels fear to tread."

"Angels don't fear much," Sam began, caught

sight of Austin's expression, and decided he'd rather be under the table.

Diana folded her arms and just managed to stop her lip from curling. Knowing they were right didn't help. "All right, fine. We'll go in the morning."

"Fine."

"Good."

"And now that's settled, I'm going to bed." Austin stepped from the table to Claire's lap to the floor, glaring at Dean on the way by. "These days, if I don't stake my claim early, all the good spots are taken."

"We'll be there in a few minutes," Claire told him, her tone very nearly making the words a warning.

"Oh, joy." He stopped, one paw in the hall, and glanced back over an immaculate black shoulder. "Don't forget to pack the cat food."

"And thus we have the subtitle for my life," Claire sighed, getting to her feet. "When you left to answer this Summons, did you tell Mom and Dad where you were heading?"

"They weren't home. I left them a note."

"You should call before you go to bed."

"Yeah. Right." Picking up her sandwich plate, Diana headed for the kitchen only to be stopped by Dean's outstretched hand.

"I've got it."

"I was just going to put it in the dishwasher. Claire said business was good enough that you guys bought a dishwasher."

"We did."

"So?"

The blue eyes behind the glasses met hers without apology. "I like to load it."

"He has a system," Claire put in.

"Whatever." Diana handed over the plate and watched Dean walk into the kitchen. "He's just a little obsessive," she murmured as Claire moved up beside her.

"A little . . ."

The faded jeans stretched tight as he bent over to set the plate in the lower rack.

". . . but there are compensations."

"Oh, yeah. I can tell you're with him for his mind." Grabbing her backpack, she headed for the hall. "So, in the interest of being rested and prepared, I'm going to grab the key to room one and crash. Come on, Sam."

Eyes still on Dean, Claire waved absently toward her sister. "Call home."

"Bite me."

Accelerating to make the end of the advance green, Dean cranked his truck hard to the left and roared up into the mall's parking lot. Just after nine *a.m.* the temperature had already climbed past thirty degrees C; unusually hot for the end of June. Three adults and two cats didn't leave a lot of room for air flow in the cab and exposed skin would have been covered in a glistening layer of sweat had not the fine patina of cat hair caught—and dimmed—the glisten.

"That's the entrance by the food court," Diana declared, pointing out the open window. "Turn here."

Dean turned.

"If it's the closest entrance to the Emporium, it'll be the most watched and therefore the most likely to be guarded," Claire argued, holding her skirt up off the damp skin of her legs with two fingers. "Turn back onto the roadway and head for the door Diana used last night. We know we can get through that one."

Dean turned.

"We don't know that we can't get through the closer one."

"We don't want to risk setting off an alarm."

"And the longer we spend wandering around the mall, the greater the chance we'll be discovered. Dean, turn here."

Dean turned.

"Charging in on a direct line to the Emporium is a lot more likely to get us noticed. Dean, turn here."

Dean stopped the truck.

Both sisters shot him essentially identical looks of disbelief as they rocked forward against their seat belts.

"You either walk from here," he told them calmly, "or you agree on an entrance."

The cab filled with overlapping protests and no agreement.

Irresistible brown eyes met immovable brown eyes.

"Okay, that's it." Austin flowed up over the back

of the seat. "Since two of us are out here sweltering in fur coats . . ."

"I'm okay," Sam interrupted.

"Shut up, kid. . . . sweltering in fur coats," he repeated, "and there's air-conditioning behind whatever door we decide to go through, I'm making an executive decision." He jumped down onto Claire's lap and put his front paws up onto the dash. "What's wrong with those doors? They're closest."

Claire shook her head. "They lead to one of this reality's anchor stores. The way things are skewed, we might not be able to get out."

"Fine. What about the next doors?"

"Same store."

"And the doors after that?"

"That," Diana told him, arms crossed and sitting as slumped as her seat belt and the crowded conditions allowed, "is where I went in last night."

"Then that's where we're going in today."

"But it's my Summons. I should be in charge."

Austin's head swiveled slowly around and caught Diana in an emerald glare.

"Okay," she muttered, wondering whose bright idea it had been that Keepers hang out with cats. "We'll go in there."

"Excellent idea. Claire?"

She decided not to point out that it was where she wanted to go all along. "I agree."

Unable to stop himself from grinning, Dean put the truck into gear. Given the nonfeline connotations, he didn't think he could say the words *pussy whipped* to his true love and her little sister—no matter how accurate the observation.

As they came around the corner of the building, he felt Claire stiffen beside him. "What is it?"

"Minivans."

"They were here last night as well," Diana said grimly.

"You should have told me."

"Why? There's nothing we can do."

"It's just . . ."

"Yeah. I know."

Minivans? In the nine months Dean had known Claire, he'd gone briefly to Hell, driven around northern Ontario after a demon, and discovered that all those clichés about regular sex were pretty much true. He'd also learned that there were some things he was happier not knowing. This seemed like one of them.

"What was wrong with that parking spot?" Claire demanded as he drove past open pavement.

"Nothing. But I can get closer."

"Okay, there's one."

"I see it."

"And you just drove by it."

"I can get a better spot."

"The doors are right there!"

"I see them."

"So *park* already."

Speeding up to cut off a circling red sedan, Dean

pulled in between a midnight-blue and a seafoam-green minivan and shut off the engine looking proud of himself. They were four spaces in, straight out from the door.

Claire rolled her eyes. "You are such a *guy*."

He grinned and threw one arm along the seat back behind her, the close quarters allowing his fingers to trail down the damp, bare skin of her arm. "You have a problem with me being a guy."

"Well, not right at this minute . . ."

Unbuckling her seat belt, Diana threw open the door and dropped down onto the pavement. "You guys are terminally embarrassing and . . . I'm sinking."

"What?" Setting Austin on Dean's lap, Claire slid across the seat and peered down at her sister's feet. "That's impossible. It's not *that* hot out."

"Hey, you don't have to take my word for it." Stepping two careful paces back, heavy rubber tread imprinting the asphalt, Diana gestured for Claire to join her.

The low heels on Claire's sandals poked square holes into the pavement. Pulling her skirt against her legs so that she could see her feet, she frowned. "This isn't good. The influence has reached the parking lot."

"Well, duh." Diana swung one arm out in a wide, demonstrative arc. "Minivans?"

"Right. We'd better carry the cats. Dean, can you get the backpacks?"

Even with the extra weight, the pavement remained firm under Dean's work boots.

"That's a relief," Diana noted as she set Sam down on the concrete pad outside the door and began scraping the felted layer of orange cat hair off her arms. "If it's only affecting us, it hasn't spread as far as we thought."

"And I'll be pleased about that in a minute," Claire muttered, glaring down at the tar stuck to her heels. "I told you those were stupid shoes to wear Otherside."

"No, you didn't."

"Didn't I? I meant to."

"I was after thinking that the whole rubber tree/hat stand thing kept these light." Stepping over Austin, who'd sprawled out on his side in the shade, Dean set both packs on the black metal bench to one side of the door. "What's *in* here?"

"A serious lackage of rubber trees and hat stands." Wondering why Claire seemed to be cat hair free, Diana crossed to her pack and lifted it. "It's against the Rules to access the possibilities once we've crossed over, so stuff like that won't work. Which means we have . . ." She swung it up onto her shoulders. ". . . a few clothes, some preset odds and ends—possibilities having been used to create them but no longer necessary, so hopefully they'll still work. . . ."

"Hopefully?" Dean interrupted with a searching glance at Claire.

"Hopefully," Diana repeated when it became obvious that Claire had nothing reassuring to say. "But mostly we're carrying food and water because it's dangerous to eat or drink on the Otherside."

"Why?"

"Are you kidding? They put sauces on everything so it's all high-cholesterol-let's-slap-the-calories-right-onto-the-hips time."

"The food changes you," Claire interjected, shooting Diana a *stop messing with his head* look. She laced her fingers through Dean's and smiled up at him. "Different foods do different things, and all of it ties you to the Otherside, making it harder to get home. You've heard of Persephone and the pomegranates?"

Dark brows dipped down under the upper edge of his glasses. "Early eighties girl band? Had one hit 'You're Not Seeing My Depression'?"

Diana snorted. "It was, 'You're Not Seeing My Repression.' Although, given the hair, I totally admit they had reason to be depressed."

"How do either of you know what was going on in the early eighties?"

"MuchMusic Classic Videos," Sam told her, sitting down by Austin and wrapping his tail around his toes. "There's, like, two hours of them every Saturday afternoon."

Claire looked from the younger cat to the older.

"Don't look at me," Austin sniffed disdainfully. "If we're not out saving the world, I'm usually napping Saturday afternoons. And speaking of saving the world, I'd just like to point out that we still haven't reached the air-conditioning. Not that I'm complaining or anything. Much."

Hearing impending volume and duration in that final pause, Claire released Dean's hand and reached for her backpack only to find Dean there before her. She turned so he could lift it up onto her shoulders and shivered as he kissed the back of her neck, murmuring, "Be careful." against damp skin.

"I'm always careful."

"What about Sharbot Lake?"

"That wasn't careless, that was just unexpectedly deep." She turned again, facing him now. "Will you be okay?"

He lifted her chin with a finger. "Without you? Probably not."

"Enough with the clichés, already." Thumbs through her pack straps, Diana paced to the edge of the concrete and back making gagging noises. "I've just figured out why Keeper and Bystanders together are such a bad idea. You're boring. And sappy enough to cause insulin shock."

Dean ignored her, his eyes remaining locked on Claire's face. "I'll be waiting here."

"We'll be a couple days; remember?"

"But only on the Otherside." When Claire shook her head, he frowned. "Time runs differently there. You can come out just after you went in. Right?"

"Probably not. Time might run faster or slower in pockets, but in order for the segue to work, they'll have to make time run concurrent on both sides." Hands flat on his chest, she studied his expression. "You knew that, right?"

"And how would I be knowing that if you didn't tell me?"

"I didn't tell you?"

"No." He sighed and pulled her closer. "You'll actually be a couple of days on this side as well?"

"Maybe more. I've set my watch so that we'll know."

"Okay, now we've got that settled," Diana prodded, "just say good-bye already, suck a little face, and let's *go* before the Otherside comes to us."

Dean stared down into Claire's face for a long moment before his mouth finally curved into a worried smile. "Got my heart?"

She laid a hand lightly against her chest. "Right here. Got mine."

He mirrored the motion. "Safe and sound."

"And did I mention, barf! Hey! I said suck a *little* face. You do know she's already had her tonsils out, don't you? So if you're in there looking for them, you're out of luck."

Claire pulled out of Dean's embrace, turned on one heel, smacked Diana lightly on the back of the head, and walked toward the doors—all in one smooth motion. "Someday, as unlikely as it seems, you're going to find someone able to overlook certain personality flaws and I'm going to be there to do the color commentary."

"As if," Diana snorted, waving to Dean and falling into step beside her sister.

"I thought the color commentary was my job?" Sam asked Austin as they followed the Keepers through the doors.

Austin sighed. "There's usually enough to go around."

Once through the inner doors, Keepers and cats both disappeared. Standing with one hand spread out on the outer door, Dean could see his own reflection and little else. It was just a trick of the light, at least that's what he told himself as he walked back to the edge of the concrete and stared out at the heat-silvered sky and the minivans keeping a silent vigil. He felt fidgety, restless—what his grandfather, an outport minister back in Newfoundland, would have called flicy. Hands shoved deep into his pockets, he turned and stared at the mall.

The vertical concrete slabs were almost the same shade as the sky.

Even without knowing what was going on inside, something about the building made his skin crawl. He would have said it was because it looked like a prison except there were two prisons within Kingston's old city limits and both of them were more attractive.

Claire figured they'd be in there for a minimum of two days.

"When do I start worrying?"

"When another Keeper shows up with the Summons," Diana snorted.

"Don't worry," Claire told him, shooting her sister a quelling glance. "I'll always come back to you."

Austin rolled his eyes and horked up a hairball.

Not an entirely comforting memory, Dean realized walking back to the bench and sitting down.

"Oh, my God. They've musaked Alien Ant Farm. It's the second sign of the Apocalypse."

"What was the first?" Claire wondered, shifting her pack straps.

"Orange polyester bellbottoms. On sale."

"How much?"

"You're not serious." A quick glance over at her sister and Diana winced. "You *are* serious. One of us *has* to be adopted."

"I tried adopting you out for most of your childhood. No one would take you."

With the cats hard on their heels, they stepped out into the main concourse and paused. Four senior citizens sat soaking up the air-conditioning on a bench close by the escalator. There was no one else in sight.

Diana pushed damp and rapidly cooling hair up off her forehead. "So much for that hiding in the crowd theory; there were more people in here last night."

"All right, we're a little early for the crowds. But as far as the Otherside is concerned, we're still just shoppers with a perfectly valid reason to be in here. Nothing for them to worry about."

"And the cats?"

"Given the metaphysical buzz this place has,

they'll never notice the trickle of power it'll take to hide the cats . . . provided one of the cats doesn't decide to use a planter as a litter box," she finished glaring at Austin who was digging in the plastic bark chips.

"Old kidneys; give me a break. Besides . . ." One last swipe with a back leg and he jumped up onto the planter's broad rim. ". . . I might have been the first *cat*, but I wasn't the first."

"That's mildly disturbing," Claire admitted, scooping him up into her arms. "Diana, where . . ."

Eyes closed, head swiveling slowly from side to side, Diana waved a silencing hand. "There's something," she murmured, trying to pin it down. "Something close."

"Something? I'm amazed you can sense anything in this."

"Feels like the bracelet. It'd be harder to find if I hadn't already touched . . . There!" Her eyes snapped open and she pointed across the concourse to Heaven Sent Cards and Gifts. "Whatever I'm picking up, is in there."

"Overpriced ceramic angels?" Claire stared at the storefront in dismay. "Lots and lots of overpriced ceramic angels?"

"They're not angels," Sam sniffed, whiskers bristling. "They're cherubs. Useless little twerps in the heavenly scheme of things."

"Well, it's not them." Diana crossed to the store, her soles squeaking faintly against the tile. The moment she stepped onto the dark gray carpet, the feeling strengthened, and she turned to face the cash desk. "It's over there." A quick glance showed Claire and the cats had followed her across the concourse and were standing just off the edge of the carpet. "I'll deal with this while you guys search the rest of the store, just in case. And Sam, do *not* spray those angels."

"Cherubs," he muttered, trying to look as though he hadn't been about to lift his tail.

Claire reached out and poked him lightly with her foot. "Come on. We'll start at the back and work our way forward."

When Diana turned to face the cash desk again, the heavily mascaraed teenager standing behind it was watching her in some confusion.

"Who was she talking to?" she asked, gesturing in the general direction Claire had taken. "If somebody sprays those angels they're, like, going to have to pay for them, you know."

Closing the distance between them, Diana smiled at her. "*Please*, don't worry about it."

"Okay." She nodded slowly, looking slightly stoned and remarkably happy. Looking, as it happened, very much like she was never going to worry about anything ever again.

"Oops." Apparently, her power problems hadn't been solved by moving off reserve status. Reaching out carefully, Diana tweaked things, just a little, and was relieved to see a frown line reappear.

"If you're looking for something, I can't, like, leave the cash desk, so you'll have to find it yourself."

"Not a problem." There were a dozen tubs, boxes, and spinners of impulse kitsch nearly covering the glass counter. If customers actually wanted to buy an item larger than a foot square, they were out of luck. Problem was, in a dozen containers of assorted bits and pieces, the thing she sensed could be . . .

In the tub of magic wands.

"You've got to be kidding me."

The clerk blinked and focused. Lips almost as pale as the surrounding skin twitched. "Kids love these."

"I'm sure." *Especially if they get one that actually works.*

The wands were about eight inches long; a hollow tube of clear Lucite partially filled with a metallic or neon sparkling gel and topped with a plastic star the same color. The fourth one Diana pulled from the tub jerked in her hand, rearranging a display of 'flower of the month' tea cups into a significantly larger porcelain cherub. She was beginning to understand why Sam disliked the things. A quick flick of the wand changed it back.

"What was that?" the clerk demanded, whirling around toward the sound of metal ringing against china.

"Falling halo," Diana told her, continuing to pull wands out of the tub.

"What?"

"Forget about it. Specifically, about *it*," she added hurriedly, heading off inadvertent amnesia.

"Forget about what?"

Nothing like a cliché to measure effectiveness. "Exactly."

The remainder of the wands were no more than they appeared.

"I'll take this one."

"Whatever. That'll be twelve ninety-five. Plus tax."

"Fourteen ninety-four," Diana complained, showing Claire the wand. "For a piece of plastic crap."

Claire stepped aside so that the neon pink star no longer pointed directly at her—she'd seen what had happened to the cups and had no wish to suddenly acquire a useless pair of wings and a winsomely blank expression. "Not a bad price for a working wand, though."

"And the plastic crap was on sale for five dollars," Sam added. "There was a whole box of it at the back of the store."

"From the Otherside?"

"No, I think it was from a Rottweiler."

Should have seen that *coming.* Reaching behind her, Diana slid the wand into a side pocket on her backpack. "Taking this across with us should neutralize it. You're sure there was nothing else?"

"A few Chia Pets left over from Christmas—made on the Otherside, but I checked their bar codes and they were all legally imported."

"Then our work here is done." Diana nodded

down the concourse toward the stairs. "Let's go close this sucker down."

"Chia Pets are imported from the Otherside?" Sam asked, as he and Austin fell into step between the Keepers.

"They were part of a whole Free Trade thing that fell apart over softwood lumber."

"That doesn't make any sense."

"And that's what I told them at the time."

"That wasn't what I . . ." A half glance over at the older cat and Sam realized that it didn't really matter what he'd meant. "Okay. Never mind."

There were more shoppers on the lower levels and a dozen senior citizens in the food court, having coffee and complaining about the way the younger generations were dressing.

"I've had it with my granddaughter," one sighed loudly as the Keepers and cats passed her table. "She's constantly borrowing my clothes."

Her companion set down her blueberry bran muffin and smoothed her *Canadian Girls Kick Ass* T-shirt over artificially perky breasts. "I hear you, Elsie. I hear you."

"That was disturbing," Diana muttered as they headed down the last short hall toward the Emporium. "Didn't you find that disturbing?"

Claire shrugged. "Not really, but then I'm not wearing the same shirt as a seventy-year-old."

"Hey, hers was red on white, mine's white on red. Not the same shirt!"

"Okay."

Marvin Travel, The Tailor of Gloucester, The Erl-king Emporium . . .

Trying to appear as though they were just resting, they sat down on the bench across from the Emporium and took turns glancing through the open door.

"Is that your troll?" Claire asked.

"Okay, first; not *my* troll. And second, why couldn't he have a part-time teenager covering the weekend shifts like almost every other store in the mall?"

"That could be a part-time teenager."

"Good point."

Given the wide variations in human physiognomy, the troll could pass—provided no one looked too closely and were willing to ignore an unfortunate truth; most humans his color had been dead for a couple of days. A couple of hot days. His head was bald, his goatee had probably come off a real goat, his sunglasses appeared to be Ralph Lauren. He was just over six feet tall and only one short third of that was leg. Huge fists dangled even with his knees.

"At least he dresses well."

"Yeah. Nice tie. I wonder what kind of leather it is."

"Not what," Austin said, jumping up onto the bench. "Who."

"Eww."

"His shoes seem to match."

"Like I said, eww."

"It's your Summons," Claire pointed out. "How do we get past him?"

"We've got someone on the inside, remember?" Diana stood, stretched, and started toward the window. Do-it-Yourself Voodoo Kits were forty percent off. Faking an interest in the display, she slid sideways until she could see herself reflected at the very outside edge of the mirror's curve. Blue-on-blue eyes drifted up from the depths.

"Hey, Boss!"

The troll's head jerked around, taking most of his upper body with it owing to a distinct lack of neck. "Are you insane? What if we'd had customers?"

"Then they'd probably be a little freaked by the way the rubber snakes are moving."

"What, again? I knew I shouldn't have trusted that warty little reject from Santa's workshop." Bitching about the way salesmen took advantage of honest retailers, he stomped out from behind the counter and across the store.

Diana, who'd returned to the bench, grabbed Claire's arm. "Now."

When they reached the store, she tugged her sister lower. "Duck!"

Claire almost pulled out of her grip. "Where?"

"Cute, but we did that one already. Just stay low."

A rubbery squelch and a satisfied, "Let's see how much moving you do with your tail stuffed down your throat." propelled them all through the door to the supply room.

There was no immediate sound of pursuit.

And the one nice thing about trolls, Diana acknowledged, *they don't sneak worth a damn.* "Do you think he saw us?"

"Let's not risk it." Claire took three long strides across the storeroom to the steel door that led to the mall's access corridors. She frowned at the hand-lettered "Staff Only" sign, then yanked the door open. "Come on. We've got to be out there to cross over anyway. This is the safest place to emerge into and in order to emerge, we have to exit."

Diana nodded. "An obvious but valid point. Sam . . ." She slipped through after the cat.

Austin followed her.

Claire followed him, checked to make sure they could get the door open again, and carefully closed it.

They found themselves in a concrete corridor where grimy fluorescent bulbs shed just enough light to illuminate a recurring pattern of stains at the base of the walls. The air smelled of old urine and older French fry grease.

Pivoting to the right, Diana took a step toward the ninety-degree turn only a few meters away. "I've always wondered what it looked like back here."

"Here specifically?" Austin snorted.

"No, you know, in back of the shopping parts of shopping malls."

"You need to get out more."

"And we need to get out of here," Claire reminded

them, her hand on the latch. "This is where the troll crosses over; there's so much power residue on and around this door, we'll be able to use it without even causing a blip on their radar."

"Unless we send up a major 'hey look at me' flare because we're going in the opposite direction."

All eyes turned toward the younger cat.

"Sorry. Bit of leftover higher knowledge. It's *possible*. But not very likely," Sam added hurriedly as Austin advanced on him. "I mean, power residue's power residue; right? And besides, what would I know."

"Austin!"

Austin shot a "spoilsport" glare at Claire and suddenly became very interested in cleaning his shoulder, his claws almost totally retracted again.

"It's my Summons." Diana reached out for the latch. "The risk should be mine."

Claire shook her head, blocking Diana's hand. "If one of us is going to send up a flare, I'd rather they knew about me—leaving the more powerful Keeper in reserve."

"That's a good point, but here's a better one. We don't know what we'll face on the other side of this door. I should cross first to make sure we're not stopped before we get started."

"Why don't we cross together. They won't get a good reading from either of us and we'll be ready for whatever we have to face."

"But I get to take it out."

"Be my guest."

On Diana's nod, Claire threw open the door.

The storeroom on the Otherside looked almost exactly like the storeroom they'd left behind. The same metal utility shelves, the same jumble of empty boxes, the same overstock. The only real difference was the light—low, diffuse, and slightly green.

The two Keepers stood weighing the silence for danger.

"Hey." Sam jumped up on a stack of old plastic milk crates. "Where's Austin?"

THREE

One minute, he had the tip of an orange tail in his face. The next, he felt the possibilities shift and he was walking alone into the storeroom they'd just left.

The door to the access corridor was closed.

The door to the store was closed.

Austin sat down, wrapped his tail around his front feet, and glared at nothing in particular. The urge to piss on something was intense. Like all cats, he knew when he was being told "No!"; he usually ignored it, but he knew.

He'd just been told in no uncertain terms.

The possibilities would not allow him to cross over.

When the door to the access corridor remained closed, his eye narrowed. Had she been able to, Claire would have returned immediately to find him. She hadn't, so therefore she couldn't. The question now became: why?

Fortunately, there was a way to find out.

Unfortunately, even up on his hind legs, he could just barely stretch to touch the bottom of the latch plate.

Okay, new plan.

Dropping to all fours, he stared at the closed door, a position proven to bring a talking monkey trotting to his assistance.

"Not a problem, ladies, I've got more T-shirt sizes in the back room."

Or possibly a talking whatever the troll claimed as an evolutionary precedent.

As the door opened, Austin slid in behind a crate marked with both a biohazard and a live cargo symbol. Curious, he took a sniff at one of the air holes, but the crate was empty and had been for some time—probably a good thing although he could easily imagine scenarios where it wouldn't be. With the troll's full attention fixed on pulling an XXX large *Astarte Fan Club* out of a shipping carton of T-shirts, he slipped through the doorway and into the Emporium.

A fast right, a dive under a raised display case, a quick creep forward belly to the ground brought him behind a basket of small plastic jewelry boxes. Head cocked, he listened for the straining gears that would indicate someone with a desire to hear music played on pieces of bent tin had wound the key. When he finally found a silent box, he flipped it open. The miniature Republican in a frilly pink tutu remained motionless in front of the mirror.

Austin smacked the tiny politician out of his way and tipped the box back until its mirror reflected only the security mirror up by the ceiling.

Fortunately, cats were masters of refraction.

The direct approach would have taken him right into the troll's line of sight now that the big guy was back at the counter explaining washing instructions to the T-shirt's new owner—apparently, the blood-stains were not supposed to come out.

Blue-on-blue eyes drifted up from the depths of the jewelry box mirror.

"What are you doing here?" the mirror demanded, its usual booming tones more of a low tinkle.

Muzzle so close his breath fogged the glass. "The possibilities wouldn't let me cross."

"Age thing?"

Austin shrugged. "Maybe. Maybe the idiots in charge think two cats would give the good guys an unfair advantage; I don't know. Can you get a message through to my people on the Otherside? I need to know that Claire's all right; she needs to know that I'm safe."

"I can do better than that. I should be able to patch you through, cat to cat. Video only, though, no audio. You want full bandwidth, you'll need a crystal ball."

"Video's fine." If Claire could see him, she'd know he was okay and could concentrate on doing her job. He scanned the store for something visual that would help get his message through and just when it seemed that nothing at all said "Dean," he spotted the rack of ceramic nameplates.

The rules governing tacky gift store purchases clearly stated that no one was to ever find exactly the name they were looking for.

Cats made their own rules.

Utilizing the speed that could hook a fry from unsuspecting fingers during the instant it passed between plate and lips, Austin leaped into the air, got a paw under his objective, and was on the floor with it before the troll could look up from making change, the impact with the carpet barely audible over the muttered, "Five and six is thirteen plus eight is twenty."

The name was right although the decoration of two obscenely cute mice eating a giant strawberry didn't exactly say six foot two, obsessively tidy, Newfie hockey player. Oh, wait, not a giant strawberry— they just had most of the skin off.

Positioning himself by the mirror again, Austin leaned in until his whiskers touched the glass.

"Do it."

"What do you mean, where's Austin?"

Sam rolled his eyes. "I mean, he's not here."

Diana grabbed Claire's wrist as she reached for the door. "Where are you going?"

"Back. He could be hurt."

"He could be anywhere. Just because the possibilities didn't bring him through here doesn't mean they left him in the other mall."

"There's only one way to find out."

"And if he isn't there?"

Pulling free, Claire took a deep breath and looked her sister in the eye. "Then I'll come right back."

After a long moment, Diana nodded.

Claire closed her fingers around the latch, and froze.

Footsteps. Marching footsteps.

Distant, but coming closer.

Hard soles against concrete.

Hard *something* against concrete. Hooves, maybe? Impossible to tell.

The Keepers could feel the floor vibrate against their feet. Sam's tail puffed out to four times its usual sleek diameter.

Diana wound her fingers through Claire's pack straps and hauled her toward the other door. "We've got to get out of here!"

Closer.

A pair of snowflake paperweights vibrated so violently they shattered, spilling out miniature Grendels chewing on the bloody ends of Viking arms.

"We don't know what's out in the store," Claire protested, as Diana yanked the door open.

"It's got to be better than what's out there!"

Sam leaped off the milk crates and raced between their legs.

"Sam thinks it's safe! Move!"

They dove through the door after the cat. Diana slammed it behind them.

The sudden silence was almost overwhelming.

The hair lifting off his spine into an orange Mohawk, Sam moved out into the store. "It's so thick, it's like walking through pudding."

"You should know," Diana muttered, hands flat against the door, straining to hear if they'd been followed.

"That was an *accident*."

"Maybe the *first* time. I can't hear anything moving in the storeroom." She turned to her sister. "You?"

"Nothing. Wait here. I'll go back for Austin."

"No need."

"Sam!" Claire glared down at the younger cat . . .

. . . who ignored her, his head raised, his eyes locked on the back corner by the ceiling.

The mirror on the Otherside was a sheet of thick, silvered glass, about half a meter wide by a meter long, in an antique wooden frame. It was currently reflecting the store they'd just left. The troll flirted with the two teenage girls standing by the counter, a woman pushed a baby stroller out into the concourse, one of the rubber snakes disappeared under the pile of stuffed toys, and Austin stared down at them from beside a basket of tiny plastic music boxes.

"He's all right." Claire released a breath she hadn't realized she'd been holding. "Thank God."

"You're welcome."

Diana rubbed her hands over the goose bumps texturing her arms. "Uh, Claire, ixnay on the anking-thay odgay while we're erehay. Attracts the wrong kind of attention."

"I know."

"I know you know. You were just relieved to see, you know." She nodded toward the cat in the mirror.

"What's he trying to . . . oh. Dean. He's going to go to Dean."

Eyes narrowed, Diana peered up at the ceramic name plate Austin had pushed out into the aisle. "Are those mice eating a pixie?"

"What? No, they're eating a straw . . . Okay, that's really, really gross."

Then they were staring up at themselves.

"Hey!" Claire folded her arms and stomped one foot—which would have been a more effective protest had the tar residue not temporarily attached her heel to the carpet. She jerked it free, caught hold of a display shelf as her backpack shifted suddenly, threatening to topple her over, and snapped, "What happened?"

The blue-on-blue eyes managed to look slightly sheepish. "Sorry. Lost the signal."

"How?" Diana demanded. "You forgot to disable call waiting?"

"No, it's a hardware problem—those newfangled convex mirrors distort everything. Look, I've got to get back on duty, but don't forget what you promised."

She nodded. "To get you out of here before we shut the place down. I remember."

"You remember now," the mirror acknowledged. "Harder to remember when you're pinned down under enemy fire."

"What enemy fire?" But the eyes were gone and her reflection looked as annoyed as she felt. "What enemy fire?" she repeated in her sister's general direction.

"What difference does it make? Stop thinking about it!"

Diana blanched. The Otherside built substance from the subconscious of its inhabitants and she was suddenly unable to think about anything else. Distraction, distraction . . . "OW!"

Looking smug, Sam removed his claw from her foot.

"So I'm suddenly less convinced that mirror's on our side." Dropping to one knee, she licked her finger and dabbed at the blood. "What do you think, Claire?"

"About what?" She forced her gaze off the mirror. "Sorry. I'm worried about Austin all alone in that mall."

"Austin's older than most of the weekend staff," Diana reminded her. "And it goes without saying he's smarter. I'm totally sure he'll have no problems getting back to where we left Dean."

"We've been here a while. What if Dean's not there?"

His biggest problem was going to be getting out of the Emporium unseen. Capture out in the mall would mean, at most, a few unpleasant hours until he escaped custody. Capture in the store would mean mustard. Trolls put mustard on everything they ate. Usually, to kill the taste. Occasionally, to kill the food. Austin had no intention of dying by condiment.

Concentrating on keeping his tail close, he crept along the floor using every bit of cover an eclectic array of merchandise provided and trying not to notice what he was creeping through. Trolls weren't known for the cleanliness of their carpets and some of the merchandise was eclectic in ways that stained. A little over a meter from the door, he ran out of things to hide behind.

No customers remained to distract the troll.

Even at this distance, the wards around the door stroked energy into his fur. If he read them right, which went without saying, they needed only a single word to close them down and create an impenetrable barrier. Given that he had to cross directly through the troll's line of sight, it would take luck as much as speed to ensure he was on the right side of the barrier when that word was spoken.

Okay. He drew his legs in tight to his body, weight to the back, ready for powerful haunches to launch him forward. *Remember, you're only as old as you feel.*

. . . ready for powerful haunches to launch him forward.

And I feel like I'm going to be eighteen in August.

. . . launch him forward.

Eighteen's old for a cat. If I was a dog, I'd probably be dead. Of course, if I was a dog, I'd want to be dead.

. . . forward.

Oh, crap.

His first leap took him nearly to the threshold. He heard the troll yell "Cat!", then he heard him yell "Endoplasmic reticulum!", saw a flash of aubergine light, smelled the unmistakable odor of burning cat hair, and was in the concourse under the bench, patting out the smoldering end of his tail. Fortunately, his fur was long enough so that no actual damage had been done.

Another flash of aubergine light and an impact that set his whiskers vibrating.

Heart pounding, he turned toward the Emporium.

The troll lay flat on his back just inside the door. Apparently, the wards were set to keep everything in.

"Idiot," he muttered, and washed a triumphant paw.

"Kitty!"

His attention had been so completely on the store that the toddler squatting down and peering under the bench, his diaper nearly touching the tiles, one chubby hand reaching for Austin's head, came as a complete surprise.

"Are you *trying* to give kitty a heart attack," he gasped when he could catch his breath.

"Pretty!"

"Don't touch that!"

"Come on, Brandon." A woman's feet came out from behind a massive stroller. Large hands tucked themselves into the child's armpits and hoisted him out of sight while ducky sandals kicked futilely in protest. "Let's get you home while you're still in a good mood."

Austin inched carefully forward until he could get a good look at young Brandon's destination. The stroller not only had plenty of room for hitchhikers but a large flat canopy. When the back rack was full of bags—which it was—the adult pushing couldn't actually see the seat. He waited while the seat belts were secured, waited while the woman went around to the handle, then, just as the stroller was about to move, he leaped.

"Kitty!"

"No kitties this trip, big fella," the woman corrected, adding with some pique, "and next time we'll stay away from the pet store."

He hadn't been seen and Brandon already had a cover story in place. "Way to go, kid," he murmured into a chubby ear. "Hey! Arm does not go around kitty's neck."

"Kitty soft."

"Yeah? Well, baby smelly." Tucking legs and tail close to his body in an attempt to look as much like a stuffed toy as possible, Austin settled back to enjoy the ride. *If they turn left once they've crossed the food court, I'll have to bail.*

The stroller turned right.

What are the chances, they'll head for the upper level . . . ?

The stroller's front wheels bumped against the escalator.

"You okay in there, Brandon?"

"Okay!" The stroller tipped back and began to rise. "Kitty?"

"I'm good. And do *not* put that in your mouth, it's attached!"

At Sunshine Records, his luck ran out.

"Just going to make a quick stop, kiddo, then we'll head for the parking lot."

With the stroller stopped, someone in the record store would be sure to do that "make faces at the baby" thing that adults found so impossible to resist. After a lifetime of similar faces looming over him, Austin had a strong suspicion the babies weren't as thrilled by it. As they began to turn, he murmured a quick good-bye and jumped clear, racing for a planter and the cover of a plastic shrub.

No hue and cry.

Now to find out exactly where he was.

It looked good. Ten meters of main concourse, then the short side hall to the doors where they'd left Dean. A little exposed until he got to the side hall, but if he remembered correctly—which, of course, he did—once there, he'd have plenty to hide behind.

Play the skulking music, boys.

Checking that no one was looking his way, he jumped down and began moving along the clear Lucite barrier that kept the careless, the stupid, and the carelessly stupid from falling through a hexagonal opening to the lower level.

Clear Lucite barrier?

"Hey!" The shout came from across the concourse. "There's a cat over there! Let's get it!"

Oh, crap.

Wondering how much longer he was going to wait, Dean tried to find a comfortable position on the metal bench and picked up his last remaining section of the Saturday paper. He'd read the comics, the sports pages, the wheels section—which was pretty much the newsprint version of infomercials but about cars so that was okay. He'd read life, and entertainment, and even the report on business. There was nothing left but the actual news.

The front page shared space about equally between a doom-and-gloom prediction of an economic slowdown caused by consumer inability to realize the need for more electronic crap and the continuing disappearance of Kingston's street kids. "Look, the day you can keep track of three hundred and ten cases and not lose a few of the mobile ones, you let me know. Until then, get off my fucking back!" a social worker was quoted as saying. Dean couldn't decide which impressed him more, the social worker for saying it or the paper for actually printing it.

The Children's Aid Society requested that anyone with news contact them at any time, day or night, where any time actually meant between eight and four Monday to Thursday, and eight to noon Fridays because of government cutbacks.

"Okay, now I'm depressed." Folding the section neatly, he piled it with the rest. Claire'd told him that they'd be inside for a couple of days; maybe it was time he went . . .

Paws drumming on glass.

Paws?

Leaping to his feet, he ran for the doors.

Up on his hind legs, his stomach fur a brilliant streak of white, Austin pounded to be let out. As Dean yanked the door open, he fell forward, hit the concrete running, and disappeared into the parking lot before Dean could get a question out.

The trio of teenage boys in hot pursuit made at least one of the questions moot. They rocked to a halt at the edge of the asphalt, stopped as much by the heat as the sudden disappearance of their prey.

"Lose something?" He had four or five years on them and a couple of inches as well as a lot of muscle on the biggest. If it came down to it, Austin was in no real danger.

"You let the cat out, man. We were trying to catch it!"

"Why?"

"Why?" The speaker exchanged a clear but silent *"Dude's an idiot"* with the other two. " 'Cause there's not supposed to be cats in the mall."

Dean glanced pointedly out at the parking lot.

"It's not in the mall now 'cause we chased it out of the mall." Eyes narrowed. "It's not your cat."

"I know." Austin considered Dean one of his ambulatory can openers, but that was beside the point.

"If it's anyone's cat, it's our cat. We saw it first."

"I don't want the damned cat, man." One of the other boys hauled up the shorts falling off skinny hips and looked longingly back toward the air-conditioning. "Come on, it's hot out here."

Under the shadow of a scruffy teenage mustache, the first boy's lip curled. "So we just let the cat win?"

The third boy sighed and scratched at the growing damp spot under his arm. "Cats always win. One way or another."

"Oh, yeah, hiding under a parked . . ." Narrowed eyes widened. ". . . minivan." He shifted his gaze across the nearly uniform rows of family vehicles until it returned, eyes wide, to Dean. "You find the cat, man, you can have it. We don't want it." Hands shoved deep into his pockets, he turned on one heel. "Come on."

Does everybody *know about the minivans?* Dean wondered as the three boys slouched back inside the mall. He waited until he heard the doors close, then he waited a few minutes more, just in case. Picking the folded newspaper up off the bench, he walked out to his truck.

As he stepped off the concrete pad and out of the building's shadow, the heat hit him like a warm, wet sponge. By the time he had the driver's door open, his T-shirt was clinging damply to his back.

"Took you long enough," Austin panted, crawling out from under the truck bed.

"Sorry." Scooping the cat up in one hand, Dean dropped him gently on the seat and slid in after him. "What happened, then?"

"The possibilities wouldn't let me through, but the others are fine, so don't sweat it." An emerald eye turned briefly toward Dean. "That was sort of a joke. Is there any water in here?"

After their last visit to the vet, Claire'd begun keeping a bottle of water and a small bowl in the glove compartment. It was tepid, but Austin drank almost all Dean poured.

"Are you okay?"

"Give me a minute." The cat sat up, rubbed a paw over wet whiskers, and sighed. "Ever notice how much a group of teenage boys resembles a dog pack?"

"Uh, no."

"So that was some other guy doing all that alpha male posturing?"

Dean thought back over the encounter and frowned. "I didn't . . ."

"You didn't sniff their butts, but other than that, it was all big dog, little dogs. Don't get me wrong.

If it weren't for my whole dogs-are-an-accident-of-nature belief system, I'd have been very impressed." He folded himself into tea cozy position. "Well?"

"Well, what?" Dean asked, still working his way through the dog thing.

"Well, why are we still sitting here? I have some serious napping scheduled for this afternoon and I'd like to get to it."

"We're just going to leave, then?"

Austin sighed. "Yes. I don't like it any more than you but that's the way it is. We leave. They stay. They save the world. We go home and you feed the cat. At least now you also have vital and important duties to perform."

"Right." Dean fished his keys from his pocket and started the engine. "Don't be taking this the wrong way, but I'd be happier if you were with Claire."

"Likewise."

"You know, I'm starting to think this isn't the actual anchor. That it's just the tip of the iceberg."

"Mixed metaphors aside, I think you're right." Claire straightened up from examining a display of remarkably realistic stone garden gnomes. "I also think they're using a basilisk, so keep your eyes peeled."

"That would explain the stone guy with the stone net and the wet stain on his stone trousers," Diana acknowledged, crossing toward her sister. "I was wondering why they'd only stock one of such a guaranteed big seller. Where do you think it is?"

"The basilisk? Hopefully, not here."

"Not the basilisk, the anchor."

"It's got to be close. It's not in the store. It's not in the storeroom . . ."

"It's probably behind the construction barrier," Sam yawned. He closed his mouth to find both Keepers staring at him. "What? It's covered in *danger, keep out, authorized entry only, this means you* signs. It seemed kind of obvious."

After a moment, Diana sighed. "He's right."

"You say that like you're surprised," the cat protested.

"Only because I was," she told him reassuringly as she shoved him off her backpack and heaved it back up onto her shoulders. "Let's get a move on. They've got to know we're here by now."

"If they don't, they will in a moment." Claire nodded toward the door. "It's warded to keep things in."

"Given the basilisk, good. Otherwise, that kind of sucks."

"And it explains why no one's shown up so far. They know they can take their time coming to get us because we're not going anywhere."

"We aren't?"

"Hypothetically. Do you think you could not want those wards there enough to get rid of them?"

"I could just *get* rid of them." As Claire turned

toward her, Diana raised both hands. "Except I'd be imposing my will on the Otherside, and that would be breaking the Rules, and so I would never, ever do it because that would make me just like the bad guys."

"Hey!" Sam bumped her in the calf with his head. "What are you talking about?"

"You can influence the Otherside with strong sub-conscious desires or by consciously wanting or not wanting something badly enough, but you can't just demand it be one thing or the other," Diana explained, bending just enough to stroke the end of his tail through her fingers. "Even if you're very young and it was sort of an accident, no matter what people say."

"Is this another doesn't-know-her-own-strength story?" the cat wondered.

Claire nodded. "Every door that had ever been used as an access was blown off its hinges."

"Okay, okay, fine. But nobody got hurt, so no harm, no foul." Diana stepped closer to the wards. "You do something once . . ."

"Twice."

"Okay, twice, and all of a sudden you can't be trusted."

"I trust you. I'm the one who asked you to not want the wards, remember?"

"Right." Her brow furrowed. The absolute last thing she wanted was to be stuck in a shadow Emporium with a possible basilisk and her sister telling remember-how-Diana-blew-up-the-sofa stories. The wards flickered. And again. And disappeared to the sound of sirens and a blinding array of flashing lights.

"I think you set off an alarm!" Sam yelled.

"What was your first clue?" Diana shrieked back at him as the three of them ran out the cleared door and into the concourse.

"It was either the sirens or the flashing lights!"

The shadow construction barrier was the same painted gray plywood as the original.

"Unless this is the original and the other one's the shadow."

"Not imortant right now!" Claire had both hands pressed flat against the wood. "We've got to get through this."

"How? There's no door!"

"Then want to get through harder!"

"I am!" Diana scanned the barrier for any kind of a seam, but all she could see were the warning signs and the ubiquitous, *Kilroy was here.* "Oh, sure, but he's not here now. The obnoxious gnome owes me ten bucks."

"What?"

"Nothing!"

Claire smacked the barrier with the palms of both hands, then backed away. "We're going to have to use the access corridor to get behind it!"

"I hate this, but you're right!"

They turned back toward the store, but before

they'd taken a single step, the door to the storeroom crashed open and half a dozen misshapen bodies in badly fitting navy blue track suits charged through. Essentially bipedal, they looked like someone had crossed a rhinocerus with a hockey player.

"Great! Not wanting *them* doesn't seem to be working either!"

"What are they?"

"Who cares?" Diana grabbed Claire's hand, yanked her around until she was facing down the concourse, and gave her a shove. "RUN!"

Sam was already almost at the food court.

The Tailor of Gloucester had become The Tailer of Gloucester with a number of samples hanging in the window. Diana would have liked a closer look at the multicolored fog swirling about inside the travel agency, but something slammed into her backpack as she passed the store and she decided that maybe concentrating on running would be the better plan. Fortunately, here on the Otherside, concentrating on running was enough to lend new speed to her feet.

"What are they throwing?" Claire demanded as they began weaving through the tables in the food court.

Something buzzed past Diana's ear with an almost overpowering scent of gardenias, dented one of the metal chairs, and bounced out of sight.

"I think it's scented candles!"

"Oh, that's just great! Those things are deadly!"

"Only in enclosed spaces!"

On the far side of the food court, they followed Sam to the right; the crashing and banging of their pursuers through the tables and chairs drowning out the distant sound of the sirens.

"Where are we going?"

"I don't know!"

"Hey! Up here!"

Both Keepers skidded to a halt and squinting up through the hexagonal opening to the upper level trying to make out the features of the person leaning over the edge.

"Are you a good witch or a bad witch?" the spiky silhouette demanded.

"We're not . . ." Claire began but Diana drove an elbow into her side.

"Good witches!"

"Then haul ass to the stairs! We'll hold them off."

"We're not . . ."

Diana grabbed Claire's hand again. "Close enough. Shut up and follow Sam!"

Something whistled through the air behind them as they pounded up the concourse after the cat. The escalators were insubstantial, but the stairs were much as they'd left them. Except for the piled barricade at the top and the half-dozen teenagers standing behind it.

Sam scrambled up and over but as the Keepers neared the top step, a genuine wood finish laminate armoire was rolled back out of the way. The packs made it a tight fit, but they both squeezed through and collapsed panting to the floor.

Candles pounded the barricade, hitting with enough force to slam through a display counter and into the piled barbeques behind it. The tempered steel rang like a gong but held.

The whistling noise was defined as the teenagers fired ceramic cherubs from heavy duty slingshots.

"Did you want these guys?" Claire murmured.

"I wanted rescue," Diana admitted, "but I don't think either of us had anything to do with this. It's too . . ."

"Clichéd?"

"I was going to say too real, but strangely enough, too clichéd also works."

"They're hitting the things," Sam reported from the top of the barricade. "It's stopping them, but they don't seem to be taking much damage."

"Nah, they never do," explained the teenager next to him, aiming and releasing again. "But if you hit them in the head, the bits of broken ceramic get in their eyes and they totally hate that. Damn! I don't know what you guys did to get 'em so worked up 'cause usually they got a zero attention span."

Another volley. And then another. And then a cheer went up.

"And we win again. The meat-minds'll mill around for a while, then they'll head home." She tossed long, mahogany dreadlocks back behind her shoulders and stared down at Sam. "You talk."

He shrugged. "So do you."

"Good point." Holding her bow across her chest,

she turned to face the Keepers. "I'm Kris, Captain of the Guard. Who are you?"

"Too real?" Claire whispered.

Although Kris and the other archers were dressed in combinations of clothes obviously pulled off the rack, there could be no mistaking the pointed ears or the great hair.

Elves.

Except, of course, that elves didn't actually exist.

FOUR

As the others moved to stand behind Kris, it became obvious that some ears were less pointed and some hair less blatantly great. Lined up in order, the seven would have looked like time lapse photography—from almost human to full elf.

Claire's eyes widened. "They're Bystanders."

"Maybe once," Diana agreed, watching one of them flick a brilliant red braid wound through with neon tubing back over his shoulder, "but not now. This place is changing them." Feeling like a turtle stuck on its back, she tried to stand, struggling against the weight of the backpack. When Kris grinned and held out a hand, she accepted it gratefully. The elf's grip was warm and dry, surprisingly callused and remarkably strong; Diana found herself lifted effortlessly to her feet.

"You're 'bout right for walkin' on the weird side," Kris observed as Diana reluctantly released her hand, "but your . . . sister?"

Both Keepers nodded. Probably because of the Lineage, the family resemblance had always been strong.

"Well, she's a little old for this sort of thing."

Diana hid a smile as she helped a glowering Claire stand. Since Dean and the seven-year age difference, the whole age thing had become a sensitive point.

"And, no offense," Kris continued, "but you're both too well fed."

"Too well fed for what?" Claire demanded, smoothing her skirt over her thighs.

"For livin' rough."

"That's because we haven't been."

"Totally obvious they didn't fall in off the street," the redhead snorted.

"No, we didn't." Diana agreed, breaking in before Claire's tone got them into trouble. "We came here deliberately."

That got everyone's attention.

A very pale blond with eyes so light only the pupils showed, stepped forward. "You can do that? Come here deliberately?"

"Well, duh." A boy who might have been East Indian jabbed him with the end of his slingshot. "They're here."

"Well, duh, maybe they're lying."

"Yeah? Maybe you're an idiot."

"Yeah, well, you're a . . ."

"Colin. Teemo."

Names held power. Whether Kris had known that before or had discovered it after crossing, she certainly knew it now. The argument stopped cold, both boys looking sheepish at suddenly being the center of attention.

"*We* can cross deliberately," Diana said into the sudden silence. "Not everybody can."

"How?"

"Did we get here?"

"Yeah. That. And why did you come? And who the hell are you?"

Diana exchanged a speaking glance with Claire. If the, well, elves—for lack of a better word—could still swear with impunity, then they were influencing the Otherside on a subconscious level only. However they'd changed, they remained Bystanders, and the Lineage worked very hard at keeping Bystanders unaware of their existence.

"Your Summons," Claire murmured. "Your choice."

"The Rules . . ."

"Diana, there's a sign in that shoe store window advertising ruby slippers for half off. Unless they're trying to attract the Otherside drag queen business, I'd say that the Rules have already been twisted pretty far out of shape."

"O–kay." Claire had been a total Rule follower her entire life. Dean had obviously loosened her up a lot more than Diana had suspected. *Bad, bad mental image. Think about . . .*

Kris folded her arms and glared. Her expression promised violence if she didn't get an answer soon.

Yeah, that works. "My name is Diana. This is Claire. That's Sam. Essentially, we're a sort of wizard called a Keeper."

"We're not wizards," Claire sighed.

"Okay," Diana muttered sotto voice, not the least surprised Claire'd had to stick her two cents in regardless of what she'd said about choices and whose they were. "*You* explain to the *mall elves* exactly what we are in three thousand words or less."

Claire's eyes narrowed, then she sighed again. "Essentially," she told their fascinated audience, "we're wizards. It's our job to make sure that metaphysical balances are kept."

"That the magical stuff between the worlds doesn't go out of whack," Diana clarified as half a dozen pairs of eyes stared at them blankly.

Kris shook her head, dreadlocks bouncing. "You're wizards?"

"*Essentially* wizards," Claire amended reluctantly.

"They're wizards," Sam snorted. "I'm a cat."

"Right." Kris acknowledged him with a quick smile and turned her attention back to the Keepers. "Well, since you're here and since we're here and since our candle throwin' friends with the negative number IQs are here and since this is a fuckin' *shopping mall*, I'm guessin' that the magical stuff between the worlds is way whacked."

"Good guess."

"Yeah, well, we're not stupid."

"Kris." One of the others, a skinny, dark-haired, androgynous kid probably no more than fifteen jumped the barricade. "The meat-minds have retreated back past the food court."

"Thanks, DK. All right, the rest of you go back to

what you were doing before Jo gave the alarm. Me and Will'll take these guys in to Arthur." She jerked her head down the concourse toward the anchor store at the far end. "Let's go."

Will turned out to be the redhead.

"Actually," Claire announced in a tone that suggested she'd neither forgotten nor forgiven the earlier *too old and too well fed* observation, "we've got to get back to the other end of the mall. We appreciate your assistance, but we have a job to do here."

Kris shrugged. "So do I. And my job says I take new people in to see Arthur."

"Claire . . ."

"Diana?"

She flashed Kris a smile, grabbed Claire's arm, and yanked her close enough to mutter into her ear. "I know that time is a factor, I mean, it is *my* Summons and all, but these guys are a factor, too, because whoever's running this segue isn't going to be able to finish it while they're still here. I mean, we weren't expecting indigenous life."

"They aren't indigenous!"

"Maybe they didn't used to be, but they are now."'

"All right, fine." Claire pulled her arm free. "But if this thing goes critical while we're talking . . ."

"Then we'll be in the right place because it can't go critical until the forces of darkness attack and destroy this last bastion of the light."

"The forces of darkness are throwing scented candles!"

"Yeah, but they're throwing them really hard. And besides, you know as well as I do how fast things can change on the Otherside." Diana patted Claire's bare shoulder in a comforting sort of way and turned back to Kris. "So, take us to your leader. He *is* your leader, right?"

Claire sighed. "Well, if he isn't, you've just wasted that line."

"He *is* our leader," Kris told them, and this time when she indicated they should start moving, there was very little room for arguing with the gesture.

As the Keepers stepped away from the barricade and Sam jumped down to walk between them, Will fell in on one side, Kris on the other. They were clearly being escorted. Diana decided to think of it as an honor guard.

"So," she prodded after a moment. "This Arthur; what's he like?"

Kris glanced over at her and shrugged. "Not like us."

"Like you are or like you were?"

"What's the diff?"

"You know; the whole ears, thick flowing tresses thing."

"The what?"

Bystanders could lie to Keepers; they just couldn't get away with it. Kris honestly didn't know what Diana was talking about. Apparently their perception of themselves had changed as they had changed. Now why they'd changed the way they had; that was a whole different question without an answer. "Never mind, it's not important. So, how *is* Arthur different from you?"

"He came from outside."

"Outside?" Diana was beginning to have a bad feeling about this.

"Yeah, outside the mall." Kris waved to the tall, slender girl standing guard at the intersection of the main concourse and the short hall leading to one of the outside doors. "We don't know how he got in, 'cause we can't get out, but he understands this place. He keeps us together; he made us strong. We were getting our asses kicked by all sorts of strange shit until he showed up."

"And he made you the captain of his guard?"

"Yeah. He did. You got a problem with that?"

"No. Of course not. You're obviously really good at it and you, you know, you're in charge and um . . ." *Babble much? She's going to think you're an idiot. Get a grip!* Diana took a deep breath and ignored Claire's raised eyebrow. "So, were you the first one who crossed over?"

A muscle jumped in Kris' jaw. "Second."

Something in her tone made Diana remember all the things Austin had listed that were worse than BAM. Splat. Crunch. Grind. Chew. For some reason, especially chew.

They were heading toward the large department store at what had been the west end of the mall. Cosmetic counters had been stacked on their sides to make a solid wall across all but a small section of the store's wide entrance. A nod of Kris's head and Will lounged in the opening.

"Just so you know," Claire said, delivering a speaking look to her sister, "you can't hold us."

Kris shrugged. "Just so's *you* know, I'm not planning on it. But I believe in coverin' my ass, just in case."

"Of what?"

"Whatever." She led Diana, Claire, and Sam into a large open area where the faint, antagonistic scents of a dozen different perfumes lingered, told them to wait, and disappeared between two racks of plus size winter coats.

"You know they might be able to hold us," Diana murmured, with a quick glance at Will's back. "This being the Otherside and all. If there's enough of them wanting us held . . ."

"You were the one who wanted to see their leader. I just think we should go in from a position of strength."

"They had to rescue us from walking cat food throwing scented candles," Sam pointed out, tail lashing as he paced the perimeter. "Oh, yeah, that's a position of strength."

Claire glared at the cat.

Diana punched her lightly on the arm. "Missing Austin?"

Claire shifted her glare up and over. After a moment, she sighed. "Yes. A lot. I hope he's all right."

"Don't worry, he's with Dean. On second thought, worry about Dean."

"Very funny. I'm sure Austin will be a huge help to Dean at the guest house."

"You're delusional. You know that, right?"

Claire smiled tightly. "It helps when you work with cats."

They watched Sam explore nooks and crannies they couldn't see and listened to the distant sound of someone beating a drum kit to death with a couple of guitars and an electronic keyboard.

"So, Arthur," Diana said at last, rubbing her nose and moving away from a particularly strong patch of Phobia™ for Men. "He came in from outside the mall to bring them together and make them strong."

"The name could be a coincidence."

"Oh, please."

Claire sighed as deeply as the weight of her backpack allowed. "They needed a leader; he's what their subconscious created."

Fur between his eyes folded into a darker orange "w," Sam frowned up at them both. "Do you guys know this Arthur?"

"Not *this* Arthur, but he's just the sort of opportunistic archetype who'd show up in this kind of story. And you never just get him, do you?" Her own brow furrowed, Diana folded her arms.

"We should be glad they're not a little younger," Claire reminded her. "Or we might have been dealing with Peter Pan."

"Yeah, but they've turned themselves into elves. Wouldn't Oberon make more sense?"

"I doubt this lot's read much Shakespeare, but you have; you'd honestly rather deal with Oberon?"

Diana considered it for a moment. "Okay, good point. Ass ears; not a great look. But still, that whole Immortal King crap just gets up my nose. Follow me, serve me, love me . . . gag me!"

"Your opinion aside, Arthur is a nice, classic, archetypal answer to a leadership dilemma."

Arthur turned out to be a tall, broad-shouldered, narrow-hipped young man in his late teens with startlingly blue eyes and a wild shock of blue-black hair that kept falling attractively forward over his face in spite of a silver circlet.

"Okay," Claire said slowly as they walked toward him, drawn by the brilliant, perfect white crescent of his smile. "So he's a nice *anime* archetypal answer to a leadership dilemma."

"And we can be grateful they're becoming elves, not pokemon," Diana added.

Dressed in black and silver—jeans, boots, T-shirt, leather jacket, lots of buckles—and wearing a very large sword across his back, he waited for them in the electronics section of the department store. The sword, at least, should have looked out of place. It didn't.

A burgundy leather sofa and two matching chairs, heavy on the rivets, defined three sides of the space.

Under the furniture, was a square of carpet patterned in shades of gray. The fourth side was a massive, rear projection television—its screen a reflective black. The mere lack of accessible electricity wouldn't have been enough to keep the TV off had enough of the mall elves wanted it on but, subconscious desires or not, the programming would have been beyond their control. Diana had seen a TV in one of the bleaker Otherside neighborhoods that showed nothing but reruns of *Three's Company*. Next to the Girl Guide camp, it was as close to actually being in Hell as she ever wanted to get.

There was no sign of Arthur's usual entourage and although the coffee table had smoothed corners, it could in no way be called round.

"When Kris said that a pair of Keepers had crossed over, I thought the news was too good to be true," Arthur announced, moving to meet them as they stepped onto the carpet. "And yet, here you are." He looked so pleased that Diana found herself grinning foolishly in response. A quick glance over at Claire showed she was having much the same reaction.

"Sire? About some us heading out scavenging?"

"Of course." Arthur nodded toward the Keepers. "If you'll excuse me." When he turned his attention to Kris, it seemed almost as though the lights had dimmed.

Oh, great. Diana scowled at her reflection in the television. *That's so* not *good.*

Wait a minute, the lights have *dimmed.*

She glanced up at the ceiling. The huge frosted squares over the fluorescent tubes were becoming distinctly gray. "Claire . . ."

"I see it. I think this store is almost real and the mall in the real world is closing down for the day."

They were right under one of the emergency lights. As the rest of the store filled with shadows, the area defined by the sofa, the chairs, and the television remained, if not bright, at least lit. "But it's barely midafternoon."

"A little past." Claire thrust her wrist and watch into Diana's line of sight. Six fifteen. The second hand swept around the dial almost too fast to see. Six sixteen. Seventeen.

"Give me one good reason why I should feed you anything different than I would if Claire were here?" Dean demanded, lifting Austin off the table and out of his supper.

"Claire's not here."

He thought about that for a moment then cut the cat some cold beef. "Okay. Good reason."

"But time was running one to one when you checked at the Emporium."

Claire nodded toward Arthur, who was still speaking quietly with Kris. "I think he's a time distortion. He's pure Otherside. Whoever's running this segue can't control him."

"Yeah, but they clearly can't control the *elves* either."

*   *   *

"It's June." Austin settled himself in tea cozy position on the coffee table. "Why are they still playing hockey?"

"Because they're not finished."

"You know, the world made a lot more sense when I was young."

Dean twisted the cap off a beer and toasted his reluctant companion. "Oh, yeah, I'll drink to that."

"They had no trouble controlling the elves before Arthur showed up. Kris said they were getting their asses kicked."

"Okay, so these kids get caught in the segue, but it happened over time, so the darkness had to know about it, which means it has to want them here to . . ." Diana glanced around at the department store, complete to the sale banners hanging from the ceiling. ". . . to help define this end of the mall—which is where they'd end up, running from the darkside at the other end. The darkness figures it can remove them easily enough before the segue's complete, but it doesn't count on them banding together and being able to bring in outside help. Darkness underestimates Bystanders, the latest in a continuing series. But it must have realized that Arthur was a threat to its plans—so why hasn't it moved to destroy him and his merry men?"

"Watch it, you're mixing archetypes."

"So? What's the worst that could happen?"

"I can think of a dozen really bad movies that essentially answer your question," Claire told her in a low voice. "And bits from any of them could show up if you're not more careful!"

Diana shuddered and checked out the surrounding shadows. So far, they seemed clear of movie clichés. "Sorry. But I'd still like to know what the darkness is waiting for."

"Maybe it's not waiting. Maybe it's just that the other end of the mall's running a lot slower than this end."

Time was relative, sure, but the Otherside took it to extremes. "Given your vast years of experience, what are the odds that our presence acts like a catalyst for a little localized Armageddon?"

"Pretty good."

"How good?"

Before Claire could answer, Arthur clapped Kris on the shoulder and sent her on her way. Forgetting Armageddon, Diana watched her leave, watched the swing of her hips and the movement of her hair against her back until she disappeared around a corner. Then she stared at the corner as though wanting could make the other girl come back. Actually wanting *could* make her come back. As Kris reappeared, looking confused, Diana forced herself to think of other things.

Like being overrun by the forces of darkness.

On second thought, let's not think too hard about that either.

"Come, drop your gear. Sit and we will speak together." Arthur's voice was deep and a little rough.

It was a voice that spoke of fairness and trust and responsibility and the kind of values people always said they were looking for but never much liked once they found them.

He sounds just like the kind of guy you'd buy a new operating system from, Diana realized suddenly. *And he sounds a lot older than he looks. Which he is. Thus the immortal part of that whole Immortal King thing. Duh.* Still, losing the backpack seemed like the best idea anyone had had in days. Diana let it slide down her arms, caught it just before it was about to drop, and fell back gratefully onto one end of the sofa.

"Here, let me help." Arthur stepped forward and lifted Claire's pack off her shoulders. He showed no surprise at the weight, merely settling it to one side as Claire thanked him.

Stronger than he looks, Diana noted. *Just another piece of the whole, too good to be true, package.*

He waited until Claire and Sam were sitting before shoving his sword back out of the way and sprawling bonelessly over one of the armchairs. Archetype or not, he still sat like a teenage boy.

A teenage boy with a big honkin' sword.

"Will you take refreshment?" He waved at a stack of juice boxes.

"No, thanks." Diana pulled a bottle of water and Sam's saucer out of a side pocket. "We brought our own. We're not staying," she added, as Arthur began to frown. "And we'd just as soon not have our ears sharpened."

*   *   *

Wrapping himself in his tail, Austin glared up at Dean. "Just so we're both clear on this, no cuddling."

"Maybe you shouldn't be sleeping on Claire's pillow, then." Setting his glasses carefully on the bedside table, Dean reached up and turned off the light. "Suppose I wake up lonely and confused?"

"Lonely, confused, and *lipless* if you come anywhere near me."

"No tongue . . ."

"Because I'll have ripped it out and batted it under the bed!"

"Good night, Austin."

"Eating or drinking while we're on this side, will make it more difficult for us to cross back," Claire explained.

"I could be insulted that you refuse my hospitality, but you are of the Lineage, so I bow instead to your wisdom." Suiting action to the words, he bowed where he sat and then straightened, flipping his hair back out of his face. His revealed expression was serious. "So, Keepers, what *are* you doing here?"

Diana passed the water bottle to Claire and told the story of the bracelet one more time.

"I don't remember your bits of the dialogue being quite so witty the first time I heard this," Sam muttered.

Ignoring him, she told Arthur about the Emporium, the mirror, and the segue.

"That explains a great deal," he said thoughtfully.

"Whoever is behind this no doubt allowed my people through in order that their beliefs hasten the reality of the mall, figuring to pick them off when their usefulness was done."

"Yeah, we think so, too." Diana fought the urge to be unreasonably pleased that Arthur agreed with her.

"They can't be happy that I have made them one people, strong and able to defend themselves."

"No, they can't—mostly because these sorts literally can't *be* happy. The best they can manage is triumphant glee."

"In order to complete their plan, they must attack us in force and wipe us from their reality."

He caught on fast. Diana reluctantly admitted she liked that in an archetype. It made for less exposition. "Yes, they must."

"You must close the segue before this happens."

"Duh."

Arthur lifted a single brow. "I'm sorry?"

"We have every intention of closing the segue before anyone is hurt," Claire explained, shooting Diana a look that promised a future lecture on the inappropriate use of the smart-ass response. "Unfortunately, the anchor's hidden somewhere in the construction zone, and when we left the Emporium, we set off an alarm. The dark guards your . . . people call the meat-minds arrived before we could get to it."

"And if that's not enough happy happy," Diana broke in, "we can't seem to influence that end of the mall, so we're going to have to go into the construction zone through the access corridor."

"Darkness has more deadly servants than the meat-minds patrolling the access corridors," Arthur said quietly.

Claire nodded. "We heard some—or one—right after we crossed over."

"Some of them *are* large," Arthur admitted, pensively rubbing a buckle between thumb and forefinger. "Some are smaller but dangerous still. We've barricaded them out of our territory, but I fear they stay away more out of their desire than ours."

"They don't push because, so far, they don't want to, not because they're afraid of you?"

"Of me and my people, yes."

"That's not good." Which, given the situation, was pretty much a gimme. Diana glanced up as the ceiling lights came on, glanced down to note that Claire's watch was still keeping speedy time, and decided not to worry about it. "So, about your people; from what Kris said about living rough, I'm guessing no one's going to miss any of them back home?"

"Until they came here, they had no home." Releasing the buckle, he curled his hand into a fist. "They are the unwanted youth of your world. Rootless and wanting to be elsewhere. With the shadow mall in place, it took only the opening of a door to cross over. Most of them crossed when leaving the public washroom by the food court."

"Oh, yeah, public washrooms," Diana snorted. "Always an adventure. The food court would put them pretty close to the Emporium and a whole bunch of the bad stuff."

"This is why not all of them survived." He studied all three of them for a long moment, his pellucid gaze moving unhurriedly from Keeper to Keeper to cat. "You told them you are wizards," he said at last, the sentence falling between question and accusation.

Diana's tone sharpened in response to the later. "Keepers, wizards—it seemed the simplest explanation since it's essentially true."

"Essentially," Claire muttered under her breath.

"Essentially?" Arthur repeated. "Are you saying then that Merlin was of the lineage?" Full lips twisted up into a half smile.

"Sorry, classified. But speaking of Merlin . . ." Diana leaned left and peered past the television, searching the shadows around the stacks of boxed DVD players. ". . . don't you usually come with a side of fries?"

Azure eyes blinked. "What?"

"Yeah, what?" Sam turned around on her lap, fabric bunching under anchoring claws, and stared up at her. "Even I didn't get that one."

"Extras. Baggage. Bad choices. Betrayal." Diana sighed. "I could go on, but we all know the story. No Lancelot? No Guinevere?"

"Not so far." Arthur looked pleased with himself and remarkably young. "I think I managed to ditch them this time. That whole star-crossed lovers thing—definitely getting tedious."

"Tedious?"

When he nodded, Diana shook her head. "Nice try. But isn't it part of what makes you Arthur?"

"Not in the oldest stories. In the oldest stories, I make one people out of a number of warring tribes and then lead them out to face a common foe. All the sex? You can blame that on the French."

"Actually, we can't; it's a Canadian thing. And," Claire continued in her best *I'm a Keeper and you aren't* voice, "none of that's important. What's important is that we close this segue down before there's an open access into our world and before your people are . . ."

"Crunched?" Sam offered helpfully.

"I was going to say 'attacked', but 'crunched' works. Maybe a little too well . . ." She started to stand. "Which means . . ."

"We're going to need your help."

Dropping back onto the sofa, Claire glared at her sister. "What?"

Diana shifted around to meet Claire's glare. The protest had been expected, an argument had been prepared. "These guys know every accessible inch of this mall. Plus, they know the safest way into the access corridors, what to expect when we're there, and how to avoid it."

"They're Bystanders!"

"So's Dean."

"I *knew* you were going to bring him up."

"Who's Dean?" Arthur asked.

"Something you can't blame on the French," Sam snickered.

Arthur looked confused, but both women ignored the feline non sequitur with practiced ease.

"Dean has nothing to do with this, Diana." Eyes narrowed, Claire punctuated her protest with a stabbing finger. "I agreed to exchange information, but I draw the line at bringing Bystanders any further into our business."

"First, it's my Summons, so it's my line. Second, this is totally their business. This is their world now, they've changed too much to go home, and they have a right to defend themselves. Their best defense . . ." She spread both hands. ". . . and I'm willing to bet that it's their only defense—is helping us to close this thing down before the bad guys make their move. Considering how complete things look—time shifts or no time shifts—that move can't be too far off."

"My scouts have reported more activity in enemy territory," Arthur allowed.

Diana jerked around to stare at him. "You have *scouts?*"

"Not the scary kind," he reassured her. "No shorts, no apples."

"Good."

"Where were you?" Austin demanded as Dean closed the front door.

"Where I told you I was going, playing ball with some friends. Just like I do every Sunday afternoon." Tossing his glove onto the counter, he headed for the kitchen. "The answering machine was on, and you were asleep."

"Well, I woke up and I was hungry."

"I left you a bowl of dry." Something crunched underfoot and Dean noticed the kibble spread evenly over the floor. "Which you obviously found. You think you could have caudled things up any more?"

"This is a big place," Austin reminded him. "But before you start looking, how about feeding me."

Head to one side, hair falling attractively, Arthur studied the Keepers. "If we have battle coming—which I'd be a fool to deny—why should I split my strength by helping you?"

"When we remove the anchor and close the segue," Diana told him, peeling her bare thighs one at a time off the leather and scooting to the edge of the sofa, "we'll be able to influence the other end of the mall. Our influence could save your butts."

"Even though our influence would be *totally* subconscious," Claire added.

Diana waved off the warning. "And besides, you said it yourself, it's part of your original raisin of the day—you make one people out of a number of warring tribes and then you lead them out to face a common foe."

"Raisin of the day?"

"I assume she means *raison d'etre*."

"Hey, I'm trying to keep the French out of it. We don't need Arthur's baggage finally making it through customs."

Arthur glanced around uneasily. "Could that happen?"

"Keepers. Otherside." Diana shrugged. "Anything could happen."

A siren shrieked out on the concourse.

In the heartbeat of silence that followed, Claire and Sam turned to stare at Diana.

"What? I didn't do it!"

On his feet and running full out between one moment and the next, Arthur charged past them, clearing Electronics in three long strides and disappearing between the racks of winter coats.

"You know that question about us being a catalyst?" Claire snarled, swinging her pack up onto one shoulder. "This answer it?"

"Unfortunately!" Grabbing her own pack in both hands, Diana pounded after Arthur, Claire behind her, Sam taking the high road over the furniture to end up leading the way.

Chaos filled the concourse. Meat-minds, some wearing a fine dusting of ceramic cherub, lumbered after the more limber mall elves. Arthur leaped forward, shouting orders and using his sword like a baton to direct a reorganized defense. Claire and Diana rocked to a halt in the entrance to the store.

Sam skidded out into the battle, claws scrabbling for purchase against the slick tile floor. When a massive foot slammed down in his path, he let his slide close the distance, bumping up against an enormous instep, sinking claws deep into gnarled flesh. Finally

able to control his momentum, he pushed off and
raced back to Diana's side.

"You okay?"

Ears saddled, he looked as though he was trying
to back away from his own feet. "Word of advice,
don't stick your claws in those things!"

The meat-mind ignored him, pounding off after
the tiny female elf in the PVC corset.

"I thought those things got easily discouraged?"
Diana protested.

Claire pointed to a tall, slender figure in black
armor. The red plume on his helm bobbed over the
battle. "Meet their motivation."

The figure turned to meet Arthur's charge.

"A dark elf?"

"Given what the kids are turning into, it almost
makes sense." On one knee beside her pack, Claire
rummaged out her bag of prepared possibilities.

"It looks like the barricade at the stairs is intact,"
Diana told her, yanking a bulging belt pouch out
from under the half a dozen cans of cat food in her
pack. "They must have come through another way."

"The access corridors?"

"No. Arthur said they're guarded. Someone
would've given the alarm."

A pair of charging meat-minds crashed to the floor
for no apparent reason. A pepper grinder in one
hand, Claire glared at Diana.

"Totally subconscious, I swear; they just look *really*
clumsy!" Here and now, she wasn't going to risk

feedback. It was one thing to break a Rule with only her own life hanging in the balance, it was another entirely to risk Claire and Sam and a group of teenagers she'd only just met. With a powerful enemy on site, any power she released would, at the very least, be sucked up and used against them. Definitely embarrassing. Probably fatal.

One of the meat-minds stepped on its own hand as the two she'd dropped scrambled to their feet. It bellowed in pain and swung what looked like a plastic tote bag at its companion, knocking it down again. One of the mall elves darted in, wielding an aluminum baseball bat, and it stayed down.

"You've got to like the kid's enthusiasm."

"I don't have to like anything about this," Claire snapped. "I'm going to try and take a few of those things out. You find out where they're coming from and close the door!" Waving the pepper shaker, she plunged into the fight.

"How is seasoning going to help?" Sam demanded as Diana buckled the belt pouch around her waist.

"Peppercorns are seeds." She stuffed the wand into a pocket, just in case. "Seeds carry certain distinct possibilities." A running dive took her past a meat-mind's outstretched arms. "Claire has hers rigged for sleep," she grunted, sliding into one of the plastic wood planters.

"But why pepper?" Sam jumped up onto the planter's edge.

"Except for the Minute Rice, it was the only seed

Dean had in the kitchen and Minute Rice comes with that unfortunate time restriction." Scrambling to her feet, she joined the cat and took a moment to study the battle. The clash of blade against blade and the distinctly less musical clash of aluminum against meat, echoed under the twenty-foot ceilings. From her vantage point, she could see that the meat-minds in the main concourse were fighting in a random pattern, but by the entrance to the short hall—the one leading to the entrance where Claire'd left Dean way back when—they all faced one way. Into the concourse. Even the bulky body stretched flat at Kris' feet and being efficiently bludgeoned pointed in the same direction.

Then, between one swing and the next, a meaty hand snaked out and closed around a slender ankle.

Kris' next swing went wide.

Then the meat-mind was on its feet and Kris was swinging, dreadlocks sweeping back and forth across the floor.

Darting into the melee, Claire pounded one of the meat-minds on the shoulder—given the location, it was probably a shoulder. When it turned, she ground fresh pepper into its face. It looked affronted, then blinked onyx eyes, scrunched up its nose, and sneezed, covering Claire in a dripping patina of snot before falling backward to the floor.

Teemo, his orange-and-yellow Hawaiian shirt clutched in bratwurst-sized fingers, went down with it. "Is it dead?" he panted, bracing red hightops against the meat-mind's stained sweat suit and yanking himself free.

"No," Claire spat, scrubbing at her face with the hem of her skirt. "Asleep."

"Bummer." Switching to a two-handed grip, he set about changing that.

Given her sudden, desperate need for a shower, Claire wasn't at all surprised when the sprinklers went off.

"Geez, these guys are clumsy," Diana muttered, as she ran. "Clumsy, clumsy, clumsy." But it was hard to hold the thought when the only thing she could see was Kris dangling by one foot. Her mouth might be saying clumsy, but her brain kept insisting, *don't stop her.*

Closely followed by: *Would you stop whaling on it! You're just pissing it off!*

Closely followed by: *I guess that answers the 'do they or don't they' genitalia question.* as Kris' flailing bat impacted between the creature's legs with no effect.

Its knees were significantly more sensitive.

Howling in pain, it whipped Kris twice around its head then threw her toward the concourse.

Diana rocked to a halt, spun around as Kris sailed by, yanked open her pouch, and broke a lime-green feather in half.

The mall elf floated gently to the floor as the sprinklers came on.

A tote bag whistled past Diana's head fast enough to part her hair, the letters on the bag a red-on-white blur. Heart pounding, she raced past the furious meat-mind while it struggled to recover its balance, the force of the swing having nearly tipped it over.

"Diana! Over here!" Sam paced in front of the optical shop, tail lashing marmalade lines in the air. "Something's happening!"

Inside the store, a multicolored fog had begun to swirl.

A familiar multicolored fog.

Diana skidded to a stop by Sam's side. "The travel agency?" All of a sudden, the whole attack made a horrible kind of sense. The red plume on the dark elf's helm, the tote bags. The darkside had chartered a trip into the mall elves' territory. "Who's coming *up* with this stuff!" she snarled, reaching back into her pouch.

"Hurry!"

As the fog grew thicker, a familiar trio of shapes began to take form.

"Not this time, bologna for brains."

As the three meat-minds charged toward the door, Diana dropped to her knees and slammed a key down on the threshold. Slamming into the barrier with enough force to vibrate glass all the way to the exit, they bounced back into the fog and disappeared. It was probably imagination that provided the crash of impact at the travel agency, one level down and a quarter of a kilometer away.

"You sure that'll hold them?" Sam demanded, looking dubious as he checked out the key.

"Hey, when I lock a door, it stays locked." She rocked back on her heels and stood. "Why aren't you wet?"

"Why should I be?"

"The sprinklers . . ."

He stared up at her, amber eyes challenging.

". . . never mind."

A quick run back to the end of the hall.

Out on the concourse, about two thirds of the meat-minds were down, those parts of their faces not being covered by the impact of baseball bats, covered in fresh ground pepper. Claire sat slumped against the art supply store, cradling one arm. Scattered, brightly colored heaps marked fallen elves, Kris and Colin weaving among them pulling downed comrades to safety.

Wet blades glistening, Arthur and the dark elf fought on.

As Diana stepped forward, Arthur danced sideways to avoid a lunge and tripped over a discarded tote bag.

He began to fall. His sword rose to block a descending blow, but the angle was wrong and everyone could see it.

The Immortal King was about to die.

A simple "no" could prevent disaster.

Diana could feel the word rising.

But that "no" could provide the enemy with power enough to complete the segue.

She had nothing in her pouch, nothing that might . . .

The wand. The wand belonged on the Otherside

Yanking it from her pocket, Diana pointed the pink star at the dark elf, tried very hard not to think of how stupid this had to look, and opened herself up to extreme possibilities.

The sudden spray of pink power froze him in place, his dark sword no more than a centimeter from Arthur's throat. Glistening lines raced over his armor, connected the water droplets, and flared into a rose-white light too bright to look at.

When the light finally faded and everyone had blinked away the aftereffects, the dark elf was gone.

The few meat-minds still standing threw themselves over the barrier to the lower level, landing five meters down with a disconcerting splat.

"Wicked."

Diana turned to see Kris smiling at her admiringly. "And thanks for that, you know, feather thing."

Diana would have liked to have spent a moment basking in Kris' admiration, but the wand dropped from numb fingers and a heartbeat later she followed it to the floor, not entirely certain if she wanted to puke or pass out. Unable to decide, she did both.

Dean brushed his palm over a depleted spray of lime-green feathers and sighed. "Austin, what happened to my feather duster?"

"Don't look at me."

"I thought you knew everything."

"I do." Rolling over, he exposed his other flank to the square of sunlight. "I just don't want you to look at me."

FIVE

"It's been three days."

"Four," Austin corrected morosely from his place on the counter. "They left Saturday, it's now Tuesday."

"They left at nine-thirty Saturday morning. It's only eight forty-five." Dean expertly worked the broom into a corner of the office, capturing an elusive clump of cat hair. "Technically, it hasn't been four days."

"You're amazingly anal about a lot of things, aren't you?"

"If I'm going to do something, I'm after being accurate."

Austin sighed and dropped his chin down onto his front paws. "You missed a spot."

Dean bent to push the broom under the desk. He knew he was displacing his anxiety, but even the hand-waxed shine on the old hardwood floor seemed less, well, shiny than it had. "I miss Claire."

"I miss her more," the cat muttered.

"I'm not arguing." Mostly because he'd finally learned there was no point in arguing with a cat but also because, in this particular instance, there really wasn't anything to argue about. Austin probably did miss Claire more than he did. The two of them had been through a lot together over the last seventeen years. In fact, given what the three of them had been through over the last nine months, Dean was willing to bet that "been through a lot" didn't even begin to start covering the highlights of the previous sixteen years.

Straightening, he glanced over at the counter. "I bet you've got a lot of great memories."

"Great memories, good memories, and a few 'holy crap I can't believe we survived that' memories," Austin agreed. "But don't get your hopes up, broom boy; I'm not sharing stories of what a cute little Keeper Claire was. Nothing against you personally, it's just not something cats do."

"Why not?"

One black ear flicked disdainfully. "Hey, I don't write the rules."

"You don't even follow the rules," Dean pointed out, frowning down at a set of parallel scratches gouged out by the desk chair. "Before Claire went in, she said they could be in there for a couple of days. We're already past that estimate."

"True. But they could still come out yesterday."

That was enough to pull Dean's complete attention from the floor. "What?"

"Time on the Otherside runs differently: four days here isn't necessarily four days there, so they could come out at any time."

"What?"

Austin sighed and sat up. "If they can come out any time," he reiterated slowly and distinctly, "then as long as they don't come out before they left, they can come out yesterday."

"But we've already lived yesterday and part of today without them."

"Doesn't matter, we won't know that we did. This particular reality will simply disappear, a new reality with Claire and Diana and that orange thing replacing it and becoming the only reality."

"Really?"

"Nah. I'm just messing with your head." He looked significantly more cheerful than he had for days. "Once time's been used, it's done. Nobody wants time with turned-over corners and pencil scribbles in the margins."

"Do cats get senile?" Dean asked the room at large. When the room didn't answer, which around the guest house wasn't always a given, he knelt to whisk the pile of dirt and cat hair—mostly cat hair—onto a dustpan. Still on his knees, he heard the outside door open and half a dozen people tromp in. Without wiping their feet. Wondering why Newfoundlanders seemed to be the only people in Canada who grasped the concept of not tracking dirt inside, he called, "I'll be right there." He spilled the dustpan into the garbage and stood.

A young woman waited in the lobby, half leaning on the counter and stroking Austin. Tied back off her face with a ribbon, her shoulder-length hair was so black the highlights were blue. Her skin was very pale, her fingers amazingly so against Austin's fur, and her lips were a dark red . . . red as blood. Dean looked out the window and once he was certain the sun hadn't set early and no unscheduled total eclipse had darkened the sky, he exhaled a breath he hadn't realized he was holding. The continuing presence of daylight came as a distinct relief. He had nothing against vampires in general, but they always drew groupies and those guys just weirded him right out.

He smiled what Claire called his innkeeper smile. "Can I help you?"

"We were wondering if you had rooms available."

We? Dean leaned forward and found himself staring down at seven muscular men in shorts and tank tops. The largest of them barely cracked four feet tall. "Uh, we only have six rooms and they're all doubles . . ."

She waved off his protest. "Not a problem. Four rooms are fine; we're not made of money, so we're used to sharing. It's just we've been on the road all night and we'd like to catch some sleep before the game."

"Game?"

"Yeah, we're basketball players," one of the men announced belligerently, weight forward on the balls of his feet as though daring Dean to make something of it.

"Okay."

"They're the Southern Ontario Midget Basketball champs," the young woman announced proudly. "I'm their manager, Aurora King."

Dean shook her hand. "Pleased to meet you."

"We have an exhibition game this evening at the community center." Leaning toward him, she dropped her voice and added, "If you can knock a little off your room rates, I'm sure I can score you some tickets."

To a midget basketball game. *Were people even allowed to say midget anymore?* Dean wondered. Although all things considered, he had to assume Ms. King would know the politically correct . . . label? Word? Description? Realizing she was waiting for his answer, he shrugged. "Uh, sure."

"Come on, come on, enough of the chitchat," yawned a member of the team. "I'm so tired I'm going to sack out right here."

"Low blood sugar," snorted the young man standing beside him.

"Premed," Aurora murmured as Dean pushed the registry toward her. "He diagnoses everything. Drives us nuts." Her voice rose back to more generally audible levels. "You guys work out who's sleeping where and with who."

A strangled cough drew everyone's attention to a redhead blushing almost the exact same shade as his hair.

"Lord fucking save us, the new guy's shy," muttered the first player who'd spoken.

Teasing the new guy kept everyone amused while Dean finished the paperwork and reached for the keys. "I'd just like to point out that there's no smoking in the rooms."

The entire team turned to stare at a diminutive blond.

He pushed short dreadlocks back off his face and shrugged. "Hey, man, I'm cool. No mellow the day of a game. I know the rules."

"Strangely enough," Aurora laughed as Dean's eyebrows rose, "he's one of the best guards we ever had."

"That's because I control my own space, Dude."

After a short tussle over the keys and a little more teasing of the new guy, they started up the stairs. Six steps up, one of them sneezed violently. "I think I'm allergic to the damned cat."

"Well, he won't be in the damned room," Aurora mocked, slipping her arm around the shoulders of the last man standing in the lobby. He wrapped his arm around her waist and they walked in lockstep up to the second floor.

"I'm guessing that one's happy," Austin murmured as they heard the fourth door close.

Dean removed his glasses and polished them against the hem of his T-shirt. "I'm not going there."

"Probably wise."

Struggling up through a pounding headache and the kind of nausea that made even breathing seem like a bad idea, Diana opened her eyes. The ceiling—

a long, long way up—didn't look familiar. Where was she? Mattress and pillow under her. Blanket over. She was obviously in a bed. In her underwear. So she'd been here for a while.

Her head flopped to the left and she could see a row of beds stretching off across a . . . store?

To the right, baby and toddler pajamas were twenty percent off.

Okay. Got it now. Otherside. Mall. Meat-minds. Mall elves. Battle. Wand. Ow.

The two nearest beds were also occupied. She identified Colin by his pale hair but didn't know who the second wounded elf was.

Raising her head, she could see another row of beds facing the first. Since all the beds were made— bedding, aisle fifteen—she assumed the elves were using it as a dormitory slash infirmary.

"Hey. You're awake."

"Claire!" A strong hand behind her back helped her sit. The world tilted. "Bucket!"

A bucket appeared with an efficiency that suggested this was not the first time.

Legs crossed, Diana grasped the turquoise plastic sides firmly and bent over.

"I can't believe you've still got that much in your stomach," Claire murmured worriedly when Diana finally sat up.

"I don't. We're on the Otherside, remember?" Diana gratefully took the offered water, poured some into her mouth, rinsed, and spat. "I could be channeling it from anywhere. Why is everything on an angle?"

"I'm guessing that when you sat up, the world tilted. It's been happening every time you vomit, but don't worry, it settles down."

"I hurl and the earth moves?"

"I know, just what you need, more ego reinforcement." Eyes averted from the contents, Claire set the bucket into the lower cupboard of the bedside table and closed the door.

Diana thought about that for a moment and shuddered. "Uh, Claire . . ."

"Do you want to deal with it?"

"Well, no, but . . ."

"Well, I don't want to deal with it either and that means we don't have to. Next time it comes out of the cupboard, it'll be a new bucket. Okay, once it was a new cauldron because a couple of the kids were hanging around, but, mostly, it's a bucket."

"Cauldron?"

"We're wizards."

"Right. Don't cauldrons go with witches?"

"I suspect the kids were a little confused by that wand trick." Arms folded, brow furrowed, Claire walked almost all the way to Baby and Toddler Pajamas, returned, and reluctantly continued. "And they were also impressed."

"I get the impression you're less impressed," Diana sighed.

"When you used the wand to destroy the dark elf,

it didn't pull power from the possibilities, it pulled it from you."

"No sh . . . kidding, Sherlock." Throwing back the covers, Diana cautiously swung her legs out over the side of the bed. The world wobbled a bit but went no farther off center. "That certainly explains why I feel like I've been puked up and left to dry on the sidewalk. Do you think the wand was a trap?"

"No, I think it was thrown together for the tourist trade with no real thought. It'd have little effect on a Bystander and a Bystander would have less effect on it, but a Keeper . . ."

". . . it sucks dry."

"It's why you collapsed."

"Yeah, I got that." She glanced around for her clothes, saw them folded neatly on the end of the opposite bed, and sent a pleading look toward Claire.

"Are you sure you're well enough?"

"My head's pounding, but I don't actually want or enjoy the feeling of my brain being ground between bricks, so I should be better soon." It wasn't until Claire picked up her shorts and T-shirt with her left hand that Diana realized her right arm was held tight against her chest. "You okay?"

Claire followed her gaze, flexed the fingers, and nodded. "I took a hit from one of those tote bags when the dark elf realized what I was doing with the pepper. It's almost healed."

"How long was I out?"

"About four hours." Three words. A whole lot of feelings.

Diana reached out and touched her sister lightly on the shoulder. "I'm okay."

"I know."

"And if I wasn't okay, it wouldn't have been your fault."

"I know."

"I'm an active Keeper now, and I'm my own responsibility."

"I *know*."

"Okay, that last one sounded like you actually believed it." Diana would have grinned, but it hurt to move the muscles of her face. "So give me a hug and let me get dressed. Since we seem to be stuck with him, I'd just as soon not appear before the Immortal King in my underpants and a sports bra."

"You saved his life, he wouldn't mind." Claire pulled her into a fiery one-armed hug. "And you haven't seen what his elves consider party wear," she added, as they separated. Scrubbing away a tear, she nodded toward Diana's clothes. "Although we do have the dignity of the Lineage to uphold."

"Right. Dignity." Carefully, she pulled her shorts up over her hips. "So. Four hours. Big delay in our plans to close the segue. That's not good."

"No. The darkside may have lost the battle, but it won time, and it has to be pleased about that."

"What about Colin and the other kid?"

"Colin took a tote bag to the forehead while he was dragging Alanyse to safety and Stewart got pounded against a wall." Claire walked around to the end of the next bed and lightly laid a hand on the blanket covering Colin's foot. "They'll both be okay, though."

"How do you figure?" Diana demanded, emerging from the T-shirt with teeth clenched. Dragging the reinforced neck over her head had done nothing to help the brick-grinding-brain problem.

"Arthur's convinced them that they can't die. As long as they believe that, everything heals."

"Nice if he could have convinced them they couldn't get hurt." A quick, careful search found her sandals under the edge of the bed.

"I think that's beyond even his powers of persuasion. These kids came off the street and before that from places even less pleasant. They *know* they can get hurt."

"Good point. Hey, where's Sam?"

"Sam's fine. He's out by the fire."

That pulled Diana's attention off her fight with a buckle. "Fire?"

"They have one every night. Here, let me get that before you vomit again." Claire hiked up her skirt and knelt by Diana's feet. "I don't know how it started, but it's become symbolic, so now it's self sustaining."

"Like the one at the Girl Guide camp?"

The older Keeper shuddered. "Different archetype, so let's hope not."

"I'm starving."

"Hardly surprising, we missed lunch and it's past time for supper. Come on, our packs are by the fire."

"My pouch? The wand?"

"I put them away. You won't be using the wand again, of course, but I thought it was safer in your pack than out where one of the kids might get to it."

Diana didn't see why if it would have little effect on a Bystander, but since her pack was still the best place for it, she didn't argue. Nor did she argue about that *of course*. It was an older sister thing and could safely be ignored. As things stood right now, she had no intention of using the wand again but, as her grade twelve sociology teacher used to say, change is the only constant. And the road to Hell was paved with good intentions. Dean had probably given them a polish on his way by.

The fire burned in a circular pit in the open area just inside the doors. There'd been no pit or even a sign of one earlier, but consistency frequently took a beating on the Otherside. They appeared to be burning charcoal briquettes, fake fireplace logs, and remaindered novelizations of *Everybody Loves Raymond*. Apparently, everybody didn't.

The party clothes Claire had mentioned seemed heavy on the high-heeled boots, leather, and lingerie. Had she ever thought about it, Diana would have said that a run of the mill, middle-class shopping mall wasn't likely to carry PVC corsets—and she'd have been wrong. Gilded by the light from the leaping flames, it looked like the elves were about to break into a coed version of "Lady Marmalade."

Arthur sat on the only chair in the circle of cushions. Although missing legs put it low enough to the ground that he had to cross his own legs in front of him, it still put him head and shoulders above everyone else. The fire reflected off his silver circlet and off the hilt of the sword thrusting up over his shoulder. He was gnawing on a drumstick and looking suitably barbaric until Diana noticed the red-and-white-striped bucket at his feet. The elves had apparently dared the food court.

A quick search spotted Sam perched on the lap of the tall, slender girl that Kris had signaled during their original walk down the concourse.

"He's telling Kith everything that's happened on *Buffy* since she crossed over," Kris said suddenly by Diana's shoulder. Diana tried not to shiver at the warm breath laving her neck. "Your cat watches too much TV."

"Tell me about it. He hogs the remote, too."

Sam's ears flicked back at the sound of her voice, and an orange blur launched itself into the air. The background noise grew richer with the sound of Kith swearing in at least two languages as Diana's arms filled with cat.

"You made me worry!" Amber eyes glared accusations at her.

"Sorry."

"Don't do it again!"

"Okay."

"Now put me down!"

"Sure." She kissed him behind one ear and stroked two fingers back over his head as she set him on the floor. Spinning around, he gave the side of her palm a couple of quick licks and then bit down—not quite drawing blood.

The moment his mouth was empty, he glared up at her. "I meant it when I said don't do it again."

"I know."

He butted against her leg, hard enough to leave the imprint of his head as a purple-and-green bruise. Tail straight up in the air, a fuzzy orange exclamation mark, he stalked back around the fire.

"He's gonna have to make with the apologizing. Kith loves her leather pants."

"Cats don't apologize," Claire said, from Diana's other side, her voice the voice of experience. "He'll convince her the whole thing was her fault."

"Yeah, but he . . ."

Diana cut the protest short. "It doesn't matter."

"If you say so." Kris' fingers were warm in the crook of her elbow. "Come on, himself wants to thank you."

"What for?"

"Duh. Saving his ass and nearly killing yourself doing it." Her grip tightened. "I'm with the cat on that bit. Don't do it again!"

"Look, if another situation comes up . . ." The dark glare from the guard captain was very nearly more heated than Sam's. *Ohmygod, she cares!* Nearly breathless, Diana maintained just enough self-control to shove her free hand into her pocket and cross her fingers. "Okay. Not doing it again."

"Good. Because I'll kick your ass if you do."

Arthur tossed a bone onto the fire as they approached and rose fluidly up onto his feet, wiping greasy fingers on his jeans.

Immortal King. Teenage boy. Mixed messages, Diana sighed silently, *that's what's wrong with the world.* And while they weren't strictly in the world, it was a universal kind of observation. Well, maybe not the Immortal King, teenage boy part but the rest of it.

A hush fell over the assembled mall elves. Arthur touched his right fist to his chest and inclined his head in a regal salute. "My heart rejoices to see you well again, Keeper. I thank you for your timely intervention. I very much regret you were injured for my sake."

His words carried the weight of ritual. Diana felt her cheeks begin to heat and sternly told herself to get a grip. Keepers didn't do liege lord stuff—totally independent contractors. *She* didn't do liege lord stuff. The blood rising into her cheeks ignored her. Nothing to do but blame the color on the fire and make the best of things. "Hey, no big." Her shrug was as nonchalant as the circumstances and the lingering effects of her headache allowed. "I knew the job was dangerous when I took it."

"Then I thank you for your willingness to do the job." His gesture included Claire in his gratitude. "We all thank you."

On cue, the elves began to whoop, then one of them flipped on a boom box and the first track off The Melvin's *Hostile Ambient Takeover* ripped through the remaining silent spaces.

"Oh, yeah, that's appealing. If they really wanted to thank us, they could find something that sounded like music," Claire muttered.

Diana snorted. "Too old to appreciate the good stuff?"

"I'll let you know when I hear some."

"People who only listen to the CBC have no grounds for criticism."

"I'm sure you're both hungry," Arthur interjected smoothly, his voice sliding through the ambient noise. One hand indicated the bucket of chicken. "I'd be honored if you'd join me."

"We'd be pleased to eat with you," Claire said while Diana swallowed an inconvenient mouthful of saliva cased by the rising scent of eleven different herbs and spices deep fried to an extra crispy goodness. "But as we mentioned before, we can only eat the food we brought with us."

"I understand." He sank down into his chair—a gold brocade wingback; the legs having very likely gone to fuel an earlier fire—and waved the two Keepers into the space on his right, empty but for two cushions, their packs, and a saucer.

"Sam couldn't wait." Claire kicked off her sandals, crossed her ankles, and descended gracefully. "I fed him while you were out."

Diana dropped and sprawled, one hand digging in her pack for food before her butt hit the cushion. "I figured. I also figured a full stomach was the only thing keeping his fuzzy head out of the chicken."

"It's not actually chicken." Both Keepers turned to

stare at the cat. Backlit by the fire, his fur looked more red than orange. "I'm not even sure it's some kind of bird."

As one, the Keepers turned to stare at Arthur who shrugged and pulled out a wing that was just a little too large and folded one too many times. "It *tastes* like chicken."

"What doesn't?" Diana muttered, biting into her tuna salad sandwich. Chewed. Swallowed. Scraped her tongue against her teeth. "Oops. My bad."

Claire flicked a coral-colored fingernail through her chicken-flavored carrot sticks and sighed. "Try to be more careful." She offered one to Sam who turned up his nose at it.

"I don't care what it tastes like," he sneered, "it's still a carrot."

On the other side of the fire, bodies leaped and twirled, flames burnishing hair, and skin, and jewelry. The more *elfin* the dancer, the wilder the dance although even Jo, whose ears had barely begun to point, moved with both grace and abandon to the pounding music. It wasn't the kind of dancing Diana was used to, that was for sure.

"Your face wears an interesting expression. What are you thinking?"

Her attention drawn back across the fire, Diana glanced up to find both Arthur and Kris watching her. The guard captain had settled a little forward of the Immortal King's left hand in order to see around the edge of his chair. "Interesting?" she asked, trying to figure it out from the inside. There were, after all, a limited number of ways two eyes, a nose, and a mouth could combine.

"Speculative."

"Okay." It seemed to have something to do with eyebrows. "I was just thinking how much these guys would have livened up one of my high school dances. You know, the kind where the DJ's playing a dance mix from when *he* was in school so the music's all at least three years old and almost no one's dancing and the jocks stand with the jocks and the geeks stand with the geeks and someone always shows up drunk and pukes in the hall and half the kids who think they're taking ecstasy are really taking baby aspirin and actually . . ." She frowned. ". . . so are the other half because that's why the 'rents force me to attend these things in the first place and the one guy who's out on the dance floor grooving to the beat is being made fun of by the other guys. The air is heavy with angst and hormones and there's enough hair spray in the girl's can to open a new hole in the ozone layer."

"It sounds . . ."

"Like major suckage," Kris supplied when Arthur seemed stuck for a word.

He nodded. "Indeed. And you think my people could help?"

Diana took another look. Feet planted, Will undulated hips and arms and scarlet braid in time to the music. "They sure couldn't hurt."

"But in your world, my people would have no reason to dance."

Street kids, CSA kids . . .

"Sure they would." She answered Arthur, but her eyes locked on Kris. "Dance to escape. Dance to forget. Dance to lose yourself in the way your body works; it's the one thing in your life a bunch of overworked bureaucrats can't control."

Kris made a sound somewhere between a snort and a sigh. Not exactly agreeing but not dismissing the observation out of hand.

Arthur glanced from one to the other and then back at the dancers, nodding thoughtfully. "Here, they dance to celebrate their victory over the dark forces."

"It's only a temporary victory," Claire reminded him grimly. "The dark forces will be back and they won't stop until you're all destroyed."

"Way to be a downer," Diana grunted, fishing a nectarine from her pack.

"Ignoring the problem won't make it go away," the older Keeper insisted.

"Jeez, Claire. Hair shirt much? They're not ignoring the problem, they're recharging so they can continue to fight."

"Well, we don't have that luxury. We have to deal with this segue and in order to do that, we have to know what's happening at the other end of the mall."

"And in order to do *that*, we'll need their help. The food court's at the other end of the mall," Diana continued before Claire could voice one of her usual "Keepers do it alone, yadda yadda" protests, "so they obviously know a way to get in and out again." She wiped nectarine juice off her chin and glanced at Kris, who nodded.

"We do."

Her gaze shifted from Kris to the King. "So we need to set up some kind of a recon mission. I suggest that Kris and I wander down for a quick look. She takes care of the navigating and any necessary bad-ass whupping, and I handle the metaphysical stuff."

Sapphire eyes narrowed in confusion as Arthur leaned forward, arms braced across his thighs. "Bad-ass whupping?"

"She means, sire, that I can smack any meat-minds we run across," Kris explained, grinning broadly. "But don't ask me why she's talking like that."

"Don't ask me either," Diana muttered weakly. She could only assume that the thought of spending time alone with Kris skulking through a dark mall had cut the circuit between her brain and her mouth. Claire was looking less than pleased with the suggestion and Sam . . . Sam was buried so deep in her backpack that only his butt and his tail showed. Grateful for the distraction, Diana tossed the nectarine pit into the fire, turned, and hauled him clear.

"Hey! I was just checking to see if you packed my hairball medicine!"

"You don't have hairball medicine." She pulled

out a second tuna sandwich. The wrapping had been holed and a fair bit of the tuna excavated. "You have your own food!"

"Yeah? So?" He licked down a bit of ruffled fur. "You going to eat that? I mean, since it's kind of covered in cat spit . . ."

Diana sighed and handed over the sandwich.

"You shouldn't let him get away with that kind of behavior."

As Sam retreated to the edge of the firelight, she turned a pointed look on her sister. "Like you're the expert. Austin totally runs your life."

"Austin and I have an understanding."

"Yeah, that he runs your life."

"A reconnaissance mission has merit," Arthur announced suddenly. From his tone, Diana assumed he'd done some thinking about it while she'd been dealing with Sam. "But are either of you well enough to go? Both of you were injured in the recent battle; perhaps two of my scouts . . ."

"No." Claire was using her don't-even-bother-arguing-with-me voice. "It has to be one of us. Your people can't see what we need to know."

"And I'm fine," Diana broke in. "Headache's mostly gone, I had a nice nap, I have two working arms . . . it has to be me."

Claire nodded agreement. "You're right."

"And Claire obviously got hit on the head and we never noticed."

Arthur turned an anxious expression on the older

Keeper, but she waved him off. "Diana's just trying to be funny."

"Now is not the time."

Apparently a sense of humor was not a requirement to be an Immortal King. "Sorry." The apology slipped out before Diana remembered that Keepers never apologized.

Still suitably serious, Arthur nodded. "Then, as you request, Kris will accompany you. She has been into enemy territory many times and is therefore your best chance to not only get in but get out again."

"Out again, that's the tricky part," Kris muttered.

"When should this . . ." He stumbled a bit over the shortened word. ". . . recon mission take place?"

Claire held out her good arm. The hands of her watch continued to spin wildly. "As soon as possible."

Kris rose fluidly to her feet. "I'm good." She raked a critical gaze over Diana's clothes as the younger Keeper stood. "You'll have to change. Dark colors, nothing to catch the light."

"I brought jeans."

She gestured back into the store, her rings glittering in the firelight. "We'll find you something better."

"You should have been there last night, Austin, those guys kicked tall ass!" Dean stepped back from hanging a signed picture of the team on the wall of the office and turned to grin at the cat. "You missed a great game."

"I also missed being smuggled into the arena in a gym bag," Austin muttered without lifting his head from his front paws. "Pass."

Before Dean could answer, the phone rang.

"If it's three bears," the cat announced as Dean's hand closed around the receiver, "tell them we're full. That one only ever ends well for the bears."

Black leggings, black tank, black zip-up sweatshirt, black socks, black canvas fanny pack, black leather driving gloves—Diana wore her own hightops and drew the line at using a black lipstick as camouflage paint. The line stayed drawn for about fifteen seconds.

"So you're not as pale as your sister . . ." Finished wrapping the last of her dreadlocks up into one long tail, Kris reached for the tube. ". . . you'll still show up in the shadows."

"I'm a Keeper . . ."

"And I know what I'm doing. Hold still."

"I'm sorry, Sam, but you can't come."

His eyes narrowed, flaying Diana with amber scythes. "You're ditching me so you can be *alone* with your new *friend*, aren't you?"

"No!" She dropped to one knee and beckoned him closer. "Look, I'm really worried about Claire. She's not used to being without Austin. I mean, one of

those meat-minds actually hit her with his little concrete bag thing. How weird is that? Claire never gets
hurt. I'm afraid of what might happen to her if
there's no cat around at all."

Sam snorted. "What a load of crap."

"Fine; I need someone here who can remind Claire
that she's not always right, that this was my Summoning. I'd rather you were with me, but I don't
want her screwing things up from this end."

He thought about it for a moment. "Okay, that one
I'll buy. Be careful."

"You, too. Remember, she gets cranky when
she's crossed."

"Please, if Austin can handle her, how hard can
it be?"

They took the first set of stairs down to the lower
level, past a pair of elves standing guard who might
have been fifteen in the outside world but here were
becoming ageless.

"It's sort of neutral territory between these stairs
and the next ones," Kris murmured as they descended toward the lower concourse. "The meat-
minds never go much farther than the stairs they
chased you and your sister up, but that doesn't mean
there isn't some nasty shit hanging around. There're
a few storefronts you don't want to get too close to."

"In a way that's a good thing."

"Yeah? I doubt you'll think that when the pieces
start rolling out of the Body Shop."

Pieces. Body Shop. Evil was remarkably literal-minded at times.

"You smell something like a seaweed emulsion," Kris continued, "you haul ass. You hear me?"

"What's a seaweed emulsion smell like?"

"Dead fish and seagull shit."

"Okay." Diana took a vigorous sniff but could only smell the perfume/plastic mix of the lipstick smeared all over her face. And maybe, just maybe something warm and spicy and slightly intoxicating rising off Kris which she was going to work very hard at not thinking about until they were safely back in King Arthur's Court.

King Arthur's Court. A legless armchair at a metaphorical fire. Somehow, and she had no idea how, that wasn't as lame as it should have been.

Two more steps. "Looking at the bright side, continuing weirdness means there's still some time before the segue. The more normal this place is, the closer the bad guys are to success."

"Yeah, well, if it's all the same to you, I'm gonna worry about what's going down *before* the muzak starts play . . . Fuck." She spat the profanity between clenched teeth.

"What?"

They were standing at the west end of the lower concourse. Behind them, what should have been another entrance to the department store the elves had claimed was, instead, a solid wall of glass. Diana could barely make out the barricade beyond it. To their right, a Mr. Jockstrap. Sporting goods. She tried to remember if the original mall held a store by that name but couldn't. In a world with Condom Shack franchises, she supposed it was possible. The lights were low, the only sound the bass beat of a fast hip-hop track pulsing down from the upper level. Nothing looked particularly dangerous.

"It's night."

"Okay."

"He's here at night."

"Who?"

"Some old security dude."

Diana felt a chill run down her spine and really hoped it was a gust from the air-conditioning. "Walks with a limp? Kind of weaves his head from side to side like a snapping turtle? Mutters things like lithe and lissome?"

"I never seen a snapping turtle, but that sounds like the guy."

"But he's not in this mall, he's in the other mall. The real mall."

"Yeah? Well, he gets around. Don't let him catch you in his flashlight beam. He nails you with that and you're gone."

"Gone?"

"Gone." Kris rolled her eyes impatiently. "Speak English much? Gone. Not here. Now come on, we got some distance to cover."

They stayed to the darker shadows of the kiosks and the potted trees; Kris leading, Diana half a pace

behind doing her best to mimic the other girl's eco-
nomical movements. Their path led down the center
of the concourse until they neared the second set of
stairs when Kris began to veer left. She tucked into
the rectangular shadow of the last storefront before
a side corridor and motioned for Diana to join her.

"Shoe stores are safe," she whispered in answer to
Diana's silent question, her mouth close to the Keeper's ear. "What's gonna come out? They watch these
stairs," she continued, softening her esses. "It's why
we couldn't use them. We have to get to that hall up
there. Where the sign for the security office is."

The sign was across the side corridor and four
storefronts farther east.

"We used to come down through the store at the
end there . . ." A quick jerk of Kris' head, the motion
felt rather than seen they were so close together, indicated the corridor. ". . . another big one, like ours,
but lately it's been locked at night. Good thing we
didn't fuckin' risk it."

"Because it's night."

The elfin captain patted Diana lightly on one
cheek. "Can't put nothing past you Keepers."

Diana felt her face heat up under its mask of lipstick. The store locked at night could only mean reality had found another foothold, but she decided not
to mention that at the risk of being thought obvious
as well as dense. She watched as Kris dropped to her
belly and inched forward toward the corridor along
the angle of floor and wall. Was she supposed to
follow?

Apparently not.

Just as she began to seriously consider dropping to her knees, Kris began to back up. Feet under her, into a crouch, standing . . . warm breath against Diana's ear. She clenched her hands to keep from shivering.

"It's clear. Move fast, don't make any noise, and try to look as little like a person as you can."

"What?"

"If they see you, you want to leave some doubt about what they're seeing."

That made sense. Although "look as little like a person as you can" didn't. Not in any useful sort of a way.

"All right. Let's . . ."

shunk kree, shunk kree

Kris slammed back against her as a line of light split the concourse.

He was coming from the west. From the same direction they had. He'd been behind them the whole time.

shunk kree, shunk kree

Unable to use the possibilities, even in the minimal way she had in the original mall, Diana was left feeling like she imagined Bystanders must feel all the time. Helpless. Angry. Vaguely pathetic. How did they manage? Kris' back pressed hard against her, warm and comfortingly solid. It helped. The cold glass and dark store behind her didn't.

Shoe store, she reminded herself as the light swept through the shadows under the stairs. *What could possibly come out of a shoe store.*

Actually, she could think of a few things.

None of them good.

All of them the *last* thing she should be thinking about right now.

shunk kree, shunk kree

She was listening so hard to the sound of the security guard shuffling down the concourse that she didn't hear the music start inside the shoe store. By the time she noticed, it had already reached the chorus.

These boots are made for walking . . .

And over the faint, tinny music, another sound. Heels. Rhythmically hitting cheap carpet.

Diana winced. *That can't possibly be good.*

SIX

Claire watched Diana follow Kris past the guard and almost instantly disappear into the shadows of the concourse. She should have been visible longer, even dressed like a department store ninja, but this was the Otherside and the usual rules of perspective and perception didn't always apply. Their farewells had been short . . .

"Remember you're only gathering information."

"My Summons, Claire."

"Just be careful!"

"Well, duh."

. . . and now all she could do was wait. And gather what information she could from talking to Arthur's scouts. And help secure this end of the mall against another attack. And find an exit that could show her what was happening outside because there might be something there she could use. And check the lock Diana had set during the battle. And lock any of the other storefronts the elves didn't actually use; the damage had sounded extensive, but the travel agency could be up and running again at any time.

But mostly, wait.

For her little sister to return safely from enemy territory.

Claire envied the other Keepers—*all* the other Keepers—who had no siblings and would never know how it felt allowing the person who'd taken their first steps with chubby fingers wrapped around yours to walk blithely into danger when every instinct screamed, *"Stay here where it's safe. I'll do it."* no matter who logic declared was the better choice for the job.

If something happened?

She had a brief, horrid vision of explaining the situation to their parents. Infinitely worse than trying to explain how she'd only turned her head for an instant and two-year-old Diana had eaten the entire tube of yellow poster paint.

And vomited it up on the white wool rug.

So nothing *would* happen. Nothing bad. This was the Otherside; all she had to do was hold tight to that belief.

Holding tight, she returned to the fire and sank down on her cushion beside Arthur's empty chair. First, she'd talk to the elves who'd raided the food court earlier in the evening. They'd have the most recent information about that end of the mall. Arthur would know who they were.

As though her thoughts had called him, he appeared, walking around the fire with the loose-limbed self-confidence of a young man who'd never been called geek, who'd never had a girl turn him down for a date, who was captain of both the football team and the debating club . . . Claire shook her head and rewound the thought. He was walking with the confidence of a young man wearing a huge, mythical sword strapped to his back. A huge, mythical sword he knew how to use.

"I have sent word to Bounce and Daniel that you wish to speak to them." Arthur sank into his chair and flipped his hair back off his face. "They'll be here shortly."

"Are they out scavenging again?"

"No. They're taking advantage of the darkness to . . ." He finished the sentence with an incomprehensible gesture.

"To?" Was he blushing? He was. The Immortal King had turned an uncomfortable looking shade of deep crimson. Suddenly, Claire got it. "Oh. To . . ." She repeated the gesture. "They're being safe, right? I mean, these kids didn't come from the best of backgrounds and you have no idea of what I'm talking about, do you?"

"They're in no danger."

"Okay." Probably best to leave it at that. Feeling, well, old in the face of Arthur's embarrassment, Claire searched for a less loaded topic. "So, the darkness—I'm a little surprised it's lasted this long. Time's been moving fairly quickly up until now."

"The darkness last as long as the fire does."

Were it not for the implications of that statement,

his relief would have been amusing. Claire glanced down at her watch. The second hand lay motionless over the two. "Great." Once Diana reached the area controlled by the dark forces, she'd be moving in a totally different time. *At* a totally different time? Prepositions just weren't set up for this sort of thing.

According to her watch, Dean and Austin weren't moving at all. On the bright side, that should keep them out of trouble.

Austin poked Dean's rigid arm with a paw and snorted. Walking around the phone, he took a closer look at the watch on the wrist below the hand holding the receiver. Stopped.

"Fortunately," he said, trotting to the end of the counter and leaping carefully down, "time waits for no cat."

And with any luck, the fridge door would be open.

The weight of a constant regard between her shoulder blades spun Claire around. "What?"

Sam blinked. "Nothing."

"Well, stop it."

The weight didn't change. She turned again. "What did I say?"

"Weren't you listening either?"

"Did Diana tell you to watch me?"

"Why would she do that?"

"Are you watching me?"

He licked his shoulder. "I don't know what you're talking about."

"A cat may look at a king," Arthur observed, grinning.

"Yes . . ." Claire shifted emphatically on the cushion, feeling a bit like a butterfly on a pin. ". . . but he's not looking at *you*."

shunk kree, shunk kree

You can't see me. You can't see m . . . us. You can't see us.

Diana repeated the mantra silently, hoping it would be enough. She could make it enough. The smallest act of will would slide that flashlight beam right on by. But the smallest act of will would break the Rules, strengthen the bad guys, and get her in major shit with Claire and the rest of the lineage.

So all she had was hope.

Hope, and Kris' warm body pressed tightly against her as they squeezed into the darkest part of the shadow.

Okay. The situation wasn't *all* bad.

The glass behind her shivered at a sudden impact, but the beam never wavered and the step/drag of the old man's approach didn't change. How had he not heard that?

"I know you're here. Soft, round flesh not to be touched."

shunk kree, shunk kree

Maybe he hadn't actually crossed over. Maybe he couldn't hear the music and the boots banging against the glass because he was walking the borderland between the world and the Otherside.

"Pliant, flexible, heated limbs. Can't hide forever. I will find you. Oh, yes."

Maybe he was a freakin' fruitcake and not the good kind of fruitcake either. No icing. The kind of dried fruit that either broke fillings or curled tongues. Cake dense enough to pound nails with . . .

And I'm so totally babbling.

She'd faced demons, disasters, and Hell itself with more composure. What was it about this guy?

For that matter, what *was* this guy?

The circle of light swept up the underside of the staircase, then flicked across the concourse to illuminate the window of a gift shop where a line of porcelain dolls sat with their eyes squeezed shut. Hard to tell for sure at such a distance, but they looked much the way Diana felt. The old man couldn't possibly be seeing the Otherside contents of the stores or he'd have surely reacted to the rude gesture being made by a well-dressed teddy bear propped up behind the dolls. First teddy bear Diana'd ever seen with articulated fingers.

If he followed the path of the light, if he kept it pointed in the same direction, he'd be heading away from them, down one of the short arms that turned the lower concourse into a weird kind of enclosed "y." He'd be heading into territory controlled by the dark side. Diana wondered how *they* coped, if his light had any effect or if his overlap only included the elves.

Did it include Keepers?

Something about the way the hair lifted on the back of her neck suggested it did.

Standing motionless, listening, he kept his flashlight beam trained on the gift shop window. Let them think the useless pieces of pretty debris held his attention. Let them grow complacent and move. Or better yet, let them grow afraid as they waited. Let their muscles tense and their limbs begin to tremble. Let breath catch in their throats and their hearts flutter as they tried to make no sound he would be able to hear.

Let them finally break from cover, unable to stand still any longer.

He would have them then.

Not sneering, not laughing. Hard/soft bodies caught and held.

They had no business being in the mall after closing.

They had no business being so young.

There.

He rocked his weight back on one heel, spun to the left, and whipped the light across the concourse.

Diana stifled a gasp as Kris jerked back against her—although whether she was gasping at the sudden increased contact or at the flashlight beam that swept the tiles inches from the toes of Kris' Doc Martens, she couldn't say for sure.

shunk kree, shunk kree

You can't see us . . .

The old man came closer. The puddle of light spread until Kris was standing with her heels together and her toes splayed almost a hundred and eighty degrees apart. Feeling her begin to totter, Diana slipped an arm around the guard captain's waist. They were pressed so closely together their hearts began to beat to a single rhythm. Why that rhythm seemed to be reggae when the boots were still banging an old Nancy Sinatra hit on the other side of the window, Diana had no idea.

Then, finally, the light began to move on down the mall; east, the way they had to go. But better to have the ancient nutbar in front of them than behind.

shunk kree, shunk kree

As he passed, his head slowly turned, and he peered into their rectangle of shadow. His eyes narrowed. His grip shifted on the flashlight.

You can't see us . . .

And he passed on by.

They listened to his footsteps fade. They took their first breath in unison. Then their second. Then Kris murmured, "He's gone, Keeper. You got reasons for hanging on that I should know?"

"No." Because, *you feel so good* wasn't really a reason Diana wanted to get into right now. She dropped her arm and tried not to feel bereft as Kris stepped away. "What should we do about the boots?"

"Do?"

"They could come right through the window."

"It's summer, there aren't a lot of them and even

if they break the glass, the security cage'll keep them in." She reached back and wrapped her hand around Diana's wrist. "Come on."

The feel of cool fingers on the skin between sleeve and glove was familiar.

"That was you, Friday night. You held Sam and me in the shadow so we didn't get caught in the beam when the security guard flashed back the way he'd come."

"Yeah. That was me. Now do me a favor and never use the word *flash* in the same sentence as that scary old dude again." Her lip curled, showing a crescent of teeth. "Bad image frying the wetware."

Diana caught the image and shuddered. "Eww."

"Big time."

"But how did you . . ." She looked down at Kris' hand, still around her wrist, and then up at the other girl's face. "We weren't even in the same reality."

Kris shrugged. "Reality's what you make it."

"True enough. You got reasons for hanging on I should know about?"

"No."

It was a familiar sounding *no*. Diana grinned as she followed Kris back out onto the concourse. *Hey, Sam, I think she likes me.*

It wasn't difficult to imagine Sam's response.

"And what am I, chopped liver?"

"No, I mean she likes me.*"*

"So what are you going to do about it?"

What *was* she going to do about it? And should

she even do anything? And when? Actually, that last question was a no brainer.

Not now.

"Remember, stay low, move fast, and try not to look like a person. We're in the bad guys' fuckin' territory." Kris dropped into a crouch and scuttled across the side corridor, one arm crooked over her head.

She looked exactly like a person in a crouch with her arm over her head, but Diana figured she knew what she was doing, so she folded herself into a mirror image of the position and scuttled after. Shadows spilled out of the far end of the corridor, but they came with no accompanying feeling of being watched—a faint feeling of looking ridiculous but that passed as she reached the storefronts on the opposite side and straightened.

Tucked up tightly against the wall, Kris moved steadily toward the short hallway leading to the security office.

Security office?

Oh, great. What's wrong with this picture?

Grabbing the back of Kris' waistband, Diana dragged her to a stop. "What if *he's* in the security office?" she hissed.

"What if he is? We still gotta go that way. It's the only safe way to the food court."

About to ask what definition of "safe" Kris was using, Diana jumped almost into the guard captain's arms as a thick, purple tentacle slapped the glass beside her. "I didn't do that!"

"Of course you didn't." The *dumbass* was silent but clearly implied. "It's the pet store."

"Right. And that's . . . ?"

"Beats the fuck out of me, but it's not a squid."

"What happened to the puppies and kittens?"

"I'm guessing it ate them."

"Of course it did."

They reached the hall without further incident. Narrow and lit by every third bank of fluorescents in the dropped ceiling, it went back about thirty feet, ending in a cross corridor. Diana could just barely make out two signs on the back wall. The first read: Elevator to Rooftop Parking and included a red arrow pointing left. The second: Baby Change Room; arrow to the right. What the babies changed into was anyone's guess. The closed door to the security office was about a third of the way up the hall, on the right. That far again was a small water fountain.

No *shunk kree*. No advancing armies of darkness.

The only sound was the hum of the lights.

Like it would kill them to learn the words? Diana wondered as Kris began moving faster and she hurried to catch up.

Both walls were covered in crayon portraits that shifted. A great many of them seemed to be of a dark silhouette, horned and cloaked and possessing glowing red eyes. None of them were particularly good.

Although the eyes seem to be following Kris, Diana realized. *Are following Kris*, she amended as a pair of crimson orbs plopped out of a portrait and rolled almost to the mall elf's heels. An emphatic poke turned Kris around as a pointing finger directed her gaze to the problem.

Kris rolled her own eyes and took a quick step back.

A sound like bubble wrap being popped.

A bit of waxy residue on the floor.

A quick glance at the rest of the portraits showed them all pointedly looking in different directions. Whatever dark power controlled them, it wasn't strong enough to overcome basic self-preservation.

Passing the security office, Diana worked at remembering trig formulas and other useless bits of high school math rather than merely trying not to think about the old man opening the door. In this situation, getting caught up in the old "try not to think of a purple hippopotamus" problem could have disastrous results.

At the water fountain, Kris indicated she needed a boost.

Diana dropped to one knee, let Kris use the other as a step, and watched amazed as, standing on the edge of the fountain, she reached up and shoved one of the big ceiling tiles off the framework. Were the elves keeping supplies inside the dropped ceiling?

Kris braced her hands and smoothly boosted herself up and out of sight.

Okay, that's not poss . . . Biting the thought off before Kris crashed through acoustic fibers and aluminum strapping that couldn't possibly hold her weight, Diana sat in the fountain, drew her feet up next to her butt and, pushing against the side walls of the alcove, stood. Apparently, she was supposed to follow. *No matter how imposs . . .* She bit that thought off, too, and concentrated instead on doing the mother of all chin ups. Sneaker treads gouging at the wall, she managed to hook first one elbow behind a cross brace and then the other. A little involuntary grunting later, her upper body collapsed across the dusty inner side of the ceiling. Strong hands pulled her farther in and dropped the open tile back into place.

For no good reason, there was enough light to see a path worn through the dust. It headed off to the right on a strong diagonal. Southeast, Diana figured after a moment. Directly toward the food court. They were going to reach the food court by traveling inside a dropped ceiling—something it looked as though the elves did all the time.

Even though it couldn't be d . . .

It could be done.

It had been done.

A lot.

Hold that thought, Diana told herself as she crawled after Kris. *Don't even consider thinking about how stu . . .*

Fortunately, crawling after Kris provided its own distraction.

Her knees were raw and the lump on her forehead

where she'd cracked it on a pipe was throbbing when the path stopped at the edge of a concrete block wall. Kris motioned for silence. Diana tried to ache more quietly.

Another tile was lifted carefully aside and, after a moment, Kris dropped down out of sight. Her head reappeared almost instantly and then one arm, beckoning Diana forward.

They weren't in the food court.

They were standing on the sinks in the women's washroom.

Together, they replaced the tile and one at a time, jumped down.

"This is the way you always go?' Diana asked quietly.

Kris nodded and pulled her bound dreads back with one hand, bending to drink from the taps. "Meat-minds have never caught on," she said proudly when she finished drinking. "It's like they can't wrap their tiny fucking brains around the idea."

That's because acoustic tiles and aluminum strapping could barely hold the weight of a full-grown mouse and certainly couldn't hold a couple of full-grown elves. Or even mostly grown elves. Definitely not an elf and a size twelve Keeper. People, or in this case, elves, who believed that a dropped ceiling provided a secret highway between distant destinations got their information from bad movies and worse television. The meat-minds, who watched neither, knew that no one could travel by way of dropped ceilings. No wonder they couldn't wrap their tiny brains around the idea.

Believing seven impossible things before breakfast was pretty much standard operating procedure on the Otherside, but even in a place where reality depended on definition, some things were apparently too much.

Diana said none of this aloud. Had no intention of ever mentioning it.

The certainty of the mall elves that it *could* be done because they'd seen a hundred heroes and an equal number of villains do it, had created the passage. She had no intention of messing with that certainty. Certainly not while they still needed it to get home.

Only the full toilet paper dispensers in every stall and the lack of graffiti scratched into the pale green paint suggested this wasn't the actual women's washroom in the actual mall—another indication of how close the segue was to completion.

Kris opened the door just wide enough for the two of them to slip through. Moving quietly from shadow to shadow, they peered out into the deserted food court.

Diana's nose twitched at the smell of freshly brewed coffee. She must have made a noise because Kris grinned and murmured, "Starbucks."

"You mean an Otherside corruption of Starbucks."

"Is that what I said? I mean an actual Starbucks."

"Man . . ." Diana shook her head in reluctant admiration. "Those guys are moving in everywhere."

* * *

Claire yawned, rubbed her eyes, and realized that the lights had come back on in the department store. The fire had gone out. She checked her watch; the second hand was revolving at significantly better than normal speed. Time had become relative again. When she glanced up, the fire pit was gone and one of the mall elves, a dark-haired petite girl who looked capable of precision kneecapping, was sweeping up the ashes. Jo, Claire remembered after a moment.

"You done with us, Keeper?"

Daniel was lounging back against the few remaining cushions, one long, denim-clad leg draped over Bounce's lap. The other boy had his eyes closed, a glistening line of drool running from the corner of his mouth and down the side of his chin. They hadn't been able to tell her much; only that the food in the food court was a lot less weird than it had been and as the food got more *normal*, the meat-minds patrolled more frequently.

"*And at certain times of the day, there's like a bazillion old people hanging around.*"

"*Are they eating?*"

"*Listen, much?*" Daniel had snorted. "*I said they were hanging around. Kind of dropped down from the ceiling like big old wrinkly spiders.*"

"*Are they dangerous?*"

"*Nah, just a big fat pain to get around.*"

"*Keeper?*"

"Thanks, guys. I'm done." A little sleep would be nice, Claire thought as she watched Daniel rouse his friend and the two of them disappeared into the depths of the store, but she couldn't risk it. The first year she was on active duty, a Keeper had fallen asleep on the Otherside; fallen asleep and dreamed. He'd woken up at his old high school . . . naked. Fixing the resultant fallout had definitely been one for the history books. Chapter seven. Right after the Riel Rebellion. Some nice black-and-white pictures, too. They'd pulled all the copies from circulation, but Claire knew a couple members of the Lineage who'd kept personal copies, allegedly for research purposes.

Arthur touched her lightly on the shoulder as someone carried away his chair. "I must attend to the business of the realm. If you require me . . ."

"I should be guarding you." Claire stood and smoothed down her skirt. "They could send an assassin." It would cost them a lot, single travelers always paid a premium, but she didn't doubt for a moment that if they could pay, the darkside wouldn't hesitate. Kill Arthur; destroy the united defiance raised against them.

"They would kill the Immortal King?"

"Don't get too attached to the label," she told him acerbically. "Just because you never stay dead doesn't change the fact that you die and kingdoms fall every time you're removed from the equation."

"I have doubled the guards on all points leading to this level and I will be careful. But if you have

nothing better to do than to act as my nursemaid . . ."
He bowed slightly, hair falling into his face and
swept up as he straightened. ". . . then I will be
honored by your company. Although I had thought
you wanted to take a look outside."

"I do."

He smiled and waited. He had a way of waiting
that reminded her of Austin.

"All right, I'll go have a look out the nearest doors,
but I want you surrounded at all times by your best."

"My very best went with your sister."

"Fine, your second best, then, until I get back. I'll
be as quick as I can. Sam, you coming?"

"Nope. Not even breathing hard."

Claire stopped, and the orange cat bumped into
the back of her calves. "What?"

"It's just something Diana says."

"Why am I not surprised?"

"If you actually want me to answer that, I'm going
to need more information," Sam pointed out as they
began walking again.

The key locking the optical shop not only continued to hold but couldn't be moved. Claire pushed
against it with one finger, then with her entire hand,
then sat back on her heels with a satisfied nod.

"So, what's it worth to you to have me *not* tell
Diana you were checking up on her work?"

She turned her head just enough to spear the orange cat with a disdainful gaze. "What's it worth to
you for me *not* to tell Diana you tried to blackmail
me?"

Amber eyes blinked. "You're assuming she'd care?"

"Good point."

On the 'better safe than sorry' principle, she locked the rest of the stores along the short corridor. Once they defeated the darkside, she'd unlock them and give the elves access to the entire mall but, for now, the last thing they needed was a horde of meat-minds charging out from behind a rack of cheap silver accessories.

The doors at the end of the corridor—the doors they entered the mall through way back whenever—were unlocked. Claire wasn't sure why. They could have been open because it was now business hours in the real mall or they could have been open because she wanted them to be. She had to be more careful about her desires before they set up a beacon the darkside could use to . . . to . . . she honestly couldn't say what the darkside would do, but it went without saying that it wouldn't be good.

"Sam, you wait in here."

"Why?"

"Because going through a door on the Otherside can be dangerous; you don't always end up on the other side of the door and I don't want to explain to Diana that I lost her cat."

"Her cat?" Sam snorted. "I am a free agent in the universe."

"Not until you can open your own cans of cat food, you aren't." Without waiting for a reply, she pressed down on the bar latch, and pushed. Her mind carefully blank, she stepped over the threshold. And then again—press, push, blank, step—for the outside door.

She was still on the Otherside. A half turn. She was outside the copy of the mall. All things considered, it wasn't a bad copy. Some of the edges in the middle where neither the elves nor the darkside held complete control were a little fuzzy, but, even so, it would pass.

The concrete pad was exactly as she remembered it: black metal bench, newspaper box. The headline GFDHK SCGH TPR! was different—most newspapers used at least a couple of vowels—but the hockey scores seemed current. That probably wasn't relevant. Or no more relevant than the appalling reality of hockey in June. The only things missing were Dean and Austin and they were safe in the guest house.

She didn't remember it smelling so bad.

Although the edges of the parking lot faded into mist—intent on their segue, the darkside hadn't bothered to anchor the mall on the Otherside—the lot itself was glossy black, the yellow lines gleaming. And steaming. And bubbling. Claire jumped back as an ebony bubble swelled to iridescence then burst almost at the edge of the concrete. The parking lot was a very *very* large tar pit. She had no idea how the yellow lines stayed in place, but at least that explained the smell.

On the bright side, there'd be no attacks coming in through this door.

As she turned, she noticed something she'd missed before. A sign and a ramp. There was parking on the roof.

Frowning, she remembered there were skylights over the hexagonal cuts through the floor. Designed to send light down into the lower level, Claire had a sudden image of dangling . . .

Not ninjas. Think old people, dangling old people. Images that were already real.

Trouble was, she remembered looking up and seeing handrails around the skylight.

There had to be a way up to the parking on the roof. Where?

"Greetings, I am Professor Jack Daniels . . ."

Far too polite to say what he really thought, Dean peered across the desk at the balding man in the tweed jacket and said, "I'm sorry?"

"Jack Daniels . . ."

"Is a kind of whiskey."

"Oh." He sighed, looked down at his hands, and up again. "Bad choice?"

"Not a good one," Dean allowed. "Besides, you gave me your real name when you called." He spun the registration book around and pointed. "Dr. Hiram Rebik."

"Right." Another glance down at his hands. "I'm uh . . . I mean, just so you know, I'm not a medical doctor. I have a doctorate in archaeology."

"Yeah? I've seen *Raiders of the Lost Ark* more than twenty times."

"Have you?"

"Maybe thirty even, it's some good. I'm Dean McIssac."

A small self-conscious smile. "Pleased to meet you."

"You wanted a room for you and your mummy."

"Yes."

"I've had the dehumidifier running in room two all day."

"Thank you."

"Did you want help carrying him . . . or her," Dean corrected hurriedly, "inside?"

"No, thank you. I'm parked in the back. I assume there's a back door?"

"Yes, of course." Coming out from behind the counter, he indicated that Dr. Rebik should follow, and led the way down the hall.

"You have an elevator," Dr. Rebik observed as they passed. "Late Victorian?"

"Sometimes." Slipping back the deadbolt, Dean opened the door out into the narrow passageway that separated the guest house from the building to the north. "I hope there's enough room."

"Plenty."

As Dr. Rebik hurried out to the parking lot, Austin appeared to wind around Dean's feet. "I wonder why he wanted to use the back door."

"Well, it's a mummy. There's got to be, you know, a sarcophagus or something."

"You think that skinny little guy could carry a sarcophagus on his own?"

"No."

"Then . . . ?"

Dean shrugged. "You're the expert, you tell me."

Two sets of footsteps approached down the passage; one slow and steady, the other shuffling along, feet never leaving the ground.

"Okay, that's . . . weird."

"I'm just guessing here," Austin muttered, backing up to cover both possible lines of escape, "but I think the phrase you're looking for is: Oh, my God! The mummy! It's alive! Alive being a relative term," the cat added thoughtfully.

"You're not helping."

"Oh. Was I supposed to be?"

Before Dean could answer, Dr. Rebik appeared in the doorway carefully supporting a slender figure wearing a floor-length, hooded cloak. *Where would you buy something like that, then?* he wondered stepping out of the way.

"Mr. McIssac, this is Meryat. She was Chief Wife to Rekhmire, Grand Vizier to Ramses the Great."

"Ma'am."

"Meryat . . ."

And that was the only word Dean recognized. Made sense; why would an ancient Egyptian speak modern English? On the other hand, why would a modern archaeologist speak ancient Egyptian? Still, that was a moot point given that there was a mummy shuffling toward the dining room. Was she hungry? What would he feed a reanimated corpse?

"Uh, Dr. Rebik, just so we're clear, the guest house has a few rules. No bloodsucking, no soul sucking, no dark magic in the room, anything that detaches while you're here leaves with you . . ." They'd added that one after a trio of zombie folk musicians had left part of the base player in the bathtub. ". . . and all long distance calls must be either collect or on your calling card. We've been stuck with the bill a few times," he expanded when Dr. Rebik looked confused. "As long as you're in the dining room, will you be wanting anything to eat, then?"

"Nothing for me, thank you, Mr. McIssac. Meryat . . ." Again a soft string of words in a foreign tongue.

This time, there was an answer.

Meryat's voice was husky—a whiskey voice, his grandfather would have called it—and a small hand wrapped in strips of yellowing linen emerged from the depths of the cloak to close gently over Dr. Rebik's. He held it as though it might break—which for all Dean knew, it might—and smiled into the shadows of the hood.

"Meryat thanks you for your consideration, Mr. McIssac, but she only wants to rest a moment before she attempts a flight of stairs. She's not very strong yet."

"Okay. Sure. Uh, when you said mummy on the phone, I was assuming it . . ."

The hood turned toward Dean.

"Sorry. . . . *she'd* have her own place to sleep. Our rooms only have one bed."

"That's fine." Another smile into the shadows. They were definitely holding hands.

It was kind of sweet. Creepy, but sweet.

SEVEN

Dean lifted Austin's chin out of his eye socket, and sat up in bed scrubbing at the cooling cat drool running down beside his nose. Something . . .

Pounding. Distant pounding. At the front door.

Groping for his glasses, he pushed the arms more or less over his ears and peered down at the clock. Six twelve *a.m.* Almost a full hour before the alarm.

More pounding.

"Why don't you just ignore it?" Austin grumbled from the pillow. "Make them come back later."

Wishing he could curl up and wrap *his* tail over *his* nose, Dean swung bare feet out onto the floor. "That would be rude." His jeans were folded neatly over the back of an old wooden chair. He stared at them stupidly for a moment, then shook them out and raised his right foot. "Besides, it could be important."

More pounding.

About to shimmy the faded denim up over his hips, his brain finally caught up to his body.

"It could be Claire!"

"Don't be ridiculous, she has a key," Austin reminded him as he tucked in and zipped up just a little too fast to be safe.

"Then it could be someone with news from Claire!" More pounding as he ran from the bedroom and across the living room, exploding out into the office. Hoping the scream of hinges hadn't woken up either of their guests—Claire referred to them as eldritch hinges; multiple cans of WD-40 had no effect—he threw himself to his knees and slid under the drop leaf at the end of the counter, a black-and-white blur barely seen in the corner of one eye. By the time he reached the door, Austin was there waiting for him.

"I thought I was being ridiculous?" he panted, fumbling with the lock.

"If it's news about Claire, you'll need me to be here."

"Why?"

Austin snorted. "Because I'm the cat."

"*The* cat?" Twist back the deadbolt.

"The only one talking to you."

He wrapped his hand around the doorknob, turned, and yanked.

The man standing on the porch was a little shorter than Dean's six feet. His hair and eyebrows had been sun-bleached to the color of straw. Sunburn lent a painful-looking ruddiness to his complexion, and the end of his nose was peeling. Bulky muscle making him appear stocky, he wore a tan short-sleeved shirt

with the top three buttons undone, matching shorts—
with all buttons safely fastened—and hiking boots. A
number of leather pouches hung from his broad
leather belt and both his arms were covered in an
interesting patchwork of scars.

"All right, where is it?"

Not Australian in spite of appearances; the accent
was Canadian heartland.

"Where is what, then?"

"The mummy!" His pause carried the expectation
of a musical emphasis, as though his life came with
its own soundtrack that only he could hear. "I know
it's here," he continued when Dean didn't immediately respond. "I tracked Dr. Rebik's car to your
parking lot!

That didn't sound good. Unwilling to give the benefit of the doubt to someone who banged on doors
at six in the morning, Dean barely covered a yawn
and decided to play dumb. "Why?"

"Because I'm hunting the mummy!"

"Why?" Maybe if he kept repeating himself, he'd
get an answer.

"It's a mummy!"

Okay. New track. "So what's Dr. Rebik's mother
done to you, then?"

"Not mother. Mummy!" Veins bulging on his
neck, mouth open to continue his protest, he paused
and glanced down. "Is that cat laughing?"

Dean shoved Austin with the side of one bare
foot. "Hairball."

"Right. Look, my name's Lance Benedict . . ."

This time both men looked down.

"Really *big* hairball." Dean shot Austin a warning frown.

"Right." Lance's broad smile showed perfect teeth. "Anyway, I realize this must all seem extraordinary to you, an ordinary kind of a guy, living an ordinary kind of life . . ."

Dean bent down and turned Austin around to face the kitchen. "You should be having a drink of water to take care of that hairball." One hand against the cat's back legs, he shoved. If looks could maim, he'd have collapsed bleeding on the hardwood.

The angle of his tail promising later retribution, Austin stalked off down the hall.

When Dean straightened, Lance sighed. "Everything will make perfect sense the moment I explain it!"

Sighing and exclaiming simultaneously *was* quite the trick, Dean had to admit.

"Evil is afoot!"

"It's not in Dr. Rebik's car, then?"

"Not on foot! Afoot!" Another, more dramatic sigh. "Can I come in? Your neighbors must not discover the darkness that hides in the forgotten corners of their little worlds!"

Curtains twitched in a second-floor window across the street and Dean realized he was standing in the doorway wearing only his jeans and his glasses. Professor Marnara had been slipping salacious haiku in the mailbox for a couple of months now and she really didn't need more inspiration. "Yeah. Sure. Come in." He stepped back and closed the door firmly behind the mummy hunter. "All right, then, explain."

"You're Irish, aren't you? I can tell from your accent; it's a skill I have! County Cork, by way of Dublin."

"Newfoundland. Harbor Street, St. John's, by way of Herring Neck."

"Right. Sixteenth-century Irish derivative. Corrupted, of course."

Dean's lip curled. Good manners only extended so far. "The explanation?"

"Right." Lance leaned forward and lowered his voice. "Dr. Rebik has been vilely kidnapped by a woman who died almost five thousand years ago! Late one night in his lab, the unfortunate doctor broke the spell confining her wretched, evil form to her sarcophagus. She rose and took over his mind, feeding off his life force to reduce the gruesome effects of centuries of decay. When I discovered what she'd done, I fought valiantly to stop her, but her control over Dr. Rebik was so strong he attacked me and left me for dead!"

"And you got messed up in this because . . . ?"

"Because I'm Dr. Rebik's grad student and I intend to save him! I am quite possibly the only person now alive who knows how to stop the foul fiend!" His hands curled into fists as he rocked forward on the balls of his feet. "Just tell me what room that pustulant monstrosity is in!"

"Meryat?"

"That's her!"

Mummies. Doctors. Grad students. Dean weighed what he knew and came to a decision. "Third floor. Room six. You should take the elevator, it'll be faster." He led Lance to the brass gates, folded them open, and waved the other man inside. "Just pull that lever over to the three. I'll wait in the lobby in case she makes a run for the front door."

"Good man!" Legs braced, back straight, Lance yanked the lever toward him. The elevator began to rise.

"Was that nice?" Austin asked as the dial showed the elevator just passing the second floor.

Dean shrugged. "Before he left, Augustus Smythe fixed it so that the third floor always opens to the beach. We haven't seen a giant not-quite-squid in months and the fire sand is all posted. There's food and water in the cabana. Lance'll do some exploring, he'll get a bit more sunburn, maybe he'll go swimming. He's safer there than back out on the street."

"So it *was* nice." Austin looked disgusted. "Just when I think you're acquiring a personality that doesn't involve cleaning products, Claire, or hockey. I suppose I should be moderately encouraged that you actually lied to the man."

"And I should be concerned that you're having a worse influence on me than Hell ever did."

"Flattery will get you nowhere, but don't stop."
He ran to catch up as Dean started back down the
hall. "What are you going to do now?"

"Put a shirt on and wake Dr. Rebik. I'm after hearing his side of the story."

Lance stood ankle-deep in white sand, staring at
the brilliant blue sky, and the turquoise breakers. A
breeze off the distant dunes caressed his cheek with
the scent of warmed sweet grass. This had to be
another one of the mummy's evil spells—a way to
turn this world into the ancient world she'd lost.
Which hadn't included an ocean or a sign that read
Please return your towels to the guest house, but that
had to be only because she wasn't yet at full
strength.

He still had time to stop her.

But first, he had to find Dr. Rebik. Or what was left
of the man.

He pulled his cell phone from its belt pouch and
punched in Dr. Rebik's number. His mentor hadn't
answered any of his previous calls, but there was
always the chance that the resurrected she-demon
had left her captive alone for a moment or that—as
he was now so close—he'd hear the ringing of the
doctor's phone.

*"We're sorry; this number can not be completed as di-
aled. You must dial bleri or syk before the number. Please
hang up and try again."*

Bleri or syk? Brows drawn in to meet over his nose,

Lance stared down at the keypad. His phone didn't come with a bleri or syk. Damn! It was the whole pizza number debacle all over again. No bleri, no syk, no eleven . . . he should never have been seduced by that "Friday the Thirteenth Free" calling plan.

No matter.

Tucking the phone back into its pouch, he pulled a bandanna from another and tied it around his neck. Although Dr. Rebik could be anywhere in this mystical world of dark magic, the cheery looking blue-and-white cabana perched just above the high tide mark seemed the logical place to start.

"Lance is . . ."

Meryat offered two words from within the shadows of her hood.

"No, he's not an idiot." Dr. Rebik smiled and stroked the back of her hand with one finger. "He's just under the impression that archaeology should be an adventure, like it is in the movies and on television. Mystic relics. Cursed idols. Dark magics. The return of ancient gods, wrathful and virtually omnipotent. He has a problem differentiating between fact and fiction."

"And yet . . ." Dean set a mug of coffee in front of the doctor and dropped into a chair across from him, cradling his own mug with both hands. ". . . you *are* traveling with a resurrected mummy there."

"Yes, well, there's always an exception that proves the rule."

"He said you broke the seal keeping Meryat in her sarcophagus."

"I did. Good coffee. Blue Mountain?"

"Organic Mexican."

"Ah." Another swallow and a happy sigh. His face puffy and deep purple bags under both eyes, the archaeologist looked as thrilled to be up at six thirty as Dean felt. "My Meryat was once the wife of Rekhmire, Grand Vizier to Ramses the Great. *One* of Ramses' Grand Viziers at any rate. He had four that we know of during the many years of his rule. She used to give the most magnificent parties—we've found records of them in a number of writings of that era—and at one of them she inadvertently insulted a High Priest by . . ."

Another word from within the hood.

Dr. Rebik cleared his throat, his ears red. "Yes. Well, there's no need to go into the specifics. The point is, the priest was insulted and, in a fit of pique, had her poisoned. Then he cursed her ka so that Anubis could not find it, confining it and her to the sarcophagus until a string of peculiar conditions were met that allowed the lock to be opened and Meryat to rise again."

"Peculiar conditions?"

"Learned man. Eyes the color of rotting reeds. That sort of thing."

"A learned man with greenish-brown eyes doesn't seem that peculiar."

"Three nipples . . ."

"Ah." Cheeks burning, Dean paid a great deal of attention to his next swallow of coffee. "Lance says Meryat took over your mind."

The doctor smiled into the shadows as desiccated fingers with blackened tips closed around his hand. "Meryat took over my heart. How could I not love a woman who'd suffered so bravely for so long? I know what you're thinking, she's not at her best physically, but every day she's in the world she gains back a little more of her beauty."

"She's not sucking the energy out of people, is she?"

"People give off energy merely by existing. She absorbs that."

"Lance said that when you left the lab, you left him for dead."

That drew his attention back to Dean. "I pushed him into a supply closet," he explained dryly, "and locked the door. Lance tends to exaggerate."

"Yeah." Dean decided he'd best keep both the foul fiend and pustulant monster comments to himself. "Does he exclaim everything he says, then?"

"Almost everything, yes. I'm amazed you managed to send him away. He's remarkably tenacious."

"I didn't so much send him away as send him on a wild goose chase. He still thinks he's after you."

"I'm glad he isn't. Well done and thank you." As Dr. Rebik drained his mug, Meryat asked a question, her words running together like liquid and music combined. "Meryat wonders if *you* wonder how we found this place. This sanctuary."

Dean shrugged, trying to look as though having the guest house called a sanctuary didn't please him as much as it did. "You'd be amazed at the people who find this place."

"In our case, it came about when Meryat's ka managed to gain a small amount of freedom even before I opened the sarcophagus. Still trapped, it couldn't touch the real world, but it could touch what she calls the possibilities. They told her of the Keepers and specifically of the Keeper who works from this inn. We were hoping you'd help us. Until she fully regains her physical form, Meryat is helpless and prey to every media influenced, addle-pated adventurer we meet."

"Meet a lot?"

"You'd be surprised."

Dean considered the hole to Hell that had once heated the guest house. "Not really, no."

"So will you?"

"Will I what?"

"Help us."

"Me? I'm not the Keeper."

Meryat's hand which had been reaching toward him, exposing more of a wrapped arm than he really wanted to see, withdrew.

"You're not?"

"No. The Keeper's my, uh, girlfriend and she's away on business right now. But I'm expecting her back any time," he added as Dr. Rebik's face fell and

Meryat's hooded head sagged forward. "The room's available as long as you need it."

"So we'll wait."

Meryat asked another question.

"No, my love, I can't think of a place we'd be safer. And now, if you don't mind, Meryat needs to lie down. As yet she can manage only an hour or two on her feet a day."

Dean stood as they did and managed to keep from flinching when Meryat's fingertips touched the bare skin of his forearm for an instant as they passed. He took a long, comforting swallow of coffee and when he heard the door close on the second floor, said, "You were some quiet."

Austin, who'd been lying on the windowsill, lifted his head from his front paws. "Something Dr. Rebik said isn't right."

"Yeah, three nipples. That's just *wrong*."

"Hey, I've got six!"

"My point exactly; nipples should come in even numbers."

Austin shot him a suspicious look but let it go. "Something else . . ."

"Last night he had to translate for her; this morning, she understood what we were saying."

The emerald eye blinked once in surprise. "You're not as dumb as you look. But that wasn't it."

"You think Dr. Rebik was lying?" Dean asked as he gathered up the doctor's empty mug and headed for the dishwasher.

"No, but I think there's stuff he's not telling us."

"He said he's sparing Meryat's feelings. You can't blame him for that."

"Why not?" Austin's tail carved a series of short jerky arcs through the air. "I wish Claire was here."

"Me, too."

"Elderly ninja assassins?"

"I didn't say that."

"Well, you kind of implied it."

"Sam . . ."

His ears bridled as he leaped to the top of Bozo's School Bus and turned to glare. "You did. You said there were handrails around the skylights and, if the way to the roof was in the wrong area, we could expect an attempt on Arthur's life. Then you said, *'but not ninjas'* and you've been mumbling about dangling old people ever since. So: elderly ninja assassins."

"Okay, you win." Claire scooped him off the ride and continued out into the main concourse with him tucked indignantly under one arm. "Just stop repeating it so I can stop thinking about it!"

"It's not the worst thing you could be thinking about," Sam muttered. "I mean if anything's got to drop down from the roof, el . . ." He squeaked as she tightened her grip. ". . . *that* would at least be easy to beat. Right?"

"Wrong. The Otherside deals with subconscious imagery, it takes what you think you're thinking about and warps it."

"So if I was thinking about a nice, juicy, unattended salmon?"

"Nothing would happen. When I say it takes what you're thinking, I don't mean you specifically. Cats live in the now, there's nothing in your thoughts the Otherside can use."

"Fine. If *you* thought about a nice, juicy salmon?"

"We'd probably get grizzlies."

Back feet braced against her hip, he squirmed around until he could stare up at her. "You're kidding?"

"Or a rain of frozen peas. Maybe even big, green, frozen grizzlies."

"Why would the Otherside want anything to do with what's in your head?" he demanded as Claire set him down. "Things aren't weird enough around here without your two cents' worth?"

"Apparently not."

"Hey, what if you thought about big, green, frozen grizzlies?"

"You wouldn't get salmon." She stroked a hand down his back. "Wait here." Kith and Teemo glanced around as she approached the barricade and then returned to staring down the stairs into the lower level. As far as Claire could tell, it looked like the lower level of the West Gardner's Mall. No eldritch mists. No skulking shadows. No shambling hulks of darkside muscle.

Nothing out of the ordinary.

That wasn't good.

"Any sign of Diana and Kris?"

"Nada." Teemo scratched in through the ripped armpit of his now sleeveless Spider-man T-shirt—looking less like the semimythical creature he was becoming and more like the fifteen-year-old he'd been. "There was some crap-ass music playing, but it stopped a while ago. Don't worry about your blood, Keeper, Kris'll keep her safe. She's one sneaky bi . . . Ow!" He shot a pained glance over his shoulder at Kith. "I wasn't gonna say bitch!" he protested. "I was gonna say . . . uh . . ."

Kith raised a remarkably sardonic eyebrow.

"Never mind what I was gonna say. I wasn't talkin' to you nohow." He turned his back on the other elf with such exaggerated indignation, he reminded Claire of Austin. "Kris'll keep your sister safe," he repeated. "Arthur already said that if we see any shit happening, we should let you know."

"Thank you." She didn't recognize the elf on guard at the hexagonal opening until she got close enough to see the features under the lime-green hair. "Daniel?"

"Hey, Keeper."

She'd only walked down to the end of the small corridor, been outside for a minute, two at the most. Three on the absolute outside. How had he had time to . . . ? "What did you do to your hair?"

He pulled a strand forward, looked at it, looked at her like she was asking a trick question. "Uh, dyed it. Wicked look, right?"

The second hand on her watch zipped around from the eight to the two, then slowed.

She hated time distortions.

"Right. It's very . . . green." And *not* something she was responsible for. "Listen, I was wondering, do you know where the access to the roof is?"

"The roof?"

Claire leaned back and pointed up. "There's got to be an access. There's parking and there's handrails."

"Okay." Daniel squinted into the gray light currently substituting for actual sky. "I never seen any stairs, but there's an elevator down by the security office. I seen the sign on food court runs."

"Where's the security office?"

Leaning over the Lucite barrier, he pointed down the left side of the lower level. "It's not too far past the bottom of the stairs 'cept you go along the other hall."

"It's on the darkside?"

"Arthur says it's sort of territory we both claim, but yeah."

"Do you know if it works?"

"The security office?"

"The elevator."

"No friggin' idea, Keeper."

"Okay . . ." This was very bad. "They could come through the skylight. You'll have to watch up as well as down."

"Through the skylight?" Daniel repeated, glancing up again.

"Yes."

"That kinda sucks."

"Yes. It does." Pivoting on one heel, Claire headed for the department store and nearly tripped over Sam.

"I've been thinking."

"Good. Think and walk; I have to warn Arthur."

"That's what I've been thinking about. Assassinating the Immortal King makes sense—cut the head off the snake and the snake dies."

"What do snakes have to do with anything?"

"Sorry, angel leftover. We . . . they . . . use snake analogies a lot. You know, *up there*. Occupational hazard." He jumped up onto the edge of a planter and hooked all five claws on one front paw into Claire's skirt, dragging her to a halt. "If I was the darkside, and if this whole segue thing meant enough to me, I'd drop an assassin in during the battle when no one would notice. If the dark elf wins, the assassin helps the meat-minds pick off the mall elves. If the dark elf loses, then it finds a place to lay low until it gets its chance. Bada bing, bada boom."

She pulled her skirt free. "Another leftover angel thing?

"No, I've been watching *The Sopranos* with your dad. Look, it makes sense for the darkside to kill Arthur, but it doesn't make any sense for them to drop an assassin in now after the battle when all the elves are on full alert."

Claire looked back at Teemo and Kith on the barricade. At Daniel. Were there more shadows on the upper concourse than there had been?

It was definitely too quiet.

"You're right," she said. And started to run.

Sam jumped down and raced after her. "At the risk of sounding last millennia; duh."

Sunlight streamed down through the skylight into the food court, bright enough to wash away the light spilling from the bulbs over each table. Bright enough to wash away the shadows.

Kris frowned. "There's never been sunlight before."

"It's probably coming through from the real world. This end of the mall's almost totally matched up. We haven't got much time."

"Is this the sort of stuff you and your sister need to know?"

"No. This is the sort of stuff we pretty much already knew. We have to go deeper in. We need to see *who* more than what." Diana dunked her face into a filled sink, trying to rinse away the soap she'd used to remove the lipstick camouflage. *Man, that stuff could remove freckles!* When she surfaced, Kris was waiting with a paper towel. "Thanks." The towel was only marginally less destructive than the soap, and they were both an exact match for supplies in women's washrooms worldwide. Diana made a mental note to check the supplier when they got home. This could be a foothold situation that the Lineage had missed for years. And the toilet paper was definitely Hellish.

"So," Kris grunted, leaning against a stall and watching Diana in the mirror, "what now?"

"Now, unless we open the door and there's a power-of-darkness coffee klatch happening close enough for us to eavesdrop on, we need to get to the Emporium. It's as close to the anchor as we've ever come." She tossed the damp paper in the wastebasket and turned to face a skeptical mall elf.

"It's where you two came through. They'll be guarding it."

"You've taken me as far as we agreed. You don't have to go on."

"Like I'm supposed to go back to the other wizard and tell her I ditched her kid sister just when things got tough? Fuck you."

"Okay. I mean, you're right," Diana corrected herself hurriedly, hoping the flush she could feel would be taken as the result of strenuous exfoliation. "Then if it's just meat-minds on guard, we'll go around them. If it's something else, then *that* could tell us what I need to know. I wish I'd been able to get a look under that dark elf's helm."

"Before you slagged him?"

"Not much point after." She glanced toward the washroom door. "There's not going to be a lot of cover out there."

"No shit. You'd think they'd leave all that sunshine for the end. Doesn't evil usually prefer darkness and all?"

"Common mistake. Evil doesn't care. The thing you've got to remember about evil," she murmured, falling into step just behind the other girl's left shoulder as they headed for the door, "is that it's an unapologetic opportunist. It'll move in wherever there's an opening."

The smell of fresh coffee wafted up the short hall.

The black clothes made them stand out against the pale green tiles like . . .

. . . like licorice in mints, like cow patties in the grass, like Goths in a flower shop, like the wipeout from the wand caused permanent brain damage. What's up with Analogies R Us?

Diana forced herself to pay attention just as Kris said, "I don't see anyone . . . anything. Let's go."

They turned left, away from the food court, staying close to the lockers and then ducking low to cross the open front of the sporting goods store. Diana thought she saw a rack of torture implements as they passed—which was actually encouraging because she was fairly certain such stores didn't usually stock thumb screws in with their free weights in the real world. *Although it certainly explained that whole no pain, no gain thing.* Vaguely human shapes moved around in the big drugstore across the hall and she could only hope they were part of a darkside patrol. Customers, even faint images of customers, would be bad. Not that a darkside patrol would be exactly good. . . .

Kris' grip on her arm dragged her attention back to their more immediate concern—the length of corridor they had to cover unseen in order to get to the Emporium. The two planters and four benches provided the only cover. But, on the bright side, the corridor was empty except for those two planters and four benches.

Nothing ventured . . . Diana shrugged free, dashed forward, dropped as she passed the first planter, slid the last five feet to the bench, and rolled under it at the last instant.

"What do you think you're doing," Kris growled into her ear a moment later.

Diana turned and tried not to think about the confined conditions pressing them cheek to cheek. "I was thinking that the Emporium wasn't going to get any closer and the longer we waited the more risk of someone coming through the food court and spotting us." So not the time to say something like "*You smell incredible.*"

"Next time, warn a person!"

"I thought you might protest . . ."

"Yeah. Good call."

". . . and we didn't have time."

The lights were off in the travel agency and a handwritten sign taped to the cracked window said only, "Closed for Renovations." A poster advertising London at $549, Berlin at $629, and Gehenna at $666 was the only other visible indication that the store had ever been used. Either she'd really done some serious damage when she smacked the travelers back or they were too close to segue for any more tours to be booked. The Tailer of Gloucester still had bits off animal butts hanging in the window, so hopefully it was the former not the later.

Hopefully and *animal bits*; not the sort of things that usually showed up in the same thought.

"Next bench," she murmured against Kris' skin. "You've got to go first."

Kris' reply was essentially unintelligible although the sarcasm came through loud and clear. Out from under the bench, she pushed herself up into a sprinter's start, and disappeared from Diana's line of sight.

Diana followed half a heartbeat behind, put a little too much push on the final slide, and would have gone right past the bench had strong hands not grabbed a double handful of clothes and yanked her sideways. Her face impacted at the join of shoulder and neck, her nose connecting painfully with Kris' collarbone.

"Is this the place?"

Blinking away tears, she lifted her head as far as the bench allowed. In the short time since they'd crossed over, the Emporium had come to look almost identical to the store in the original mall. "This is it."

The corridor was still empty. But then, why wouldn't it be? Why would the darkness bother running patrols this deep inside their own territory? They were a lot safer here than they'd been out in the lower concourse.

"I'm going to take a closer look."

"We're going inside?"

"We have to. We haven't actually learned any-thing yet."

"I've learned that you got no sense of self-preservation. I'm not going in there."

"Good. You keep watch." She was out from under the bench on her hands and knees before Kris could stop her, then quickly crawled across to the window for a careful glance inside. The window display was pretty much as she remembered it and so was the stock beyond. In the back corner . . . She shuffled forward just far enough to get a better angle. In spite of other changes, the mirror remained the Oth-erside edition, thick silvered glass in an antique wooden frame. She couldn't see any indication of Jack but figured he was probably watching the other store.

Dropping back below the window ledge, Diana crawled to the edge of the open door and, lying down, peered around the corner. No troll. Not even the shadowy suggestion of customers. Better still, no wards keeping people from entering—although the exit wards were still in place and would need to be dealt with later.

She flashed a quick thumbs-up back at Kris—who did *not* look happy—and slipped over the threshold into the store. The fairies on a stick had been marked down and the frogs in military uniforms had been joined by newts in science fiction costumes.

Who buys this stuff? she wondered crawling toward

the back. The newts were a little weirder than even she could cope with. Skirting the rubber snakes, she sat back on her heels and peered up at the mirror. "Pssst, Jack!"

The blue-on-blue eyes appeared almost instantly. "Where the hell have you been?"

"At the other end of the mall."

"Doing what?"

"Getting caught in time distortions and fighting off a pack of traveling meat-minds. It's not like I forgot you or anything; this is the first time I've been able to get back."

"They know you're here."

"Here, here? Like here and now? Or just in the mall here?"

Faint blue frown lines appeared as he worked that out. "In the mall."

"Well, gee, that alarm we set off probably had something to do with that."

"You th . . . Who's that?"

Diana jumped as Kris' hand came down on her shoulder. "You're talking to a mirror?"

"You're turning into an elf?"

"Yeah. Okay. Fine. Your point."

"I thought you weren't coming in?"

"You were taking too long."

"Hey!"

Both girls looked up.

"You want to save that? This is not a place you should be hanging around."

Diana nodded. "You're right. We've got to go farther in."

Jack's eyes widened. "Are you nuts?"

"Exactly what I keep asking," Kris muttered. "But she's not answering me."

"Look, both of you, we're on a scouting mission, trying to find out who or what we're dealing with darksidewise, and so far, we have found out nothing. There's nobody around. Nobody lurking. Nobody skulking. Nada. I keep going until I get a look at something. No farther . . ." She raised her hands as both Jack and Kris began to protest. ". . . so I don't cut off my escape route. Unless . . ." Locking eyes with Jack. ". . . you've got new information for me."

"About who's behind this?"

"Well, yeah."

"No. He's never come out this far, but I have heard a compelling kind of voice coming out of the storeroom, so he could have been there."

"A compelling kind of voice?" Diana repeated. "What does that mean?"

"A voice that compels. A voice belonging to the kind of guy who could put all this . . ." His eyes rolled around the mirror. ". . . in motion."

"If not *the* big cheese; one of?"

"That'd be my guess."

"Okay, I'll check the storeroom for residual energy."

"Be careful. If you access the possibilities, they'll know exactly where you are."

"Really?" She frowned at the mirror. "I never would have remembered something so crucial to my own survival."

"Well, excuse me for being concerned."

"Sorry. It's a polarity thing. They're bad, I'm good. Opposites attract. Good can, therefore, track evil, no accessing of the possibilities necessary." Turning to Kris she nodded at the storeroom door. "You coming with?"

"Not so fast." The mall elf held up a cautioning hand. "Good can track evil?"

"Yeah."

"Then evil can track good. Can track you."

"Only if they know I've been there. But unless they walk in *while* I'm there, why would they know that?"

"You make it sound so easy," Kris snorted. "And we both know it isn't."

"Well, yeah. But why make it harder than it has to be? You don't have to come . . ."

"Right. Again with the ditching as things get tough; not going to happen."

"Good."

"Yeah, good."

Still on her hands and knees, Diana headed for the storeroom, not entirely certain if anything had actually been resolved.

The storeroom seemed empty of anything relevant although it was difficult to tell with all the basilisk sculpture stacked along the walls. She walked to one end then zigzagged her way back. Nothing. No sign of major evil. No minor evil. Not even a hint of meta-physical PMS.

"Where is everyone?" she demanded, yanking at the locked drawers of the filing cabinet. "This is nuts!"

Kris snorted, leaned back against the door, and folded her arms. "Stress much? Look you've got to get a bit more relaxed."

"No. I've got to get farther in."

"Yeah." The mall elf sighed. "I knew you'd say that."

Abandoning the files, Diana crossed to stand in front of Kris, her eyes narrowed. "You don't have to . . ."

". . . come with, I knew you'd say that, too." She straightened, then leaned slightly forward, capturing Diana's gaze with hers and holding it. "Now, what am *I* going to say?"

Hopefully not "get your hands off me you lezzy pervert." Their faces were so close together, their breath mingled.

Diana moved just a little bit closer.

As first kisses went, it was kind of a nonevent, but no noses ended up out of alignment, no teeth got cracked, and Kris seemed, if not enthusiastic, at least receptive. Diana would have considered it a promissory kiss except she knew the danger in fore-shadowing.

"You're thinking," she said quietly, "that you'd rather be with me than waiting here in the storeroom all alone."

Kris nodded, her expression confusingly noncommittal. "Close enough."

Reminding herself that closing the segue and saving the world had to remain at the top of her to-do list, that she and Kris were now literally from two different worlds, that she was an idiot, Diana stepped back, turned, and cracked open the door to the access corridor. Her line of sight was limited, but she couldn't hear anyone—or anything—hanging about. When Kris moved up close behind her, a crystal shot glass in the B cup of her slingshot, she opened the door the rest of the way.

The access corridor was just as she remembered it, an empty concrete tunnel; although a little darker and a little smellier and the stains seemed to be from something a lot less pleasant than merely urine. Going left would take them back into the mall. Right would take them behind the construction barrier.

Which was where they needed to go.

Touching Kris lightly on the arm, Diana pointed to the right. The mall elf nodded and moved out in front, silently indicating it was the best place for the person with the missile weapon to be. Given that the alternative would be the perfect setup for a shot glass in the back of the head, Diana decided not to argue.

Moving silently, they slipped along the wall and around the corner. Unfortunately, the meat-minds were waiting just as silently.

The shot glass thudded into the middle of an approaching body without slowing it down.

"Run!"

It wasn't meat-minds behind them, cutting them off. Meat-minds didn't move that quickly or look that dangerous.

Hanging from the taloned grip of her captor, Diana shot a glance at Kris who had finally worn herself out and was dangling quietly. Nothing they'd been able to do had had any effect on the grip of the long legged, multijointed, vaguely buglike bad guys, so she'd stopped struggling early on and tried to memorize the path they'd taken down past the construction barrier and into this ornate and, frankly, overdone throne room. Walls of etched gold, a floor of polished marble, the heads of various creatures displayed on wooden plaques, torches—who used torches in the twenty-first century?

Her nose was bleeding again. All she could do was let it drip.

Claws skittering against gleaming black stone, the two bug things carried them toward the massive jeweled throne and the silver-haired man who sat on it, one elegantly clad leg crossed over the other. He smiled, showing very white teeth as they were dropped unceremoniously to the floor, and then leaned forward with pale hands spread in a mock welcoming gesture.

"I knew you would come to me eventually, Keeper."

Diana blinked, took a second to make sure Kris

was moving, and sat up to find cold, corpse-gray eyes staring down at her with triumphant familiarity.

"Right," she said, wiping her nose on her sleeve. "Who are you?"

EIGHT

"You ask who I am?" The silver-haired man with the corpse-colored eyes leaned forward. "I am your worst nightmare."

"My worst nightmare?" Diana repeated. She hauled herself up onto her feet, hoping Kris realized that, as much as she wanted to spend the next ten minutes doing nothing but reassuring herself that the other girl was okay, duty called. "Dude, you've never been to high school. You've never had that 'sitting down to a final exam and realizing you never actually went to the class' dream, have you? Or had your bladder haul up the 'I really have to pee, but the only toilet I can find is in the middle of the main hall and classes are changing' scenario. Or done the 'scenes from the most boring Canadian short stories ever written start coming to life in freshman English.' Oh, wait . . ." She frowned, wiping her bloody nose on her sleeve. ". . . that last one actually happened. But the point is . . ." Arms folded, she met the eyes of the man on the throne. ". . . you are so not my worst nightma . . ."

The front pincers of her buglike captor smacked her behind the knees, and she went down hard.

Ow. Ow. And OW! Marble floors didn't get softer with repeated impact. Hissing with pain as she propped herself up on a bruised elbow, she gave the enemy her best "get over yourself" expression. Six months with Sam had made it pretty effective. "If it means that much to you, you can be a bad dream and work your way up."

He smiled almost pleasantly. "I recognize bravado when I hear it, Keeper. Brave words from a little girl in way over her head."

Diana sighed. "Look, seriously, I really don't know who you are. If you want me . . . us," she corrected as, beside her, Kris struggled to her knees, "to cower in terror, it would work a lot better if we knew to whom we were cowering. So, if you could, *please* tell us your name."

"Please?" His snort was elegant, aristocratic, and dismissive. "Did you honestly think so simple a magic would work on me?"

"Can't blame me for trying."

"I could kill you for trying," he pointed out reasonably. "And if you do not know my name, I am not so foolish I will give you the power of it."

"Okay, but head bad guy? Nasty number one? So not terrifying."

"Not," Kris agreed, and Diana flashed her a pleased smile for being willing to play. If they could get the guy's name, if they could find out *anything* about him, she might be able to do something. Given that she wasn't allowed to access the possibilities, she wasn't sure what, but something. She was fairly sure her subconscious agreed his ass needed serious kicking. Unfortunately, at the moment, her subconscious was busy having mild hysterics about the giant bugs.

"If you want terrifying, Keeper, I'm willing to oblige, but, for now, there are only two things you need to know." Sitting back, he flicked a pale finger into the air. "The first is that you live now only because I have not ordered your death. The second . . ." A second finger joined the first. ". . . is that you have failed. You have not shut down the segue, and the darkness will gain entry through it to your world."

"Okay, one . . ." Diana flicked the second finger on her right hand back at him. ". . . I haven't failed yet, *and* I'm not the only one fighting you."

"If you speak of your sister, we can defeat her as easily as we have defeated you. More easily, I suspect, as you have by far the greater power. It was your Summons; you were your world's best hope, and here you are. If you speak of your little friend . . ." He inclined his head graciously toward Kris and then jerked it back a lot less gracefully as she spat a mouthful of blood almost into his lap. ". . . her companions, or the Immortal King, they are even now being dealt with. The Immortal King will die and after, as always happens, the fellowship of those he leads will not survive his death. That is, after all, in the Rules."

"What's he talking about?" Kris demanded.

Diana touched her lightly on the arm. "I'll tell you later."

"You may not have a later."

"Up yours."

A brilliant and speculative smile. "Perhaps."

Was he hitting on her? He was hitting on her. Eww.

"But for now, let's have a look at the weapons you brought to the battle."

"What weapons?" Diana demanded. "Your bugs totally trashed Kris' slingshot and dumped her quiver back in the access corridor when they grabbed us."

He shook his head and pointed at . . .

She couldn't stop herself from looking down.

. . . her belt pouch. So much for subterfuge. Still, in order to take it off her, he'd have to come close enough to grab. It was possible that direct physical contact could work in her favor—darkside and lightside canceling each other out until only the more powerful remained. While willing to admit that finesse was not her strong point, Diana was fairly sure that in a contest involving raw potential, she'd be the last one standing.

Unfortunately, it seemed that she wasn't the only one who thought so.

The bug shoved one of its smaller serrated legs between the strap and her waist. A quick sawing motion and it caught the belt pouch in its pincer as it fell. A quick twist scattered bits of the pouch and her defensive possibilities over the base of the dais.

"A few keys. Some seeds. Thread. A watch face. All primed and ready to be used. Such a shame if these fell into the wrong hands, Keeper." He laughed at the wand which looked even more pink and plastic than usual against the black marble. "Oh, wait; you also brought a toy sent out to spread discord amongst the great unskilled." He shook his head. "You thought you could defeat me with this?"

Since it seemed to be a rhetorical question, Diana settled for glaring. He would have felt the power discharge when she defeated the dark elf, but he clearly didn't realize the wand had directed it. That might give them an advantage later. If they had a later . . .

Frowning, he looked down at the last item, a white, paper-wrapped cylinder that had bounced away from the rest. "And what," he demanded, "is this?"

"You don't want to know."

Kris snickered.

"On the contrary." A gesture brought a meat-mind out from where it had been lurking, the torches throwing its shadow around the room as it moved. Another gesture had it bend and pick the paper cylinder off the floor. "Do you tell me, or do I have my minion use it against you?"

Diana sighed. "It's a tampon."

The meat-mind blinked, looked down at what it was holding, and dropped it, shaking its fingers free of any contamination.

"Oh, please. It's not like it's been used."

"Guys," Kris snorted.

"Really."

"Perhaps," snarled the man on the throne, his lip curled in disdain, "you'll find the situation less amusing after a little torture."

"With a tampon?"

The disdain became confusion. "What?"

"You're going to torture us with a *tampon*?"

Became distaste. "Stop saying that!"

"Saying what?" Diana asked. "Tampon?"

"Feminine hygiene product?" Kris offered.

"Maxi pad?"

"Cramps."

"Bloating."

"Clotting."

"Yeah, I hate it when that happens."

He stared at them for a long moment, eyes wide and disbelieving. "Nice girls do not talk about those kinds of things!"

"But torture, that's okay?"

"Double standards of the patriarchy," Kris growled.

His grip tightened on the arms of the throne to the point where already pale knuckles whitened. "Get them out of here!"

Diana yanked at the chains securing her wrist cuffs to the wall and sighed. "I hate to say it, but the nameless nasty was right; this is already less amusing."

"Are they really going to torture us?" Kris panted, hanging limp and exhausted. It was fairly clear they wouldn't be able to kick, twist, or thrash their way to freedom.

"Probably." If she only had the wand. It was times like this, chained to a wall by the nameless evil who planned to use a shopping mall to take over the world, that a few hours of unconsciousness followed by a little puking started to look good. "First they'll leave us here to think about it for a while."

"You know what? I'm thinking about it. And you know what I'm thinking? I'm thinking I don't want to be tortured!"

"Who does?"

Kris found the strength for another yank at the chains. "So do something!"

"Like what?" Diana demanded, sagging back against the rough rock. "If I reach into the possibilities to free us, I break one of the big Rules. If I break a big Rule, that opens the way for them to break a big Rule and you really don't want that to happen."

"Hey! Read my lips, I really don't want to be tortured either!"

"So *you* do something!"

"You're the freakin' wizard!" Kris slapped her chains against the wall for emphasis.

"It's Keeper! Now stop yelling at me and let *me* think! Just because you couldn't come up with something useful doesn't mean I can't!"

Their breathing sounded unnaturally loud in the silence that followed.

Finally, Diana sighed. "Sorry. It's just . . ."

"Yeah. I know."

She turned to see Kris frightened and battered but almost smiling at her.

"You're supposed to be saving the world, not just hangin' around here with me."

"For what it's worth, I'm glad you're here. Not, here . . . here." Diana winced as Kris' eyebrows rose. "I mean, I'm glad I'm not alone."

"For what it's worth, I'd rather you were."

Diana sighed again as Kris returned to yanking the chain. This was not going well on a number of levels; personal, professional, and probably a few other "p" words she'd come up with later. If they had a later.

They'd been chained in an alcove hacked out of the limestone walls not far from the throne room. Chained and abandoned; they hadn't seen meat-minds or bugs since.

"How long do you think we've been here?"

Diana twisted her wrist until she could see her watch. "About six minutes."

"Seems longer."

"Yeah."

The torches across from their alcove flickered although the air was still. In the distance, something screamed.

"So, about those Rules."

When Diana turned, Kris' expression announced *I'm not fuckin' scared* as loudly as if she was shouting the words. The profanity was particularly obvious. "You want me to tell you about them *now*?"

Her upper lip curled. "You going somewhere?"

"Well, no." Maybe defining a few metaphysical parameters was just the kind of distraction they needed. Maybe not, but it was all she had. Kris didn't seem like the type to be interested in "the cute things my cat's done lately" or what Ms. Harris and the graduating president of the chess club had been doing with two tubes of acrylic paint and a number three sable in the art supply closet on the last day of school. Which had only been. . . ? Diana counted back. She'd traveled to Kingston on Friday; the same day school'd ended. They'd crossed over into the Otherside mall on Saturday. Was it still Saturday and, if so, which Saturday? That whole "time was relative" thing made her want to hurl—although in this instance the urge to hurl likely had more to do with the bug leg—arm? limb?—that had impacted with her stomach. Bruises were rising even . . .

"Hey!" Part summons, part protest, it yanked her wandering attention back to the alcove.

"Right. The Rules. The uh, the Rules impose order on the chaos of metaphysics. Magic," she amended catching sight of bravado becoming impatience. "Right here and now, the biggest Rule to remember is that the Otherside is neutral ground, so neither good nor evil can control it."

"Why would evil give a shit?"

"'Because when you break the Rules, you sow the seeds of your own destruction. That's also in the Rules."

Kris snorted. "I think I read it in a fortune cookie."

"Could have." The lineage liked to spread the platitudes around.

"Although I'm sure it would be all awe inspiring or something if we weren't chained to a fuckin' wall."

Diana thought about it for a moment, squinting up at the flakes of rust raining off the eyebolt as she yanked her chain against it. "Probably not," she admitted.

"So what about that whole 'bad guys gotta gloat' thing?"

"Just basic psychology according to my mother. What's the point of being an evil genius if there's no one to tell?"

"No point, I guess."

They hung in silence for a few minutes, then Kris muttered, "That dude on the throne, he didn't seem like the genius type."

"He didn't seem like much of anything," Diana agreed. As far as a meeting of good and evil was concerned, it was kind of a nonevent. "The bugs were cool, in an *oh, gross, get it off me, get it off me* kind of way, but he was bland. Boring. Disappointing, even."

"Except that, you know, he won."

"Yeah. Except for that."

Off to the left of their alcove, claws skittered against stone, evoking an interlude of panicked struggles to be free. After a while, when the claws came no closer, both girls relaxed.

"It's the fuckin' waiting," Kris snarled, kicking at

the wall with the heel of her cross trainers. "Why didn't they just whack us and get it over with?"

"I think they need us for something."

"What? Getting their rocks off while we get peeled?"

Diana considered that for a moment. "No," she decided at last, "that's too direct for the Otherside." The first time she'd crossed over, Claire had tried to make her understand that the shortest distance between two points was usually the long way around. Then she'd added that Diana was never, ever to think about the Smurf village again. Their mother had been furious about all the blue gunk on their shoes. "Plans on this side are always a lot twistier."

"Okay, so if you breaking a Rule lets them break a Rule, then maybe they're putting you in a spot where you gotta break a Rule to get free. You know, so they can break a Rule."

Diana turned to stare at the other girl. "That's brilliant."

"Don't sound so fuckin' surprised," Kris snorted. Her eyes widened. "Wait; you mean I'm right?"

"Probably."

"Wicked."

"Although it's insulting that they think I'd break the Rules just to escape torture and death."

" 'Cause that's not a good reason?"

"No."

'Keepers could lie to Bystanders without breaking a sweat. To balance that, they could speak the kind of Truth that went straight to the heart.

Kris stared at her for a long moment. Then nodded. "Right." And another long moment. "Okay. So, *now* how long have we been here?"

"Since the last time, about another eight minutes. Fourteen minutes all together."

"Seems like longer."

"Yeah."

"Looking on the bright side, it's a lot cooler down here."

"Cooler than what?"

"Than it is back home."

"Your home?"

"Yeah."

"I wouldn't know."

"Right."

One of the torches sputtered, almost went out, then began to burn steadily once again. They could hear nothing but their own hearts beating. Smell nothing but themselves and each other.

"What's your mother like?" Kris threw the question out like a challenge.

"What?"

"Your mother. You said she was into that psychological shit. What's she like?"

Diana shrugged as well as her position allowed. "She's a Cousin."

"Your mother's your cousin? That's got a whole unexpected squick thing goin'."

"Not my cousin. A Cousin. It's kind of an auxiliary Keeper. Less powerful."

"You're more powerful than your old lady?"

"I'm more powerful than the entire lineage. All the Cousins. All the Keepers."

"And how's that workin' for you?" Kris snickered. Bugs. Chains. Torture. "Not real well."

"You look like her?"

"Not really, Claire and I both look like our dad which is kind of funny in a way because Claire's so little and he's n . . ."

"He's what?"

Diana chewed on her lip. She almost had it. "You've been fighting the darkside in this mall for a while now, right?"

"Yeah."

"Have you seen any women, human-looking women, fighting on their side?"

"No. Sexist bastards. They think a sister can't be evil enough? They never met my Nana, that's for sure."

"Do they ever take any of the elves prisoners?"

"No."

"So if they're going to chain something up, they'd be chaining up their own guys."

Kris glanced up at the chains, then back at Diana. "Okay, but why would they do that?"

"They're evil."

"Right."

"And all of their guys are a lot bigger than we are."

"Yeah."

"And these manacles are two solid halves of iron. Not adjustable. In order to hold their guys, they've got to be a certain size." Diana folded her thumb in against her palm and slid her right hand free. "They're too big to hold us." Sliding out her left hand, she beckoned to Kris. "Come on."

"But . . ."

"I'm out, aren't I?"

Frowning, Kris worked at her lower lip with her teeth and slowly slipped both hands free. "So how come they *were* holding us?"

"Because we believed they would." It was *twistier* than that, but not really by much.

"If that's a Rule, it's a fuckin' stupid Rule."

"So not arguing here."

They stepped out of the alcove together, but as Diana began to turn right, Kris' fingers closed around her arm, dragging her to the left with a terse, "Come on."

Diana dug in her heels. "No. We need to go the other way."

"Delusional much? We need to get back and warn the others." Her grip tightened. "That guy, he said they were being dealt with."

"Except that we don't know how time's running in that end of the mall. They might've been dealt with days ago."

In the barely adequate light from the torches, Kris' eyes looked completely black with no differentiation between iris and pupil. "Then it might not have happened yet." She gave Diana's arm an impatient shake. "We need to get back and help them! I'm Arthur's captain. I need to be there."

If anyone could understand the pull of responsibility, it was a Keeper. Still . . . "There's nothing you can do. You . . . we, have to trust that Claire handled it. Can handle it. Will handle it." She wanted to sound comforting but suspected she sounded as though she were trying to convince herself. "Besides, she has Sam with her."

"And what's he supposed to do?"

"Probably nothing, but that's not the point. The point is I have to go on. The anchor's that way and unless we at least get a look at it, we don't know any more than we did when we left."

Kris shook her head. "We know there's an old white guy in charge—big surprise—and he's got bugs."

"But that tells us nothing."

"It tells me I should be hauling my ass—and yours—out of here."

"No. You can haul your own—I can't make you come with me—but I'm going farther in." Diana pulled her arm free and half turned; enough to make her choice of direction obvious but not enough to turn her back on the other girl.

"It would help if I knew . . ." Kris drew her lower lip in between her teeth; the most vulnerable move Diana had seen her make. "It would help if I knew if he was still alive."

"Look, whatever the processed cheese spread of evil out there is planning, it definitely hasn't gone down because if Arthur was dead, *things* would be happening."

"*Things?*"

"*Things.* Bad things."

Kris' gesture covered the alcove, the chains, and the general dungeonlike tone of the décor. "Worse than this?"

"Much. Season finale of Buffy kind of worse."

"Which season?"

"Does it matter?"

"I guess not."

Right or left, the passage looked identical; equally grim, equally foreboding.

"Look at the bright side," Diana offered after a moment, "When they discover that we've escaped, they'll never think of searching for us deeper in their territory. They'll assume we headed out."

"That's because they're not as stupid as they look and we are." She drew in a deep breath, slowly releasing both it and Diana's arm. "Fine. Let's get going, then. Standing around 'looking at the bright side . . . '"

She had the most sarcastic air quotes Diana had ever seen.

". . . is exactly the sort of shit that calls wandering mons . . . Where are you going?"

"Farther in."

"Fine." A none too gentle shove pushed Diana up

against the wall and out of the way. "I'm the one with the pointy ears. I'm out in front."

"And that's connected how?"

"Ears. Elf. Never get lost. Unless you don't *want* to eventually find your way out?"

"We may have to go all the way in to get out."

Kris shot her a look, equal parts irritation and exasperation, as she pushed by. "Man, I am so not envying your cat if this is the shit he has to put up with."

Sam raced past and disappeared behind the winter coats as Claire slowed to avoid trampling the elf on guard at the entrance between the cosmetic counters. It seemed as though he might try to stop her but clearly thought better of it as he got a closer look at her face.

"Shit, Keeper . . ."

"Arthur!" She spat out the name. "Where is he?"

"Large Appliances."

"And that's where?"

"Straight to Children's Shoes, hang a right, then a left at Women's Accessories and straight to the back. You want I should sound the alarm?"

"No." The alarm would only warn the assassin she was coming. Hopping on first one foot then the other, she slipped her sandals off—bare feet would make a lot less noise—then, hiking her skirt up above her knees, lengthened her stride.

Children's Shoes, Women's Accessories . . . The floor was cold, and the air smelled like overheated

Teflon, like someone had left a nonstick frying pan on the stove and not realized the burner was still hot. As she ran, Claire hoped the smell was seeping through from the other mall. She didn't like the implications if it wasn't.

She could hear voices up ahead.

Arthur asked a question about fabric softener.

One of the elves snickered.

A cat screamed.

Sam.

Heart racing, she tried to remind herself that cats screamed as much for effect as affect and were as likely to scream in rage as in pain. It didn't help. Death of the Immortal King, successful segue, end of the world aside, if Sam got hurt, Diana was going to kill her.

Large Appliances. Buy the washer; get one hundred dollars off the ticketed price of the dryer.

Sam crouched on top of a washing machine, tail lashing, fur straight up along his spine, ears clamped tight to his skull. He didn't look injured. He didn't sound injured. He sounded like a cross between a rabid raccoon and a civil defense siren.

Arthur had his sword out.

Facing them both was . . . at first Claire thought it was the shadow of the assassin, then it moved, an almost fluid flow from one shape to another, and she realized it *was* shadow and it *was* the assassin.

The shadow feinted right; Arthur moved with it, keeping his blade between them.

The shadow rose up ten, fifteen feet, stretched into a thin line, then whipped forward. Arthur dove out of the way, one hand reaching out to the mall elf beside him and dragging her behind a free-standing dishwasher.

Claire pulled a length of white thread from her belt pouch, tied two quick knots, and threw it into the darkness.

It froze, shivered once, shifted shape, and turned toward the Keeper, the thread anchoring it in place. Given the power pulling against it, the thread wouldn't hold long.

Shrieking a challenge, Sam launched himself off the washing machine.

It arched just enough of itself out of the way.

Rising up on one knee, Arthur swung. Missed. Leaped to his feet. Swung. Missed. Nearly had his head taken off by a sudden side shot. Got his sword around in time to cut off a piece eight inches long by about three inches in diameter. It hit the floor, flattened, and shimmied its way almost too fast to follow back into its dark bulk.

Claire winced. *That's not good.*

The thread was beginning to give.

Light could defeat it. Shadows disappeared in the light.

Unfortunately, the closest thing to a light source was in the refrigerator beside her and it went off when the door closed.

. . . door . . .

It could work. If she could get it to chase her. If the shelves hadn't been put into the refrigerator. If she hit the back of the fridge with time enough to set a second path.

An ice cream scoop flew through the center of the shadow, whistled past her arm close enough for her to feel the breeze, and clattered off white enamel. The good news; the cavalry had arrived. The bad news; it was half a dozen mall elves with slingshots and bats. *They couldn't have brought flashlights?*

"Careful!" Arthur's voice rising above the sudden babble.

And a voice out of the babble. "Fuck! What is this thing?"

"An assassin!" Claire snapped. "It's here to kill Arthur, but it'll just as happily take any of you. Don't let it touch you; it'll suck your life out through any exposed skin!" If she'd thought—suspected even— that they'd be fighting shadow, she'd have brought along some lotion with an SPF of at least 30. Rummaging in the belt pouch, she pulled out her compact. "Get back! All of you. You, too, Arthur. In fact, you especially."

He shook blue-black hair off his face. "Your spell will not hold it for much longer, wizard. I would rather be facing it and ready to fight when it breaks free than running away with my back exposed."

"Fine." He had a point. "Then *back* away, but give me some room to work and try to remember that you must stay alive."

"What are you planning, Keeper?"

Switching the compact from hand to hand, she wiped her palms against her skirt. "I'm going to get it to chase me into this refrigerator."

"Are you totally *mental*?"

A good question. Exactly what Diana would have asked were she around. Claire spent a moment believing her little sister was up to whatever she might have to face, then flashed the assembled mall elves a confident smile. Belief and confidence both for the benefit of the Otherside. "Trust me. Just don't close the door until I find my way out."

"Of the refrigerator?"

"Yes."

The shadow swayed left, the elves shifted right, and Claire felt a cold wet nose bump up against her shins. "I'm going with you."

"No, Sam, you have to watch out for Arthur and the elves while I'm gone."

Amber eyes narrowed. "You can't tell me what to do!"

The shadow rose up, then snapped flat. Arthur swung his sword like a nine iron and sliced a piece off as it tried for his ankles.

"I'm not." Too many years with Austin for her to even attempt it. "I'm just telling you what the right thing is and hoping that you'll do it."

"But what . . ."

No time for extended arguing. "You attacked the shadow, didn't you? Kept it from sneaking up on Arthur from behind?"

"Yeah but . . ."

One of the knots released. Held at only one point, the shadow lashed out at the elves, fell short, and gathered itself up for another attack.

"You kept him alive. We need him alive."

"Fine, but . . ."

Claire took that as an agreement and shoved Sam aside with one leg just as the second knot gave way. Snapping open the compact, she caught Arthur's reflection in the mirror and wrapped the seeming around her. This wasn't exactly what this had been intended for, but . . .

. . . *close only counts with horseshoes and hand grenades.*

Which wasn't at all reassuring.

"Hey! Tall, dark, and two-dimensional! Over here!"

A choice between two targets.

But only one of them with a blade sharp and shiny.

Claire threw herself sideways as the shadow attacked, yanked open the refrigerator door, stepped up onto the top of the double crispers, and dove inside. Substance began to distort. Caught her. Then, as an icy touch stroked the bottom of one bare foot, caught the shadow. She jerked her foot away, tumbling through the unformed reality. Allowing the path to take her where it would, she concentrated on splitting it off behind her, on sending the shadow to its ultimate defeat.

Nothing definite. Not *exactly* imposing her will— Her subconscious was in full agreement with her conscious when it came to destroying that thing.

For an instant, she smelled woodsmoke and burning marshmallows and heard high, girlish voices singing rounds. Then smells, sounds, and shadow were gone.

Another slow tumble and there was water all around her.

She dropped the compact and began kicking for the surface.

"How much longer until the Keeper emerges?"

Sam's ears flattened, but his gaze remained locked on the half-open refrigerator door. "I don't know."

Arthur crouched down beside the cat, stretched out a hand to stroke him, and thought better of it. "I think that she is safe. I think that she has defeated the shadow. I think that even now, she makes her way back to us." When Sam's only response was his tail tip, jerking back and forth, he sighed and straightened. "I will leave you, then, to your vigil. I think that the Keeper will be pleased to see you here when she returns."

As the footsteps of the Immortal King faded into Women's Accessories, Sam sighed. "*I* think that Austin's going to kill me."

Head up, Austin remained motionless on Claire's pillow sifting the night for what had awakened him.

Dean? No. One arm stretched up over his head,

bare chest rising and falling in the slow rhythm of sleep, Dean hadn't moved for hours.

Something outside? No. He could hear the occasional car going by on King Street, two raccoons up a tree arguing about whose turn it was to dump the garbage but nothing unusual. Nothing to lift the fur along his back.

He glanced toward the wardrobe, Claire's preferred entrance to the Otherside. The door was closed. Even if there was trouble, nothing could seep through.

But something *had* wakened him. Something *had* lifted the fur along his back. Therefore, something was wrong.

He stood, stretched, walked over Dean's stomach to the edge of the bed, and jumped cautiously to the floor. Over the last year or so, the floor had developed a nasty habit of being farther away than it should be.

The bedroom door was open. Whiskers testing the air with every step, Austin crossed the living room, the light spilling in around the edges of the blind just barely sufficient. Except for Dean's unfortunate taste in artwork—who really believed dogs had enough imagination to play poker—and Claire's equally unfortunate inability to say no to him, everything seemed fine.

The door between the living room and the office was closed, but it had been years since Austin had allowed that to stop him.

With no blind on the front window, the office was lighter than the living room. And empty.

The elevator?

No.

The basement?

Not this time.

The kitchen?

He was too unsettled to be hungry.

Only one place left. Only one room occupied.

Usually, Austin preferred to stay away from the guests but tonight, he'd make an exception. Slowly and silently he slipped up the stairs, along the hall. Another closed door.

There were two bodies in the bed, the perpetually nervous scent of Dr. Rebik as distinctive as the dust and desiccation scent of his companion. His tail lashing from side to side, he crept closer, unable to shake the feeling that something was wrong but willing to believe it could be prejudice on his part. He'd half expected Meryat to have been up and *walking*, arms outstretched, a bit of musty linen trailing off one heel. The whole concept of the undead annoyed him. Nine lives and it's over, that was his motto.

A tray on the small table by the bed held two empty mugs and a plate covered in muffin crumbs. Under the table, crumpled up against the table leg, was a dead mouse.

Okay, not so much wrong as embarrassing.

The mice had come to his aid after his . . . *meeting* with the Keeper who'd been interred in room seven and when he and Claire had returned to the inn just after Christmas, they'd come to an understanding. He would see to it that they were left in peace and, in return, they would be circumspect in their foraging, stop shitting behind the microwave, and never again wear orange waistcoats with blue breeches. Mice had appalling color sense and *The Complete Tales of Beatrix Potter* that had been left in the attic had only black-and-white illustrations.

This particular mouse looked to have died of old age.

Austin looked from the body up to the top of the table and shook his head. A mouse that age had no business even attempting such a climb. *Stupid little bugger's heart probably gave out on him*, he thought as he sank his teeth through the tail of the brocade frock coat.

He carried the tiny corpse over to the dresser and set it gently on the floor. A strong smack with his right paw and it slid out of sight. When he heard it whack lightly against the baseboard, he nodded in satisfaction and left the room. The mice had an exit under there; now they could retrieve the body without the possibility of a guest being subjected to the sight of a tiny funeral cortege.

Nothing looked more asinine than a mouse in a black top hat and crepe.

He was halfway down the stairs when, between one heartbeat and the next, he felt something pass.

Something old.

And hungry.

And gone so fast he might have imagined it.

Except that he was a cat and cats knew . . .

Dean!

Heart pounding, he raced back to the bedroom and bounded onto the bed.

"Ow! That was my arm!"

"Yeah, whatever." He freed his claws from the surface layer of skin and walked up Dean's chest until he could stare into his face. Blue eyes blinked myopically back at him.

"What?"

"You're okay?"

"I'm bleeding and I'm after being awake when I'd rather not be, but yeah." His voice softened, and one hand stroked gently along Austin's spine. "What's wrong, then?"

"Nothing. Why should anything be wrong?"

"I just thought . . ."

"Well, don't." A purposeful climb over an inconvenient shoulder and onto Claire's pillow. Snuggling down, he glared at Dean, now gazing at him with concern. "I thought you were sleeping?"

"I was."

"So sleep."

"All right. But we'll talk about this in the morning."

"Not so smart to warn me," Austin muttered. Not one of his best comebacks but he was shaken. He watched Dean until he went back to sleep. Watched him sleep. Could see nothing wrong.

He'd been so sure on the stairs.

So sure.

He thought about the mouse lying dead under the table and sighed.

Maybe he was just getting old.

NINE

A pale and slightly murky green, the water had never been treated by chemicals or filtered through anything but a fish bladder. As Claire's head broke the surface and she sucked in a welcome lungful of air, a light caress trailed down the inside of one leg.

Oh it's fresh water. Great.

Pushing her dripping hair out of her face with a quick swipe of one hand, she began treading water and trying to figure out exactly where she was. A combination of sunshine and a gentle swell threw reflected light up into her eyes, making her squint.

Outside.

Far enough beyond the segue for there to be actual weather—not the neither/nor sort of sky that had been draped over the mall—but still on the Otherside.

She'd been lucky. With both her conscious and subconscious preoccupied in sending the shadow assassin to a place where it would be no threat, she could have ended up anywhere. Stepping through a door on the Otherside with no clear idea of a destination could have resulted in a visit to any number of unpleasant places, not only on the Otherside but in the real world as well.

She could have ended up on the south side of Chicago.

Vancouver's Downtown Eastside.

The West Bank.

The north of Afghanistan.

At a second-run theater screening of *Attack of the Clones*.

Claire shuddered.

A little water was a small price to pay.

She was wet and her batik silk skirt might never recover but she was safe. Arthur was safe. She had defeated the shadow. All that remained was to find her way back to the mall, which shouldn't—wouldn't—be a problem for a Keeper of her abilities.

The Otherside was no place for false modesty.

Or actual modesty.

Kicking harder lifted her head above the swells. Unfortunately, it didn't change what she could see—water and sunlight. She turned slowly. Water and sunlight. Water and sunlight. Water and sunlight and . . . something. It might have been fog. It might have been land, lying low along the horizon. She sank down until her chin settled just under the water, rested for a moment, then took another look.

Something.

Exactly what I need, she amended silently and started to swim, the water lapping at her in a vaguely lascivious way.

Years of practice kept her from thinking about all the many things that could go wrong before she made it back to the mall. Plenty of things were likely to go wrong without her help.

"No, you cannot go after Diana. I forbid it."

"You forbid it?" Sam's ears flattened as he glared up at Arthur. "News flash; you're not the boss of me!" Tail lashing from side to side, he stalked toward the door.

Only to find himself lifted off the floor by strong hands tucked into his armpits.

Folding himself almost in half, he got a back paw between his fur and an unprotected palm, got a claw out, and raked it downward.

Anyone else would have hollered and dropped him. Screamed and thrown him aside. Cursed and pitched him. All possible reactions and all a variation on a theme resulting in his freedom. Arthur jerked a little at the sudden pain but held on, and Sam realized he'd continue to hold on even if his hands were ripped to bloody shreds. For a moment, he considered testing that conclusion, then the moment passed and he found himself dangling helplessly.

"I'll put you down if you give me your word you'll remain in the store."

"And if I don't," Sam sneered.

"Then I'm afraid I'll have to put you somewhere secure until you give me your word or until one of the Keepers returns. They both wished you to remain here and I will not risk their wrath."

"And my wrath?" He had a feeling his look of disdain would have been more successful had Arthur not been holding him so he could see only the back of his head.

"Your wrath, I'm afraid, I will have to risk."

He flexed his claws. "Big mistake, bub."

"Do I have your word?"

"No." He needed to be free. He couldn't be bound to the store by his word when either Diana or Claire might need him. *Austin* would never allow himself to be held. Too late, he realized Austin would have lied—given his word, and then broken it with a perfectly clear conscience. He could almost hear the older cat's voice as the door to the pet crate closed behind him.

"What part of 'cats make their own rules' did you not understand, kibble-for-brains?"

"I changed my mind. You want my word, you've got it!"

Arthur shook his head. "Too convenient a conversion, I fear, but we'll speak again later."

"I saved you from that shadow! You owe me."

"I do."

"And this is how you repay me?"

"The two are not connected."

Sam watched the Immortal King head out of Pet

Supplies and searched for a sufficiently scathing last word. Unfortunately, nothing came to him. One paw braced on a crossbar, he rose up on his hind legs and studied the latch. It could only be opened from the outside.

"Hey, little furry dude. What're you in for?"

Sighing, he dropped back down to all fours and glanced mournfully up at Stewart. "I wouldn't promise Arthur I'd stay in the store."

"Oh, for crying out loud; what part of 'lying' did you not understand?"

Oops.

"Couldn't lie to him, eh? Yeah, I know how it is. He's the kind of guy you can't lie to because this little voice in your head just kind of chimes in and says he deserves the truth."

"The little voice in *my* head keeps calling me kibble-for-brains."

"Harsh."

"Yeah, but cats are supposed to be good at lying. And they're supposed to only think of themselves, but I can't stop worrying about Diana. And Claire. And you guys."

"Us guys? Hey, we're fine."

Sam swept an amber gaze up one side of the mall elf and down the other, getting full mileage from the disdainful expression Arthur hadn't seen. "No, you're not. The only person I'm not worried about is Dean, and that's because he's got Austin with him and Austin knows what he's doing. He can keep bad things from happening. I can't." The stripes on his forehead folded back into a worried frown. "I just haven't been a cat long enough."

"Yeah?" Stewart picked up a tiny purple mouse on a scarlet string, looked at it thoughtfully for a moment, then began attaching it to a braid. "What were you before you were a cat?"

"An angel."

"An angel? A real angel? No shit?

"Not until I got a body, then it came as a bit of a surprise."

"Okay." Reaching into a birdcage, the mall elf pulled out a tiny mirror. "Why do you suppose birds want to look at themselves?"

"I have no idea."

"Are they just, like, really vain? Or do they think the mirror's some kind of, I don't know, magic window to another bird?"

Mirror's some kind of magic window.

Magic mirror.

Sam padded over to Stewart's side of the crate. "Can I have that?"

"The mirror?" He finished checking the position of the purple mouse, flipped the narrow braid back over his shoulder, and shrugged. "Sure."

That was easy.

"Can you unlatch the crate?"

"Sorry, little furry dude, not unless Arthur says it's okay."

Oh, well. Worth a try.

Back in the Emporium, Austin had used a mirror to talk to the magic mirror and then used the magic mirror to connect to him. Well, technically, Claire; but the basics were the same. If he could use the budgie mirror to contact the magic mirror, then he could find out where Claire was and if Diana was okay. Sam ran through that one more time, just to be certain it made sense, then had Stewart hook the mirror over the crossbar. Ignoring the dangling bell and bits of fake feather, he stared at his reflection.

His reflection stared back.

Apparently, there was a trick to it.

He leaned closer until his breath fogged the glass. Leaned a little closer until there was less than a cat-hair's width between his nose and the mirror. He was *not* in the mood for tricks. "HEY!"

Blue-on-blue eyes snapped up out of nowhere. "I'm not deaf! Or I wasn't," Jack added petulantly as Sam jumped back. His eyes slid from one side of the mirror to the other, then widened. "Okay, this is new. Hold it!"

Sam froze, one paw in the air.

"Don't move your reflection off the glass. It's all that's holding me here. Not that it *should* be holding me here. Or that I should be here at all." The eyes narrowed speculatively. "Who knows, maybe our earlier connection left some residue or something. So what do you want?"

"Information."

"Yeah? Well, I'm a mirror—not a database."

"Information on Claire and Diana."

"You lost *both* Keepers?"

Sam really didn't like the way that sounded. "You know something."

"Not about Claire, I haven't seen her since you guys crossed over, but . . ."

Jack's pause suggested all sorts of horrible possibilities. "But what?" Sam demanded, surging back toward the mirror.

"Diana was in the store; her and some elfin cutie. They stopped and talked, I told them what I knew, and they went into the back room. I don't know how to break this to you, kid, but from the buzz I picked up later, they got caught."

"By the bad guys?"

Blue-on-blue eyes rolled. "No, by the Publishers' Clearing House prize patrol. Of course by the bad guys!"

"And?"

"Sorry, kid. That's all I know."

"Okay." Sam stepped away from the mirror, and the eyes disappeared. Tail whipping from side to side, he caught Stewart in an amber gaze and growled, "Get Arthur."

Dean knew he was dreaming because, although he had once played hockey in his underwear, he'd never had so much trouble covering the ice. It had to have been five or six kilometers between the goals and by the time he crossed the blue line, he could barely put one skate in front of the other. With all his remaining strength, he drew back his stick, set up for a slap shot, and stared in amazement as the blue light around the puck turned white and sparkly and, for no good reason that he could determine, it ascended, becoming a higher being.

"Hey, McIssac!"

He looked down at Austin, wondering how he could actually blow a whistle without lips.

"What have I told you about keeping your stick on the ice?"

It took him a moment to remember how his mouth worked. "Nothing."

"Fine. If that's the way you're going to be about it, get up and feed me."

"What?"

"I said, get up and feed me!"

A sudden sharp pain on his chin jerked his eyes open in time to see Austin pull back his paw, claws still extended.

"What's a cat got to do to get some breakfast around here?"

Rubbing his chin with his left hand, Dean reached for his glasses with his right. "That'll do it." The sheet felt like it weighed a hundred pounds and after he swung his legs out of bed, it took him a moment to remember what he was supposed to do next.

"Are you all right?"

"Just some tired." He squinted toward the bedside table. "Is that the time, then?"

"Let's see . . ." Austin walked across the pillows. "Numbers on a clock; yes, I'd have to say that was the time."

"It's seven thirty. I slept through the alarm." He never slept through the alarm. *Had* never slept through the alarm. Ever. It bordered on irresponsible. Two tries to stand up, but once he was actually on his feet, his head seemed a little clearer. Washing, shaving, dressing, refolding perfect hospital corners; by the time he set Austin's saucer of cat food on the floor, he'd shaken off the sluggishness and was feeling more like himself.

Moving the fridge out from the wall and vacuuming the cooling coils banished the last of it.

It had probably been nothing more than a reaction to the uncomfortably warm temperature in the bedroom. He hated sleeping with a fan on and the air outside was so still and hot, an open window made little difference.

"Good morning."

A pleasant soprano voice but not one Dean recognized unless Dr. Rebik had woken up in even worse shape than he had. He finished shouldering the fridge back against the wall, turned, and was surprised to see Meryat's shrouded form standing alone at the end of the counter dividing kitchen and dining room.

"It is a . . . beautiful day."

It was already 29 degrees C, the sun so bright on the front of the guest house he'd nearly been blinded stepping into the office. Still, for someone used to the weather in Egypt it probably felt like home.

"You're speaking English."

Although he still couldn't see her face, the tilt of her hood looked confused. "England?"

"No, Canada."

"But . . . English?"

"Canadians speak English. Except for those of us who speak French. We have two official languages, see, and we have people who speak both. And a Prime Minister who speaks neither. Sorry, that was kind of a joke," he added hastily as he felt her confusion level rise. Taking a step toward her, he tried to explain. "He's after having this accent that's uh . . ."

Her hand rose toward his chest.

His voice trailed off and he froze, trying to decide which would be ruder, backing away or shuddering at her touch.

Fingertips, a little less black than they had been, stopped just above his T-shirt. Close enough that he could feel body heat filling the space.

"You are . . . strong."

"Strong?" Then he remembered she'd seen him move the fridge and blushed. "Well, yeah, I guess. Thank you."

"Strong is . . . good."

There was a note in her voice that deepened the color of his ears. Nine months ago, he wouldn't have even realized she was hitting on him, but since Claire . . .

"Your Keeper . . . will return . . . soon?"

"I hope so."

She was smiling. He *knew* she was smiling. He just wished he knew what to do about it.

"Meryat?"

Her hand fell, but the heat lingered. She turned toward Dr. Rebik and murmured something in her own language. When he shook his head, she repeated it. Or something so close to it Dean couldn't tell the difference.

The archeologist sighed and motioned toward the dining room, allowing Meryat to precede him. "Would a little breakfast be possible, Mr. McIssac?"

"Sure."

"I'll have what I had yesterday, and Meryat would like to know if there's any chance of chopped dates and honey on a flatbread."

Why didn't she ask him herself?

"Sorry, no, but I could do up some grape jelly on Melba toast."

Dr. Rebik glanced down at his companion then back at Dean, and shrugged wearily. "Close enough."

"I don't trust her. You're too tired to get up this morning, and suddenly she's able to complain about the food."

"It's not what she's used to."

Austin sighed and walked over to stand on the dishwasher where he could look Dean in the face.

"You're missing the point. You're tired. She's got new skills. She's a mummy. Mummies are known for sucking the life force out of the people they come in contact with."

"We're not in a cheesy horror movie here," Dean protested as he straightened.

Austin merely stared.

"No matter what it seems like most of the time," Dean amended. "And besides, you said you checked on her and she didn't leave her bed. She'd have a little trouble sucking my life force from the second floor."

"You don't know that."

"Why are you so suspicious?"

"Why aren't you?"

"Austin, I can't be after accusing her of something without proof. It doesn't do any harm to think the best of people."

"Yeah, tell that to your dried and desiccated corpse," the cat muttered. Jumping carefully down, he followed Dean out into the hall. "Now, where are you going?"

"Up to the third floor." He hauled back the elevator door. "I can't just leave Lance at the beach indefinitely. You want to come, then?"

"No . . . yes."

"You're thinking he'll be an ally in this sudden antimummy thing of yours, aren't you?"

Austin wrapped his tail around his toes and snorted. "I don't know what you're talking about."

*   *   *

By concentrating on what a pleasant swim she was having, Claire managed to have pretty much exactly that. Granted, the water had a tendency to throw in a grope or two when she was least expecting it, but she was a strong swimmer and, bottom line, it made what could have been a tedious hour a little more interesting.

When she could hear the breakers folding against the shore, she stopped and had another look, checking out potential landing sites. The white sand beach stretched in a shallow arc for six or seven kilometers rising up from the water in a series of staggered dunes, sand giving way to grasses, to low ground covers, to aspens, and a good distance inland to the darker blur of a mature forest.

The blue-and-white–striped cabana, flags flapping, sides billowing in the gentle breeze, looked ridiculously out of place.

Blue-and-white–striped cabana?

Claire lost her stroke, got smacked in the face by a wave, choked, coughed and started swimming with everything she had left. Assumptions, conscious or subconscious, were no longer relevant. She *knew* what lived here.

The first time they'd used the elevator, the first time they'd stepped out on this beach, had nearly been their last. While she and Dean had been wading, taking a bit of a break from the extended responsibilities their lives had become bogged down in, a giant not-a-squid had heaved itself up through the surf, attacked, and almost crawled—squelched? flopped?—back into the elevator with them. It had moved terrifyingly fast even on land, out of its natural habitat.

Did an unnatural creature have *a natural habitat,* Claire wondered, sucking in a lungful of damp air and then burying her face again for another dozen strokes. *Or would it be an unnatural habitat?*

Not that it mattered. It was fast on land. In the water . . .

The gentle touches had become motivating rather than interesting, each bringing with it the image of a tentacle tip rising from the depths.

Or the shallows.

The waves were stronger this close to shore and gritty with sand scooped up from the bottom. Claire crested a breaker, let it carry her forward, tumbled out of it, rolled once, got her feet under her, planted them firmly, and pushed off. It wasn't quite body surfing, but it was faster than swimming.

Still not as fast as the not-a-squid.

Would you just shut up!

Subconscious, conscious; she neither knew nor cared.

During the brief time Augustus Smythe had been back in charge of the guest house, he'd killed three. In the first two months they were back, she and Dean had taken out two more. They hadn't seen one since.

Which didn't mean anything, really.

What part of shut up are you having trouble under-standing?

The next time her feet touched bottom, she was standing in water only thigh-deep and it was faster to run. Her skirt, which had been floating free and in no way impeding her kick, had decided to buy into the general sense of urgency by wrapping around her legs. Wet silk had the tensile strength of 80s hair spray and, unable to get the knots untied, she finally hoisted it to waist level and made it ashore.

Well aware that collapsing at the edge of wet sand, sinking down, gasping for breath, and giving thanks for her survival would have been the proper dramatic gesture, Claire kept moving until she got to the cabana. A dramatic gesture on the Otherside tended to call an appreciative audience. She did *not* need to deal with any more weirdness right now.

Throwing back the flap, she stared down at the large blond Bystander lying on one of the air mattresses, his left arm tucked up behind his head, his right curved around an inflatable shark. Even in the dim light filtering through the canvas, all his exposed skin was a deep, painful red; Claire'd seen rarer steaks.

His eyes were a brilliant blue.

Eyes?

"Nice underwear!"

Dropping her skirt, she wondered why she'd expected him to be Australian. "Who are you?"

"Lance Benedict!" Tossing the shark aside, he bounded to his feet. "You escaped from her, didn't you?"

"Who?"

"Meryat!"

"No." She stepped inside and let the flap fall. "How did you get here?"

"The same way you did, I imagine!"

"Do us both a favor and don't imagine anything." Technically, Bystanders couldn't affect the Otherside, but in all the times she'd taken the elevator to the beach, Claire had never realized it was on the Otherside so . . . wait. Could there be more than one Otherside? Would that not depend on how many sides reality started with? And did that not depend on an agreed upon definition of reality?

My head hurts.

"Did she throw you from her dahabeeyah?"

"Her what?" With any luck, there was some variety of painkiller in the first aid kit.

"Her boat. You're wet! Did she throw you from her boat?"

"Who is *she?*"

"Meryat, the reanimated undead! I'm the only one who knows how to stop her!"

Claire looked down at the two aspirins in her hand and realized they were going to be insufficient. "*Please,* tell me everything from the beginning."

"In the beginning, only the ocean existed, and on this ocean appeared an egg from which was born the

sun-god, Atum. He had four children, Geb and Shu,
Tefnut and Nut. Planting their feet on Geb . . ."

"Lance."

"Yeah?"

"Skip ahead."

Okay. There was a 3,000-year-old mummy and the
archaeologist who'd freed her from her cursed existence in the guest house with Dean and Austin.
Given the type of clientele the guest house attracted,
this was in no way surprising. A pair of Shriners and
their wives, yes. Reanimated Egyptian noblewomen,
no.

But Lance believed that Meryat was dangerous,
that she would suck dry the lives she came into contact with until she regained her former power, that
she would then use that power to take over the
world. He also believed that Dr. Rebik was under
some kind of mind control that kept him from seeing
Meryat as she really was and that the beach was her
initial attempt to bury the world under the sands of
ancient Egypt.

Just because he was wrong about that last point,
did that automatically make him wrong about the
rest?

Claire glanced across the cabana at Lance; currently making entries in a PDA he'd pulled from a
belt pouch. She wanted to believe he'd spent way,
way too much time in the sun, but the fact was that
here *he* was.

Dean obviously hadn't believed Lance's story, or he wouldn't have sent him on his little elevator ride. As Dean gave pretty much everyone he met the benefit of the doubt, he had to have doubted Lance more than Meryat and Dr. Rebik.

Conclusion; Dean and Austin were in no danger. Lance was merely a Bystander who'd applied a Saturday Afternoon Movie explanation to his first contact with the metaphysical.

And he'd spent way, way too much time in the sun.

Since they knew they were being hunted, she couldn't come up with a reason for the mummy and Dr. Rebik to stay at the guest house for more than one night. As soon as they were safely away, Dean would be up to retrieve Indiana Lance from his sandcastle of delusion.

Although the thought of seeing Dean made her heart beat faster, and she missed Austin with an almost physical ache, she had to get back to the mall. She'd left an eighteen-month-old cat guarding an Immortal King, her little sister was out scouting the darkside, and, if not stopped, the post-segue owners would not be exaggerating when they advertised the "sale to end all sales."

If this was the Otherside, then she could lift the stack of extra towels and find a pen and piece of paper tucked beneath them. Holding that image in her mind, she lifted the towels. Three tiny bones, a catnip square, and what looked like the spleen of a small animal. Either Austin had found something to hunt on their last visit, or he was casting auguries again. Either way, she didn't want to know.

Claire let the towels drop and turned to Lance who was stowing his PDA in its pouch. "I don't suppose you have a pen and some paper? I need to leave a note."

"Better!" He crossed the cabana in two long strides, holding out a small black book and a pencil. "When you're on a dig at Karnak, you need a writing implement you can fix with a knife!"

"Do you have a knife?"

"I have a pencil sharpener."

"Okay."

She'd entered by water; she'd have to exit by water. Unfortunately, that meant a sudden and total immersion with no thoughts of vicious not-a-squids waiting for her below the surface.

"Where are you going?" Kicking out a fine spray of sand, Lance hurried to catch up.

"To the headlands."

"Great idea! The high ground will give us a chance to see where Meryat's hiding. She's sneaky, but there's got to be a palace around here somewhere."

Claire sighed. He was consistently delusional at least.

Eventually—after embalming, ancient Egyptian magic, and the tracking of the risen undead had been thoroughly explained—the soft sand gave way to pebbles and then to the ridge that jutted out into the water. She winced as a sharp rock dug into the bottoms of her feet.

"I bet you wish you had shoes on!"

Actually, she was trying very hard not to wish he'd fall and break his neck.

The rock smoothed out on the top of the ridge and she was able to move quickly out to the end. They were twenty, maybe twenty-five feet above the water.

"Long walk back," Lance observed, one hand shading his eyes as he gazed toward the distant cabana.

"Not necessarily."

"The sun hasn't moved!"

"It never does."

"I don't see Meryat's palace."

"As Diana would say, 'Quel surprise. Not.' "

"Who's Diana?"

"My sister." Who needed her. In the mall. Not standing here trying to see past reflections to what might be lurking below the surface. Fortunately, she didn't need to convince herself that there was nothing there, only that it didn't matter. She wasn't jumping into water; she was using the change, the line between air and water like a door. "Go back to the cabana and wait for Dean."

"I think I should keep searching for Meryat."

"Whatever." This Bystander, at least, was not her responsibility. Stepping back half a dozen paces, she ran for the edge of the rock and jumped, folding her knees tightly against her chest, arms holding them in place in order to cross the line as *simultaneously* as possible.

Just before she hit the water, she heard:

"Cannonball!"

"Lance!" Dean moved a little farther away from the propped-open door of the elevator and yelled again. "LANCE!"

"Maybe Meryat ate him."

"Not funny, Austin."

"Not joking."

"He's not answering and I don't see . . . Austin!"

"I know, I know." Austin stepped off the path and began digging a new hole. "Just because this place looks like the world's biggest litter box doesn't mean I should yadda yadda." After checking depth, he stepped forward, positioned himself, and glared up at Dean. "Do you *mind?*"

"Sorry." Ears red, Dean headed for the cabana. "I'll be after checking if Lance is inside."

"Yeah, you be after doing that, then."

There were a suspicious number of footprints around the cabana's flap. A large bootprint—Dean dropped to one knee and measured it against his hand—probably belonging to Lance, and a small bare print that appeared to have come up from the water.

"Hey, Claire's been here."

"Claire?" Heel, toes, instep; still anonymous to him. "How can you tell?"

"I'm a cat." Flopping down, Austin rolled over on

his back, sunlight gleaming on the white fur of his stomach as he rubbed his shoulders into the compacted sand. "And I'm generally a lot closer to the ground than you are."

Hard to argue with. Leaping to his feet, Dean grabbed for the canvas. "Claire!"

"She's not here, hormone-boy. Look there, the same footprints heading out. She's been and gone."

"How long ago?"

"About thirty-one minutes. She was walking quickly, carrying a ham sandwich, and humming *The 1812 Overture*."

"You can tell all that from her footprints?"

"No, you idiot, I can't. But I'd be just as likely to know the last two as the first." Shaking his head, the cat slid through the break in the canvas.

Because he couldn't think of anything better to do, Dean followed. "Still no Lance." But there *was* a note on the beer cooler. *"Just passing through. Still working on the mall. I agree with your assessment of Lance. Austin, you're eating the geriatric cat food and that's final. Love you both. Claire."* He folded his hand around the paper.

"Are you going to do something sappy, like hold the note up to your heart?"

"No." Not now he wasn't. "Do you think she took Lance with her?"

Wrapping his tail around his toes, Austin looked thoughtful. "They definitely headed off together, and she said she trusted your assessment of him."

"Well, after hearing Lance's story, it wouldn't be hard for Claire to figure out that I sent him up here to get him safely out of the way."

"So maybe she took him with her because this place is no longer safe."

Dean's brows drew in and he studied the cat. "Facetious comment?"

"Experienced guess."

Fair enough. "And if this place is no longer safe . . ."

". . . we should go." Austin finished, jumping down and running for the cabana's flap.

Dean caught up to him halfway back to the elevator. "Did you know there was a back way into this beach?"

"Sure."

"You lying to me?"

"You'll never know."

"It's like a fucking maze down here. What do they need all these tunnels for?"

"Nothing. It's what *we* expected to find." Specifically, it was what she'd expected to find, unable to shake the feeling that they couldn't just go straight to the anchor—way too easy. About to suggest they stop wandering and start coming up with some sort of a plan, she snapped her mouth closed as Kris raised a silencing hand.

Voices.

Angry voices.

Not very far away but bouncing off the rock.

Head cocked, ears fanned out away from her skull, Kris slowly turned in place. Barely resisting the urge to make beeping sounds, Diana waited. After a long moment, Kris pointed to the left. "That way."

"I guess Chekhov was right."

"What does *Star Trek* have to do with this?"

"Not *that* Chekhov. The Russian writer—we studied him last year in English."

"You studied a Russian in English?"

"Yeah. Go figure. He said that you never hang elf ears on the wall in act one, unless you're going to use them in act three."

"You're not making any fucking sense. You know, that, right?"

The tunnels to the left slanted away on a slight downward angle—just enough to be noticeable. Heading down toward evil . . . it was annoyingly clinchéd and beginning to make Diana just a little nervous. She'd cop to the maze but not the slope, she just didn't do symbolism that blatant. Which meant something that did was in control of this part of the Otherside.

The voices grew louder, and Kris pointed to an inverted, triangular-shaped fissure in the rock.

And this is why I get the big bucks, Diana reminded herself, kicking the toe of one sneaker into the bottom of the crack and heaving herself up into the passage. It took her a moment to figure out how to tuck herself inside, but she finally started inching sideways toward the distant argument. Rocks jutting out from the sides of the fissure scraped across her stomach, laying out what she was sure would be a fascinating pattern of bruises, and there were one or two places where she was positive she lost chunks of her ass. *Memo to self: lay off the ice cream and thank God I don't have much in the way of breasts.*

She didn't expect Kris to climb in after her but couldn't do much about it since she'd reached a spot without enough room to turn her head.

Stretch out left arm, stretch out left leg, anchor both, and shimmy sideways.

And then she ran out of fissure.

Dipping her left shoulder, Diana forced herself close enough to the outside edge to get a look around.

They were in a crack about twenty feet up the wall of a huge circular chamber.

The generic nasty from the throne room was standing just off center.

In the center, in the exact center, was a hole. Not a metaphysical hole, an actual round hole. Like a well.

Before she could follow that new information through to any kind of a logical conclusion, a piece of shadow fell screaming from the ceiling. Shuddering, she had to admit it had reason to scream. Reasons. Reasons that started with the baby doll pajamas, worked through the lopsided braids, and finished at the residue of melted marshmallow, chocolate, and graham cracker crumbs.

No Name Nasty didn't seem to have much sympathy for it.

"I don't care how many boxes of cookies you have to sell! You're pathetic. You were sent to assassinate the Immortal King . . ."

Diana felt Kris' gasp by her right ear and managed to wrap a hand around the other girl's arm. Now was not the time.

". . . and you failed!"

There. It failed. Good news.

"YOU HAVE BOTH FAILED."

Diana stiffened. "Oh, Hell."

"I thought you weren't supposed to swear," Kris muttered.

"I wasn't."

TEN

Backing out of the fissure scraped and bruised a number of interesting new places, but given what she now knew, Diana found the pain a whole lot easier to ignore. *There's was nothing like finding yourself right back at a potential apocalypse to put a bruised boob in perspective.*

"FEE, FI, FOE, FEEPER . . ."

That didn't sound good. She poked Kris, trying to get her to move a little faster. Kris flashed her a one-finger answer.

"Feeper? What's a feeper?" The guy from the throne room, now positively identified as a Shadowlord, had become a lot harder to hear.

"IF I COULD FINISH!"

"Sorry."

"NOT YET, YOU AREN'T. BUT YOU WILL BE."

With any luck, the punishing of the unnamed Shadowlord would distract . . .

"AS I WAS SAYING; FEE, FI, FOE, FEEPER, I SMELL THE BLOOD OF A NEARBY KEEPER!"

. . . or not.

Kris dropped down into the corridor.

"We have a Keeper in chains . . ." the Shadowlord began.

"NO, YOU DON'T."

"Yes, we . . ."

"NO."

"But . . ."

"YOU'RE AN IDIOT."

Diana stumbled as she landed, cracked her knee against the stone floor, and told herself to ignore it. "Come on." Grabbing Kris' hand, she dragged the mall elf into a run. "We've got to get out of here."

"Haven't I been saying that?"

"Yeah, but now I'm saying it." First, up the slope. Then, when the floor leveled out, she'd follow the signature of her scattered stuff back to the throne room. After that, a fast run through the construction site and into the access corridor. Granted, the last time she'd covered that particular bit of the escape route, she was being dragged by a giant bug, but she was fairly sure she remembered the pattern of water seepage on the ceiling.

As they turned the first corner, Kris leaned in close and said, in an urgent whisper. "Who was that talking?"

"I told you."

"You said; oh, hell."

"Close." A short pause at the second corner to make sure the way was clear. "I said, oh, Hell."

"And the diff?"

"Capital letter."

"So that was really. . . ?"

"Yeah." At the third corner, the floor leveled out. Diana reached out, feeling for possibilities out of place. Not surprisingly, it wasn't hard to pick up the signature of Keeper-designed weapons over the general hum of evil.

"But Hell's a place. Places don't talk."

"It's not so much a place as it's a metaphor."

"Whatever. Just so's you know, I don't believe in Hell."

"Just so *you* know, that doesn't matter.

"It isn't real!"

Diana sighed. "Six months ago, you were freezing your ass off, trying to survive on the streets during a Canadian winter. Now, you're an elf, living in an evolving shopping mall, having been made the Captain of the Guard for an allegorical king. All things considered, I think you should be a little more open-minded about the parameters of reality."

"All things considered, I think I have the right to be fucking terrified!"

On a list of bad times for a second kiss, a kiss intended to fall between attraction and relationship, standing in a torchlit tunnel, deep in territory controlled by the dark side of a segue that could allow Hell itself into the world, ranked up there near the top—above "during the funeral of one of the participants" but definitely below "in the holding cell at a maximum security prison."

Figuring that there wasn't likely to be a right time

any time soon, Diana closed her eyes and leaned in. After a moment—a long moment of soft lips and gentle pressure and just a little tongue—she pulled back and murmured, "Still terrified?"

"Yeah."

"Oh . . ."

"But if you were trying to distract me, I gotta say it was a better idea than more stupid stories about your cat."

"Hey, that's Claire! I don't tell stupid stories abo . . ."

The third kiss involved a little more tongue and strong fingers cupped around the nape of her neck. Diana's left hand buried itself in the warm mass of mahogany dreads and her right spread out to touch as much of a narrow waist as possible.

"I'm not sayin' this is anything more than a reaction to that whole Hell thing."

Still close enough that Kris' voice was a soft warmth against her face, Diana murmured, "I'm not asking it to *be* more than a reaction to that whole Hell thing."

"I'm not sayin' that it isn't either."

"Okay."

"I thought we had to get out of here?"

"We do."

"You can beat this thing, right?"

"Sure."

Kris' eyes widened and she stepped back, breaking the heat between them. "You don't know, do you?"

"Look, I'm the most powerful Keeper in the lineage right now, and Claire's already closed this thing down once. Anything's possible, so all we have to do is find the right possibility. Which we won't find standing here." Taking a deep breath, she added a little more distance between them. "Let's go."

By the time they reached the alcove where they'd been chained, they could hear the distant sound of pursuit behind them.

"I guess it's stopped arguing," Diana muttered as they began running faster.

"You mean they've stopped arguing."

"No. The guy from the throne room is a Shadowlord, as much a shadow of Hell as the assassin; just bit more formed, is all."

"Hell was arguing with itself?"

"It's a thing it does. It doesn't get out much."

"And that's good, right?"

Diana shot a quick, disbelieving glance at the elf. "Generally speaking, yeah." They took a small flight of stairs two steps at a time. "This also explains why the Shadowlord thought I should know him and why he lacks a name. Bits of Hell don't get names until they've really distinguished themselves in some truly disgusting way."

"So Jerry Springer's pretty much a gimme?"

"Pretty much, yeah."

They were running between walls of dressed stone now. Walls that had been built rather than carved out of the bedrock. They were very close to the throne room.

"Good thing . . . the torches are still . . . lit," Kris panted.

"Yeah. They're lit . . . because I expect them to . . . be. We need them . . . to get out of here."

"Wouldn't Hell . . . know that?"

"Probably. But I don't . . . think it has direct influence . . . this far out yet."

Between the time her right foot rose and she brought it under her body, ready to stretch it out front once again, the torches went out.

"Of course, I could be wrong."

The bedroom was dark when Austin woke. The day just passed had grown overcast, although no cooler, and that overcast had lasted into the night, blocking starlight and moonlight and, very nearly, streetlight. Eye open the merest slit, he could see Dean's darker-on-dark silhouette on the other pillow and not much else, but he knew they weren't alone. Something stood beside the bed.

Something satisfied . . .

He sprang without warning, over Dean and off the edge of the bed. So positive that his claws would connect with linen bandages, he was taken completely by surprise when he hit the floor.

And was blinded an instant later.

"Austin?" One hand on the switch for the bedside lamp, Dean blinked down at the cat. "What's the matter, then?"

"She was here. Just a second ago."

"Who was?"

"Who do you think?"

"Meryat?"

"Give the man a rubber mouse." He stalked stiff-legged out into the sitting room. "She's gone."

"I didn't hear the door . . ."

"Neither did I."

"So how did she leave without opening and closing the door? She couldn't go through it—she's touched me, you know. She's solid. And slow. You've seen how she walks."

"Maybe she's just pretending to be slow."

"I think I'd know if she was faking it."

Austin snorted. "You'd be surprised." He padded back to the bedroom and stared up at Dean. "I don't know how she's doing it, but she's been sucking your life force!"

"You sound like Lance."

"Yeah?" Hooking his claws into the edge of the mattress, he rappelled his way up the side of the bed and stood on Dean's thighs. "You look exhausted. Explain that!"

Dean squinted at the clock. "It's three forty-seven *a.m.*"

"You were sleeping; you should be rested."

"I should still be *sleeping*." Settling back against his pillow, he gently stroked the spot behind Austin's left ear with his thumb. "Has it occurred to you that maybe you're having mummy nightmares because you're a cat and cats have this whole Egyptian connection going?"

Eye narrowed, Austin glared. "You know nothing about that."

"Not true. When I had the new strut put in the truck, there were *National Geographics* in the waiting room and I read this article on cats in ancient Egypt."

"How old was the magazine?"

"Some old, but they were talking about 1,500 BC; does it matter?"

"I am not having nightmares. I am not imagining things. And I did not tell you to stop doing that."

"Sorry." Dean started stroking again as Austin stretched out.

"I will get to the bottom of this," he vowed, sweeping his tail across Dean's legs.

"Sure you wi . . . OW! Lord t'undering Jesus, cat! I'm attached to those!"

"Then maybe you should consider where my claws are before you make another patronizing observation." Having leaped safely away from any physical retaliation, Austin curled up into a tight ball on Claire's pillow and closed his eye. "Turn out the light, would you. It's the middle of the night."

"Where are we?"

"Based on the cannons, the parapets, and that big guardhouse," Claire hissed, grabbing a handful of Lance's wet shirt and dragging him down behind the buttress, "I'd say we were in a fort."

"Which fort?"

"I don't know." They were still on the Otherside,

although which Otherside she wasn't entirely certain—
a concept she'd take the time to find disturbing the
moment she was no longer personally responsible for
an idiot Bystander. Motioning for him to follow, she
murmured, "Stay close," and led the way along the
inside curve of the outer wall. When she paused in the
triangular shadow of a small lean-to, he tucked up tight
behind her. She reached back and shoved hard enough
to break the contact between them. "Not *that* close."

He inched in again. "What are we doing here?"

"You yelled cannonball as you hit the water and
that influenced the path."

"This is Meryat's doing, isn't it?"

"No." Claire measured the distance between their
hiding place and the guardhouse and decided a
sprint across open ground with a Bystander in tow
was just too dangerous—no matter how much she
would dearly love to lose said Bystander. They
hadn't seen any actual guards, but that didn't mean
there *weren't* any actual guards.

"But . . ."

"Would you *please* shut up."

"But why is it dark?"

"It's night." She didn't know why the magic word
wasn't working—whether it was her, or him, or a
combination of them both—but only an urgent need
to return to the mall kept her from trying out a few
more words. Any delays at this point would only
serve the segue.

"It wasn't night at the beach."

Any delays at this point . . . "No, it wasn't." She'd be willing to detour and take him back to the beach, but that didn't seem to be possible. That path had closed behind them. And taking him back to the real world would take far too long. Time she—and the world—didn't have.

"This is Meryat's . . ."

"No, it isn't. Shut up."

On the other side of the lean-to, the wall curved out to the left. Wet skirt clinging to her legs, she crept forward, stumbled as Lance grabbed hold of the fabric, and managed to regain her balance without doing anything Lance would regret for the rest of his very short life. She followed the wall into a shallow alcove and began running her hands over the stone.

Lance crowded in with her. "What are you looking for?"

"A door."

"Why?"

"So we can go through it."

"And then we'll be on the other side of it!"

"Yes . . . no." She didn't know what the alcove was for, but it wasn't an access to anything. "Didn't I tell you to shut up?"

"Yes!"

Turning brought them almost nose to chest. Claire glared up at the oblivious grad student. "How many times am I going to have to say shut up before you actually do it?"

Lance looked thoughtful. "I don't know."

*   *   *

"So you used this budgie mirror to contact a magic mirror in the Emporium . . ." Frowning at his reflection, Arthur turned the tiny mirror between long fingers. ". . . which is both the store nearest to the darkness anchoring the segue and the place where you and the Keepers crossed through to this side."

Sam hooked his claws on the crossbar of the crate and stared at Arthur—who'd crouched just out of paw reach, his sword point on the floor, pommel jutting up at a sharp angle over his left shoulder. "Yes."

"And this mirror said it saw Diana and Kris pass through the store?"

"Yes."

"But that it later heard gossip suggesting they had been captured?"

"Recap much? Get on with it!"

"And this . . . story isn't merely a ploy intended to secure your release so that you can run off after Diana?"

"No." In all the time he'd been a cat, he'd never realized just how satisfying a good tail lashing could be. If he moved it any faster, he was afraid it might come off his butt. "Would I do something like that?"

Arthur straightened, reached back, and adjusted his sword. "As I understand cats, yes, you would."

"But I'm not!"

"And you heard this conversation with the mirror?" Arthur asked, flipping his hair back off his face as he turned to Stewart.

The mall elf froze in mid squeak of a rubber fire

hydrant. "No words, sire, 'cause the mirror's real small and it was down by him, not up with me, but I heard the talking."

"Hey!" Sam drew the attention of both the Immortal King and the elf back to the crate. "You know I suck at lying. If I was any good at it, would I be in here?"

"You have a point," Arthur acknowledged after a moment's consideration.

"I have a whole lot of points," Sam muttered, "and I know where they'll hurt the most."

Sapphire-blue eyes narrowed. "What was that?"

"Nothing. Look, it's real simple. The bad guys have Diana. We have to rescue her."

"We?"

"I'm smart enough to know when I need help. You can't just leave her there! And what about Kris. You can't leave her! You're supposed to be this great leader, but isn't abandoning your people a bad thing?"

"Yes." Arthur bent and opened the crate.

"Finally." Sam raced out and up onto a stack of dog food, reclaiming the high ground. "What convinced you?"

"With one Keeper taken and the other gone, the darkside will want to close the segue as soon as possible, before the light has a chance to send other wizards. In order to succeed, they must remove us. They will, therefore, be massing to attack. I have always preferred to attack on my terms, not the enemy's."

"I didn't say any of that."

"I know."

"But Diana . . ."

"Will be freed when we defeat the darkside."

Sam opened his mouth to ask what would happen if they didn't defeat the darkside, but he closed it again when he realized he already knew the answer. And he didn't like it much.

"What a lovely cat."

Dean glanced down in time to see Austin pointedly cross to the other side of the dining room—as far from Meryat as he could get and still be contained within the same four walls.

"I don't think he likes me."

"Foolish kitty," Dr. Rebik murmured, bringing the blackened tips of the mummy's fingers to his lips.

Trying not to shudder, Dean developed a sudden interest in cleaning nothing off a spotless floor. He was doing his best to be open-minded about this— he was involved with an older woman himself—but he just couldn't get past the reanimated corpse part of the relationship. When he straightened, all ancient digits were back within the masking folds of Meryat's cloak and Dr. Rebik was finishing his oatmeal.

"As Meryat would like to remain here until your Keeper returns," the archaeologist began, setting his spoon aside, "I was wondering, Mr. McIssac, if you could do me a favor."

Ignoring Austin's warning twitch, Dean nodded. "I'd be happy to."

"It's just I don't have a lot of clothes with me and, were I to go out to a coin laundry, I'd have a choice of either not washing my trousers or not wearing them while they washed. And they do need washing."

From what he could see of the cream-colored chinos, that was an unfortunately accurate observation. "I'd be happy to do a load for you. Put everything you want washed in one of the pillowcases and set it out in the hall."

"Thank you, Mr. McIssac." He set both palms against the tabletop and pushed himself to his feet, then tucked a hand under Meryat's elbow to help her stand.

"Yes, Mr. McIssac." The morning light illuminated the depths of her hood as she turned and Dean got an unwelcome education in what bits rotted away even in a very dry climate. The dark eyes looked out of place amidst the lack of cartilage and fat. "Thank you."

He assumed she was smiling although the words "rictus grin" couldn't help but come to mind. "You're welcome."

"You know, *I* was wondering something myself."

All three heads rotated toward the cat, the new angle throwing Meryat's face back into shadow.

"Why is it that you want to see the Keeper?" Austin continued, suddenly sitting at the end of the long table. Dr. Rebik looked startled, a ripple traveled the length of Meryat's cloak, and Dean tried to pretend that he didn't usually let the cat sit with the breakfast dishes. Not that "let the cat" was in any way pertinent to cats in general and this cat in particular. "She's on assignment. You could have quite the wait."

"I am willing to wait." Meryat folded her hands into her sleeves. "I am hoping she will be able to give me back all I have lost."

"You seem to be doing fine without her."

"But so, so slowly. I look forward to the day when I can . . ."

"Rule the world?"

"Go out in public."

Shooting a "now see what you've done" look at Austin and another at Dean, Dr. Rebik slipped his arm around Meryat's bowed shoulders and led her from the room. During their slow shuffle down the hall and up the stairs, Dean loaded the dishwasher, swept the dining room floor, polished the table, and did his best to ignore the expression on Austin's face.

The distant sound of a door closing on the second floor brought the cat to his feet. "Convinced? It's going too slowly and she needs to suck the life out of Claire to finish rebuilding herself."

"I thought you said she was after sucking the life out of me."

"Yeah, but *slowly*. She doesn't want to spook Claire the moment she gets in the door. Trust me, Claire'll notice if you're a desiccated corpse propped up in the corner, but a couple of missing years'll slip on by."

"That's reassuring."

"Yeah, well she's not going to be too happy that another woman's su . . ."

His ears scarlet, Dean clamped a hand over the cat's muzzle. "There was no one in the bedroom last night and you said Meryat was asleep when you heard something moving around the night before. Drop it. You're imagining things. You're some worried about Claire and it's stressing you out. Giving you nightmares."

He removed his hand.

Austin shook his whiskers back into place. "Cats don't have nightmares," he hissed. "Cats have premonitions of disaster, and I'm having one now. Gag me again, and you'll lose the hand."

"Stop touching me!"

"Sorry. It's just this is a little . . ." Lance waved a hand at the milling herd of purple hippopotamuses. ". . . weird."

"Yes, it is. But it's only weird because you seem to be incapable of doing what you're asked."

"You told me to think about nothing."

Claire slapped a hippo on the rump and moved it out of her way. "These aren't nothing."

"I tried to think about nothing, but that made me think of how difficult it was to think about nothing and that made me think about that whole 'don't think of a purple hippopotamus' thing."

"You know, I figured that out without the explanation."

"How?"

She exchanged an exasperated look with a lavender cow. "It wasn't hard. We're in a herd of purple hippopotamuses. Who usually live in water. And aren't purple."

"I don't see any doors."

"Shut up and keep walking." On the one hand, they were definitely back in the right Otherside so if nothing else, the last path took them closer to the mall. On the other hand, there was nothing like walking through a herd of herbivores in bare feet to put a person in a really, really bad mood.

"Where did you guys find armor in a department store?"

"Sporting Goods." Will flipped his braid out from under the edge of his shoulder pads. "There's enough hockey gear in there to outfit the entire NHL."

"In June."

The elf shrugged. "End of season sale?"

"Okay. That makes as much sense as anything else around here." Sam tucked his tail carefully out of the way as more and more elves wearing hockey equipment returned to the area by the fire pit. "Now correct me if I'm wrong, which I'm not, but didn't you guys used to be twenty-first-century street kids?"

"Yeah. So?"

"So how do you even know what armor is?"

"It's all in the book, man." Reaching behind him, he pulled out a familiar orange-and-blue book.

"*The Dumb-ass Guide to Elvish Armor*," Sam read, squinting a little in the uncertain light.

"Kris found a bunch of these in the bookstore back in the day. You know, while we were still getting stomped by the bad guys. She used *The Dumb-ass Guide to Not Getting Your Butts Kicked* to start bringing us into one group. Then, when Arthur showed up, she checked him out against *The Dumb-ass Guide to Leadership*. Lately, we've been using *The Dumb-ass Guide to Living in a Magical Freakin' Shopping Mall* as a kind of Bible."

"Really?"

"Nah, I just like saying dumb-ass. We figured out the whole living in a shopping mall thing on our own."

"What's the skateboard for?"

"Sort of our version of cavalry." He flipped the board up on end. "Makes us a lot faster than the meat-minds, more mobile. And it comes straight out of *The Dumb-ass Guide to Making the Most of the Skills You Got Handy*."

Orange stripes folded into a "w" between Sam's ears. "Really?"

Will grinned. "Man, you are one gullible cat."

"Ow! Try walking on your own feet, why don't you!"

"Sorry." Adjusting her grip on Kris' arm, Diana continued moving them as quickly as possible along the wall. As long as she didn't lose the signature of her stuff, they were fine. Well, maybe *fine* was stretching it a bit.

"I don't see how you can be so freakin' calm about this!" Kris ground out through what were clearly clenched teeth. "Fact, I don't *see*! I can't see! We got shadows from Hell coming after us—really from Hell, not just from some bad-ass place people are calling Hell—and we can't see squat because it's pitch-black down here!"

"That's one of the reasons I'm calm."

"What is?"

"Shadows are impotent in total darkness. They lose all definition, all ability to act. In order to actually do anything to us, they'll have to turn the lights back on. If I can see them, I can fight them."

" 'Cause you're the most powerful Keeper in the world."

"Yeah."

The mall elf snorted. "Like I'm so impressed."

"Look, you've got every right to be scared, but don't take it out on me just because I'm the only one here."

The only sound for a few long moments: the pounding of their hearts, the whisper of their breathing, the shuffle of shoes against a stone floor, the soft hiss of fingertips against a stone wall.

"Sorry."

"It's okay. I understand."

"I still shouldn't have said it."

"I'm not arguing."

"So what's the other reason?"

"What?"

"You said that shadows what can't get it up is *one* of the reasons you're calm. What's the other reason?"

Diana worked "shadows what can't get it up" back to impotent and grinned. "Just that I've been training for this my whole life."

"This?"

"Yeah."

"Your whole life?"

"Uh-huh."

"Damn. You must've gone to one bitch of a nursery school."

"Fine. Not my *whole* life." Her right fingers ran out of wall. She braced her knee and reached around the corner. "Doorway."

Kris leaned close enough to breathe a question into her ear. "Throne room?"

"With any luck."

"Oh, yeah. And our luck has been so good."

Reaching back, Diana stroked two fingers down the other girl's cheek. "I'm not complaining."

"Man, you are one cheap date."

But she traced a smile before she took her fingers away. The silence on the other side of the doorway felt bigger, like it was filling more space. She counted thirty heartbeats, then sighed in relief. "I don't hear anything. If we follow the wall around, we'll eventually trip over the dais. Once I have my stuff, we'll make a run for the access corridors. If we can get into the Emporium, I think we'll be safe."

"You think?"

"Jack said the big boss has never come out into the store." Careful not to lose contact with the stone, she moved them through the doorway and along the wall of the room.

"Always a first time."

"Here's a thought. Why don't you say something positive?"

"Positive?"

"Yeah, like not negative." Diana rolled her eyes as the pause lengthened. Three steps. Four. Five . . .

"If memory serves, you got a wicked ass in those pants."

Ears burning, she stumbled, recovered, and mumbled "Thank you."

"So, about that training," Kris prodded, sounding much happier. "Any actual experience?"

"I was with Claire when she closed Hell down the last time, I helped integrate a demon into a small town in northern Ontario, and I . . ."

"Hawaiian pizza!"

"That wasn't me. And besides, what's wrong with . . ."

"No! I can smell Hawaiian pizza!"

All at once, so could Diana. Spinning around, she scooped Kris' feet out from under her and followed the mall elf to the floor.

Which was when the lights came on . . .

. . . and the Shadowlord smacked a large club against the wall right through the space they'd just vacated.

From her position half sprawled over Kris, Diana could see all four bugs and half a dozen meat-minds waiting motionless in front of the dais. Nearly motionless. One of the meat-minds was chewing in a decidedly guilty way.

Three guesses about what he's eating, and the first two don't count. Diana was fairly certain there were stranger things than feeling grateful to ham and pineapple in tomato sauce, but right at the moment she couldn't think of any.

Grateful wasn't even close to what the Shadowlord seemed to be feeling.

Pivoting away from the wall, he heaved his club at the chewing meat-mind and screamed, "I don't care what your union says about lunch breaks!"

"Union?" Kris asked as the gnarled wood smacked meat-mind skull and the two girls scrambled to their feet.

"Otherworld Pan-dimensional Service Employees Union."

"You're fucking kidding me."

"Yes. Run!"

"I'm glad to see you're taking me seriously."

Dean dropped the pillowcase into the washing machine. "How's that?"

"I just saw you go through Dr. Rebik's pockets."

"And how is that taking you seriously?" he asked, reaching for the laundry detergent.

Austin jumped onto the dryer, walked over, and peered into the tub. "You're looking for clues."

"I'm looking for tissues."

"To send away for forensic testing?"

"To keep from filling the washing machine with little bits of wet tissue." He closed the lid, checked that the water temperature was on cold/cold, and started the timer. "I know I'll be after regretting this, but what kind of clues did you think I'd find? If Meryat's the bad guy . . . girl . . ."

"Corpse."

Given the look he'd got at her face, that was hard to argue with. ". . . then isn't Dr. Rebik the victim?"

"So?"

"So what kind of clues would he have in his pockets?"

"An amulet controlling his free will. A note written in a moment of clear-headedness begging for rescue. And maybe he's not a victim at all; maybe he's helping her in return for a slice of the world domination pie."

"Maybe I should never have taped that *Scooby Doo* marathon for you."

"He's a dog," Austin snorted, jumping down and following Dean up the basement stairs. "He's not going to notice anything he didn't sniff off someone's butt. *I'm* telling you there was something in the bedroom last night and probably the night before!"

"Okay, let's say there was." Dean bent and lifted the cat up onto the kitchen counter, sanitary issues losing out over the inconvenience of holding a conversation with someone six feet closer to the floor. "But just because you sensed something, that doesn't mean it was Meryat. It's not like this place hasn't had *visitors* before. Ghosts, imps," he added when Austin merely scowled at him.

"I knew what you meant; I just think you're an idiot." Sitting down, he swept his tail regally around in front of his paws. "I talked to the mice."

After a moment spent trying to match up the end of that declaration to the beginning, Dean surrendered. "Okay."

"The mice," Austin told him in a tone that suggested *idiot* was actually a little high on the scale, "said that the dead mouse I found in room two was just a kid; six months old, prime of his little rodent life."

"And?"

"Oh, for the love of kibble, would you at least try to connect the dots!" Leaping to his feet, he paced to the end of the counter and back again, his tail covering twice the horizontal distance. "That mouse had his life sucked out right next to the mummy!"

"So you're saying that sucking the life out of that mouse gave Meryat—who can barely walk at the best of times—enough energy to get downstairs and then back upstairs again moving so fast that you couldn't see her? Some mouse."

"You're forgetting her visit to you. The mouse only had to get her downstairs."

"And you don't think I'd notice if a reanimated Egyptian mummy was su . . ." Cheeks flushed, he suddenly decided there'd been a little too much use of the verb *to suck* in recent conversations. ". . . absorbing my energy?"

"You spent six months not noticing a hole to Hell," Austin muttered, "I'm not sure you'd notice if a reanimated Egyptian mummy was doing the Macarena."

"Hey! I'd notice. Nobody does the Macarena anymore."

"Oh, give her a break! She's been dead for three thousand years, it takes a while to catch up."

"If we're talking three thousand years," Dean snapped, "she'd be doing the hustle!"

The silence that followed was so complete, the distant sound of skateboarders in a neighbor's pool came clearly though the open dining room windows.

"Dude, what's with the water?"

After another long moment during which it became clear that neither skateboards nor skateboarders could float, Dean managed to find his voice.

"Did I just make a disco reference?"

Austin nodded.

"Lord t'underin' Jesus."

Austin nodded again. "If that's not a sign there's evil energies about, I don't know what is."

"Granted. But that still doesn't mean it's Meryat."

"Why are you so resistant to the obvious?"

"Maybe I just like the thought of people being in love without any sucking going on!"

Oh, yeah. Definitely too much use of the verb *to suck.* He kind of wished he'd remembered that.

But all Austin said was, "I wish Claire was here."

ELEVEN

Claire closed her fingers just a little too tightly around Lance's arm. They were standing at one end of a massive hall—although massive didn't really do the place justice—on a pair of circles made of the only red tiles visible in a blue-and-gold mosaic floor. Just to be on the safe side, she looked up and breathed a sigh of relief. So far, no falling anvils. Behind them was a set of what looked like fifty-foot-high, solid gold doors. In front of them, a double line of huge pillars disappeared into the darkness above. If they were supporting a roof, Claire couldn't see it. The walls behind the pillars appeared to be covered in tiny black dots although, given how far away they were, it was entirely possible they were covered in huge black dots. Light levels were comfortably bright in spite of no visible light source—which was hardly surprising as ambient light was the one thing pretty much every reality took a crack at. If she'd been in one cave with phosphorescent fungus, she'd been in fifty.

"So. Where are we?" she asked, a little surprised by how calm she sounded. They were no longer on the Otherside—either Otherside—that much and that much alone she was sure of. Well, that and how much she'd like to kick Lance.

"I don't know!"

Not exactly a surprise.

"What were you thinking when we went through the door?" Maybe calm wasn't exactly the right word. *Tight* was closer.

"That if I didn't get it right this time, you were going to give me hell."

"This isn't Hell."

"How can you be so sure?" Lance demanded, turning to stare down at her with wide eyes.

"It's my job to be sure."

"Of Hell?"

"Of what isn't Hell." While he was thinking about that, she turned to face the doors. Doors were doors. Fifty feet high and solid gold, two feet high at the end of a rabbit hole—it didn't matter. If she could get them open and fit through over the threshold, she could use them. In this particular instance, getting them open might be tricky since the doorknobs were a good twenty feet above her head.

A quick glance around determined the area was unfortunately empty of a small table holding a bottle and a note that said, *Drink me.*

"Incoming!"

Does he have to sound so cheerful about it? Claire

turned again and watched as two figures approached from the far end of the hall. Of course, since she couldn't see the far end of the hall that was an assumption only. Wherever they'd come from, they were moving fast.

Very fast.

Impossibly fast.

One moment they were barely visible in the distance. The next, they were standing barely two meters away.

On the left stood a cat-headed woman, barely covered from neck to ankles in a sheer linen shift. Her fur was pale brown with darker fur outlining golden eyes, lighter fur around the mouth, and two large pointed ears; both pierced, with a small gold ring in each.

On the right, a jackal-headed man, naked to the waist, wearing a pleated linen skirt held in place by a wide leather belt. Two small metal disks, stamped with hieroglyphs, hung from the front of the belt.

Do not go there, Claire warned herself. *It doesn't matter what it looks like, just do* not *go there.*

"I know where we are," Lance offered helpfully.

"So do I." When PhD candidates in Egyptology thought about Hell, they didn't think about Dante. Granted, neither did Keepers, but that was mostly because they preferred not thinking about hell at all and they sure as . . . heck . . . had no intention of handing it helpful definitions.

"They aren't dead," Anubis growled.

Bast shot him a disdainful golden glare. "And once again I marvel at your grasp of the obvious."

"If they aren't dead, why are they here?"

"Since they aren't dead, why don't we ask *them*? Or maybe you could fill in the details with a little butt sniffing."

His eyes narrowed. "It doesn't work that way."

Claire bit her lip to keep from laughing. Apparently jackals were just as clueless about sarcasm as dogs. She'd seen Austin reduce Rottweilers to twitching bundles of confusion with only a few barbed comments about their bathroom habits. Of course, the chances were good Anubis didn't drink out of the toilet.

As though thoughts of Austin had pulled her attention, Bast turned the full force of her golden gaze on Claire. "You're a Keeper, but this isn't one of the realities you Keep. Why are you here?"

Lesson number one in dealing with gods: don't lie to them. "I'm trying to return to a *situation* on the Otherside, but circumstances have landed me with a Bystander and his thoughts keep turning the paths."

And the corollary to lesson one: keep it simple.

The cat goddess glanced over at Lance. "He holds his thoughts strongly?"

"Oh, yeah. Once he gets something into his head you can't shift it."

And right on cue:

"*I* know why we're here. This is Meryat's work!

She's trying to stop me from stopping her by sending me to the Hall of Osiris!"

"Lance . . ."

"No! It all makes perfect sense!" He gripped her shoulder with one hand and waved the other around the Hall. "She's trying to cheat the afterlife by sending me . . . us . . . in her place."

"When the ka is strong enough . . ." Bast began.

"This ka has been bound between life and death for three thousand years," Lance interrupted. He ignored Claire's elbow in his ribs—interrupting gods was never a smart action in her experience—and continued. "As soon as it was freed, it sucked the life out of Dr. Rebik."

Anubis shrugged. "It happens."

"It does?"

"Sure. Not as much as it used to, though."

"But that's not what happened this time," Claire insisted. "I don't know about Dr. Rebik and the life-sucking part . . ." Although, given that Meryat was staying at the guest house, she really hoped Dean was right and Lance's lunatic theories were just that. Lunatic. She *had* to get back to the mall and Diana, so she'd have to trust Austin to keep Dean safe. ". . . but I do know exactly why we're here." She pointed at Lance. "Bystander. Path. Idiot."

Bast nodded, gold ring swinging as she flicked her ear. "I believe you. After three thousand years, this Meryat would have to absorb a truly powerful ka, the ka of a Keeper, say, in order to have enough strength to rip the veil between the world of the living and the world of the dead."

The pieces began to fall together. If Meryat would be that strong after absorbing the ka of a Keeper . . . "She's waiting for me to return to the guest house. Dean's safe enough until I get back, and then she'll take him in order to take me."

"I can stop her."

Claire turned to glare at Lance. "You're not there. And unless you get a grip on your thought processes, you may never be there!"

"That's not our concern," Bast pointed out a little sharply.

Right. Don't ignore the cat goddess . . .

"No, it's not your concern, and I apologize for taking up your time. If you can point us to a door, we'll be on our way."

Anubis pointed over Claire's shoulder.

Right. "A smaller door?"

"That's the only door in the Hall of Osiris and only Osiris himself can open it. If you were dead, we'd take you before Osiris to be judged, but since you're not dead . . ." His muzzle wrinkled as he tried to work it out.

Bast sighed. "Dead or alive, it doesn't matter; in order to leave the Hall, they have to be taken before Osiris."

"But we're only supposed to escort the dead. We could kill them," he added, looking hopeful. At least Claire thought it was hopeful; she wasn't too good at reading jackal physiognomy.

"Or we could just escort them to Osiris and let him work it out."

"I'd be honored to meet the Lord Osiris!" Lance declared, striding half a dozen quick steps forward and five back. "He'd appreciate my plan for dealing with Meryat! I could show him my thesis! No, wait." He bounced up and down on the balls of his feet. "I don't have my thesis with me!"

"Does he exclaim everything he says?" Bast asked Claire her ears slightly saddled.

"Pretty much."

"We could just kill *him* if you like. No bother."

Without Lance, the next door would take her back to the mall. The door after that, back to Dean. "Thank you for the offer." And she meant that sincerely. "It's tempting, but Lance knows how to deal with Meryat and besides—that whole Keeper thing—I'm not allowed to have even the most irritating Bystander put down."

"Pity."

"Sometimes."

It was a long walk to the other end of the Hall. The tiles were cool underfoot and it would have been a pleasant journey but for the heavy scent of embalming spices in the air and the sound of distant lamentation that started up the moment they'd both left the squares of red tile. At that, the lamentations were preferable to Lance's running commentary on the Egyptian afterlife.

When Bast's ears flattened against her skull, Claire grabbed Lance by his much less indicative ear and yanked his head down beside hers. "I've come to realize that telling you to shut up doesn't work, so instead I want you to remember everything you've ever heard about the dangers of pissing off gods." Not to mention cats. "Remember that the gods are invariably described as cruel and capricious and remember that everything you've ever learned about them is true."

"But a lot of the information contradicts . . ."

"Doesn't matter."

"But . . ."

"It's *all* true."

"Even . . ."

"*All* of it."

He straightened rubbing his ear. "So you're saying I should shut up?"

"Yes."

"Okay."

For a while, Lance and Anubis walked on ahead, circled around, walked with them for a few paces, walked on ahead, and Claire finally realized what Lance reminded her of. A half-grown, golden retriever puppy.

"His heart's in the right place," Bast murmured.

Claire waited.

The cat goddess didn't disappoint.

"That'll make it a lot easier to remove."

About the time they began to see their destination at the far end of the Hall—although it was still little more than a big golden wall with some smaller unidentifiable things in front of it—Lance returned to walk by her side, allowing the two gods to lead them the rest of the way into Osiris' presence.

"When we arrive," Bast announced as it became obvious that one of the distant objects was a huge throne, "I'll do the talking."

Anubis turned his head far enough for Claire to see a flash of teeth. "Why?"

"Because you've been known to leave out important bits of information about the deceased, and it would be unfortunate if that happened this time."

"Unfortunate?"

"Very."

"Why? Dead's dead."

"These two are alive."

"Oh, yeah . . ."

"They're not how I imagined gods," Lance said almost quietly.

Claire shrugged. She didn't want to get into it.

"I mean, they look like gods," Lance continued, clearly not picking up the subtext, "but they don't sound like gods. First of all, they use contractions."

That was unexpected enough to get Claire's attention. "What?"

"Contractions. You know; don't instead of do not. Or we're instead of we are. Or . . ."

"I know what a contraction is."

"They use them."

"So?"

He exhaled explosively. "So who ever heard of a god using contractions? It just isn't godlike."

Claire'd heard of gods who took their own names in vain three words out of seven, but she decided not to mention that to Lance. "What's second?" When he looked confused—well, more confused than usual—she expanded the question. "You said *'first of all,'* so there must be at least a second."

"Right!"

And the exclamations were back.

"It's the two of them, the way they interact. They're like *Ruff and Ready!*"

"Who?"

"You know; the cartoon!" Waving his hands from side to side, sketching out the beat, Lance sang, "They're Ruff and Ready. Always Ruff and Ready. They sometimes have their little spats, even fight like d . . ."

Up onto her toes, she got her hand over his mouth just in time. Anubis was showing rather a lot of teeth, and Bast's ears were flat against her skull while the triangle of fur that touched the top of her spine had lifted. Lesson . . . actually, Claire'd lost track at this point, but it had to be around lesson seven or eight in dealing with gods. Do not *ever* compare them to cartoon animals.

"Please . . ." No power, just a heartfelt plea. ". . . ignore him. He's just a Bystander."

"He is . . ."

". . . annoying." Anubis finished, the word emerging as one, long growl.

"I know. But we'll be gone soon and—gross!" She snatched her hand away and wiped it on her skirt. "You licked me!"

Lance grinned down at her. "It worked."

"How'd she taste?"

Bast and Claire turned as one toward the jackal-headed god.

"How did she taste?" Bast demanded.

Anubis shrugged. "I'm just curious."

"Pretty good," Lance allowed thoughtfully. "A little salty."

His muzzle wrinkled as Anubis took a step toward her, and Claire was ninety percent sure she was about to be licked again. *Oh that's just great. I am so not a dog person.*

Bast's hand on his arm yanked him to a halt. "The Lord Osiris is waiting."

Sure enough, there was now a figure sitting on the distant throne.

Sighing deeply, Anubis began walking again. "You never let me have any fun."

"Oh, yeah? Who throws all those damned balls for you?"

Instead of growing larger, the throne grew smaller as they approached until it, and the male figure sitting upon it, were only slightly bigger than the human norm. Osiris wore a pleated linen skirt similar to Anubis' but with a cloth-of-gold overskirt.

Gold sandals laced up around muscular calves, and a huge gold-and-obsidian collar rested on broad shoulders over impressive pecs. In spite of the traditional stick-on beard, the god of the underworld was a piece, no question about it, although Claire was fairly sure she'd seen the same outfit while closing an accident site at the Pyramid Club in Las Vegas.

Before either of their guides could speak, Lance pulled his PDA from its belt pouch, hit a quick sequence of keys, and read, in what Claire assumed was ancient Egyptian, "Praise be unto thee, O Osiris, lord of eternity, Un-nefer, Heru-Khuti, whose forms are manifold and whose attributes are majestic. It's a hymn to Osiris from the Book of the Dead," he added, sotto voce in English. "I've got the whole thing in here! Had to get extra memory! It goes on for a bit."

"I think you hit the high points."

"You understood that?"

"It's a Keeper thing." One golden-shod foot had begun to tap. "I'll explain later. Why don't we let Bast speak now?"

"Why do you need *me*?" Bast wondered pointedly. "You seem to be doing so *well* on your *own*."

Seventeen years with Austin had given Claire seventeen years of practice groveling, and a cat goddess was by no means as picky an audience as an actual cat—particularly one who'd accidentally been shut outside in the rain. Austin had made her pay, and pay, and pay for days, but by the time Bast turned to Osiris, she was almost purring.

Claire tuned out the story of their arrival in the Hall and worried about Dean instead. It was her fault he was in danger, her fault he might get his life sucked out by a reanimated Egyptian mummy. Women who went away on business and only worried about the man they left behind compulsively gambling away their savings or getting involved with the floozy at the coffee shop had no idea how good they had it. At least they had better-than-average odds that the man they loved wouldn't end up as bait in a deadly plot that involved power sucking and world domination. Well, better than average odds everywhere but New York and LA.

"It has been a long time since the living came to my Hall," Osiris said thoughtfully as Bast finished. His voice reminded Claire of that velvet glove/iron fist combination and while he was speaking, she couldn't take her eyes off him. "You are not on the Otherside, Keeper. You could reach into the possibilities here. Why haven't you?"

"This is your domain, Lord Osiris. To breach your parameters would be at best very stupid and at worst, incredibly rude."

He frowned. "Don't you mean that the other way around?"

"No. It's a Canadian thing," she added when he continued to look confused. "Lord Osiris, all we want to do is to leave. I'm in the middle of trying to stop a shopping mall from taking over the world, and Lance here . . ."

"Isis embraceth thee in peace and she driveth away the fiends from the mouth of thy paths."

"Not now, Lance."

"If not now, when?" he asked.

Clarie admitted he had a point. Unfortunately, she had no idea how long they'd been traveling as her watch had stopped working between the beach and the hippos and she couldn't risk squandering the time. "Probably never. Sorry. Lord Osiris, if you could point us toward a door . . ."

"Unfortunately, there is only one door out of my Hall and to go through it, you must be judged."

"But we're not dead."

"I would so have remembered to tell him that," Anubis muttered.

"Living or dead, it doesn't matter," Osiris pointed out. "Judgment is the only way out. One at a time, your hearts will be weighed against a single feather. If your heart is lighter than the feather, you will be declared *maa kheru* and the door will be opened. If it is heavier, then you stand condemned and will be devoured . . ." He gestured toward a triangle of deep shadow to the left of his throne. ". . . by the Eater of the Dead."

"But we're not dead," Claire repeated, enunciating carefully.

NOT A PROBLEM. I'LL FIGURE SOMETHING OUT.

"Claire?" Lance grabbed her shoulder and shook her hard enough to rattle her teeth. "Your mouth is open."

She closed it. Opened it. Closed it again. "What are you doing here?" she demanded at last.

DARKNESS. CONDEMNED SOULS. I GET AROUND.

Obviously."

I KNOW SOMETHING YOU DON'T.

Claire snorted. Only a rookie would fall for that.

IT'S ABOUT YOUR LITTLE SISTER.

Her toes were at the edge of the shadow before she was even aware of moving. "You stay away from my sister!"

OH, I'M SO SCARED. MAKE ME.

About to reach into the possibilities, Osiris' voice snapped her back into reason. "You two know each other?"

"We've met." Walking carefully, deliberately, back to Lance's side, Claire turned on one bare heel and glared at the shadow. "Last couple of times it happened, I kicked metaphorical ass."

YOU KNOW WHAT THEY SAY, THIRD TIME LUCKY.

"Really? You know what else they say?" She folded the fingers of her right hand into an "L" and tapped it against her forehead. "Loser. Loser. Loser."

"Keeper!" The Lord of Judgment's voice had picked a tone somewhere between Darth Vader and her mother. "Stop taunting the Eater of the Dead."

"Sorry."

YOU WILL BE.

"And that's enough out of you as well." Osiris stepped down off the throne, his size changing from gigantic to merely tall. "Anubis, bring out the scales."

Claire didn't exactly catch where Anubis brought the scales out from. It appeared between one heartbeat and the next, the onyx center post exactly as tall as Osiris, the onyx arms, the same measure. Shallow golden bowls hung at the end of golden chains.

"Thou turnest thy face upon Amentet and thou makest the earth to shine as with refined copper."

"Lance, what are you doing?"

He lifted his eyes from the small screen. "Sucking up!"

This had to be the most sensible thing he'd said since the beach. "Carry on."

"Those who have lain down, rise up to see thee, they breathe the air and they look upon girls, girls, girls. You wanna see girls? We got the best at www.ohmama.com. Wait a minute, that last bit's something else I downloaded!"

"I guessed."

"How'd it get into this file?"

"Shut up, Lance."

"But I have more!"

It was always hard to tell with anthropomorphic personifications of gods, but the expression on Osiris' face was making Claire just a little nervous. "No, really, Lance, shut up."

Maybe she'd finally reached the magic number.
Maybe he was trying for a satellite uplink. Whatever
the reason, he actually stopped talking.

"Bast. The feather."

Bast pulled a white feather from the air and laid
it in one of the shallow bowls.

"This feather is from the Sacred Ibis." Osiris shot
Bast a look as he spoke. Claire knew that look although the accompanying dialogue had gone *This
feather is from Mrs. Griffon's canary!* "Who will go first
to judgment?"

"I will!"

When Osiris turned his dark gaze on her, Claire
realized she must have made some small sound of
protest. But did it really matter which of them went
first? This wasn't something she could protect a Bystander from and, who knew, maybe enthusiasm
would count for something. Still . . . "If he passes
and I don't, do I have your word you'll send him
home? To *his* home," she added hastily. Rule whatever—be specific.

"You have my word," Osiris answered solemnly.

"Good enough."

Anubis beckoned Lance forward.

"This is amazing! I mean you can read about this
sort of thing and study it, but to actually be a part
of . . ."

The jackal-headed god's hand sank into Lance's
chest and emerged clutching his beating heart.

". . . ow! You know, I thought this would be a
little more metaphorical!"

Osiris shrugged. "I weigh your heart against a feather. Seems fairly straightforward to me. Anubis . . ."

Lance's heart landed in one of the shallow bowls with a moist thud as Osiris laid the feather in the other. The scales began to shift.

"Wait a minute! That's my . . ." Pale blue eyes rolled up so only the whites showed.

Claire danced back as Lance hit the floor. "You know, up until now, he'd been taking this whole experience annoyingly well."

"He's not the first fainter we've had," Osiris said matter-of-factly as he watched the bowl holding Lance's heart begin to rise. "He'll be fine once he gets his heart back. I'm getting the impression he doesn't worry about much," he added as the feather continued to drop. "He treats his life as a series of grand adventures; this one merely a little more grand than usual. Besides, I can feel a place where his ka was brushed by a dark ka. As long as that shadow remains, he'll be . . ."

"Distracted?"

"Focused."

Well, that explained the Meryat obsession. "Does the shadow affect . . ." She waved a hand toward the scales . . .

. . . which had stilled with Lance's heart holding steady a good six inches above the feather.

"Not in the least. I judge this man to be *maa kheru*. He is free to go. Anubis."

Anubis, who'd been licking his fingers, leaped forward, retrieved Lance's heart, squatted down, and pushed it carefully back into his body.

"Bast . . ."

Caught between bracing herself and trying to relax, Claire missed Bast's hand plunging into her chest, but she certainly felt it coming out. Ow! was a bit of an understatement. The cat-headed goddess frowned slightly as she crossed to the scale and Claire began to have a bad feeling about how this was going to turn out.

Of course her heart was heavy. She was a Keeper. She was responsible for the metaphysical protection of a good chunk of southeastern Ontario and upstate New York. And then there was the guest house and Diana, and being away from the segue, and dragging Lance around the Otherworlds, and not even knowing there were Otherworlds until she found herself plunged into the middle of them. Or maybe it. And she'd left Dean alone to face a reanimated mummy. Sure, Austin was with him, but he wasn't supposed to be, and what had she been thinking dragging a seventeen-year-old cat into an evil shopping mall anyway?

"Well. This is . . . interesting." All three gods were staring at the scales. The bowl holding the feather was brushing the floor. The bowl holding her heart was an arm's length above Osiris' head.

"Is this happening because I'm a Keeper?" Claire hazarded.

"No. This is happening because this isn't your heart."

She glanced down at her chest and up at the bowl. "Pardon?"

"It appears you have given your heart to another. This heart is his."

Dean stared down into Claire's face for a long moment before his mouth finally curved into a worried smile. "Got my heart?"

She laid a hand lightly against her chest. "Right here. Got mine."

He mirrored the motion. "Safe and sound."

"A most unusual young man."

He'd lived next to a hole to Hell for six months and it hadn't even convinced him to drop his underwear on the floor.

"He is, yes."

The Lord of Death dragged Dean's heart down to where Bast could reach it. "You realize you're getting off on a technicality."

"Yes, I do." The return was painless. It was a pity Lance was still out; Claire had a feeling things couldn't get much more metaphorical than this.

HEY! THIS ISN'T FAIR!

Osiris shot an exasperated look toward the shadow. "Death seldom is."

SHE CHEATED!

"No one cheats death in the end."

WHAT, I'M SUPPOSED TO EAT PLATITUDES NOW?

"If you like."

And you can choke on them, Claire thought as Lance's eyelids started to flutter. Dropping to one knee beside him, she shook his shoulder. "Come on, big guy. We're leaving."

"Going home?"

"Not right away. I've got some shopping to do first."

"I like shopping."

"Great. Hold that thought."

It took Anubis and Bast helping to get him to his feet. He swayed slightly and blinked at Anubis. "Hey, who's a good OW!"

Violence against Bystanders was permitted only in circumstances where it saved said Bystander, or Bystanders, from a greater violence. Claire figured calling Anubis a "good doggie" was definitely in the greater violence category.

"You pinched me!"

"Yes, I did."

"Okay, then. How did we do?" he asked, rubbing one cheek.

"Neither of you were found wanting," Osiris answered. He stepped forward, and Claire wasn't surprised to find the three of them suddenly standing in front of the huge golden doors. Only now the doors were a standard height.

"Hey! We grew!"

Okay. That worked, too.

*   *   *

"Dr. Rebik?" The cleaned and ironed chinos hanging over his arm, Dean knocked on the door to room two. "Dr. Rebik, your pants are ready."

"Maybe they're having a nooner."

Dean turned to stare at Austin in disbelief.

The cat shrugged. "Why not? They're young and in love . . . oh, wait, my mistake, he's having his life sucked out and she's a reanimated corpse."

"And it's twenty after ten." He knocked again.

"I find it disturbing that you're more concerned with the time than the corpse."

"I find it disturbing that you know what a nooner is." About to knock a third time, he lowered his hand as the door opened and Dr. Rebik slipped out into the hall. Dean caught a quick glimpse of Meryat lying on the bed, wrapped arms crossed over her breast, then Dr. Rebik pulled the door closed.

One hand clutching the waistband of a pair of borrowed sweatpants, he stared up at Dean through bloodshot eyes as if unsure of who he was speaking to. "Yes?"

Dean held out the chinos.

"Ah. Yes." Comprehension dawned slowly. "You were washing them for me." His hand trembled slightly as he reclaimed his clothing.

"You all right, Dr. Rebik? You're looking some poorly."

"Some poorly?" The archaeologist managed a tired smile. "It's the waiting. It's hard on Meryat."

"Looks like it's hard on you."

"We are as one in this."

"Okay. Sure." Frowning slightly, Dean watched as Dr. Rebik slipped back into his room. Meryat hadn't moved. If he didn't know better, he'd have to say she looked dead. As he stepped away from the door, he noticed a worn, brown leather wallet lying on the floor.

The way those sweatpants had been sagging, it had probably fallen from a pocket.

Dean bent, scooped it up, and lifted his hand to knock again.

Austin cleared his throat.

Don't look at the cat. Just give it back.

As subtlety didn't seem to be working, Austin sank a claw into Dean's ankle just above his work boot.

"Son of . . ." He danced down the hall, collapsing against the wall by room one. "What'd you do that for, then?"

"Aren't you the least bit curious?"

"About what? Tetanus?"

"About what's in his wallet."

"An amulet controlling his will? A note asking us to save him?"

Austin speared him with a pointed gaze. "You didn't used to be this sarcastic."

"I didn't used to live with you!"

"Maybe he dropped it on purpose, did you think of that? Maybe it's a cry for help."

"You're reaching."

"You're opening it."

And he was. He didn't know what he expected to find, but he found he couldn't give the wallet back unexamined. It *had* fallen some conveniently. "I can't believe I'm after doing this."

"I can't believe it's taking you so long."

Credit cards. Health card. Driver's license . . . His eyes widened. If forced to guess, he'd have said Dr. Rebik was in his mid to late sixties.

According to his driver's license, he was thirty-eight.

And he looked worse than his picture.

"I was right."

"I know."

"You were wrong."

"Yeah. I got that."

"There's a song, you know. When I'm right and you're wrong."

Dean stopped pacing long enough to glare at the cat. "Don't sing it."

Austin sat down on the dining room table, stuck a foot in the air, and began washing his butt.

"Very subtle." The dining room was exactly fourteen paces long. Provided he shortened the last step. "What do we do now?"

"You mean now that you admit I'm right?"

"Yes!"

"Well, we have to stop her. She's sucking your life force out and what's to say she won't get tired of waiting for Claire and start sucking harder."

"Lance said he knew how to stop her."

"Which would be relevant if Lance wasn't off with Claire."

"Can we use the elevator on her?"

Austin sat up and shook his head. "It's a little obvious. I suspect she'd sense it. What are you doing?"

Dean paused in the middle of crumpling up a sheet of newspaper. "I'm going to clean the windows. It's what I do when I need to think."

The two huge windows in the dining room were already spotless, but he sprayed them with a vinegar-and-water solution and began to rub.

"That's a very annoying noise."

"Sorry."

"You're not going to stop, are you?"

"No."

When the paper was wet, he tossed it into the garbage and reached for another sheet. As he pulled it off the early edition, Austin's paw snaked out and smacked it back down.

"There's our answer!"

Dean scanned the headlines and frowned. "The waterfront renewal project?"

"No. The life-sized stone statue found at the mall!"

"*The* mall?"

"The very one! And you know what a life-sized stone statue means."

"Bad garden art?"

"Basilisk! We go to the mall. We capture it. We turn Meryat to stone!"

"Claire . . ."

"You want Claire coming home to find Meryat waiting for her."

No. He didn't. "How do we capture a basilisk without turning to stone ourselves?

Austin stared up at him in disbelief. "Do I have to think of *everything*?"

TWELVE

While Keepers spent pretty much their entire lives fighting to keep the world safe, they didn't usually get involved in *actual* fighting of the hand-to-hand, teeth-to-arm, knees-to-groin variety. And no matter how many Saturday afternoons got wasted watching badly dubbed kung fu movies, it didn't help.

Diana realized this about ten seconds into the fight. She couldn't reach the possibilities, she'd lost her prepared defenses, and she had no idea how to disable her opponents with a shopping cart. Not that there was a shopping cart handy.

Running, while the intelligent response, had got them exactly seven paces closer to the throne before two of the giant bugs—moving in that creepy, skittery, *fast* way that giant bugs had laid claim to since the old black-and-white movie days—had cut them off. Diving out of the way of a flailing forearm, or foreleg, or sixleg or whatever it was called on a bug, Diana smacked her head against the floor and, just for an instant, heard the voice of Ms. McBride, her last biology teacher.

"*. . . size to mass ratio . . .*"

Yeah. That was helpful.

Fortunately, her belief that the meat-minds were too clumsy to simultaneously walk and breathe made them an avoidable threat for the most part. The bugs were the problem. Just as the bugs had been the problem in the access corridor.

"*Diana, are you listening?*"

Apparently not.

She caught a quick glimpse of Kris going up and over a meat-mind, her black hightops digging into knees, thighs, hips, chest, and shoulders like they were part of her own personal jungle gym. As the mall elf leaped clear, the pursuing bug knocked the meat-mind ass over tip and got itself tangled in the sudden barricade of flailing arms and legs. Diana wasted a moment imagining what Kris could do with a shopping cart, then, at the last possible instant, dropped flat and slid under a descending carapace.

And let's hear it for polished marble floors! she noted as her slide put her considerably closer to the wand. She could see it, lying all pink and plastic on the steps of the throne, but she couldn't . . . quite . . . reach . . .

The bug's leg caught her a glancing blow, skidding her a couple of meters in the wrong direction.

"*This* will *be on the final exam.*"

What will?

She'd written her final biology exam only ten days ago. *You'd think I'd remember more of it.* Which was either a scathing indictment of the public school system, or she should start worrying about her short-term memory.

Curved, swordlike mandibles cut through the back of her sweater and hoisted her onto her feet.

Mandibles. Maxillae. Labium or lower lip.

Her final exam'd had an entire section on bugs. Class Insecta. A useless spewing of information she assumed she'd never need again—her present situation having been unanticipated at the time. Evidently, a little shortsighted of her.

Insects. Nearly a million known species.

Every kind of land environment supports a flourishing insect population.

"So, Ms. McBride, if bugs are so great, how come they aren't taking over the world like in them old movies?"

Diana smiled and mentally thanked Daryl Mills. The bug holding her shuddered as its exoskeleton cracked in a dozen places with a sound like cheap wineglasses hitting a concrete floor. She jumped clear as it collapsed under its own weight. Most of a sperm whale's weight was supported by water. Elephants had evolved massive bones and muscles to deal with their bulk. Size/mass ratio.

Giant bugs were impossible.

So there.

The sound of breaking glass filled the throne room and pieces of chitin buzzed around like shrapnel. The

Shadowlord shrieked like a hockey mom after a bad call.

Three steps and she'd be at the dais. Up two stairs and she'd have the wand. One moment after that, it would all be over but the fat lady singing. Whatever that meant.

Three steps and . . .

Something caught her between the shoulder blades and she went down, hard.

Epicuticle, she thought muzzily as it bounced and landed about two centimeters from her nose. *This isn't . . .*

A booted foot pressed hard against the back of her neck.

. . . good.

She swung out as a hand in her hair dragged her up onto her knees but only succeeded in overbalancing and nearly scalping herself. Blinking away memories of grade school ponytails so tight she looked like Mr. Spock's kid sister, Diana screamed "RUN!" over the Shadowlord's ultimatum that Kris surrender.

"What did you listen to him for?" she demanded a moment later as two meat-minds dropped Kris beside her.

The mall elf got shakily to her knees. "Like I was going to leave you here alone?"

How romantic. *Well, since you asked, not very.* "You could have gone for help!"

"As if. It's wall to friggin' wall of meat-minds out there. Couldn't get past them."

Okay. Even less romantic.

"So I remembered something I was told, way back," Kris continued. "If you're going to lose anyway, surrender *before* they kick your ass—not after."

"Arthur?"

"My mom."

"Smart lady."

"That time."

"Are you two finished catching up?" the Shadowlord snarled.

"So, 'rents still together?" Diana asked, shuffling around so that she was facing the other girl.

The mall elf stared at her for a moment, then disbelief disappeared behind a gleeful smile as she caught on. When it seems like there's no options left, there's *always* the option of being a pain in the ass. "Nah, my dad split about six years ago. I'm guessin' you've got the whole happy suburban family thing going down?"

"Oh, yeah. We're a walking, talking WASP cliché except for that whole Keeper, Cousin, cat thing."

"Silence!" At some point the Shadowlord had retrieved his club, and he was stroking it as he loomed over them.

"You know if you think that looks threatening . . ." Diana nodded toward the club. ". . . you're so wrong. It's screaming, 'hey, girls, look at my big substitute . . .'"

She'd been a little worried she might provoke him into actually using the club, but, fortunately, he went with the personal touch. The backhand lifted her off her knees and threw her back over the steps of the dais. Moving around to face Kris had placed her at exactly the right angle—no brainer to figure he'd lash out—and she grabbed the wand as she sprawled over it, stuffing it down into the front of her pants.

Diana'd seen the same stunt on a television show once. On a seventeen-inch screen it hadn't looked as painful as it really was. Bells and whistles were still going off inside her skull as a pair of meat-minds hauled her onto her feet and dragged her back before the Shadowlord.

"Foolish little girl. I should kill you where you stand."

"Not actually standing here . . . Ow!" The dangling she could cope with, but the shaking was a bit over the top. "Besides, you can't kill me or you'd have already done it. And do you know why you can't kill me?" For the same reason she hadn't used the wand the moment her fingers closed around it. "Because you're not the Big Bad." She was not wasting their one chance on a flunky. "Killing me would release all sorts of energy down here. Energy you can't control. That's why you didn't kill me . . . us," she corrected, glancing over at Kris. ". . . before. That's why you can't kill me now."

"I can't, but that from where I came, can."

Diana blinked. Even her eyelashes hurt. "What?"

"I speak of the Pit. The Darkness. The . . ."

"Yeah. Okay. I get it. You can't. Hell can. It may have split you off, and given you a personality—of sorts—but it still keeps you under its thumb."

"That's not . . ."

"Hey, denial; not just a river in Egypt. Face it, Hell's just using you. In fact, there really isn't a *you* at all. You don't have a name, you don't have an identity; you're just an itty-bitty part of a greater whole. Hell doesn't trust you with any *real* power." As the last words left her mouth, Diana knew she'd made a mistake. The Shadowlord had been frowning as he listened to her, clearly not liking what she had to say—possibly not liking it enough to challenge Hell and cause a distraction, allowing her to seal the hole and shut down the segue thus saving the world—but at *trust*, he smiled.

"Of course, Hell doesn't trust me," he said calmly. "Hell is me. And I am Hell."

"A little-bitty part . . ."

"Enough. Your blatant attempt to drive a wedge between me and my origin might have worked were we in the sort of fairy tale where the good guys always win, but we're . . ."

"In the subbasement of an imaginary shopping mall," Diana finished as dryly as her current position allowed. *Oh, great, I'm starting to sound like Claire.*

He stepped forward and pressed the end of his club under Diana's chin, forcing her head back. "What part of 'enough' are you having difficulty understanding?"

"Well, duh; the part where I do anything you say."

"Then perhaps you should consider this . . ." Had he been breathing, his breath would have caressed her cheek. As it was, she felt a faint frisson of fear spread out from the closest point between them, as though his proximity caused an involuntary physical reaction. ". . . I can't kill you, but I can bludgeon you senseless."

"Right. Enough; adverb. To put an end to an action." Clearly she'd been paying more attention in English than biology, and she really *really* wished he'd back away. "As in enough taunting the Shadowlord. I should stop it. I can do that."

"Good."

"Is there any particular reason you asked the three-thousand-year-old, reanimated Egyptian mummy that's been sucking out your life force if there was anything we could get her while we're at the mall?"

"I was just being polite," Dean protested as he turned off Sir John A. MacDonald Boulevard and onto Highway 33.

"She's sucking out your life force," Austin repeated, enunciating each word with caustic clarity.

"And that's a reason to be rude, then?"

"Some people might think so."

"Some people might be after jumping in the harbor; that doesn't mean I'm going to do it."

"So, just out of curiosity . . ." He hooked his claws in the seat as the truck maneuvered around another corner. ". . . what would be grounds for rudeness in your book?"

Dean's brow creased above the upper edge of his glasses as he thought about it.

After a few moments, Austin sighed. "Never mind."

There'd been discussion about Austin remaining at the guest house to keep an eye on things, but in the end they'd decided it was too great a risk. Without Dean there to snack on, there was always the chance that Meryat would turn to the cat and the cat didn't have life force to spare.

"Although it's entirely possible she can't feed from me."

"Why?" Before Austin could answer, Dean had raised a hand, cutting him off. *"Because you're a cat."*

"Does there need to be another reason?"

"Is there ever another reason?"

The guest house had proven it could take care of itself.

The mall parking lot was about half full. Fully three quarters of the parked vehicles were minivans, which was disturbing mostly because Dean didn't know how disturbed he should be. Or why. Just to be on the safe side, he parked next to a white sedan with Ohio plates.

"I'd feel better about this if I could go in there with you," Austin muttered as Dean pulled an empty hockey bag out from behind the seats. "Do you remember the plan?"

"Find a spot by the food court, place the bag on its side with the zipper open, place the dish of cold Red River cereal in the bag, close the bag while the basilisk is eating, only look at it with this piece of mirror." Dean held up the sideview mirror that had broken off the truck on his first drive to Ontario a year and a half ago. The support had snapped, but the glass was fine, so he'd hung on to it. "You're sure it'll come to the cereal, then?"

"It's got to be hungry, and that stuff's close enough to chicken feed it'll never know the difference."

"I can't believe we're . . ."

". . . utilizing local resources to disable a meta-physical threat."

Dean stared at the cat.

Austin stared back.

"Well, when you put it like that," Dean said at last. He opened the door and stepped down onto the asphalt. "Try to stay out of sight. The windows are open and you've got lots of water, but I don't want some good Samaritan calling the cops on me because they think you're suffering."

"Nobody understands my pain."

"You can say that again," Dean sighed as he closed the door.

The parking lot felt soft underfoot. It wasn't the heat, even though it was hot enough to paint his T-shirt to his body, and bright enough to light it up like Signal Hill; it was as if the asphalt *itself* was rising around each boot and trying to drag him down. Not exactly what had happened to Claire and Diana the morning he'd dropped them off since they'd left visible footprints in the tar and he had no actual evidence that this was going on anywhere but in his head. No footprints. No smell of melted tar.

Just a feeling. Accompanied by the certainty that things on the Otherside had gotten worse instead of better.

Things always get worse before *they get better*, he told himself and didn't find it very reassuring. He wanted to help. He couldn't help. All he could do was make sure that when Claire came home, she wouldn't be facing a life-sucking reanimated mummy. Given the condition of the parking lot, it didn't seem like enough.

He found himself walking with an exaggerated, high-stepping gait. And he wasn't the only one. Across the lot, two kids, one around three, the other no more than five, were walking the exact same way. The funny thing was, their mother—Dean assumed it was their mother although she could have been a babysitter—didn't seem to notice. Her feet were dragging with the unmistakable exhaustion of someone who'd just spent the morning with two pre-schoolers in a shopping mall.

Were children more open to the extraordinary?

He flushed as he realized the mother—or babysitter—was aware of his attention. Flushed darker when he realized she was staring at his . . . uh, jeans . . . and smiling in a way that was making him distinctly nervous. Picking up his pace, he made it to the concrete in time to turn and see all three of them pile into a later model station wagon.

Not a minivan.

Which was good; right?

Feeling vaguely nostalgic for the days when he knew what the hell was going on, he went into the mall.

The air-conditioning hit him like a dive into the North Atlantic, and the sweat dribbling down the sides of his neck dried so fast it left goose bumps behind. A trio of fourteen-year-old girls burst into high-pitched giggling as he stepped back and held open the door for them, the giggling punctuated by "Oh. My. God." at frequent intervals as they passed. Dean had the uncomfortable feeling they were referring to the rip in the right leg of his jeans. Maybe he shouldn't have worn them out in public, but after years of being washed and ironed, they were so thin that they were the coolest pair he owned in spite of how tightly they fit.

He'd parked by the food court entrance, having a strong suspicion that a man carrying a basilisk in a hockey bag was going to need to cover as short a distance as possible inside the mall.

By the time he reached the edge of the seating area, he remembered what he hated about these kind of places. He'd seen dead cod with more personality.

Actually, in this kind of weather, dead cod had personality to spare.

Only the fact that the forces of evil were using this mall as part of their attempt to take over the world made it any different than a hundred malls just like it. Although not a lot different.

Austin had been certain the basilisk would be hanging around the food court.

Dean studied the area carefully, walked over to the ubiquitous Chinese Take-Out, and bought an egg roll and a coffee. He couldn't just sit down at a table in the food court without food, taking up space he had no real right to; that would be rude. Tray in one hand, hockey bag in the other, he made his way through a sudden crowd of teenagers toward the more thickly filled of the two planters—the perfect basilisk hiding place.

The good news: the table closest to the planter was empty.

The bad news: either a chicken-lizard combo smelled like the shallows after one of the big boats had just flushed her bilges on a hot day or the basilisk wasn't the only thing the planter was hiding.

It certainly explained why the statue they'd found had been holding a trowel and a bucket.

He wasted a moment wondering why they'd positioned plastic plants under a skylight, then reached into his bag and took the top off the container of cooked cereal. With the open bag carefully braced between his feet, he set the mirror in his lap, and opened his coffee.

As he took his first sip, he heard his grandfather's voice, *"Fer the love of God, bai, you don't go buying coffee from a Chinese Take-Out! That's why the good laird gave us Timmy Horton's!"*

Dean put the lid back on his cardboard cup, forcing himself to swallow.

His grandfather had been a very wise man.

The egg roll probably would have tasted better if

his sense of smell hadn't gone numb. On the other hand, had his sense of smell still been functioning, he wouldn't have been able to eat the egg roll, so he supposed it evened out.

How long was he supposed to be waiting, then?

"Dean McIssac? Christ on crutches, it is you!"

The young woman who dropped into the other seat had a blaze of red hair over startlingly black eyebrows and breasts that threatened to spill out over the top of her . . . Actually, Dean had no idea of what she was wearing. He remembered the breasts. When he wasn't playing hockey, dreams of those breasts had pretty much got him through his last year of high school. And occasionally when he *was* playing hockey, which was how he'd dislocated his shoulder. Unfortunately, she'd been dating the same guy since grade nine and no one else stood a chance. She'd been the perfect, safe, unattainable fantasy. "Sherri Murphy. What're you doing so far from home?"

"Working. Same as. Got a job out at the nylon plant." Sherri grinned across the table at him. "Damn, it's some good to see a familiar face. You here alone?"

"Yeah . . ."

Her grin sharpened.

Dean wondered why he'd never noticed the predatory curve to it before. No wait; he knew why. "Uh, Jeff . . ."

She shrugged, and he missed the first few words. ". . . boat with his dad. Like you can support a family fishing these days." Her gaze turned frankly speculative. "What about you?"

"Me?"

"You got a girl?"

"A girl . . . yes." Floundering without knowing how he'd gotten caught up by the surf, he clung to the thought of Claire. "She's around here somewhere." Which, if *somewhere* was stretched about as far as it could go, was the absolute truth.

Head cocked to one side, Sherri studied his face. "You know, word was, Dean McIssac couldn't lie to save his life." The tip of her tongue traced a moist line over her lower lip.

Something warm and soft brushed up against Dean's ankle, and he felt his cheeks begin to burn. "Listen, there's a, uh, bar down in Portsmouth Village, the, uh . . ." The pressure against his leg increased, moving softly up and down his calf. ". . . Ship to Shore. Bunch of us from home are there most Saturdays."

"Talking about when you're going back east?" Her voice had picked up a wistful tone.

"Yeah. That, too. The owner has a load of Black 'Arse trucked up from home about once a month."

"Beer and nostalgia, hard to resist."

The lightest touch against the inside of his knee. Dean's whole body twitched although, crammed into the seat as he was, he couldn't jump back. He was amazed she'd found enough room to maneuver under these tiny tables.

"I'm not remembering you as being this jumpy."

Smiling like she knew a secret, she stood. "Saturdays, eh? Maybe I'll be stopping by, then. I'd like to meet the girl who finally got you."

More than a little confused, he watched her walk away.

Got me wha . . .

A gentle caress against his other leg.

Sherri had disappeared into the drugstore.

How did she . . . ?

Oh.

Ears on fire, he glanced down at the mirror in his lap. The chicken half of the basilisk was in his hockey bag eating Red River cereal. The lizard part, a long, prehensile, bright green scaly tail, was rubbing up and down his leg.

She must think I'm a total idiot.

Leaning forward, both hands under the table, he gently shoved the tail into the bag.

Claire could never find out about this.

A warm beak investigated his fingers. He pushed it back down toward the cereal.

Austin could never find out about this.

Holding the zipper clear of stray feathers, he quickly closed it.

The squawk was remarkably loud. Half a dozen heads turned toward him.

"Just caught my basilisk in the zipper," he explained, threw the bag over his shoulder and hurried for the door, his ears so hot he was sure they were leaving a thermal trail behind them.

*　　*　　*

Dean listened to the flat, definitive click in disbelief and then turned the key again, just in case. Another click followed by a silence so complete he could hear feathers being rearranged in the hockey bag now tucked behind the seats. "I don't believe this. The battery's dead."

"You were gone for a long time; I got bored." Austin licked his shoulder. "I was listening to the radio."

"But I have the keys, and you couldn't use a key if you had one." Click. Nothing. "How did you even turn the electrical system on?"

"It's a cat thing."

He laid his head against the steering wheel and jerked it back almost immediately as the black plastic branded the arc of its upper curve into his skin. "You're telling me cats can hot wire cars, then?"

"Don't be ridiculous," Austin snapped. "This is a truck."

"Right." Because that was all the explanation he was ever going to get. *Okay.* He got out of the truck and stared across the parking lot, watching the heated air rise up off the asphalt and shimmer like a curtain between worlds. If only it was that easy. Kevin had borrowed his jumper cables back in March and never returned them. He'd be smacking the buddy upside the head for that come Saturday, but it wasn't going to do him any good now. *A basilisk, a talking cat, and a dead battery walk into a bar . . .*

Turning his back on the minivans, he banged his head against the hood of truck.

"You look like you're having a bad day. Is there something I can do to help?"

She was about his age, her name was Mary, she was up from the States for a music festival, and she had, not only a set of jumper cables, but a set long enough to reach from her battery to his. "My brother bought them for me," she told him tossing a waist-length braid back over her shoulder as she efficiently hooked the two vehicles together. "There, try it now."

The truck turned over on the first attempt. Dean hit the parking brake, put it in neutral, and got out to help Mary coil her cables.

"Is that your cat?" she asked as Austin put his paws up on the dashboard and peered out at them.

"Not exactly."

"Ah." She nodded wisely. "Your girlfriend's cat. You have the look of a man in over his head."

As she bent to put the cables in the trunk, Dean was horrified to see the hockey bag rise up from behind the seats and attempt to take flight. He gestured wildly at Austin, who made a rude gesture in return just as the bag slid forward, hit the seat, and knocked Austin's feet out from under him. On the bright side, bag and cat were out of sight by the time Mary turned. Dean thanked her in a hurry, shook her hand, yanked his feet out of the tar, and dove back into the truck.

The bag was on the floor on the passenger side. Austin was on the bag, smacking random bits of covered basilisk. "I'm getting too old for this kind of . . ." A fast right, quickly followed by a left hook, quelled an incipient uprising. ". . . shit."

"If you hadn't run down my battery, we'd be home by now!"

"Oh, so it's *my* fault you had to be rescued by a girl?"

"Yeah. It is. Your fault." He glanced up, noticed Mary frowning at him, waved, put the truck in gear, and started for home. In over his head. That pretty much summed up his life of late.

He needed Claire back in the worst way.

Sam knew he was supposed to be calm, cool, and collected—although he had no idea of just what he was supposed to collect. He knew that he, as a cat, should be an example of self-confident serenity to the horde of mall elves, armed and armored from sporting goods, who were about to go into battle against the forces of evil.

Sporting goods aside, this wasn't going to be battle by Disney.

He had a feeling that even as an angel, he'd sucked at serenity. Unfortunately, since that whole Soldier of the Lord thing would come in handy right about now, the more time he spent in fur, the less he remembered about his life BC. Before cat.

Back and forth across the top of the shelves that

defined the open court around the fire pit. He couldn't stop pacing.

The unmistakable of sound of a two-fingered whistle echoed through the enclosed space, instantly silencing the babble of conversation. A dozen heads of exotic hair turned toward the sound.

"Dudes! Listen up." Red braid swinging across the broad shoulders of his hockey pads, Will nodded toward Arthur, who stood beside him on a chair pulled away from a kitchen set in home furnishings. "Our fearless leader's got something to say!"

The Immortal King looked out at the crowd, his blue eyes sweeping from face to face, refusing to be hurried. Under his black leather jacket, he was wearing an umpire's padded breastplate. In his left hand, he held a pair of heavy leather gauntlets from gardening supplies. In his right, he held Excalibur.

It was so quiet Sam could hear only the faint creak of plastic padding. It was almost as though the mall elves were holding their breath, waiting for their leader to speak.

The ringing crash of the aluminum bat bouncing loudly across the tiles spun everyone around. They watched in unison until the bat finally hissed to a stop under Kith's raised boot. Then they all looked at Sam.

He hadn't even noticed the bat before he knocked it off the shelf.

Ignoring the pounding of his heart, and pretty sure he'd just lost the first of the alleged nine lives, he sat down and wrapped his tail pointedly around his front paws. Given the overwhelming, all encompassing level of noise, he didn't think he could pull off the classic "I meant to do that" expression, so he settled for the slightly less difficult "What?" aimed directly at Arthur. Unable to help themselves, the elves turned again, searching for what he was staring at.

Poets knew that cats looked at kings because poets were no more immune than anyone else when it came to discovering what cats were staring at.

Arthur sighed. "You called me here," he said after a moment, "to make you one people. To stop the bickering that made you easy prey for the darkside. To teach you how to hold the line against the darkside and say, this far you shall go and no farther. This I have done. You are one people. You act as one against the darkside. You hold the line. But it is no longer enough. The darkside has taken one of us and one of the Keepers who came to set us free. We cannot just hold the line while Kris and Diana are in the hands of our enemies. It is time we take the fight to them!"

"Fight! Fight! Fight! Fight!"

Caught up in the rhetoric, it took Sam a moment to realize why the response made him so edgy. He'd seen much the same thing on a grade-school playground while waiting for Diana to close an accident site under the slide.

Tossing back his hair with one hand, lifting Excalibur above his head with the other, Arthur yelled out, "Who is with me?"

All the hair lifted along Sam's spine and in the second between the question and the answer, he shouted, "Wait!"

"Ow! Where are we?"

"In a refrigerator." Bent nearly double, Claire reached for the door, hoping it was still open. "I'd have told you to duck, but I didn't want to end up on an extended visit to Donald, Daisy, or Howard."

"So, Meryat's not in here?"

"No. Meryat's not in here." There was focused and then there was obsessive. Lance had crossed the line some time ago. "Hands off!"

"Sorry! There's not much room!"

"Well, it's a *refrigerator*," she muttered, flicking the edge of the egg tray and trying to remember if it was on the door in this particular model. They had more than the actual room available but not by much.

"Would this be a good time to tell you that I'm a little claustrophobic?"

"No." Okay. That was the butter thingy. Had to be the door. Both hands against it, Claire pushed.

"We need to get out now."

"I'm working on . . . Hey!" Those were hands where they had no business being. Not that Lance seemed to notice as he began to throw himself against the sides of the fridge. "Careful! You're going to . . ."

Too late.

The fridge went over, the door flew open, and Claire spilled out into Large Appliances wrapped up in a panicking grad student. She slapped him purely for medicinal reasons.

Rolling free, she found herself staring up at a pair of worried amber eyes, cinnamon nose nearly touching hers. No mistaking the tuna breath. "Sam! Ow!" Half a heartbeat later, she had an armful of marmalade cat and a row of bleeding puncture marks along her collarbone. "Oh, baby-cat, you have no idea how glad I am to see *you*."

The ecstatic purring stopped. Sam squirmed free and backed up until all four feet were each applying approximately ten pounds of pressure to Claire's chest. "Baby-cat?"

"Term of endearment."

"*Baby*-cat!"

"I'm sorry. I was caught up in the moment. It will *never* happen again."

Whiskers bristling, Sam stared at her with such intensity, her eyes started to water. "See that it doesn't," he snorted at last and walked away muttering, "Baby-cat? I'd like to see what'd happen if she tried that on Austin. He'd remove her spleen . . ."

Claire smiled and sat up. It was good to be back.

"What's with the elves in hockey gear?" Lance demanded, bouncing up onto his feet, panic forgotten.

Actually, that was a good question.

White, plastic shoulder pads gleaming under the

store's florescent lights, the mall elves pushed their way between the washers and dryers and surrounded the open area in front of the toppled fridge. Whatever they'd been doing, it had certainly got them worked up; Claire'd never seen them so excited. They were in constant movement, all talking at once. Half a dozen hands reached down to lift her to her feet.

"Thank you, okay, that's great, I'm fine, yes it's good to be back . . . Hey!" An elf she didn't recognize backed away, hands in the air. Sure, he *could* have just been smoothing down the back of her skirt and she *could* have just spent a couple of hours with the gods of ancient Egypt. *Oh, wait . . .*

"They're happy to see you!" Lance pointed out, accurately but unnecessarily.

"He's not Australian?" Stewart asked, shooting a disbelieving glance up at the taller blond.

"Not so that you'd notice."

"Weird." He handed over her sandals. "You left these here."

Claire thanked him, bent to slip them on, and straightened as the surrounding babble rose in volume.

Lance's fingers closed over her shoulder. "Meryat!"

She sighed. "Arthur." And stepped forward to meet the Immortal King.

He clasped her wrist in a warrior-to-warrior move Claire'd only ever seen performed in old movies. It was moderately reassuring that he hadn't changed enough from his basic parameters to greet her with a high five. "I am truly glad to see you back, Keeper."

"I'm truly glad to be back." She glanced at his chest. "Decided to have a sports day while I was gone?"

"We are armored for battle."

"Battle? The darkside is attacking?"

"No." Blue-black hair fell over his eyes as he shook his head. "We take the fight to them."

It seemed like she'd managed to find the mall just in time. "No, we don't . . ."

"Your sister, the Keeper Diana, and Kris, my captain, have been captured."

"Yes, we do. How do you know this?"

"A budgie mirror gave the news to Sam."

"Okay, then." That was just ludicrous enough to be a reliable source. She waved toward the various bits of surrounding padding. "Can I assume you were about to leave?"

"We were."

"Just let me get my stuff . . ."

"Claire?"

Right. Lance. Her own personal albatross. Except that an actual albatross would be significantly less annoying. Still . . . Bystander. Keeper. Responsible. Yadda. "Lance . . ." She reached back, got a good grip on his sleeve and dragged him forward. ". . . this is Arthur. He's in charge of the elves."

"*The* Arthur?"

"Yes."

Lance frowned. "I would have thought Oberon . . ."

"Apparently not."

"He's younger than I imagined him being."

"That's because you *didn't* imagine him." She gestured toward the kids. "They did. Arthur, this is Lance. He's a very confused grad student looking for his professor and a reanimated mummy."

Arthur stared up at the large, blond man and his pale cheeks paled further. "Lance?"

"Yes."

"Du Lac?"

"Benedict."

The Immortal King released the breath he'd been holding. "Thank God."

YOU'RE WELCOME.

THIRTEEN

"You locked Sam in a crate?"

"With both you and your sister missing, I felt responsible for his safety. I asked him to give me his word that he'd remain here, in the store. He wouldn't." Arthur glanced over at Claire, his expression somewhere between concerned and defiant. "I thought I was doing the right thing."

"You were," Claire told him reassuringly. "But that's not actually relevant. If I were you, I'd check your bedding before getting into it and your shoes before putting them on."

A quiet voice murmured "Ooo, shoes . . ." from around ankle height but when Claire looked down, Sam was nowhere to seen.

"Sorry."

Arthur waved it off. "It's all right . . ."

He was lying, but she appreciated the effort.

". . . we have greater troubles now facing us than possible retribution by one annoyed cat."

And if Arthur was very lucky, Sam hadn't heard

that. "So you've armed your people and are about to . . . ?"

"Meet the enemy head on, rescue your sister and my captain, and end this once and for all."

"That's the plan?"

"No, those are our objectives. How we achieve those objectives—that's the plan. Once we have drawn the enemy into battle, Teemo and Kith will take the scout's route in behind their lines and effect the rescue."

"And ending this once and for all?"

"I will be leading my people. Once I am on the darkside, I do not doubt their leader will personally try to kill me. We will meet in battle and in single combat decide the fate of this mall."

Claire stopped walking and turned to stare at Arthur. "I beg your pardon?" She could almost hear Diana asking him if his baseball equipment was cutting off the oxygen supply to his brain.

"I have been in these situations before, Keeper. This is what always happens."

"Yes, and you *lose*."

His smile was almost condescending. "There is no Mordred in this reality."

"Okay, first of all, you don't know that. We don't know who or what is pulling the strings on the darkside. That's what Diana and Kris were supposed to find out instead of getting themselves captured and possibly tortured, and it's all very well for you, but what on earth am I supposed to tell my mother if I come back without her?"

Arthur blinked, glanced back at Lance, who shrugged and finally offered, "Tell her that Diana gave her life in the service of the greater good."

"Uh-huh." Claire chewed a bit of nail polish off her right thumb. "And on a pure Keeper/Cousin level that might work but I'm talking about my little sister and my *mother*." She spat a bit of Midnight Coral out with the last word, then sighed. "I'll be going with Teemo and Kith. If Kris and Diana have been taken by the enemy, there isn't a chance of getting them back without my help."

"Then your help is gratefully accepted."

"Good." They began walking again, skirting the edge of Giftware and cutting through Leather Goods. Given what the elves considered party clothes, Claire wasn't surprised that particular section had been emptied out. "Where was I? Rhetorical question," she added quickly as Lance made an *I know, I know!* kind of noise. "The whole Mordred thing is irrelevant. You're the archetypal symbol for one side, and if you face the archetypal symbol for the other side— we can call it Big Bird if we want to, but it won't make a difference—you'll die. This is the Otherside. I am a Keeper. I believe this, so it *will* happen. If it makes you feel any better, you can blame Mrs. Saint-Germaine and grade eleven English."

"But . . ."

"No."

"If I . . ."

"No."

"It isn't . . ."

"What part of 'no' are you having trouble understanding? You *must not* face the leader of the darkside in combat." Claire ran both hands up through her hair and sighed again. "All at once, I understand exactly how Yoda felt."

"Who?"

"Not important."

Arthur looked as though he was about to protest, then clearly thought better of it. "Okay."

"I'm going to go get changed."

"Petite Sportswear is against the far right-hand wall."

"Thank you. Lance . . ." A half turn to find him smiling down at her. She had a sudden vision of him let loose in the mall and shuddered. ". . . you'd better stay with me."

"Sure! Hang on a minute!"

Since she didn't have a hope of moving him, she folded her arms and waited as he stepped forward, his pale blue eyes locking onto Arthur's azure ones.

"You're the actual Arthur?" he asked.

"I'm a version of the archetypal Arthur."

"Cool! Can I ask you something?"

"Yes."

"What the hell are you doing here?"

The broad brow under the silver band wrinkled. "I am making a fractured people one. I am a leader where there is need."

"But here? In a shopping mall?"

"Yes."

"With elves?"

"Yes."

Lance frowned. "I'm confused."

"You're not the only one." Claire patted him reassuringly on a sunburned forearm. "Come on . . ."

Black stretch pants, black tank, black hood, black running shoes, black belt pouch . . . Claire had no idea if the real-world store carried the same selection, but on the Otherside this was clearly the place for one stop skulking. She either looked like she was going to a very casual funeral or about to fill her evening with a little B&E—she couldn't decide. Maybe both; B&E at a casual funeral . . .

Stop it. Do not think of funerals. You'll get Diana back.

Her hands were shaking as she dropped to tie her laces. "Is this really necessary? Ninja dressing didn't keep Kris and Diana from being captured."

"I totally doubt it was the clothes that got them snagged," Kith snorted, tying off the end of her braid with a black elastic. "You walk the walk, you wear the cloth."

"Excuse me?"

"You gotta dress like you do."

"Yeah. Okay." Communication between seventeen and twenty-seven occasionally took place in two distinct languages. Buckling on the belt pouch, she hurried out of the dressing room in time to smack a piece of chocolate away from Lance's mouth.

"Hey!"

"If you ever want to go back, you can't eat or drink *anything* on this side that you didn't bring with you."

"But I'm hungry!"

Actually, so was she. "I've got food in my pack. Come on."

Her pack was with Diana's, just inside the front door. Claire dragged Lance through the milling crowd of mall elves, tossed him a power bar and a bottle of water, and began filling her belt pouch with preset possibilities.

"I'd send you back to Kingston if I could," she told him, tucking a folded piece of paper behind three glass marbles, "but with the darkside influencing the paths, I can't guarantee where you'd end up."

"I'm willing to take that chance in order to stop Meryat!"

"Since you're the only one who *can* stop Meryat and since she's with Dean, I'm not. We rescue Kris and Diana, we stop the darkside, we stop its influence, I send you to the guest house, you stop Meryat, and . . ."

"We all live happily ever after!"

"Sure. Why not." The small plastic packet of cayenne pepper got slid very carefully up against the flat side of the pouch. "But for now, you'll have to stay here in the store where you'll be safe."

"I'm not afraid to fight!"

"Good. If the store gets attacked, you'll have to." Fortunately, with Arthur out in the mall, there'd be no chance of that. Claire unzipped an outside pocket on Diana's pack, reached into it, and froze as her fingers closed around air. "The wand. Diana took the wand."

"That's bad?"

"When she used it against a minion, it nearly killed her. If she uses it against the darkside . . ."

"But I thought she was captured?"

"So?" It took all of Claire's strength to push that single syllable out against the certain knowledge that her little sister was as good as dead.

"So if it's that powerful, then she didn't get to use it before she was captured. After, well, they'll have taken it away from her so she *can't* use it. Right?"

Claire actually felt time start up again. "Right." For the first time since the beach, she looked at Lance with something other than pique. Like he was something other than an unwanted responsibility. "Thank you."

His cheeks flushed under the sunburn.

"So what's the holdup?" Sam jumped up onto the top of Claire's pack. "Why aren't we moving out?"

She zipped the belt pouch closed. "We?"

Amber eyes narrowed, and his tail traced one long, slow arc from side to side.

"You're right." Claire raised both hands in surrender, ignoring Lance's questioning glance. Some arguments didn't require actual dialogue. "But you're not coming with me because I need you go with Arthur. If he's challenged to single combat, he'll forget everything I've told him about why he shouldn't and leap forward to do what he considers the only honorable thing."

"I want . . ."

"Sam, there has to be someone there to tell him when he's being an idiot and that's one of the things cats do best."

"But Diana . . ."

"Needs my full attention. I can't be worrying about what Arthur's going to do if I'm to have a chance of saving her."

Sam's ears saddled. "You're that sure he'll answer a challenge?"

"I am. It's one of the benefits of working with an archetype." As Arthur climbed up onto the chair, she frowned thoughtfully and added, "Actually, it's pretty much the only benefit."

Arthur stared out at his assembled elves, raised his sword, opened his mouth, and closed it again.

The moment had long passed.

He jerked his head toward the mall. "Let's go."

"So, we're winning, right? And this is part of your plan?"

Diana glanced over at Kris as the surrounding meat-minds shoved them along familiar corridors. "This?"

"Yeah. This." Her gesture took in the meat-minds and the back of the Shadowlord walking up ahead. "You know, being captured and taken back to that . . . hole. 'Cause that's where you want to be, right?"

"Kris, that hole is essentially an entrance to Hell."

"So, as a plan, it sucks. But it *is* a plan, right?"

Since the other girl so clearly needed to hear a specific answer, Diana smiled and lowered her voice. "Yeah, it's a plan. It's not much of one now, but it will be by the time we get there."

"Wicked."

Actually, yes, it being Hell and all, but Diana figured Kris *didn't* need to hear that right now. Closing Hell down in the real world had been difficult enough, closing it on the Otherside without access to the possibilities would be almost impossible. Rules would probably have to be broken. *Hey, it's not like I haven't broken rules before.*

Although not big ones.

Not on purpose anyway.

And intent counted.

I'm intending to save the world. That ought to count for something.

Destroying the bugs had been easy—once she'd plugged the small memory leak—as easy as tripping up the meat-minds by noticing how clumsy they looked. but Hell hadn't given either the bug or the meat-minds substance. People preferred their world to have form and function and by giving darkness definition, they gave it a physical presence. The mall elves had created their own monsters. Giant bugs, skittering around inside the walls, and big, slow-moving guys with short hair, beady eyes, heavy guts and hands that were too big for their bodies.

The mall elves had been street kids before they found their way through to the Otherside.

The meat-minds were broad stereotypes of bad cops.

Maybe we should throw coffee and donuts at them. Answer one bad stereotype with another.

"You just had an idea."

"What?"

Kris dug her elbow into Diana's side with unconcealed glee. "You grinned. And your eyes were gleaming. You just had an idea. Hey, you! Piece of Hell Guy!" She raised her voice. "My girl's gonna kick your Metamucil ass!"

He turned, his expression so affronted Diana couldn't stop herself from laughing. "My what?"

"I think you meant metaphysical," she murmured into an elven ear.

"Metaphysical, metamorphosis, metronome, *The Metropolis Daily Planet!*" Kris snorted. "The *point* is the ass kicking."

His lip curled. "The point is that you are my prisoners, and I know a great many ways to make you scream."

Remember the meaning of enough, Diana pleaded silently with Kris. *If you push him too far . . .* She'd only get one chance to use the wand and the last thing she wanted to do was weigh the life of one beautiful, funny, interested girl against the world.

And, for a change, it really *was* the last thing she wanted to do.

When neither Keeper nor elf responded, he nodded, turned, and the whole procession began moving again.

About five minutes of shoving later, Kris sighed.
"I should've said it'd take more than an old white
guy to make me scream. Wrong color. Wrong gender.
Wrong wang."

"Yeah, you always think of the good lines when
it's too late."

"Truth."

"Wang?"

"You know." She pumped her hand at her crotch.

"Ah. Wang."

By the time they reached the cavern, the wand had
slid out from under her waistband and started down
her right leg. It would have slid farther, but one of
the points got caught on the leg elastic of her underwear. Diana half expected Hell to say, *Is that a wand
in your pocket or are you just happy to see me*, but the
pit remained silent as they were marched toward it.

She'd only get one chance.

One.

As the meat-minds released them, the Shadowlord
stepped back and wrapped long pale fingers around
their upper arms, dragging them to the edge.

Diana could feel Hell watching her. She was going
to need a diversion. Meanwhile, there was no point
in cowering. "So . . ." Given the way the hair was
raising off the back of her neck in reaction to Hell's
attention, bored was a bit more than she could man-

age but—thank God for being seventeen—insolent was no problem. ". . . what are you going to do with us?"

WHAT DO YOU THINK?

"Don't tell me. Not the virgin sacrifice again."

APPARENTLY NOT.

Hell sounded put out about her moral failings? "Oh, ha ha."

THANK YOU. I'VE ALWAYS PRIDED MYSELF ON MY SENSE OF HUMOR.

"That explains a whole lot about Comedy Central."

HEY, DON'T BLAME JON STEWART ON ME. I DON'T EVEN GET CABLE.

"Well, it's *Hell*."

AND YET YOUR LOT ALWAYS SEEM SO SUR-PRISED WHEN I TRY TO EXPAND MY HORIZONS.

"You're trying to take over the world for cable?"

NOT *JUST* CABLE. YOU MAKE IT SOUND SO PETTY.

"Sorry."

NO, YOU'RE NOT.

Diana sighed. "You're right. I'm not sorry." She tried to yank her arm free without success and sighed again. "Could we get on with it?"

IT?

"The part where you gloat about what you're going to do to us."

YOU'RE IN A HURRY?

"I just thought we should get it out of the way."

She leaned forward far enough to catch Kris' eye around the Shadowlord's black-clad body. "It's in the Rules."

"Gloating?"

"Yeah."

"I always wondered. And the giant snow-cone machine?"

Diana grinned. She was so definitely in love. "That's optional."

YOU'RE BAIT!

That's what she'd been half afraid of. But this was not the place to let fear show. "Sorry?"

YOUR SISTER WILL COME FOR YOU AND THE IMMORTAL KING WILL COME FOR HER. UNPREPARED TO FACE ME, THEY WILL BE DESTROYED.

There was her diversion.

While Hell's attention was on the destruction of Arthur and Claire, she'd take her one shot with the wand and pour everything she had into closing the hole.

And it would take everything, too.

As plans went, it sucked—worst case scenario left the ground littered with bodies—but at least now she *had* a plan.

"I'm after having second thoughts about this plan. That is one pissed-off basilisk!"

Austin smacked at another bit of rolling canvas. "You're surprised? You don't go zipping mythological creatures into hockey bags and expect them to be pleased about it." He dug his claws into the upholstery as Dean turned the truck into the guest house driveway. "Later, when we've got the time, remind me to tell you about what happened when Claire stuffed a pixie into her purse."

"Messy?"

"In a manner of speaking." The truck rocked forward and back, the jerky stop giving Austin some indication of the state of Dean's mind. He didn't really *care* about the state of Dean's mind, but he had a pretty good idea of what was going on up there. "You're wondering if you can go through with this."

"Yeah."

"You're concerned because, sure she's an evil, life-sucking mummy, but is that any reason to turn her to stone."

"Yeah."

"And you're thinking that a life-sized statue of a reanimated corpse is not only going to destroy the ambiance of the guest house but will probably gouge the hell out of the hardwood floors when you try to move it."

"I'm *not* thinking ambiance!"

Austin took a swipe at the immaculate white fur on his shoulder. "Too many syllables for you?"

"I'm thinking . . ."

As the pause extended, he looked up to see Dean clutching the sides of the steering wheel, his head bowed and resting against the top curve. "Stop."

"Stop what?"

"Stop thinking." He stood, stretched, smacked the

hockey bag again, and put his paw on Dean's thigh. "Look, you're just a Bystander and you should never have had to deal with anything stranger than laundry instructions. That said—although I'll call you a liar if you ever repeat this—you're dealing with it admirably. Just *keep* dealing with it and you'll be fine."

"I don't look like a man who's in over his head . . . OW!"

Austin retracted his claws and muttered, "You look like a man with blood on his jeans and a basilisk in a hockey bag. Get over yourself and let's get on with this. I'm hot, I'm hungry, and I'm missing Oprah."

The guest house was cool and quiet as Dean pushed open the back door. With the curtains pulled across the dining room's big windows, the sun hadn't had a chance to heat things up. And that was good because the air outside was rapidly approaching dry roast. He wasn't so sure about the shadows, though; they made the place look mysterious, spooky even and, all things considered, that wasn't exactly reassuring.

Grunting as a tail or a foot or a wing or *something* caught him in the stomach, he heaved the hockey bag up onto the dining room table. Then grabbed it as the basilisk's struggles sent it skittering across the highly polished surface. Okay, maybe he had gone a little overboard with the wax.

"Dean."

Heart in his throat, he whirled around. "Jaysus, Dr. Rebik, don't be sneaking up on me like that!"

The old man managed half a smile. "Sorry."

Old man.

They'd been gone for—Dean glanced down at his watch—just over two and a half hours. In that time, Dr. Rebik had aged a good thirty years. Actually, a *bad* thirty years.

He blinked rheumy eyes. "What's in the bag?"

"You know, word was, Dean McIssac couldn't lie to save his life."

"Well, it's uh . . ."

"Personal," Austin snapped. "Just a little cat business Dean's helping me out with." He stalked past the professor, tossing an imperious, "Let's *go*, Dean," back over one shoulder.

Dean shrugged apologetically, picked up the bag, and started to follow, his eyes flicking back and forth from one shadow to another. If Dr. Rebik was here, the obvious question became, where was Meryat?

Right on cue, she stepped out of the shadows, blocking his way. He could push past her, even though she looked significantly less dead than she had, he was still twice her size. But that would be rude. Clutching the handles of the hockey bag in suddenly sweaty hands, he stopped.

"You seem distracted, Mr. McIssac." She smiled. Her lips went almost all the way around her mouth. "Were you looking for me?"

*   *   *

"What's he looking for?"

"Us." Teemo squirmed a little farther into the shadows, only stopping when Kith squeaked a protest. "Well, not like totally us. But, you know, *us*."

Claire frowned and peered out past the elves at the elderly security guard. "He's not even in this reality."

"Doesn't matter. He's got this kind of . . ."

"Teenager sense," Kith finished. "It's like he hates us, and that helps him find us."

"Really?" She could feel her eyes narrowing all on their own.

"Yeah. Really. He's the freakiest thing in here, and that's saying something."

But exactly *what* it was saying, Claire wasn't certain. Had the old man been changed as the mall changed? Over the years, had he allowed his job to define him until he became his job and the job became his definition of reality? Was there darkness enough in him that the darkside had been able to hire him to work the segue as well as the original mall?

Using *hire* in the broadest sense of the word.

"Fuck, he's coming this way!"

He was. Then he paused and turned and stared into the shadows where Arthur's army was hiding.

Trying to hide.

There were too many of them for the nooks and crannies of the concourse to hold, so they stood and silently watched the old man approach. As the beam of light swept up, three of the skateboarders sped out from under the stairs.

Drawing his fire.

As she watched them cut the concourse into wild patterns, staying inches ahead of the light, she realized, for the first time, that the good guys might stand a chance. This was their mall now and although they were going to take on the darkside with skateboards and baseball bats, they believed they could do it. On the Otherside, belief was everything.

Two of the boarders went over the beam. The third went under.

Now, *she* believed they could do it.

Given who she was and where they were, that might be enough.

And it might not, but the point is they're farther ahead than they were . . . oh no.

Someone zigged when he should have zagged. Golden hair blazed out under the edge of the helmet as the light caught one of the elves, holding him in place six inches off the end of the metal bench. Stewart. Half a heartbeat later, both Stewart and the old man were gone.

"Where . . . ?"

"We think he'll go back to the other mall." Kith sounded very young as she stepped out of the shadows. "But we don't know for sure."

Across the concourse, Arthur's army began to move out.

Claire looked for Sam but couldn't see him in the

crowd. She did see Jo raise her bat to the place Stewart disappeared. From the look on her face, the security guard should thank any gods willing to listen that he *wasn't* in this reality and that Jo could never cross back.

But I can.

Claire added another note to her mental to-do list—after *rescue Diana* and *save the world* but before *pick up dry cleaning.*

"Come on." A hand on skinny shoulders got her escort's attention. "Let's do this."

IT BEGINS.

The declaration jerked Diana up out of her slump, spilling Kris' head off her shoulder. "What does?"

WHAT DO YOU THINK? *IT!*

"Right." It. The battle. Her diversion. She shuffled around toward Kris, using the motion to cover an attempt to move the wand a little farther up her leg. "You okay?"

"Oh, yeah, fuckin' great. I wasn't asleep."

"Okay."

"I was just . . . you know."

Looking for an excuse to cuddle. Diana grinned. "Okay."

Kris flipped her dreads back off her face and sighed. "You have to sound so smug?"

"Pretty much, yeah." Keeping her back against the wall of the cavern, she got to her feet and held a hand down to the elf.

"So this where all Hell breaks loose?"

Someone had to say it, Diana reminded herself. It wasn't exactly a Rule. Some things didn't have to be. "Not yet."

With any luck, not ever.

Leaning out around the quartet of meat-minds left to guard them, she watched as the Shadowlord came into the cavern—not walking, *striding*, and being pretty da . . . darned obvious about it, too. Over the whole black-on-black wardrobe, he was wearing greaves, vambraces, and a polished breastplate. Also in black. He pulled his sword—not black, Diana was happy to note, although it wasn't like he hadn't already beat the theme to death—and knelt by the edge of the pit.

"Is it time?"

IT IS. ARE YOU READY?

"I am."

"Who writes their dialogue," Kris muttered as the Shadowlord stood, his blade lifted in salute.

Diana had a witty comeback ready, but it slipped off her tongue. The Shadowlord's hair, definitely blond on all other occasions, was looking more than just a little red. It might have been reflected light from the pit, but she had a horrible feeling he was about to earn a name.

Given who he'll be fighting, three guesses as to what name and the first two don't count.

Sam trotted along at Arthur's heels, vaguely aware that this wasn't the first time he'd gone to war— Angels being soldiers of the Lord and all that. He just wished he could remember more of his life before he became a cat. Well, he remembered the few days he'd been essentially a human teenage male, but since that had mostly involved being confused, hungry, and obsessed with genitalia, it wasn't a lot of help.

He would rather have been with Claire, rescuing Diana. He would rather have been *with* Diana right from the start, but no one ever listened to him.

This made his ability to stop Arthur from doing a little one-on-one whacking with the Big Bad just a little suspect. The access to higher knowledge he retained in this form was no help at all.

So.

What would Austin do?

"The trick in getting them to listen is making sure you've got their attention before you start."

"But how?"

Austin stretched out a front leg and flexed the paw. His claws sank a quarter inch into the sofa cushion. "Use your imagination, kid. That's what it's there for."

Well, if a cat could look at a king, he supposed it was only a small step from there to leaving scars. Feeling more confident, he began memorizing the places Arthur's padding didn't quite cover. Just in case things got unpleasant.

"Did you have a pleasant time at the shopping mall, Dean?" Meryat's voice was low and musical, her movements graceful, even considering she was still more than half corpse.

Dr. Rebik stared at her in open-mouthed fascination.

Dean stared in horror.

Austin seemed to have disappeared.

"You seem to have done some shopping," she continued, her eyes following the movements of the hockey bag. "Is it another kitty?" Her arm whipped forward with snakelike speed and one finger poked the canvas. The answering squawk was more indignant than pained. "No, not a kitty. If I didn't know better, I'd say you'd bought yourself a chicken."

Dean really didn't like the way she'd emphasized *If I didn't know better . . .* His grip tightened around the straps of the bag, the wrapped canvas growing damp under his fingers.

"Why don't you show me?"

Okay. He thrust the bag toward her. Austin's plan had involved getting Dr. Rebik out of their room, leaving the bag outside the door for her to find, assuming she'd go after the life force of whatever was in it. She'd drag it inside, and open it, never suspecting a Bystander capable of delivering a mythological creature capable of turning her to stone. The threat of life sucking would be over and the basilisk would be safely contained until Claire came home.

Still, as long as he closed his eyes and got Dr. Rebik to close his eyes *and* assumed that Austin was somewhere safe, this should do as plan B. Given that the basilisk had been hiding out in a shopping mall with minimal statuary happening, it clearly preferred hiding over stoning. Stoneage. Turning people to stone.

Meryat pushed the bag back toward him. "You open it."

That would make things a little trickier.

Meryat was a foot shorter than he was, slim, and not entirely alive. If he shoved her out of his way, could she stop him? If he shoved her into the wall, was she still brittle enough to break?

"You can't, you know."

Dean swallowed and found his voice. "I can't what, then?"

"Just charge past me." His eyes widened and she smiled. "No, I'm not reading your mind; I'm reading your face. Everything you're thinking, everything you're feeling is right out there."

"You don't ever hit someone smaller than you."

"What about Brad Mackenzie? He's smaller than me, but he's plays for St. Pat's, and if I don't hit him, we'll . . ."

His grandfather sighed. "All right, fine. You don't ever hit someone smaller than you unless they're wearing hockey skates."

From the way Meryat was smiling, that had shown on his face, too. He was some screwed because he'd never get her into hockey skates.

"Every hero needs a fatal flaw. Now, for the last time, Dean, open the bag."

"And what if I'm after saying no?"

"Then I'll suck my darling Dr. Rebik dry, right in front of you." A gesture brought the archeologist around to her side. She slid a slender arm through his and smiled. "Your choice."

Dean set the hockey bag down on the kitchen counter and began fumbling with the zipper. "She's killing you, you know!"

Dr. Rebik matched Meryat's smile. "I die of love."

"Yeah, right . . ." The bit of basilisk he'd caught back in the food court was jamming the zipper closed. If he kept his eyes shut . . .

Would Claire be able to fix him if he was turned to stone?

If she couldn't, would she put him out in the garden?

Would pigeons shit on his head?

It'd be sea gulls back home, so he supposed pigeons would be an improvement.

"Are you stalling, Dean?"

Dr. Rebik moaned low in his throat and a patch of hair fell out, slid down the curve of his head and off his bowed shoulder to the floor.

"I'm going as fast as I can!" he cried, yanking at the zipper and fighting the urge to go for the whisk broom and dustpan. "It's stuck!"

"I see. We'll just have to . . ."

Out in the office, the phone rang.

"Where are you going?"

"I'm after answering . . ."

"No."

"But this is a business," Dean protested indignantly. "You can't be letting the phone ring!"

"I can and I will."

Four rings. Five. Six.

The machine should have picked up on five. As it didn't . . . "Look, it's Claire's mum. As long as there's someone here, it won't stop ringing."

Meryat frowned thoughtfully. "Is the Keeper's mother also a Keeper?"

"No!"

Seven rings. Eight.

The frown lines deepened with a faint crinkling sound. "Then how does she know there's someone here?"

"Claire's her daughter!" Which was the absolute truth. Maybe not the whole truth but the truth, so with any luck at all, that whole lousy lying thing wouldn't come into it.

Nine rings. Ten. Eleven. Twelve.

"This grows very annoying. Go!" A fingernail flew off with the expansive force of her gesture. "Answer it!"

Dean took two grateful steps toward the office.

"Mr. McIssac, aren't you forgetting something?"

Biting back a curse, he returned for the hockey bag.

Thirteen rings. Fourteen. Fifteen.

Closely followed by Meryat and Dr. Rebik—too closely followed as far as Dean was concerned—he set the bag on the desk and reached for the phone.

Sixteen.

"Elysian Fields Guest House."

"Dean, it's Martha Hansen. I've got this terrible feeling that the girls are in trouble. Not that the girls being in trouble is ever a good feeling, but this is remarkably strong considering that they're still on the Otherside and I'm worried. You haven't heard from them, have you? That's not why you were so long answering?"

"Uh, no, it's not." He had no idea what, if anything a Cousin could do over the phone, but this was his one chance to get help. "You just called at a bad time. There's . . ."

". . . no need for further explanations," Meryat said as Dr. Rebik's shaking finger came down on the disconnect. "The noise has been stopped, and we have business to conclude." She glanced around the office, and her eyes narrowed. "Although this is not the best place; we could be interrupted, and that has already happened once too often."

Dean suddenly realized she wasn't talking about the phone. "Lance."

"Yes. When my binding came undone, he was partially caught by my counterspell. It seems to have unbalanced him."

"He's not Australian," Dr. Rebik announced calmly.

Meryat rolled her eyes. "He might as well be. Now then, I think we'll take this someplace more private." Her gaze traveled slowly down the length of Dean's body and he shuddered. Before Claire and he had . . created an angel, he'd never noticed that sort of thing. After, he realized—to his intense embarrassment—it had happened a lot. "Let's go to your bedroom."

Suddenly, being a statue didn't look like such a bad future.

He only hoped Claire remembered to dust him.

*   *   *

Claire stifled a sneeze against her shoulder unable to believe the amount of dust in the dropped ceiling. She stopped herself from wondering where it came from before the Otherside provided an answer, and concentrated on crawling after Teemo's narrow backside.

Fortunately, Diana had already taken this route, so she didn't need to worry about securing its reality.

The drop down into the bathroom was a little farther than she was comfortable with. One foot slid off the edge of the soap dispenser and into the sink, but Kith steadied her as she landed, averting disaster with a steady grip above both knees.

The room smelled of cleaners and disinfectants, and all at once she missed Dean so badly it was like a physical ache. In fact, it wasn't *like* a physical ache at all. It was a physical ache. Austin would do what he could, but a reanimated mummy was a just a little beyond what snark and sympathy could hope to deal with.

She had to defeat the darkside and return to them before it was too late. Or get Lance to them if that was all she could manage.

Save the world.

Save Diana.

Save Dean.

At least this time, there'd be no nasty surprises in the final inning.

And that was an unprovoked sports metaphor. Even her subconscious missed Dean. At one time, she'd thought maintaining a relationship would be a distraction. It wasn't, it was a goal. Something she could use as incentive to charge right through the worst the possibilities could offer.

Memo to self, she sighed, following Kith and Teemo out into the hall, *watch a little less Oprah with the cat*.

They were almost to the food court when a rumble of thunder flattened them back against the wall, Teemo raising an unnecessary finger to his lips.

No. Not thunder. Meat-minds. A whole herd of them pounding purposefully past the food court in ranks that were more or less even. Claire thought very hard about saving the world; thinking about how clumsy they looked would only set up a chain reaction of vaudevillian proportions and give away their position.

Bringing up the rear between four meat-minds more defined than the rest was a vaguely familiar warrior dressed and armored all in black. His skin was milk pale and his hair a deep red. Really red. Blood red. Bad fantasy cliché red.

That couldn't be good. Claire sent a silent plea that Sam remembered what he had to do.

On the bright side, if their leader had taken the field, both Diana and the segue would be minimally guarded. Pulling Kith and Teemo closer, she whispered, "From here, I go on alone."

"No way, Keeper. Arthur . . ."

". . . is going to need you. You saw the size of the army he's facing; pull some weapons from that sporting goods store, and attack from the rear. Remember, as soon as I shut down the segue, the meat-minds will fall apart, so you don't have to win so much as you have to not lose."

"What?"

Okay. That hadn't made a lot of sense to her either. "Look, I usually work alone. I clearly suck at motivational speaking. Just be careful." She put a hand on each of their shoulders, squeezed lightly, then turned and raced down the hall toward the Emporium.

They hadn't come through the store. The plywood construction barricade was gone; in its place was a dark tunnel leading down under the mall.

Only one meat-mind on guard.

He saw her, turned, and, because she believed he would, tripped over his own feet.

Getting past him was as easy as dropping a marble on his head.

The passage ended in what was obviously a throne room. Kicking through bits of shattered chitin, Claire approached the dais where she found, amid the broken insect bits, a tampon lying crushed and forgotten.

Diana.

She paused and quickly checked her memory of the charging meat-mind army. Well, the odds were very good it was Diana's anyway.

A few scorch marks against the polished stone showed where preset possibilities had been destroyed. None of them looked large enough or scorched enough to have been the wand.

Then there was a chance Diana still had it.

Definitely a good news/bad news scenario.

Only one exit from the throne room. A stone corridor leading even farther down. The moment she stepped into it, Claire felt a familiar pull.

Running as quietly as she could under the flickering torches, Claire hurried toward it. This wasn't her Summoning. She shouldn't be feeling a pull, familiar or otherwise.

It was possible that she was sensing Diana's presence by the segue.

But she didn't think so.

FOURTEEN

Diana could feel the power fluctuations. They filled the cavern, rippling from side to side, up and down, raising all the hair on her body. Not exactly a pleasant feeling. They were strong enough that she suspected she could see them if she just unfocused her eyes the right way.

The good news was they weren't all coming from the pit.

Most, but not all.

Some of them were coming from her.

Some from outside the cavern.

She felt it the moment the armies joined. Felt it as the weight of Hell's attention grew lighter. Soon.

Only one small problem.

She stood, stretched, and beckoned for Kris to join her. "There's a few thing I'd like to do before we die."

Which was the absolute truth and always the best way to deal with Hell. No point playing in its court.

I'M SURE THERE ARE, Hell snarked as Kris put

her hand in Diana's and allowed herself to be pulled to her feet. BUT YOU CAN'T DESTROY ME, AND IF YOU TRY, I WILL MAKE YOU VERY VERY SORRY. I NEED YOU ALIVE AS BAIT, BUT I DO NOT NEED YOU UNHARMED.

Hands on Kris' hips, Diana snorted in the general direction of the pit. "It's not always about you, dude."

The kiss had a touch of desperation about it—the odds were extremely good this would be one of their last, after all—and things heated up a little past the point where brain cells started to fry. Somehow, Diana managed to keep a small fraction of her mind on something other than the way Kris' lips felt under hers and got them turned around until the mall elf's body was between hers and the pit. Chewing along her jaw, Diana sucked the lobe of a pointed ear into her mouth and murmured, "Slide your hand down the back of my pants!"

And let's hear it for enthusiasm.

"Farther . . . oh, yeah . . . no . . . down the leg." Diana squelched a sudden desire to giggle at what sounded like bad porn dialogue. "The other leg."

As Kris' fingers touched the top of the wand, she stiffened, suddenly realizing what this was about. From the way she began to pull back, she wasn't entirely happy about it either.

Diana tightened her grip and yanked their bodies into even closer contact. Licking her way around the inner curve of Kris' ear, she sighed, "If I survive this, I promise I'll make it up to you."

Kris' answer was an emphatic wriggle.

Probably trying to get a better grip on the wand.

Probably . . .

She could feel the wand begin to move up her thigh, toward her waistband and couldn't resist. "Oh, yes! Yes! That's it!"

OH, FOR . . . GET A ROOM!

Staying close to Arthur wasn't easy. The Immortal King moved through the battle with archetypal skills and the flexibility of a teenager. Sam did the best he could, and if he took a few detours to avoid being pounded into marmalade-colored kitty paste, well, he figured he was entitled. Squashed flat was not a good defensive position.

The trick was to see the pattern of the battle and then become a part of it.

The trouble was that his part of the pattern took him across the concourse at the same time Arthur's brought him face-to-face with the tall redhead in the so cliché black armor. Who was very definitely not a meat-mind. And who looked vaguely familiar.

The hair rose along Sam's spine.

He leaped a fallen elf and darted between two massive legs. He had to get to Arthur before . . .

"What say you? Your sword against mine. Let us leave the young and the stupid out of what we both know is our battle." The redhead's voice filled a lull in the fighting; everyone froze for a heartbeat, then dark and light turned to face the middle of the concourse.

Sam raced up and over a planter and found himself peddling air as Will grabbed him and clutched him tight against his hockey jersey.

"Put me down!"

"Shhh, it's a challenge."

"I know it's a challenge! I have to . . ."

"You have to wait," Will said, cutting him off. "When a challenge has been made, everything stops until it's been answered."

The mall elf didn't add that it was a Rule, but then, he didn't have to. Sam could feel the Rule holding elves and meat-minds both in place. Fortunately, he was neither.

"Put me down, or I'll add a few new piercings to your nose."

"What?"

A claw hooked into the inside of Will's left nostril.

"Right."

And Sam was back on the floor.

"So, do you accept my challenge?"

Arthur's back was to him. Sam had no way of knowing what his answer would be, but something in the redhead's pale eyes suggested he was about to get the response he desired. Too far away to stop Arthur from speaking, Sam did the only thing he could. "I accept!"

Everyone blinked in unison.

The redhead recovered first. "I was not speaking to you, cat."

"Should've been more specific, then." Sam walked

out into the open space between the two, sat down, and washed his shoulder.

Arthur shook himself and took his eyes off the redhead for the first time since the battle had brought them face to face. "Sam, you can't . . ."

"And I won't!" the redhead snorted.

"I can and you will." Sam stood and stretched, butt in the air. "The challenge has been made and answered. You can deal with him . . ." A jerk of his head toward Arthur. ". . . later, but the Rules say you have to deal with me first."

"The Rules . . ."

"You break them, we get to break them. Up to you, crud for brains, but you know who's here and you know what she's able to do if you give her the chance."

The redhead frowned and suddenly squatted, peering into Sam's face. "I get the feeling we have fought before, you and I. A long time ago, before all . . ." His gesture managed to encompass the elves, the meat-minds, the mall, Arthur, and their own bodies. ". . . this."

"Well, at least one of us has come up in the world," Sam snorted. "We gonna fight, or were you planning on talking me to death."

"When I kill you," the redhead purred, straightening, "I will have my name. I will use the subsequent death of the Immortal King to gain the kind of power that will cause whole kingdoms to tremble before me!"

"Subsequent death? You pick up that word-of-the-day toilet paper at the Emporium?"

"No, at the stationery shop."

"Ah."

"Sam." Arthur stepped forward, Excalibur a gleaming silver line across his body. "I can't let you do this."

"You have no choice," the redhead snarled, shifted his weight, and swung.

Sam leaped left. Then right. Then left. Then up and over another planter.

"Damn it, cat! Hold still!"

"You think I'm going to hold still because *you* want me to?" Sam ricocheted off a meat-mind and folded back on himself. "You're not only evil," he snorted, raking his claws across the redhead's wrist as he rocketed by, "you're not too bright. . . ."

"You, turn on the lights." As Dr. Rebik stretched a palsied hand toward the switch, Meryat sat down on the edge of the bed. "You, put the bag on the floor and open it."

"I don't think," Dean began, searching for a protest that would carry some weight.

"Good. You're not supposed to think. You're supposed to do as I say." She smiled and brushed dry, brittle hair back off her face with fingertips that were still a little black. "So what did I say?"

"Put the bag on the floor."

"Do it." Her hand closed around Dr. Rebik's arm.

"Or have you forgotten the consequences? He dies, and it's all your fault."

There had to be a way out of this. There had to be. Unfortunately, Dean had no idea of what it was. Coming up with a last minute solution wasn't in his job description. Run the guesthouse. No problem. Anchor Claire in the real world. Got it covered. Get a high enough gloss on the dining room table that he could stop nagging about coasters. Almost there. He even did windows. Pull a brilliant plan out of nowhere just as things were about to land in the crapper—not likely.

Where was Austin? The wardrobe door was open about six inches. Was he inside? Waiting for the perfect moment?

Dean set the writhing bag on the floor.

Meryat smiled. He really wished she'd stop doing that—although all things considered, her teeth were remarkably good. "Open it."

Austin needed to hurry it up. They were rapidly running out of perfect moments.

Dean dropped to one knee—the last thing he wanted was to be bending over the bag as the basilisk emerged—closed his eyes, and yanked the zipper open.

The scream of an enraged cat filled all the empty spaces in the room. Adrenaline surged through Dean's body demanding flight or fight and getting neither. He jerked his eyes open in time to see a scaled tail disappear into the wardrobe.

Austin leaped from chair, to dresser, to the top of the wardrobe and sat there looking smug. "The half with the brain is a chicken," he said.

"You do realize that a basilisk would have no effect on me," Meryat murmured conversationally.

"Obviously not," Austin purred in much the same tone.

"But since there's one available, I was thinking that turning Dean here to stone would reverberate through their bond and bring the Keeper racing back believing she was about to face a basilisk."

"Whereas sucking Dean dry would bring her back prepared to face you."

"Exactly. While she's dealing with the lesser threat, I will . . ."

". . . suck her dry and regain youth, beauty, and power in one fell swoop."

"What a smart kitty you are. I think the Keeper might miss *you* more. Get down from there."

"Or you'll what?" Austin snorted. "Suck Dean dry? You're going to do that anyway. Kill Dr. Rebik? Talk to someone who cares."

"I see cats haven't changed much in three thousand years."

He looked seriously affronted. "Why should we?"

"Excellent point. All right, if you won't cooperate, I suppose I'll have to return to my original plan. Dean, get the creature out of the wardrobe. Try to pick an attractive pose; you'll be holding it for very long time."

Turned to stone, he'd have a chance at being

turned back when Claire kicked mummy butt. With his life sucked out . . . Dean glanced back at Dr. Rebik who seemed to have fallen asleep propped up against the wall. He stood and headed for the wardrobe where he found seventeen pairs of shoes, a crumpled pile of Claire's clothes . . .

"What are you doing?" Meryat demanded.

"Hanging things up."

"Well, stop it!"

. . . but no basilisk.

The wardrobe was Claire's usual access to the Otherside. He'd used it himself once, following the path Claire had laid down. But this time, Claire'd crossed over in the mall, so no path. No escape for him. Apparently, basilisks were mythological enough to make their own way over. Dean pressed his hand flat against the back wall, the wood rough and reassuring under his palm. *That's it, Lassie* . . . Collies. Basilisks. Whatever. . . . *bring back help*.

Oh, Hel . . . p. Claire stood at the entrance to a huge circular cavern and stared at the pit in the middle of it. No wonder the power fluctuations seemed so familiar. *Been there. Done that. Should've got the T-shirt.*

Not a segue, a hole. A hole capped only by an incomplete segue. The moment the segue was finished, Hell itself would have unlimited access to four acres of suburban Kingston. Which was *not* a redundant observation, no matter how much Claire hated the suburbs.

The problem was: how did she close a hole to Hell

without access to the possibilities? Marbles and spices were not going to be enough.

The wand.

If Diana still had it, it was their only chance.

If.

Belief in this instance would accomplish nothing, but as it would do no harm, Claire decided to believe, with all her heart, that Diana had the wand.

She leaned a little farther around the edge of the cavern entrance and finally spotted her sister by the side wall. Not injured. Not even confined. Her hands were wrapped around various bits of Kris and Kris' hand were . . . actually, Claire couldn't see what Kris' hands were doing, but the result seemed to be a fair bit of wiggling. Neither of them seemed too upset by their captivity.

TEENAGERS, Hell sighed. If the pit had eyes, they'd have been rolling.

The groping had to be part of Diana's plan.

Forcing Hell to underestimate her.

Lulling Hell into a false sense of security.

Convincing Hell there would be no attack.

Of course, there was always the possibility that Hell was right and, when faced with their imminent death, the two girls had decided to get in one last . . .

No.

At the very least, they were creating a distraction. She'd have never gotten this close unchallenged had the darkside been paying attention.

Time to return the favor.

The cayenne pepper in one hand, a marble in the other, Claire sprinted for the edge of the pit.

She made it about two thirds of the way.

One of the wand's points had snagged on the inside of Diana's black stretch pants and wriggling didn't seem to be freeing it.

"Harder!" she growled, her mouth against Kris' ear.

"I don't want to hurt you!"

"I can take it!"

OKAY, UNDER THE CIRCUMSTANCES, I HAVE TO SAY THAT THIS IS INAPPROPRIATE BEHA . . . AH!

Between one heartbeat and the next, Diana felt the power fluctuations stop and the cavern fill with a grid of dark bands. She saw Claire snatched up into the air and held writhing. She heard Hell begin to laugh.

Then the wand ripped free.

She met Claire's eyes.

Said a silent good-bye.

And shoved Kris out of the way.

With its pink star pointed toward the pit, the wand bucked in Diana's hand like a living thing, fighting to find the possibilities through the power of Hell.

Hell's first attack slammed her to her knees. The pain of impact almost broke her concentration, but four years of enforced PE lent her strength. If she could work through the pain of field hockey, she could work through this.

Had to work through this.

She touched the edges of the possibilities.

Not enough.

Hell's second attack slid shadows through her mind.

THEY WILL PAY FOR EVERY MOMENT YOU FIGHT ME!

Images of Claire, of Kris, of her parents, of Sam broken and bleeding.

With Hell's attention split, Claire managed to open her hand although she broke a finger doing it. The marble rolled from her palm, fell too slowly to the stone, and shattered.

Brilliant white light burned the shadows away.

It only lasted for an instant.

It lasted just long enough.

Free of the darkness, Diana touched the possibilities and threw herself open to them. No fear. No doubt. No regrets.

This had been her Summoning not because she was closest but because she was youngest and most powerful.

All that she was.

The end of the wand erupted. Streams of pink luminescence sizzled and danced their way down into the pit.

NO!

Diana reluctantly admitted to a brief moment of sympathy—it *was* disturbingly pink.

Then the pink began to mute as lines of gray snaked up from the pit, twisting and spiraling around the light toward the wand. Toward her hand. Toward her heart.

HA! NOT GOOD ENOUGH.

Blood in her mouth. The taste of iron. Her vision began to blur.

"Get . . . stuffed."

Her Summoning because she was youngest and nothing but possibilities.

All that she would be.

Bubble gum pink. Barbie pink.

The scent of brimstone disappeared. The flickering red light against the cavern's roof began to brighten.

The pit began to fill with glittering, gleaming, shimmering, incandescent pink.

Diana could no longer tell where her hand stopped and the wand began. At the edge of her vision, she saw Claire fall, missed her impact with the floor, but saw the remaining shadows given form. Had to trust her sister would stop them. At this point, she could no more stop the flow of possibilities than Hell could.

She didn't realize she was moving until her toes stubbed hard against the edge of the pit.

IF I GO, YOU GO WITH ME!

Well, duh.

All she was, all she would be, given to save the

world. How hard was that to understand? It was, after all, what Keepers *did*. Evil had a distinct tendency to keep missing the obvious.

She wasn't so much falling forward as moving through the wand.

And then . . .

. . . falling back.

She saw Kris poised on the edge of the pit, the wand raised in a defiant fist.

Saw her totter.

Saw her fall.

Pink light filled the cavern.

When Diana could see again, the pit was closed.

Someone, she thought it might be her, threw themselves forward, pounded bloody fists against solid rock, and screamed "No!"

There were Rules to follow, after all.

The problem was, Sam couldn't just run. The Rules said he had to engage in battle or he wasn't actually answering the challenge. The problem was, although he had *more* pointy bits, he was fighting a Shadowlord with a great big sword.

He zigged.

The Shadowlord zagged.

A great big sword *and* opposable thumbs.

Dangling by the scruff of his neck, Sam struggled to fold himself in half and get a claw into the hand holding him. Shrieking defiance, he felt the sword begin to descend.

Flash of silver.

He felt the impact reverberate through fingers buried painfully deep in his fur. Hissed and spat as he was thrown aside.

Twisting in the air, he landed on his feet. Tail lashing, singing his challenge, he spun around.

"Let it go, Sam. I am permitted to intervene at the last instant in order to save the life of my champion." Arthur stared over his blade at the Shadowlord. "Let's get it on." When his opponent looked confused, he sighed and translated. "It's our fight now."

Not quite human teeth flashed in a brilliant smile. "I have always killed you."

"Yeah, yeah. That was then."

"Fear me."

"Bite me."

Sam had to admit the dialogue was less than archetypal. Maybe, hopefully, *possibly* that would be enough.

Or not.

As swords clashed overhead, hilt caught on hilt, body slammed against body. Eight inches from the floor, his angle unique, Sam saw the Shadowlord pull the dagger from his belt. Saw a black-clad elbow pull back. Slam forward.

My bad.

His failure.

I'm sorry. I'm sorry. I'm sorry.

Then the world turned pink.

Really, really, *really* pink.

When he could see again, the Shadowlord had vanished and Arthur was standing with Excalibur over his head, hips canted back, staring down at a hole in his chest protector.

The circle of mall elves seemed frozen in place as Sam crept forward. "Are you . . . ? Did he . . . ?"

Holding his position, moving only his left arm, Arthur slid a finger into the rent.

Pulled it out again.

The tip was red.

A strangled cry from a dozen throats.

"No, no, it's okay." Excalibur's point clanged against the tiles, as Arthur relaxed. "He barely pricked me."

They were all still too close to the edge for cheers.

Then someone sighed, "Close one, dude."

In the joyful chaos that followed, Sam lifted his tail and sprayed the place where the Shadowlord had been standing.

"Enough of this!" Meryat rose from the edge of the bed and locked Dean in place with a pointed finger. "These games no longer amuse me. I will take your life *now* and face your Keeper stronger because of it!"

"Not so fast." Austin crouched at the edge of the wardrobe and stared down at the mummy/Dean tableau. "If I'm not mistaken, which I'm not, so don't go there, the Rules state you, as the villain of the piece, have to brag about how you defeated us before you administer the coup de grace. That's the finishing stroke," he added for Dean's benefit.

Dean's expression suggested he didn't appreciate the translation.

"The point is," Meryat sneered, the missing piece of her lip adding further scorn to her expression, "you have *been* defeated. What difference will bragging about it make?"

Austin shrugged. "Well, I personally could care less, but if you break the Rules, we get to break the Rules."

"You? What can you do?"

He licked his shoulder at her.

"Fine! I've waited three thousand years; I can wait a few more minutes."

FIFTEEN

"Come on, Diana, you've got to run. This whole place is coming down!"

Diana twisted free of Claire's grip and headed back toward the center of the cavern. "We've got to get her out!"

"We can't." Claire hooked her fingers into the waistband of Diana's pants and yanked her to a stop. "You know as well as I do that there's a hundred ways to go to Hell—hand baskets, good intentions— but we can't use any of them if we've been crushed under a pile of . . ." She threw herself sideways, taking Diana with her as a piece of the cavern ceiling crashed down. ". . . rock."

Considering where they were, the light bulb wasn't entirely unexpected. Claire batted it out of the way with her good hand as Diana surged up onto her feet.

"We'll go after her!"

"Yes, but . . ."

"But nothing." Diana's hand closed around her wrist and yanked her up. "Let's move!"

It seemed that their presence alone had been maintaining what little stability the cavern still had. As they crossed the threshold, the rest of the ceiling crashed down. Coughing and choking in the billowing clouds of faintly pink stone dust, they ran faster, the tunnels collapsing behind them.

Which is certainly better than in front of us, Claire acknowledged as they raced toward the throne room . . .

. . . only to find the entrance blocked.

"Is there another way out?" Mouth close to Diana's ear, she still had to shout to be heard over the roar of falling rock.

"This is the only one *I* know!"

"Oh that's just great!" One-handedly fighting the zipper on the belt pouch open, she found Diana there before her. "What are you doing?"

"If we don't get out, we can't save Kris. So we're getting out!" Snatching out the folded piece of paper, Diana knelt and stuffed it between two of the rocks that blocked the door.

"Diana, that won't work! Rocks can't read!"

"I'll read it for them." Yanking Claire out of the way, she pointed back toward the oncoming destruction and yelled, "Move!"

The paper released the possibilities it held.

The rocks moved.

They moved as though they knew full well they'd be pounded to sand if they didn't.

The black marble floor had cracked and buckled

and the wall behind the throne had canted inward
at an impossible angle, but structural integrity was
being maintained. Provided the definition of both
structural and integrity was less than precise.

And then, lungs burning, they were running on
concrete, not stone.

Almost out . . .

They missed the turn that would have taken them
through the construction zone and found themselves
in the access corridors instead.

The troll was waiting at the back door of the
Emporium.

Before Claire could stop her, Diana grabbed him
by the tie and shoved her face up into his, snarling,
"Your choice, Gaston! The Otherside's a big place.
You can lose yourself in it, or you can deal with me."

His eyes widened, showing pale yellow all around
the gray. "But . . ."

"Billy goats *but* as you very well know. I'm count-
ing to three. One . . ."

On two, he chose to leave the tie in her hand and
pound farther up the access corridor into the mall.

Diana dropped the piece of pale leather and
swiped her hand against her thigh, moisture drawing
darker lines through the pale pink dust. "Eww."

"Definitely," Claire agreed, using the moment to
catch her breath. Not the way she'd have handled it,
but since it worked . . . "What are you doing?"

"This is where we came in. This is the best place
to cross back!"

Bad hand cradled against her chest, she stepped between her sister and the steel door. "We're not done."

"The Summoning ended when that hole closed; *I'm* done!" Dark brows drew in, their challenge plain. "And *I'm* going after Kris!"

Claire had her choice of half a dozen good arguments. She used the only one that would work. "What about Sam? He's still in the mall. I left him guarding Arthur."

"*You* left him," Diana snapped. "You go . . . you . . ." She blinked. Swallowed. Scrubbed her hand across suddenly wet eyes. "Sorry. I just . . ."

"I know."

"You *can't* know."

"Dean . . ."

"Didn't go to Hell for *you*! I'm sorry." She scrubbed at her eyes again. "But he didn't."

"I know," Claire said again, because it was pretty much the only thing Diana was willing to hear at the moment. She jerked open the steel door with her good hand. "Let's go get Sa—" A crack opened suddenly in the concrete floor. Somewhere, not very far away, a steel reinforcing rod snapped with an almost musical twang. "Not good!" Shoving Diana into the storeroom, she slammed the door shut with her shoulder and locked it.

It sounded like someone was playing a steel guitar in the access corridor. Playing it badly.

"How far do you think the destruction will come?"

Diana demanded as they charged through shards of broken garden gnomes toward the store.

"It's already come farther than I thought it would."

"Great."

"Not really. I was wondering, last time you used the wand, it knocked you flat. This time . . ."

"I think Kris' sacrifice caused a backlash. I got—I don't know—refilled. I'm feeling . . ." Diana flashed half a pain-filled grin and straight-armed the door out into the Emporium. ". . . in the pink."

Claire managed a nearly identical smile. "We'll get her back."

"I know." Easily clearing the fallen T-shirt rack, Diana lengthened her stride and raced for the concourse. One foot out the door, she stopped, turned, and ran back.

"Where are you going?" Claire figured she had grounds for sounding shrill. From behind them, one small room away, came the unmistakable sound of a steel door buckling.

"Promises to keep." Dragging a wooden crate of resin frogs under the antique mirror, she climbed up, and slapped the glass. "Jack! Hey! Time to go."

The blue-on-blue eyes popped into view so fast they came accompanied by a faint *boing*. "The whole place is falling apart!" Jack also sounded a little shrill, Claire noted. "What did you do?"

A green glass ball fell from a shelf and shattered. Something hissed and scuttled away.

"We won. Sort of."

"How do you *sort of* win?"

"I don't want to get into that right now."

"Yeah, but . . ."

A muscle jumped in Diana's jaw. "I said, I *don't* want to get into it." She ducked her head behind the edge of the frame. "Is this all that's holding you on?"

"How should I know?" Shrill had given way to slightly panicked. "I don't have eyes in the back of my glass."

"Fair point. Claire . . ."

No time to argue. Claire reached up, noted somewhat absently that much of her left hand seemed to be purple, and grabbed the lower edge of the carved and gilded wood. "I've got it."

Jack was a lot heavier than he looked. They dragged him past the writhing box of rubber snakes, past the toppling display of scented candles, and reached the concourse just as the windows started to shatter. As the first triangular piece of glass whistled past, Claire spun him around, his back to the store, and pushed Diana down behind him.

"Claire, we haven't time . . . !"

"To get cut to ribbons? You're right."

"Hey!" Jack's eyes were as wide as Claire'd seen them. "Get me farther away! I'm breakable here!"

Barely enough room for them both but barely was better than the alternative. "Calm down. You've got a wooden backing."

"Calm down? That's glass breaking! Lots and lots

of breaking glass! Do you know how that makes me feel?"

"Do I care?" Claire snapped. As Jack's eyes fled to the far corner, two tiny blue pinpricks deep in the glass, she sighed. "I'm sorry. I do care. We've just had a . . . bad time."

"Sort of winning?"

"Yeah."

Sort of . . . Diana lifted her head out of the shelter of her arms and stared into the mirror. She didn't look any different. She should have looked different. Wasn't that the sort of thing that changed a person?

It took her a moment to realize that the mall was totally silent. No more crashing. No more breaking. No more dying. Apparently, this was as far as it went. "Claire?" She almost didn't recognize her voice. She sounded about seven. "Why did she do it?"

Carefully brushing aside broken glass, Claire sat down cross-legged on the floor. It wasn't quite a collapse. "I don't know. I guess she didn't want you to die."

"Yeah, but it's part of the whole 'saving the world' thing. It's in my job description. Our job description."

"And it seems that saving you was in hers."

"I didn't want her to."

"She didn't ask you." Claire reached out and wiped away a tear with her thumb. "We'll get her back."

"Because you promised?"

"Because it's part of our job description."

"Right." Diana dragged her sleeve under her nose, leaving a smear of darker pink across one cheek. "Time to sit around and sob about things later! Let's get Sam and . . ." She paused, half standing, and cocked her head. "Is there a reason you're flipping me the finger?"

Swelling had moved the second finger on her left hand out from the rest. "It's broken."

"It's *what*?"

"Broken."

"Why didn't you tell me?"

"When?"

"Before!"

"During our copious amounts of spare time? While we were running for our lives, saving Jack, or trying not to be julienned?"

"Yeah, then."

"Sorry, next time. Don't touch it!" She leaned back away from Diana's questing fingers. "I'll fix it as soon as we cross back."

"Does it hurt?" Jack wondered, coming out to the front of the glass.

Did it hurt? There were a number of things Keepers weren't permitted to say to Bystanders. But since Jack was a metaphysical construct . . .

"Diana!"

Claire closed her mouth, words unsaid, watched Sam race toward them, and sighed. Probably for the best.

*   *   *

". . . and then, he just vanished!"

"You accepted a challenge from the Shadowlord?"

Sam squirmed around in Diana's arms. "For the three hundredth time, I'm fine."

"You could have been killed."

"For the five hundredth time, I wasn't!"

Continuing to ignore the post-fight metaphysical analysis going on around her, Diana buried her face in Sam's fur and held on tight.

"Ow, that was a rib."

"Sorry." She loosened her hold just a little and drew in a deep breath of warm cat. He smelled like safety and comfort. Okay, scraping the clump of shed cat hair off her soft palate wasn't exactly comfortable, but still . . . She didn't know what she would have done if she'd lost him, too.

Too.

Right.

As they reached the stairs, the whole procession moving at the snail-like pace of the most seriously wounded elves, she tucked Sam back under one arm and grabbed Claire's sleeve. "Let's go."

"Diana, you have no idea how much I wish we could. While you were gone, I found out that Dean is in danger of . . ."

"Overfeeding the cat? Stepping on a hairball? Austin's with him, how much danger can he be in?"

They were facing off at the bottom of the stairs, Arthur's army breaking into two streams around them. The two elves carrying Jack set him down and leaned on the top of his frame.

"There's a three-thousand-year-old life-sucking mummy staying at the guest house."

"A three-thousand-year-old life-sucking mummy?"

"Say that three thousand times fast," Sam muttered.

"No." Diana absently stroked a marmalade shoulder and frowned at her sister. "Since when?"

"Impossible to tell with the time distortions."

"How did you . . ."

"Claire!"

Claire nodded toward the sunburned blond starting down through the climbing elves, her pack in one hand and Diana's in the other, declaiming apologies with every step. "He told me."

"Who's he?"

"Lance."

"A lot?"

Arthur stopped beside them and visibly shuddered. "Fortunately, no."

"While you were gone," Claire explained, "I went on a little tour of the Othersides and . . ."

"The Otherside's what?"

"The Othersides plural. Long story."

"Then skip it. You found him . . . ?"

"At our beach."

"The one in the guest house?"

"Yes. Longer story."

"Skip it, too."

"He's not Australian," Sam announced as Lance reached the lower concourse and set the packs down.

Diana looked confused. "Why would he be?"

The cat shrugged as well as his current position allowed. "I have no idea."

"He's a Bystander. Wait." She raised a hand cutting off Lance and Claire together. "I don't care why he's here, but as he obviously can't stay, we've got even more reason to leave immediately. He's got to go back, Dean's in danger, Kris is in *Hell*—three strikes, let's motor!"

Without the time to count to ten, Claire counted to three. "Believe me, Diana, I *want* to, but the injured elves are our responsibility."

"No, they aren't." Diana nodded toward the Immortal King. "They're his responsibility. We did our bit. The hole's closed. The segue's been disrupted, and without an anchor the two malls will continue to drift farther and farther apart. Street kids looking for a place to belong will have to look somewhere else—not necessarily a good thing but a thing. *Our* work here is done."

Claire sighed, cradling her left hand in her right. The pain in her broken finger—which was now hurting up her arm, across her shoulders and into her right ear for reasons she wasn't entirely clear on—made it difficult to concentrate, but Arthur *was* alive, Hell *had been* defeated, and the world *had been* saved from a shopping mall where midnight madness sales meant exactly that. However, while Diana had a point, she'd missed one as well. "Diana, Kris . . ."

"Now, Claire! Or are you tired of Dean already?"

Even the ambient noise of bells in elvish hair quieted. Lance opened his mouth. Arthur shook his head. He closed it again.

There were also a number of things Keepers didn't say to other Keepers. Claire made a mental note to say most of them to her younger sister at a later time. "I'm going to allow for the stress you're under," she said quietly. "Pick a door." Any door would take them back to the access corridor in the actual mall. The point of departure remained the point of return regardless. "Let's go home."

"Fine!" Pivoting on one heel, shifting Sam's weight against her hip, ignoring the little voice that told her she'd gone too far, Diana scanned the lower concourse stores. "There, that kid's store, the Rainbow Wardrobe. Nothing bad should come out of it."

"How responsible of you."

"Don't patronize me!"

"Fine." Claire turned toward Arthur. "The mall is no longer a segue, so we can come and go the same way we can from any other place on the Otherside. I'll be back to check on things."

The Immortal King glanced at Diana, his blue eyes sympathetic, then turned his gaze back to her. Less sympathy, more understanding, Claire noticed. "When?"

Her watch appeared to be keeping time to a rhumba beat. "Unfortunately, I have no idea."

"Claire! Now, or I'm going without you!"

Under no circumstances was Claire allowing Diana

back into the world unsupervised. Even standing right beside her, it would be hard enough to keep her from making a foolish attempt to rescue Kris the moment she could manipulate the possibilities—on the other side of reality, it would be impossible. Claire picked up her pack, wrapped her good hand around Lance's arm, and hurried to join Diana at the store.

When the door flew open on its own, they stepped back together. Jumped back together. Fortunately, Lance was in hiking boots.

A sound spilled out first—like a terrified chicken being chased by a snake.

Dropping her grip on Lance, Claire shoved her hand into her belt pouch. She hadn't closed the zipper after the throne room and for one, heart-stopping moment she thought it was empty. Then her fingers closed around a peppercorn. Enough? It had to be. Releasing the contained possibilities, she yelled, "Everyone close your eyes!" as something squawked and exploded out into the lower concourse.

A moment.

Two.

Cats hunted by sound. "Sam?"

"I don't hear it."

"I can't open my eyes!"

She signed and opened hers. "Yes, you can, Lance."

"Oh, this is just great . . ." Diana would have thrown up her hands had she been willing to put

Sam down. ". . . Hell's gone, and this place makes even less sense. I don't see the connection between a basilisk and a children's st . . ."

"So you're saying that while your body stayed in the room, your ka moved around sipping off bits of Dean's life and spying on us?"

Austin's voice ghosted out the open door.

"That's exactly what I'm saying. I knew everything you had planned from the instant you planned it."

"Meryat!"

Claire and Diana together grabbed Lance as he surged forward.

"Wardrobe-to-wardrobe connection?" Diana asked, brow furrowed, curiosity momentarily flattening the peaks of other emotions.

"Seems like."

"I think that fulfills my part in this foolishness, cat. I have explained, I have gloated, now I will have what I want."

The sound of a struggle.

"A valiant attempt, Dean. But you are mine."

"I don't think so, bitch!"

Diana's eyes widened as her head snapped around toward her sister. "Claire!"

"Lance . . ." Claire yanked him free of Diana's grip, her fingers dimpling his arm. Yanked him around to face her. ". . . can you stop Meryat?"

He pulled a roll of ancient linen out of his right front pocket with his free hand. "Yes!"

"Then go!"

Diana grabbed too late as Lance raced for the storefront, so she grabbed her sister's shoulder instead. "Claire, that isn't where he came in. There's no way to be sure he'll come out in your bedroom! Not without . . ." Her voice trailed off at the look on Claire's face.

Claire reached into the possibilities and set Lance's feet on a single path.

Rules broke.

Dean's hair had begun to gray.

Since it seemed to be his only remaining option, Austin launched himself from the top of the wardrobe, screaming a challenge.

Meryat swatted him aside. Lost a little flesh tone in the use of power but quickly gained it back as Dean seemed to shrink in on himself.

"Hold hard, you ancient and perfidious evil!"

Her attention lifted off Dean. "What?"

Austin muzzily wondered much the same from where he sprawled against the headboard. When *he* was a kitten, perfidious and evil meant the same thing.

Bounding out of the wardrobe, Lance twirled a line of linen across the room.

Meryat stared at him in disbelief for a heartbeat, then laughed and raised a hand. "Foolish b . . . OW!"

As the linen looped around her neck, Dean slid off the edge of the bed. It had taken everything he had left to overcome the years of training that Meryat had called his tragic flaw but, in the end, he'd managed a solid kick in the ankle. Now his back hurt, he had an intense craving for prune juice, and he couldn't actually hear what Lance was shouting. Wasn't entirely sure it was English. *That's the trouble with kids today, talk a language all their own. It's all the fault of that MT . . . Whoa.* Suddenly, he felt a lot better.

Meryat wasn't looking too good.

A finger dropped off and shattered to dust against the floor.

Lance wrapped another loop of linen around her body and kept shouting.

Another finger fell. The rest of her followed about seven syllables later.

Dean covered his mouth and nose as a fine particulate rose and settled.

"Dr. Rebik!"

The archaeologist now looked only five or six years older than his driver's license picture. Which wasn't exactly good, but he inarguably looked better than he had been.

"Lance!"

In turn, Lance no longer looked like he'd taken too many hits from a croc.

Although he still looked Australian.

As the professor and his grad student caught up, Dean stood and leaned over the bed. "You all right?"

Austin checked extremities, sneered in the general direction of the reunion, and reluctantly admitted he was fine.

"Good. I'll be after getting the vacuum, then."

*   *   *

The sheer enormity of what her sister—her older, responsible sister—had done shouldered its way past loss and grief. Diana felt as though she was thinking clearly for the first time since Kris' sacrifice. And Claire *so* didn't want to know what she was thinking. She'd been hurt before, upset, now she was angry. "I can't *believe* you did that!"

"Believe it!"

When Rules were broken, there were consequences.

Claire slammed the door closed, counted to ten, and yanked it open. They stepped through together.

They stepped from the lower concourse into a children's clothing store.

"You've permanently warped it," Diana snapped as she tightened her hold on Sam and they ran for the next storefront.

"I had to save Dean!"

"Sure you did!" Because Claire could do what Claire wanted and too bad if anyone or what anyone else needed to do got in her way.

Jeans store.

Fabric store.

They ran past the watching elves and tried the other side of the concourse.

The doors opened only to their singular, prosaic destination.

They couldn't cross back over.

When Rules were broken, there were consequences.

Squirming free, Sam jumped up onto the edge of a planter and looked from Claire to Diana. "So, we're stuck here?"

"Looks like!" Diana's lip curled. "Because Ms. I Always Have to Have My Own Way had to save Dean at the expense of everyone else!"

"I was not going to let him die!"

Less than an arm's length between them now. Voices raised and getting louder. The mall elves started studying the tiles, the light fixtures, the cat.

"Did you even *once* think of me?" Diana snarled.

Claire snorted. "Do *you* ever think of anything but yourself?"

Sam dropped back onto the floor.

"Oh, fine talk from someone who goes on and on about sacrifice to the greater good and who just condemned my . . . condemned *Kris* to save her boyfriend!"

The shrieks of pain sounded pretty much simultaneously. In the silence that followed, Sam returned to the planter.

Claire rubbed at the blood on her ankle, looked up to see Diana doing the same, realized the tears were not from the cat scratches and reached out. "Oh, Kitten, I'm sorry."

Things got a little damp and mushy for the next few minutes, embraces awkward because of the packs but determined.

"Well done," Arthur murmured by Sam's shoulder. "I had begun to think I should intervene."

"That would have worked, too," Sam admitted. "But you probably wouldn't have liked the result."

"Oh?"

"Common enemy."

"But you . . ."

"Are a cat."

"Right."

Caught up in the circle of Claire's arm, Diana sniffled and raised her head. "You haven't called me Kitten in years."

"You started hitting me when I did it."

"Oh, yeah."

"And then you filled my bed with butterscotch pudding."

"Technically, I turned your sheets to pudding, but I can see why you stopped."

They separated slowly, wiped tears, and mirrored watery smiles.

"Rough day."

"Yeah."

"Diana, Kris . . ."

"I know. We'll save her. And I've figured out how to get us home."

"Diana, I'm not a teenager."

Diana straightened her pack straps, then bent down and scooped Sam off the floor. "Look, it's after hours, you're with a teenager and a cat, and we've got a mirror we definitely didn't pay for—it's covered."

Shunk kree. Shunk kree.

"That certainly sounds like it's covered," Claire admitted. She closed her good hand around the edge of Jack's frame. "Jack, are you sure?"

"I just want out of the mall. The guesthouse sounds fabulous and . . . Hello! Fingerprints on my glass!"

"Sorry."

Shunk kree. Shunk kree.

Sam tucked his head up under Diana's chin. "What's taking him so long?"

They were alone on the lower concourse, Arthur and the elves back in the department store in an effort to minimize time distortions. Good-byes had been perfunctory at best.

"I'll be back with Kris as soon as I find her. Now go away, or this will never work!"

Claire thought she could smell the fire, could definitely hear the music. Actually, now that the mall was nothing more than a place on the Otherside, they could probably hear the music at the Girl Guide camp. The mall elves were great kids, but she could see why Jack didn't want to stay

Shunk kree. Shunk kree.

The circle of light swept across the concourse.

Swept back.

His eyes widened as he stared at the two girls and the cat. Twenty-one years he'd been patrolling this darkness, finding the hidden ones, dragging them out to face the consequences. Girls. Boys. Young bodies. Lithe bodies. Hard bodies. All their possibilities caught and held.

They thought they were better than him. They laughed. Here, in the darkness, he made sure they stopped laughing.

Not the first time he'd caught two at once.

Not even the first cat.

The first pair with a cat. And a mirror?

Caught himself, he stared at his reflection and almost saw something stare back.

"That was unpleasant." Although she hadn't actually touched the old man, Claire wiped her fingers against her thigh as they hurried toward the nearest exit, Jack riding the possibilities behind them.

"Yeah, lots of waxy build up in there. How much did you wipe?"

"His memory of us."

"And that whole 'geeks that hunt the night' thing?"

"Couldn't touch it. It was tracked in too deep."

"That's almost . . . sad."

"Might be for the best, though; Arthur will have an easier time with the elves if they continue to face a common enemy."

"That's an interesting definition of 'for the best.' "

"Remind me to check at Children's Aid tomorrow and find out where they're holding Stewart."

"You'll send him back?"

"Of course I will. If he wants to go."

"Can't see why he would," Diana snorted. "I mean, reality's just so much more meaningful than a life you've made for yourself." Barely slowing, she popped the lock on the exit's inside door and held it open. "How's your finger," she asked as Sam raced through their legs and off the concourse.

Claire flicked it at her sister. "Good as new."

Grinning, Diana flipped a finger back as Claire dealt with the outside door. "Sam, she'd be a little faster if you weren't quite so underfoot."

"I just want to get out of here."

"I hear you." Bending, she picked him up again and rested her chin between his ears. "I'm totally web shopping from now on."

Jack glanced up at the security mirror as he passed between the doors. "Is that what I looked like on this side?"

"Pretty much, yeah."

He frowned. "Did that curvature make me look fat?"

The heat outside the mall hit them like a wet sponge.

"Oh, man, I so didn't miss this." Diana waved the hand not holding Sam between their black-on-black outfits. "And we're so not dressed for it."

"Not a problem. First, it's the middle of the night. Second, if anyone does say anything, we'll tell them we're from Toronto."

"Works. Now . . ." Deep in Diana's pack, her cell phone began to ring, the sound remarkably loud in the empty parking lot. She touched the possibilities. "That's Mom."

Claire winced. When Rules were broken, there were consequences. "I don't suppose . . ."

The ringing stopped. "Battery must've gone dead."

"Thanks."

"De nada."

"It'll be something when your mother catches up to you," Sam muttered.

Diana ignored him. "So, like I was saying; now what?"

"Home."

"The guest house?"

"Yes, because . . ."

"Because the residual power signature in the furnace room will lead us right to Kris! And you have to check on Dean and Austin," she added hurriedly as Claire's brows drew in. "I understand. But you know; two birds, one stone. Let's move!"

Claire reached into the possibilities and called a cab.

Chin resting on one hand, Dean covered a yawn with the other and watched Austin eat a sausage he wasn't supposed to have. After everything they'd been through, it was reassuringly norm . . . "Austin?"

Both ears were up. His head turned suddenly toward the front door. A heartbeat later the rest of his body followed.

With a shriek of wood against wood and a crash as his chair hit the floor and bounced, Dean followed.

Claire stepped out of the taxi and braced herself as a black-and-white streak flew down the front stairs of the guest house and into her arms. She winced as

claws sank deep into both shoulders but only murmured reassurances into the top of a velvet head.
After a moment, Austin calmed enough to pin her in
an emerald gaze.

"Never go away for that long again!"

"I missed you, too."

"We could have been killed!"

"I'm sorry."

"If you hadn't sent Lance back . . ."

"I know."

"I had everything under control."

"Of course."

"If that's Dean I hear pounding toward you, put
me down before I get crushed."

It was, so she did.

Sitting on the sidewalk, Austin finished smoothing
rumpled fur and looked up to see Sam watching him,
head cocked to one side. "I'll make her pay later,"
he said.

The younger cat nodded. "I never doubted you."

"I assume there's a story behind the whole
'dressed like they're heading out to do some second-
story work'?"

"Yes."

"Well, skip it."

Diana wrestled Jack out of the back seat—bending
half a dozen or so possibilities in the process—and
shoved him toward the guest house as the cab roared
off, the cabby remembering only the twenty percent
tip. The possibilities were cheaper, but their mother

had called twice more on the ride home. Once on the cabby's cell phone. Once using a phone booth near the intersection where they were waiting for the light.

Sooner or later, one of them would have to answer.

Claire would have to answer, Diana corrected glancing over at her sister and Dean. About to suggest Claire leave tonsillectomies to the medical profession, another phone rang. Actually, not another phone. Her phone. In her pack. Mom had clearly found a way around the dead battery.

At this point, the fastest route to Kris might be to answer it. While *she* hadn't broken any Rules, at this point in the proceedings, she was likely to catch just as much Hell. Leaning Jack carefully against the porch railing, Diana slipped off her pack and began to search for her cell. Finding it at last under a tunaless tuna sandwich, her thumb was poised over the connect button when the sound of squealing tires drew all eyes to the street.

A minivan pulled up in front of the guest house and stopped on a dime. With a tinkle of nine cents' change hitting the pavement, the side door opened and a familiar body exploded out onto the sidewalk.

"Freakin' OW!"

"Kris!" Diana raced forward as the van roared away. Throwing herself to her knees, she gathered the crumpled body of the elf up into her arms. "Kris say something!"

Kris blinked, and looked around. "This is Hell?"

"No, this is Kingston!"

She was still holding the wand, now flaccid and more puce than pink. "I was falling and this is where I landed."

"You were in a minivan."

"No. I think I'd remember that. Cavern. Falling. Pink stuff. Here."

Diana twisted around to stare at Claire.

"I kept trying to tell you." She leaned back against Dean's chest and wrapped herself in the safety of his arms. "Rule one . . ."

"The possibilities are not to be used to bring in HBO?" Diana asked, unable to see the relevance.

"Okay, rule two. Hell can't hold a willing sacrifice. It couldn't hold Kris any more than it could hold Dean."

"And you tried to tell me that?"

"A couple of times."

Diana's heart felt like it was beating normally for the first time in days. "Next time, try harder."

"You guys want to keep it quiet out there!" The voice drifted down from one of the surrounding windows, open because of the heat. "It's three in the morning and some of us are trying to sleep!"

"You want to sleep?" Claire reached into the possibilities.

"Then sleep." Diana added her two cents' worth as she helped Kris to her feet.

From where Diana had dropped it at the base of the steps, the phone began ringing again. She looked at Claire. Claire took a step forward, turned, and looked at Dean. Who took two steps sideways and brought his work boot down as hard as he could. Sam batted the pieces down into the area by the basement door.

"Might as well be hung for a sheep as a lamb," Claire said with satisfaction.

"I could go for some lamb," Austin murmured as he followed Sam up the stairs.

"I don't know about lamb," Diana sighed as she led Kris into the guest house, "but I could eat."

Claire waved Jack in ahead of them—time for introductions when there was less chance of being overheard—and laid her head on Dean's shoulder as he slipped an arm around her waist. They climbed the stairs together. "Where's Lance?"

"He and Dr. Rebik are . . . Uh . . . Sleeping."

A half turn, and she could see his ears were pink. "Sleeping?"

"Probably. By now."

"What?"

His eyebrows made an appearance above the upper edge of his glasses.

"Oh. Happy endings all around, then."

"Well, Dr. Rebik definitely lost a few years and Lance—actually, since I wasn't after knowing him before, I don't want to assume . . ."

"Happy endings," Claire repeated, leaving no room for postgame analysis.

"Yeah."

"Good. I want to hear everything that happened while I was gone, but for right now, there's just one thing I have to know."

He kissed the top of her head as they stepped over the threshold. "What's that?"

"What were you doing with a basilisk in the bedroom?"

The door closed on his answer.

From King Street came the faint sound of a mini-van being pulled over by the police.

And for the first time in days, a cool breeze blew in off the lake.

Tanya Huff

Victory Nelson, Investigator:
Otherworldly Crimes a Specialty

"Smashing entertainment for a wide audience"
—*Romantic Times*

"One series that deserves to continue"
—*Science Fiction Chronicle*

BLOOD PRICE
0-88677-471-3

BLOOD TRAIL
0-88677-502-7

BLOOD LINES
0-88677-530-2

BLOOD PACT
0-88677-582-5

To Order Call: 1-800-788-6262

Tanya Huff

The Finest in Fantasy

To Order Call: 1-800-788-6262

DAW21

Tanya Huff

The Confederation Novels

"As a heroine, Kerr shines. She is cut from the same mold as Ellen Ripley of the *Aliens* films. Like her heroine, Huff delivers the goods." --*SF Weekly*

VALOR'S CHOICE
0-88677-896-4

When a diplomatic mission becomes a battle for survival, the price of failure will be far worse than death...

THE BETTER PART OF VALOR
0-7564-0062-7

Could Torin Kerr keep disaster from striking while escorting a scientific expedition to an enormous spacecraft of unknown origin?

To Order Call: 1-800-788-6262

DAW 19